The Innkeeper

Lou + Wade

Dr. Rebecca Sharp

The Innkeeper (The Kinkades, Book 4)
Published by Dr. Rebecca Sharp

Cover Design:

Sarah Hansen, Okay Creations

Editing:

Ellie McLove, My Brother's Editor

Printed in the United States of America.

Visit www.drrebeccasharp.com

Chapter One

Lou

"Oh my goodness, your wedding was beautiful," Mrs. Tisdale exclaimed as she stood at my reception desk. Her eyes were wide and adoring at the photograph on the wall behind me as I checked her in for her stay through the long weekend.

The middle-aged woman had her hair pulled back in a tight, crystal-covered clip, her make-up painted on thick, and she was branded head to toe in designer monograms. From the moment she'd stepped through the front door of the Lamplight Inn, I knew exactly what kind of guest she was. After over a decade in customer service, I wasn't phased in the slightest when she began telling me exactly what she'd thought of the place.

From the "strikingly historic" red brick exterior, to the "eclectic" interior vintage décor, to the "quite sweet" smell, and right down to the "quaint but tarnished" lamppost that marked the entrance at the gate, no inch of my new business escaped her noticed. And, unfortunately, neither would I.

"Oh, that's not—"

"And a baby, too," she gushed, reaching for the silk scarf

around her neck and adjusting it. "How old is he now? Or she? Do you have photos?"

My smile flickered, going from easy to requiring some effort. Unfortunately, I knew where this conversation was headed. I'd been down the same path countless times since I'd put my sister's wedding photo on display a few months ago.

"Actually, that's my—"

"That was recent, wasn't it?" Her verbalized thoughts continued like a runaway train. "I can tell from your pants."

My pants?

I looked down to where my white blouse was tucked into the high waist of my loose beige trousers, the outfit completed with a matching oversized beige blazer.

"I wore so much of that style after I had my children. A lifesaver until my body snapped back," she went on blithely, though if the tight, immovable skin of her face was any indication, her body probably had some help 'snapping back.' "But you look great, dear. If it wasn't for the photo, I'd never think you even had a baby—"

"That'snotmywedding!"

Guilt flooded my cheeks for my sudden forcefulness, but it was the way her expression dried up and she stared at me blankly that made my heart start to hammer.

Oh, no.

I adjusted the rims of my glasses and forced my nervous smile wider, the ends spearing painfully into the borders of my cheeks.

"That's my twin sister, Francesca, with her husband, Chandler. They were married here in January and had their son, Logan, back in March."

The revelation was met with a few punctuated blinks.

"That's your twin?"

Did she think I was lying?

The notion made my chest tighten. "Yeah."

She rested her jewel-encrusted fingers on the edge of the

counter and narrowed her gaze. "Why do you have your twin's wedding photo behind your desk?"

"Oh." I exhaled with a small laugh. "I'm going to be opening the inn for weddings and events starting this fall. Since they got married here, I thought the photo would be a nice advertisement."

It was a good thought, but in practice, it was turning out to be more misinterpretation than marketing. This wasn't the first time—wasn't even the dozenth time—someone had made this same mistake and thought Frankie was me.

It was my own fault. I'd put the photograph front and center in the main hallway so it would get the most views, even from day-trippers who wanted to stop in and see the historic inn, and Frankie and I were identical twins. Of course, I'd thought about the possibility of this happening, so I'd chosen one of their wedding photos, which was a side-profile shot of her and Chandler standing in front of the fireplace in the living room. With the scene and the candles and the side view, I thought it was enough to obscure the similarities. I was wrong.

Frankie thought the whole thing was comical. *"Too bad you can't make the picture talk. Then no one would get confused."* A photo was about the only time and place she and I could get mistaken for one another; as soon as anyone met us in person... Well, it was impossible to conflate my twin's personality with my own.

Everyone in our family had their own way of describing the two of us. The calm and the storm. Toil and trouble. The truth of it was simple: I lived from a "worst-case scenario" perspective, whereas my sister was more the "you only live once" kind of person.

"Oh, I see." The tinge of disappointment in Mrs. Tisdale's voice was pointed, drawing me back to the moment with a sharp prick.

I turned and scanned the set of small cubbies anchored to the wall. My oldest brother, Jamie, was a carpenter—a woodworker—

and he'd custom-made the small shelving unit for me to house all ten room keys for the inn. The keys were the vintage metal kinds with deep green tassels attached to the ends.

When I'd bought and remodeled the inn last year, I'd had the option to switch all the door locks over to digital, but I couldn't bring myself to do so despite all the advantages. I'd gone into this venture wanting to preserve the old inn's history and restore its prestige as one of the main landmarks in Friendship, and in my opinion, there wasn't a whole lot of character to a keycard.

"I have you in room 210, Mrs. Tisdale—"

"So, you're not married then?"

My pulse tripped. The strength it took to hold my smile now was Olympic. "No, ma'am," I murmured and stepped out from behind the desk, grabbing a small welcome bag from the shelf for her. "I have a little welcome gift for you. There's a water bottle in there and a little baggy of fresh chouquettes. They're a French puff pastry with a little custard inside."

"Oh, interesting." I couldn't contain my sigh of relief when she took the bag from me and peered inside. "I don't know that I've ever had one of those, and I do love Paris in the spring."

"It's hard to overshadow the croissant, but I love lesser-known pastries, so you'll find a different international pastry at breakfast every morning, all made fresh by a local baker for me." The nervous vise around my throat eased along with the strain of my smile.

"How delightful." Her genuine excitement managed to flutter the previously immovable muscles on her forehead.

"Here. Let me take your bag, and I can show you to your room," I offered as she fished out one of the puff pastry balls.

"So, do you have kids, Elouise?"

I was already bent over, reaching for her brown monogrammed duffel bag, when the question made me wince. I hung my head for a second and squeezed my eyes shut. *So much for escaping this conversation...*

I didn't know what it was that made people like this. That

made strangers breeze along this line of questioning—*Are you married? Do you have kids? Do you have a house?*—as though that was all life was. A checklist. No one ever asked if you were happy.

And the thing was, I *was* happy.

Unlike Frankie, who knew from the time we were sixteen that she was going to open her own candle store, I had no idea what I wanted to do. So, while my twin made candles, I started working, first at Mom's homemade jam company, Stonebar Farms, and then at the local juice bar and coffee shop, The Maine Squeeze.

For eight years, I worked in customer service, and I loved every minute of it. I loved meeting people—meeting visitors. I loved sharing with them the history of Friendship and recommending all my favorite things to do, see, and eat in my hometown. It was through The Maine Squeeze that I met Ella, the lovely Ukrainian baker who made the chouquettes and all the other treats I served. Every Sunday, Ella would deliver a different batch of special pastries to the coffee shop, sharing with me what they were and where they came from. That was where my pastry obsession began.

While I was working at the coffee shop, my second-oldest brother, Kit, needed my help. My choice, not his. Kit was a phenomenal artist. After the trauma and injury he'd sustained in the military and afterward, he painted to cope with the stress and was content to throw his paintings away when he was finished. I couldn't let that happen. He was too good. They were too good. So, I found a space in town and told him he was going to open an art gallery, and I would manage it during the hours I wasn't at The Maine Squeeze.

All those years, I worked and lived at home and saved for a dream I might never have.

But then it happened. The idea of restoring the historic Lamplight Inn appeared in front of me like a giant red stop sign, and suddenly, everything clicked into place. I worked and saved, and after some of Frankie's shenanigans, I bought the old inn from Frankie's now-husband, Chandler, and my dream became reality.

And I was happy. No boyfriend. No kids. No house. But happy. Shouldn't that count for something?

Apparently, not to Mrs. Tisdale.

"No, I don't, and please, call me Lou," I said, keeping my tone breezy as I picked up her bag and beelined for the main staircase just to the left of the desk.

The front door of the inn opened then and my cousin, Max, stepped inside dressed in a navy suit and holding a huge bouquet of flowers.

"Oh my, what are these?" Mrs. Tisdale exclaimed as he approached.

"Mrs. Tisdale, this is my cousin, Max Hamilton. He owns a local flower shop and delivery service, MaineStems," I introduced, and Max tipped his head in greeting. "All the fresh flowers here at the inn are catered by his company, and he is responsible for all of the fresh, seasonal blooms here at the inn."

"They're absolutely gorgeous."

In spite of her line of questioning, I was excited for Mrs. Tisdale to see the fresh bouquet waiting in her room. It was the little authenticities that had started to make a name for the business even though I'd only been open less than six months.

"Thank you," Max rumbled. Ever the gentleman, he paused obligingly and let her smell the blooms as he introduced them all. "We've got some roses, mini Callas, Veronica, Delphinium, Alstroemeria..."

While I could go on for hours about all different kinds of lesser-known baked delicacies, flowers were Max's domain. I was lucky I could tell a rose from a rhododendron.

I inched all the way to the first landing on the stairs before Mrs. Tisdale took the hint and began to follow me.

"I'll be right back down, Max," I told him, leading her the rest of the way upstairs.

"Oh, what a lovely idea for fresh flowers," the woman chortled. "Does he deliver them to your house, too?"

I was sure I would've stumbled on the last step if I hadn't already stopped, seeing the door to room 201 left ajar.

Gritting my teeth, I scurried over and closed it, making a mental note to speak with Mr. Stevens about it when he returned. I saw him rush out of the inn not long ago. He'd looked upset, but even if I hadn't been in the middle of giving Mrs. Tisdale a tour, he was out of the building before I could check and see if everything was okay.

This wasn't okay, though. Guests were responsible for closing and locking their doors. If anything happened to his things—if anything was taken from him of all people—I swallowed and shook off the thought.

"Elouise?"

Lou. I flipped my frown and faced her. *I was happy.*

"I live here at the inn," I answered and breezed straight to the last door on the right. "Here is your room. If you need anything while you are here, you can press 0 on the room phone which will either connect you to the reception desk or will forward to my cell phone during off hours."

I unlocked and opened the door, revealing the soothing pastel blue room with brocaded wallpaper and white curtains.

"Oh, wow. And the flowers," she said, heading straight for the blue-hued bouquet on the nightstand and completely forgetting about me.

I wasn't sure my sigh of relief could've been big enough.

"You're welcome to leave your key at the desk with me if you are going out. There is a door hanger on the nightstand there that you can place outside your door if you'd like the room cleaned. Otherwise, we won't disturb you." I set the key on the small table by the door as I went through my usual spiel, though at a slightly more rapid pace. "You can just give me a call at reception if you'd like fresh linens, and there is also a continental breakfast available every morning from seven to nine a.m. in the dining room."

"Wonderful." She turned back to me, and I saw the moment her distraction started to wane.

"If you have any other questions about your room or things to do in town, feel free to stop by reception, and I'm happy to answer any of them for you. For now, I'll let you get settled in, Mrs. Tisdale. It's a pleasure to have you staying with us," I barreled on, hoping a big smile and friendly tone would obscure how I shut the door before she could respond and rushed for the staircase.

I. Was. Happy.

Before I could even get back to my cousin, the newlywed couple I'd checked in yesterday were waiting at the reception desk for me.

"I'm here. Thank you for your patience," I said, speeding back to my post with a smile. They were spending their honeymoon here at the inn. "What can I help you with?"

The woman, Cynthia, smiled. "We were thinking about heading to the beach but wanted your recommendation for the best spot that might not be as crowded."

"Absolutely."

"And dinner suggestions," her husband added.

I beamed. "Of course."

I pulled out an illustrated map of town Kit had made for me, circled the landmark of the inn, and then began to mark my recommendations.

"If you head to your left just outside, past the center square, you'll see a directional sign pointing out the way to the Friendship lighthouse. Right behind that, there is an unmarked entrance to the beach that only locals really know about since everyone coming in for the day lands in the first parking lot and follows the town's signs for the main beach entrance." I dragged my red pen in a circle around the secret entrance and then drew a line along the path down to the rocky shore.

"Wonderful."

"If you want to picnic on the beach, I'd recommend sandwiches from the shop just across the street, or if you want to do wine and charcuterie, my family owns the Stonebar Farms store right here"—another circle—"and we sell our homemade jams, crackers, a selection of cheeses from Vermont."

"Oh, Oscar, that sounds amazing."

I glanced up just in time to catch the look she gave her husband, and my chest twinged.

But I was happy.

"And then, for dinner, I would highly recommend Brazos. It's a local steakhouse, and it's just amazing." I marked that on the map, too, and then capped my pen.

"Sounds great." Oscar smiled as Cynthia took the map, folded it, and put it in her purse. "Thank you."

"Of course," I said and gave them a small wave goodbye, but they were already too engrossed with each other to see it.

Sighing deeply, I finally turned my attention to my cousin, who was working quietly at the table in the entryway, switching out the flowers from a week ago with the new arrangement.

"Sorry about that."

"Don't worry about it." He hugged me and then went back to styling the flowers in the vase until they were perfect. "Everything okay?"

"Yeah. Perfect." Even as I said it, I tipped to the side and gave myself a once-over in the vintage, gold-framed mirror that hung on the wall behind the bouquet.

I ran my hands down the braids on either side of my head, the honey-brown ends landing in the middle of my chest, and then straightened the collar of my blazer. Other than the flush of frustration on my cheeks, I looked otherwise unscathed from Mrs. Tisdale's probing questions.

"I wasn't expecting you to come today."

Normally, Max swapped out my flowers every other week, which meant this bouquet was a week early. On top of that, he usually texted to let me know when he was coming. A partially selfish courtesy since I'd make sure to have a cup of coffee and a small bag of pastries to sustain him for the rest of his day of deliveries.

"Yeah. I'm sorry for not texting..." he murmured and stepped back to assess the final product. He looked for long enough I realized there was another reason he was here.

"What's going on?"

"I actually came early because I have a favor to ask." He folded his arms, his eyes darting around sheepishly.

"A favor?" My brows peaked. "Of course. Anything." I wasn't sure what I had to offer except a room at the inn, but whatever it was, I was happy to do it.

"I know you haven't finalized the options and packages yet, but I want to book the inn for a wedding."

My jaw dropped and then snapped shut. "You? A wedding? You're getting married?" I clamped my mouth shut and then shook my head. "Sorry." I pushed out a breath. Clearly, Mrs. Tisdale had frazzled my brain. "Not for you. Obviously. I mean—I don't mean it like that—"

"Lou." Max chuckled and put his hand on my shoulder. "Take a breath."

"I'm sorry. That woman from earlier thought I was Frankie—that it was my wedding photo on the wall, and she wouldn't stop asking me questions."

"Ahh. Got it."

"Please. Continue," I begged and gave my head a little shake. "So, you want to book the inn for a wedding?"

He smiled again, but unlike earlier, it didn't quite reach all the way to his eyes. "Yeah." Even his voice sounded a little...raw. "Todd just proposed to Daisy, and they want to get married in September."

Todd was Max's best friend. They'd started MaineStems together, and then Max bought him out when Todd wanted to pursue a different venture.

"This September?" My eyes went wide when he nodded. No wonder he was asking for the inn to host it. September was only four months away. To find a venue with availability in that short of time... "I mean. Sure. Of course. I don't know what I'll have ready by then or be able to offer exactly—"

"It's fine." He waved away my worries. "Todd is trying to tell me they're just going to go to the courthouse, and I keep arguing with him that he's going to regret that. Daisy deserves more—" He broke off with a shake of his head, something hard flashing in his usually carefree gaze. "Anyway, it'll be a relief for the both of them if I can offer that they can have it here."

"Absolutely."

"Thanks, Lou." He hugged me again. "Knew I could count on you, and I have no doubt you'll make it perfect."

My smile broadened at his confidence. *I was happy.*

As soon as Max left, I pulled out my laptop and opened up the *Weddings* folder. Running an inn and having guests was one thing, but being an event venue was a whole different ball of wax. Something I'd found out firsthand when Frankie and Chandler had their wedding here in January. The vendors. The food. The seating and space for dancing...

I opened up my massive spreadsheet of all the local suppliers and vendors I was in the process of reaching out to and scrolled to the next on the list. *Coastal Cakes.* The owner, Bea, was the daughter-in-law of the Fullers, a local Friendship family who lived close to Mom. I'd just created a new email, my fingers drumming on the keys to try to wake up the idea of what I wanted to say when the front door swung open, hitting the doorstop with a violent thud.

I jumped and stared at the culprit. *Mr. Blaze Stevens.*

There were many things—so many possibilities I'd tried to plan for and pitfalls I'd tried to avoid since opening the inn—but in none of my scenarios had I planned for him.

Hollywood heartthrob. Celebrity Casanova. And former train wreck.

Back in March, I received an urgent email about a longer-term booking. At that point, we were just coming out of winter, the

Lamplight Inn had only been open for about two months, and even with the marketing I'd started, my reservation book was still mostly empty. A long-term reservation seemed like a good opportunity, but still, I was wary. However, when Mr. Stevens offered double my nightly rate, I couldn't afford to be that cautious, not with the massive loans I had for the mortgage and renovation. So, I agreed.

In my defense, I didn't know who Blaze Stevens was until he walked through the door. And technically, not even then. It was only when Max's younger sister, Harper, who'd been here helping me that day, squealed in excitement that I realized I'd missed something. A very big something when a very official non-disclosure agreement was handed to me before he even said hello.

Later, after settling him into the largest suite I had available, Harper gave me the full rundown on movie star Blaze Stevens. Her eyes practically turned to hearts when she'd equated him to her generation's Leonardo DiCaprio or Brad Pitt. In my mind, with his tousled light brown hair and blue eyes, he looked more like Bradley Cooper.

I tried to find the same appeal she did, but I couldn't. He was handsome in the way that most movie stars are, and I recognized it the same way I recognized when a piece of furniture was good quality. With an objective appreciation, not a physical attraction.

She went on about the films he'd been in, scolding me for not having watched any of them. She gushed about the characters he'd played and the fandom he'd achieved. Apparently, there was a rumor he'd been at some ski resort out west a couple of months ago, and the place got so flooded with fans and reporters the cops had to be called to secure the place and check IDs, allowing only registered guests to enter. The craziest part? Blaze was never there. Never had plans to go there. Just the rumor of his presence was enough to turn everything upside down.

And that famous movie star was staying at my inn. What would happen to Friendship if the world realized he was here? What would happen to the inn?

Later that night, after Googling him and reading far too many things I shouldn't, I panicked over the situation…and all the possible consequences.

What if he didn't like something? What if something got messed up, or I didn't fold his sheets the right way, or the coffee wasn't a precise temperature in the morning?

What if something went wrong, and the reputation of the Lamplight Inn was ruined before it even got off the ground?

All the tabloids were filled with stories about Blaze's reputation for being a party boy—for being so wasted and getting himself into so much trouble that the rumors were his family's law firm existed solely for the purpose of covering up his messes.

What if he tried to have a party at the inn? What if he trashed his room? What if he damaged everything I'd just invested all of my hard-earned savings on?

But my panic turned out to be unfounded.

Not only were there no parties, but my famous, long-term guest stayed holed up in his room most of the time and disappeared on the days he wanted me to clean it. And even though I'd strictly informed Harper she wasn't allowed to ask Mr. Stevens for an autograph or photo, she never even had the opportunity.

He was the first down for breakfast, gathering what he wanted just as I finished putting everything out, and then retreated back to his room. And for lunch and dinner, there was a steady stream of delivery people dropping off food he'd ordered. Chinese on Monday. Mexican on Tuesday. Sushi on Wednesday. Italian on Thursday. And pizza on Friday. On the weekends, he'd switch it up, but invariably, right around seven o'clock, I'd be bringing some takeout bag up to his door and leaving it with a gentle knock.

For two months, I'd had no issues. He'd cause no problems. But for him to leave the way he did earlier in the middle of the afternoon and leave his door open…Even if nothing was wrong, I had to say something about the door.

"Excuse me! Mr. Stevens!" I called after him, taking the stairs two at a time to catch up, only to hear his door slam just before I reached the second floor. Gritting my teeth, I went to the door and knocked. "Mr. Stevens, it's Lou from reception. If I could have a moment—"

The door swung open so quickly that I jumped, my hand smacking to my chest as my heart raced.

He looked like a completely different person. Like a method actor taking on a darker role, his soft smile had become a scowl, and his sad eyes had turned to shadows.

"What?" he demanded, but it wasn't the tense frustration in his tone that worried me. It was the alcohol on his breath. *And the half-drunk liter of vodka still in his hand.*

I swallowed over the lump in my throat. *Stay cool, Lou.*

"I'm so sorry to bother you. Did you leave your door open when you left earlier? I came upstairs, and it was ajar, so I just wanted to make sure everything was okay..."

"It's fine," he snapped.

"Oh. Okay." It was not fine.

He shook his head and muttered something I was sure was a curse. His agitated movements gave me a glimpse of the room behind him, and my heart dropped to my stomach. Everything was everywhere. Clothes. Sheets. Garbage. The desk chair was tipped over.

"Mr. Stevens—"

"Don't do that," he snarled and drove a hand through his hair so roughly I half-expected his scalp to start coming apart at the seams.

"I'm sorry?"

"Don't look at me like that."

I shivered. As afraid as I wanted to be—felt like maybe I should be—the emotion that surged inside me was sympathy. This man wasn't okay. After seeing what my brother, Kit, went through when he came home, I recognized trauma. I recognized when someone was haunted by demons they thought they couldn't control and feared they'd never escape. And I recognized it now on Blaze Stevens.

Something had happened, and he was suffering, and I just... wanted to help. Maybe if I kept him talking...

"I'm sorry. What do I look like?"

"Like you're not surprised I fucked up again," he rasped, his voice catching. "God, you're just like my brother."

And then the door slammed in my face.

His brother? I didn't even know he had a brother, let alone who his brother was. *And what look?*

I shivered, hearing the distinct sounds of stomping and cursing from inside the room. Rolling my lip between my teeth, I raised my hand, tempted to knock again, but then thought better of it. The more we tried to coddle Kit when he was struggling, the more he pushed us away. Maybe in the morning, I'd bring him up a tray for breakfast and see if he was more willing to talk. Sometimes, people just needed to be alone.

I retreated back to my desk, and between the wedding vendor worksheet and attending to other guest needs—*thankfully, not Mrs. Tisdale's*—it seemed like the next time I looked up, it was going on eight o'clock.

I hung up the phone, my eyes darting to the ceiling, hearing another thump from room 201 above me. *What was he doing up there?* I didn't want to bother Mr. Stevens, but something wasn't right. Our interaction earlier was so different than how he'd been in the past. Not that I'd spoken all that much to the movie star during his stay, but he'd never been...looked...smelled like that.

Space had been a good idea until the intermittent thumping began as I started making calls to potential vendors, making me wonder if the infamous actor had turned into an ogre while left alone in his room.

The deepest breath wasn't enough to settle or stop my resolution: I had to go up there. At this point, it wasn't wrong to want a well-check...on him and my furniture.

And I could bring some water bottles with me. Maybe that would soften the intrusion. Oh, and a bag of chouquettes. Those would definitely help.

The kitchen was at the back of the building, just underneath my bedroom on the floor above. I grabbed two bottles and the box of remaining pastries when I heard the thud of a door closing. I rushed back toward the reception desk as heavy footfalls descended the stairs. No, not descended. He collided down the staircase. Into the wall. Then the railing. Then the wall again. Like a bowling ball bouncing back and forth between bumpers along the lane. Only bowling balls didn't curse with each impact.

No, no, no. What was he doing?

My feet moved quicker, a familiar hot and dizzying sensation growing inside me. It was like all the times Frankie had gotten into trouble when we were growing up, and I knew she was about to get caught. She was always cool as a cucumber, but I, on the other hand, would start to shake and sweat. I would panic for her, knowing a consequence was coming her way. Only this time, my panic was for me.

"Mr. Stevens?" The pitch of my voice was higher, my lungs absorbing only quick, shallow breaths.

There was an even louder thud followed by a pained groan and then the distinct sound of either a body or a sack of potatoes falling down the stairs.

"Oh my god!" I cried out, the water bottles sliding from my damp palms and rolling on the floor as I rushed to him. "Mr. Stevens!" My knees would hate me tomorrow for the way I crashed onto them by his side. "Mr. Stevens, are you alright?" I grabbed his shoulders. *No response.* "Mr. Stevens? It's Miss Kinkade. You fell..."

Did he pass out?

"Mr. Stevens, can you hear me?"

No response.

Was he dead?

I shoved my trembling hand under his nose and felt the weak rush of air. *Not dead.* But not moving either. *Oh god.* I went to my desk, my hand shaking so badly it was a miracle I was able to dial 911.

"Hi, yes. A man—one of the guests at my inn—just fell down the steps. He's breathing, but I can't wake him," I stammered to the operator, my sentences just as choppy as the breaths I took.

"Did he hit his head?"

I swiveled my gaze. There was blood on the floor. Blood on the side of his head. How had I not seen... "Yes. There's blood. A lot of blood—" I broke off with a cry and clutched the desk like it was the only thing holding me upright.

"I have an ambulance on its way to your location. Don't try to move him in case there's an injury to his neck."

"O-okay." The line clicked off.

Oh god. Oh god. Oh god. I covered my mouth with my hand, my heart pounding like an avalanche in my chest. *Oh god.* This was the bad thing—the thing that would ruin the reputation of the inn. *Beloved Hollywood actor falls and dies in historic Maine inn.*

"He's not dead. He's not dead," I repeated over and over, a kind of mindless chant to will it into reality as I tried to make another call. I was still shaking so badly that I tapped on Max's name instead of my oldest brother, Jamie's.

"Hello?"

"Max. Something happened." I kneeled back beside the unconscious man, resting my hand gingerly on top of his. I didn't know what else to do. I didn't know how else to help.

"What? What's wrong, Lou?"

"One of my guests...he fell down the stairs. Th-the ambulance is coming. I need to go to the hospital. If he sues me, there's nothing I'll be able to do. He's famous, and I don't have that kind of money. Oh, god," I gasped, the memory of what I'd read months ago hitting me like a punch to the stomach. "His family are lawyers, Max. If he's injured or brain dead or paralyzed—If he dies—"

"Lou," Max's voice hit me like a wall, stopping me from going completely over the edge into the sea of worst-case scenarios. "I'm coming there now. Just keep breathing."

"Max..."

"I'll be right there. It's all going to be okay."

I nodded, but no more sounds could come out. My cell landed on the floor, and I cupped my hand over my mouth, tears threatening to spill.

I should've knocked again. I should've knocked and tried to talk to him—tried to help him. What if this is all my fault?

I stood rooted to the same spot in the hallway, my mind spiraling a mile a minute for the entire five minutes it took the ambulance to get there. The whole time, Blaze didn't move. Didn't wake up.

The only small miracle I was afforded was that none of the other guests were disturbed until the sirens blared outside, and by then, Max rushed in behind the EMTs.

"Are you okay?" He took my shoulders, but I couldn't tear my eyes away from the paramedics as they assessed Blaze and then started to put a brace around his neck.

"Fine," I said when Max shook me again. "I'm fine."

"Oh, my word. What is happening?" Mrs. Tisdale exclaimed, standing on the landing of the stairs in her pink silk robe.

"Can you handle her—them? I have to go..." I don't think I waited for Max's confirmation before I moved around him and followed the EMTs and the gurney out the front door.

I quickened my pace down the stone walk in front of the inn to where the ambulance was parked, reaching the curb just as they lifted Blaze into the back.

"Is he okay?" I rushed in front of the one EMT.

"He's not responsive. Until he gets to the hospital and the doctors there can run tests, I can't really give you much more information," he said apologetically, shutting one of the doors.

"Can I go with him to the hospital?" I said, standing in the way of him closing the other door. "Please. I have to go with him."

I had to know he was going to be okay. I didn't even know who his emergency contact was or how to contact them.

"I'm sorry, ma'am. The only people I can bring in the ambulance are family."

My jaw went slack. Everything slowed until I was sure time had come to a standstill, just waiting for my next move. I couldn't swallow. Couldn't breathe. And the only thing I could think about was my sister. My wild, crazy, brazen twin sister who'd looked me in the eye when she fake-haunted my inn and told me—warned me, *"I think you could pretend if your life...if your dream depended on it."*

What would Frankie do?

"Ma'am, are you alright?" A hand gripped my shoulders as the world started to tip.

Yes. No.

"Ma'am," he repeated, just as my chin started to dip and the gears of my tongue fumbled to catch. "Are you alright? Are you his girlfriend?"

"Yes," I answered before he finished—an answer meant for the first question, but he assumed it was for both.

"That's all you had to say. Here, climb up in there with him." He guided me into the ambulance where the miscommunication gagged me into a lie.

I'd let him think I was Blaze Stevens's girlfriend because the future of my inn depended on it.

Chapter Two

Wade

The phone on my desk beeped with an incoming call, drawing my glare until the red light came on, indicating that the system immediately sent it to voicemail.

Who the hell was calling at ten at night?

Almost instantly, my cell started vibrating on my desk. I'd set it earlier to *do not disturb* so whoever it was had called multiple times to try and reach me.

"Dammit," I swore, my gut turning in a way that usually meant something wasn't right. I shoved aside the mess of paper on my desk, having written and rewritten my line of questioning at least a dozen times.

Stevens, Stevens, and Heller was the largest anti-trust law firm in Boston, and right now we were trying a huge case against an insurance company, so every word, every statement had to be perfect. Monday morning, I'd scheduled a mock jury to hear my arguments and gather their feedback. *Suits* might've done a shit job portraying what being a lawyer was really like, but *Bull* and the idea of trial science was no joke, especially in cases where everything was on the line.

The other partner at the firm, Tim Heller, wanted to argue the case, but I'd insisted I could handle it. Even though Dad wasn't here, it was like I still had something to prove to his name on the building.

"Shit." My shoulders immediately slumped when I found my phone and saw who was calling. *Mom.* There was only one reason Joanna Stevens called this late at night. *There was only one reason Joanna Stevens called me, period.*

"What did he do now?" I answered, the tiredness in my voice having nothing to do with physical fatigue but the mental and emotional exhaustion of preparing to have to clean up yet another of my little brother's messes.

"It's...Blaze." She was sobbing.

I sat forward in my chair. The level of emotion in her voice was...different...than the times she'd called before. It had been years since Blaze himself asked me for any help. It was always Mom who intervened on his behalf.

"What happened?"

Drug possession? Car wreck? Drunk and disorderly? Sex tape scandal? What would the wheel of misfortune land on this time?

The rest of the world might know Blaze as Mr. Hollywood, but in the Stevens family, he was Mr. Misdemeanor. He was the classic consequence of a father who was too hard on him and a mother who babied and catered to him to compensate. Being in Hollywood only nurtured the catastrophe of his nature.

"He's...in the hospital." She choked out the words and then sobbed again.

"Not again." I closed my eyes and pinched the bridge of my nose. *Of course, he was.*

There was a cycle. Blaze would do a movie. It would blow up the box office. The press and attention afterward would consume him. He'd go hard, soaking up all the love and attention that Dad never gave him, and then he'd crash and burn in some kind of spectacular public spectacle.

The first time, he'd almost ended up in a Mexican prison. The next, he'd tried to have his own 'night at the museum' in New York and was found drinking out of a gold chalice that once belonged to Napoleon. Thank God, it had been a replica on display at the time. His most recent scandal had been a few months ago. He'd been heading to Aspen to meet some friends but never made it beyond Denver. I'd been called when he'd been picked up strolling through downtown Denver as the 'naked cowboy,' drunk as all hell and so high he could've visited with the International Space Station.

I hated that I wasn't surprised to get these calls anymore. Hated that I was only called when he was in the hospital or in a holding cell. But most of all, I hated that trying to help him only made things worse between us.

Two—three months ago, after I'd gotten Blaze off on all charges for the naked cowboy incident, we'd had a huge argument. I told him all this had to stop.

"You can't keep pulling shit like this, Blaze. You have to grow up."

"Wow, you really are just like Dad, aren't you, Wade? All high and mighty, judging everyone else who's different than you."

"That's bullshit, and you know it."

Dad was always the one to yell at Blaze. When he was younger, it was for failing a test, skipping school, not doing his homework, or being caught in the bathroom smoking weed. When he got older, it was for not having a real career. For using his good looks to get by. And no matter how hard Blaze worked, no matter how famous he got, Dad never wasted an opportunity to remind Blaze that fame wouldn't last, and when his star stopped shining, he would have nothing to stop his crash and burn back into reality.

I didn't agree with the old man. He was from a different generation, and he didn't understand Blaze. Meanwhile, I was smart. Analytical. By the book. All things Dad valued and knew how to handle. Unfortunately, it not only drove a wedge between Dad and Blaze but also between my brother and me. No matter how many times I stood up for Blaze or bailed him out, he resented me for being Dad's favorite. Even when Dad died five years ago, it wasn't enough to heal the rift he'd caused.

"You're right. You're not quite like Dad. Dad never would've bailed me out in the first place. But don't worry, there's still time for you to elevate into a complete asshole. God forbid Dad learns you haven't upheld the entirety of his reputation since he's been gone."

By that point, Mom was crying and begging me—*me*—to make it stop. Like I was the reason my brother was drunk and insolent and doing his damnedest to ruin the impressive career he'd built for himself.

"Fine, if that's what you want me to be. Fine. Don't fucking call me for help again."

"I'll do you one better. I won't fucking call you, period."

And that was the last time I'd spoken to Blaze. Mom, on the other hand, called a few weeks after the argument to tell me she'd enrolled Blaze in a rehab program and that he was going to get better. I didn't even get a chance to consider getting my hopes up before the second call came in a few days later that he'd checked himself out of the program, told her he was going to get better on his own, and then disappeared to God knew where.

"Are they detoxing him? Is he injured? Who is suing him now?" I managed to filter out a curse.

"How dare you?" Mom sobbed, and I felt my jaw tighten. *Here we go.*

Mom tried to compensate for the way Dad reprimanded Blaze. She coddled him. Gave him extra attention—extra love. She never really caught on that Dad's attention to me didn't equate to affection.

So, here we were. A prestigious lawyer. A famous actor. A wealthy widow. One big, wildly dysfunctional family.

"I'm sorry," I ground out, knowing there was no point. There would never be any sympathy for the man who had to bend over backward to make sure my brother's reputation remained spotless. Only for him, forever her broken little boy. "What do I need to do?"

"Nothing," she choked, sniffling. "You don't need to do *anything—*"

"Mom—"

"I was calling because your brother is in a coma, and I'm on my way up to Maine, but no, sweetheart, there's nothing *you* need to do."

"Jesus. A coma?" I snapped, standing instantly and grabbing my jacket off the back of my chair. I was frustrated, not fucking heartless. "What the hell happened?" I asked, and then thought better about where she'd assume that question was coming from. "Where in Maine?"

"A small town on the coast. Friendship. But he's at the Stonebar Ridge Hospital."

"Where are you?" I shoved more papers around until I found my keys.

"I'm having a car take me up there. I already rented a hotel room."

"Okay, I'll meet you up there. I'm leaving the office now." I grabbed my briefcase and hit the lights, saying goodbye as I locked up my office and then headed downstairs to the parking garage. Looked like Heller was going to get to handle the mock trial on Monday after all. I was going to be in Maine for the foreseeable future.

My BMW beeped as I locked the doors, the sound strikingly invasive to the small-town silence surrounding the hospital. I couldn't remember the last time I was outside of a major city, couldn't remember the last time I was able to see more stars above me than streetlights around me. It was...unnerving.

"Why the hell did you come here, Blaze..." I muttered, glancing upward before heading toward the entrance.

Stonebar Ridge Hospital was as small and sleepy as the town it was stationed in. It was only three floors, and the parking lot had maybe only a dozen cars parked in it. There wasn't even a separate emergency room entrance. It was all just...one. And if all of that hadn't made the whole place seem a little unreal, the fact that there was no one in the waiting room definitely did.

After shoving my way through enough ER crowds to get to the check-in desk and ask about my brother, I was on the cusp of believing I'd just entered the twilight zone, seeing row after row of empty chairs when a very normal, very friendly voice drew my attention.

"Can I help you, sir?"

I looked toward the desk. The receptionist was just returning to her seat with a steaming mug of coffee in her hands. *Damn, that smelled good.*

I hadn't eaten dinner before or on my way up here. Usually, on late nights, I'd just microwave a frozen meal at the office, but I couldn't even spare the three and a half minutes for that before hopping in the car and driving up here.

Three hours to get to Maine, and now my stomach—and brain—felt the toll of 1 a.m.

"Yes. I'm here to see my brother. Blaze Stevens." I pulled out my wallet and my license, showing her my identification as I searched for her name badge. *Kim.*

"He's a popular man," Kim murmured with a smile and then sighed. "Too bad he's taken."

I had no idea what the hell she was talking about, and if I was being honest, 1 a.m. Wade didn't care...and didn't like the way her appreciative look suddenly took a bend toward me.

"I can definitely see the resemblance." Her gaze raked over me like it was seeing a lot more than that.

I swallowed my groan. We were brothers. We looked enough alike at any distance that if we were in the same place, people would pick up on the relationship, and I'd invariably get the questions: *"Do you get to watch him be filmed? Do you get to see his movies early? Are you an actor, too? His stunt double?"*

Because I was good at my job, I was good at deflecting. The last thing I needed was our strained relationship to take the front page of the tabloids. No one wanted to hear that I didn't get early access or have the inside scoop on anything having to do with my brother because he didn't want me there.

"Are you his older brother or younger? Older, I'd bet," she asked and ruefully answered.

"I'm his lawyer brother," I added and pulled out a document from my bag. "So, if you wouldn't mind, Kim, I'm also going to need you to sign this NDA just to protect my brother's privacy at this vulnerable time."

Was it sad I kept extra copies in my briefcase for situations like this? *Because of all Blaze's situations like this? Yes, it was.*

"An NDA?" Her eyes went wide.

"I'm sure you wouldn't say anything, but when it comes to my little brother, I need to do my best to shield his condition and whereabouts from everyone who would exploit the information."

Even though HIPAA was a very real thing, a patient couldn't personally sue for a HIPAA violation. The violation could only be reported to HHS, who would then have to act. And in my brother's case, by the time that happened, every tabloid, newspaper, and blog around the globe would know Blaze Stevens was unconscious in some podunk hospital in Maine. Handing out an NDA didn't eliminate all risks of that happening, but it certainly lessened it.

"I understand, hun. Anything I can do to help." She signed her name with a flourish and handed me back the paper.

"If you could just point me in the right direction," I prompted, using my last grain of effort to smile back.

"Of course, hun. He's being held through those doors, first hallway on your right, fourth door on the left." Kim leaned over the back of her chair to point to the only doors, other than the exit, inside the waiting room.

"Thanks." I tipped my chin and headed for the doors, my loafers obnoxiously tapping on the linoleum. A sound I'd never heard before over the chaos of a busy hospital. My hand landed on the doorknob, and I stopped, turning back to her to ask. "Did my mother get here yet?"

Kim nodded while taking a sip of her coffee, holding up a finger that signaled me to wait for her to finish. I regretted asking.

"Yes, she did," she replied. "About fifteen minutes ago, I believe. It was right before I went to grab a coffee. She was pretty upset. I'm sure she'll be glad you're here now with them."

Them? Who the hell had Mom dragged with her?

An exhale barreled from my chest, my gaze anchoring on the mug in her hand. *That was what I needed.* "Any chance that coffee is available for hospital guests, too?"

"For Blaze Stevens's family, it sure is," she said coyly and winked. "Through the doors, walk straight until you hit the nurse's station, and you'll see the fresh pot behind it."

"Thank you." Just the thought of coffee had my brain coming back to life.

The sterile, whitewashed arteries of the hospital looked just like every other, and there were more signs of life happening beyond those gateway doors. Nurses. Doctors. A few other visitors stationed in chairs outside of rooms. I kept my focus trained ahead of me, not even chancing a glance in the direction of my brother's room. If Mom saw me, that would be it. No escape. No mercy. And since there was no chance of finding something stronger to drink at the moment, a large cup of coffee was essential.

The nurse's station was all the way at the end of the hall. As I approached, I heard whoever was behind the desk before I saw her, the soft mutter, "*You can do this. Just go back there and tell her what happened.*"

I rounded the corner and collided with the source of the

mutter—the soft, petite source whose arms I caught to stop her from crashing into me.

"Oh, no!" Big hazel eyes went wide behind square glasses, her full, pink lips parting.

I had a split-second to be stunned by her beauty before the pain hit. I'd stopped her from running into me, but not the wave of hot coffee from sloshing over the lip of the mug in her hands. *Not exactly my preferred method of coffee absorption.*

"Shit—" I broke off with a hiss, my stomach tightening as scalding hot coffee landed on the front of my shirt. My tie. The lapel of my jacket.

"Oh my god, I am *so* sorry." The woman—who somehow managed to come away unscathed and unscorched—stepped back like a deer in headlights. "I'm so, so sorry." She set the mug on the desk and spun, grabbing a stack of napkins so fast a few of them blew onto the floor in her tailwind. "I didn't see you. I'm so sorry."

She couldn't stop apologizing as she smashed the napkins into my chest, pushing hard enough to make me grunt in an effort to soak up the stain.

"It's fine," I rumbled, trying to stop her, but she was in a trance, her small hands rubbing over my chest and abdomen.

"Oh, no. It's on your tie, too." She bit into her bottom lip, and my dick twitched.

Fuck, it was not a good time for this—for any of this.

She grabbed my tie between two napkins and, in the process of squeezing it dry, yanked my head down until it almost collided with hers.

"Stop." My hands covered over hers, and her breath caught.

One a.m. It had to be 1 a.m. in this twilight zone that made my skin come alive to touch her, that made my blood start to pump a little faster, and that made other, lower parts of me stir that definitely should remain sleeping.

Her head tipped up, eyes meeting mine. "I'm sorry," she murmured for the thousandth time, and for a second, I had the insane thought that if this were one of Blaze's movies, I'd be a half-second from kissing her in the scene.

One a.m. Twilight zone.

"It's fine," I rumbled, peeling my hands and my tie from hers and stepping back. "It's late, and I could probably use all the caffeine I can get right now."

She smiled at that. Small. Shy. I let my eyes roam over her while she gathered all the dirty napkins and threw them in the garbage underneath the desk.

She clearly wasn't a nurse or doctor. No scrubs. No name tag. Her loose pants and shirt were paired with an oversized blazer, the ensemble professional yet relaxed. Her soft brown hair was collected in two braids along the sides of her head. With her glasses, she reminded me of this demure librarian Blaze's character had been attracted to in his movie *More Than a Bet*, another modern adaption of George Bernard Shaw's *Pygmalion,* following *She's All That,* way back in the nineties.

I rested my shoulder against the wall, perfectly able to imagine some handsome dick like my brother wagering they could transform this bookworm into a beauty.

"Can I at least pour you a mug?" She surprised me by asking.

"You don't have to do that," I said, but she'd already stationed herself in front of the coffee pot, and as evidenced by our run-in, there wasn't room for two.

"Please. It's the least I can do," she said, the slight catch in her tone telling me there was more to it than that.

"Sure," I conceded. "Just black, please."

I watched her grab a fresh travel cup and fill it to the brim, noting with each movement how much more petite she was than she first appeared. My head tipped, assessing her further. Her clothes weren't so big that they looked ill-fitting, but they were big enough to conceal the slender curves I'd momentarily held against me. Even her braids obscured the length and texture of her hair. Her glasses muted the expressions of her eyes. She was hiding in her own skin—hiding in plain sight.

Approachable but also invisible, and I couldn't help but wonder why.

My tongue ran along the insides of my teeth, itching to ask who she was here with. But if I did that, it invited questions in return, and with Blaze involved, they would all be questions I couldn't answer.

"Is it decent?"

She set the pot down and looked back at me, confused.

"The coffee?"

"Oh." Her head bobbed. "It... it'll get the job done."

My lips quirked. "Got it."

"If you want good coffee, I'd recommend The Maine Squeeze. It's about fifteen minutes south of here in Friendship," she said as she handed me my cup.

"Oh?"

"We have the best coffee on the coast. And the best pastries."

"We?"

She sighed and shook her head. "I worked there for a long time. Old habits..." Her small smile was adorable, the way it drew the tiniest dimple on her left cheek...

What the hell, Wade.

A low noise rumbled from my chest as I took a healthy sip of the bitter liquid and winced. The only way I could describe the quality of the coffee was that it was clinically acceptable.

Her gaze rose to mine, pink dusting her cheeks as she waited for me to say something next. She caught her bottom lip between her teeth, worrying the flesh just long enough to make my cock more uncomfortable. *Dammit.* My throat tightened. I could—I wanted to continue the conversation. God, I couldn't remember the last time I stopped working long enough to even have the energy to be attracted to someone...

But 1 a.m. in the twilight zone when I needed to take care of my brother wasn't the time.

I stepped to the side so she could exit the desk area. "Thanks,"

I said, lifting the cup in my hand slightly and then dipping my chin. "Have a good night."

The flush in her cheeks deepened as her head bobbed. "You, too," she murmured and quickly stepped through, her feet padding softly down the hallway.

I watched the sway of her hips all the way until she rounded the corner in the same direction as my brother's room. Groaning, I turned in the opposite direction and quickly adjusted my dick, muttering a curse as I saw the distinct coffee stain all over the front of my shirt.

I was a fucking mess.

Rolling my shoulders back, I followed the same path as the woman—I hadn't even gotten her name. *For the best,* I quickly decided. Sure enough, I was hardly two steps into the hallway to Blaze's room before Mom's wail of relief or dismay, it was anyone's guess, bounced off the walls.

"Oh, Wade. Thank God."

Of course, Mom was dressed to the nines at one in the morning, her navy pantsuit accented with an army of gold jewelry given to her by Dad. Her blond hair was curled like she'd just taken it out of rollers, but it was her make-up that gave away her distress. Mom cried a lot—wailed, whimpered, pleaded—but she rarely, truly shed tears. However, tonight, the normally precise lines of her eyeliner and armor of mascara were smudged, marred, and, in some areas, missing entirely because she'd actually been crying.

Shit.

I barely managed to hold my coffee mug out of the path of her embrace before she gave me a brief hug and an air kiss on the cheek. Even the way she hugged Blaze and me was different. He always got lingering bear hugs while mine were over before they began. Was it because I didn't need bear hugs? Or was it because I was taught not to need them?

"I'm here. How is he?" I took a half step back from her and gulped down another mouthful of coffee. This time, the liquid wasn't as bitter.

Her hand flapped in front of her face before landing with a thud on her chest. "He's...in a coma." Another cry escaped her. "They don't know..." she paused, unable to continue without drawing a trembling breath. "They don't know when...or if...he'll wake up."

My jaw flexed hard. *Dammit, Blaze.* Pain wrapped like a band around my chest, worried about my brother. No matter what he thought of me, from the time we were little, all I ever wanted was to protect him. From Dad. From bullies. From the world. From himself.

"What happened?"

"He fell. Down the staircase. At the inn. He was staying at." Her answer was broken up by uneven gasps for air.

Before I could respond to her, an older man in a white coat approached us. "Mr. Stevens?"

"Yes." I took his outstretched hand.

"I'm Dr. Cooper. It's a pleasure to meet you, though I'm very sorry for what happened to your brother."

"Thank you," I murmured as Mom let another cry escape. "What exactly is his condition?"

"He hit his head pretty hard on the fall. That, combined with the level of alcohol in his blood, caused a good amount of swelling in his brain."

Alcohol. It was more than frustration that bottled behind my lips. It was fear. Drunken escapades were one thing, but ending up in a coma.

"Will that go down?"

"In most cases like this, the swelling from the trauma abates on its own, and your brother will wake up once the brain feels safe enough."

"And how long does that usually take?"

The doctor grimaced. "That can vary. Anywhere from days to months—"

Mom sobbed again at the mention of months, and without a thought, I reached out and grabbed her shoulder, giving it a squeeze as she dabbed her cheeks.

"Should we move him to a different hospital? Maybe Mass General—"

"He's stable right now, Mr. Stevens, so I wouldn't risk any further trauma by moving him. Right now, it's a waiting game regardless of what hospital he's at."

"I understand." Unfortunately, it wasn't only my brother's care I had to think about, but also his safety. And my options for security in a small-town hospital were vastly different than the ones I had access to back in Boston.

"And there's nothing you can do for my son?" Mom's lip quivered. "No medications? No treatment?"

"None that I would recommend at this time, Mrs. Stevens," the doctor said kindly but firmly like he'd answered these questions from her a few times already. "If we don't see steady progress over the next couple of days, we can explore alternatives."

She nodded wordlessly.

"Thank you," I said the words she couldn't. "We greatly appreciate your help...and your discretion."

Dr. Cooper nodded. "We're a very small community up here, Mr. Stevens. I can't speak for everyone, but I can say that most folks around here would never intentionally invite attention to someone—anyone—who's going through a hard time."

I thanked him again, deciding to give it a day before I still asked him to sign an NDA. As much as I wanted to believe him, I couldn't. The only answers I ever took at face value were the ones delivered under oath, and even then...

"Why don't you take a seat, Mom? Take a breath?"

Her shoulders slumped. "My poor baby boy. This is horrible, just horrible, Wade. How could this happen to him? He has such a good heart..."

I gritted my teeth. She was getting worked up again, the tears welling in the corners of her eyes.

"Let's go sit with him for a few minutes. It's"—I flicked my wrist to see my watch—"It's almost two in the morning. You need to sit." Mom needed sleep. We both did. But there was no way to convince her of that until she calmed down. "Let's get out of the hallway so you can sit, and we can talk."

I needed a couple of minutes and another large cup of bitter coffee to figure out what the hell we were going to do.

"You're right. Of course, you're right," she said and sighed, as though my being right always came at the expense of my brother and his happiness.

I downed the last dregs of coffee and threw the cup in the trash.

"Oh, Wade," Mom said and paused, her hand on the door to Blaze's room. "I completely forgot. Blaze's girlfriend is in with him. She's an angel...a true angel," she gushed, attempting a watery smile.

I stared at her. Blinked a few times. And then decided I hadn't heard her right.

"I'm sorry." I shook my head. "Did you say his *girlfriend*?"

"Yes. Elouise." Mom nodded. "She's lovely."

Lovely Elouise.

No. Not a chance. Blaze didn't have girlfriends—didn't do girlfriends. He did hook-ups. I knew because I had a whole server dedicated to NDAs from women Blaze had slept with. For some inexplicable reason, it was like women were *more* turned on by the idea that they had to keep the fling a secret.

"That's why he's been up here so long," she went on with a trembling smile, seeing how I stood frozen in disbelief. "Because he finally found someone."

I knew for a fact that wasn't true. I knew just like I knew he wasn't going to listen to me. I knew just like I knew there was either alcohol or drugs involved in what had happened to him. I knew because I knew my brother. I knew how he lived, and I knew how he struggled. And while there might not be a single other similarity between the two of us, the one trait—or trauma—that we did share was that neither of us knew how to let someone in.

Not like that.

But I kept my mouth shut because Mom's baby boy was in a coma, and she was obviously clinging to this like it was some kind of silver lining—that Blaze had finally fallen in love. She didn't need to know this silver lining was nothing more than a silver *lie.*

Mom opened the door and walked inside. "I'm back, Elouise," she greeted, a hiccup in her voice. "This is Blaze's brother, Wade. We were just talking with the doctor."

I kept my head down as I entered, making sure the door was firmly shut before I searched for the woman who was invariably trying to take advantage of my brother's fame or fortune or both. And just like everything else in my brother's life, I'd handle this problem for him, too.

From the side of the bed, she looked at me. Big hazel eyes behind square frames. Hair braided back on either side of her head. And full, pink lips parted like they were just waiting to be kissed.

"You?" I croaked.

The unassuming coffee nymph was Blaze's supposed girlfriend?

Chapter Three

Lou

"You?"

There was no mistaking the accusation in his tone. Wade Stevens. The gorgeous man I'd spilled hot coffee on was my comatose, fake boyfriend's older brother.

Oh god, Lou. What have you gotten yourself into?

I never lied—never successfully, anyway. Any and all liberties with the truth had always been fully and unequivocally assumed by my counterpart, my twin sister. Growing up, Frankie was the one who played pranks. Who treaded the line between white lies and lies of omission as expertly as a circus tightrope walker. Meanwhile, my body came with its own lie detector. Cheeks blaring red in alarm, pupils dilating wide with panic, skin breaking out in a sweat, mouth fumbling over the simplest of words.

I couldn't lie to save my life...until I'd stood on the curb and been faced with the choice to lie for my dream.

Yes.

For a brief moment, I tried to lean on the technicality that I hadn't lied. I'd wanted to tell the EMT I was okay, and he assumed it was the answer to the wrong question. But that technicality crumbled under the weight of my silence afterward. I hadn't corrected him, and a lie of omission was still a lie.

It was wrong. I'd never deny that. But in my weak defense, I also thought it was harmless. Just enough avoidance of the truth to get me to the hospital so I could make sure Mr. Stevens was okay.

I didn't expect the paramedic to hop out as soon as the doors opened and declare to the nurse waiting, "We've got an unresponsive male from a fall down some stairs. Laceration to the temple. BP is elevated. We stabilized his head and neck, and his girlfriend is with him."

How was that medically relevant?

I couldn't even make it out of the ambulance before the falsehood spread like the flames of a wildfire. From that nurse to her colleagues, then to the receptionist at the desk, and by the time it reached the doctor, it was safe to say the entire hospital was apprised of my relationship status with the unconscious Blaze Stevens.

It would still be okay. They'd admit him, do their testing, and then tell me what was wrong with him and how soon he would be better. As soon as I knew he wasn't going to die, I could leave. When he woke up, he could break the news that he didn't have a girlfriend, and it would just be a harmless misunderstanding.

I started to rationalize my level of panic. I had to, or the next person they'd be moving into a hospital bed would be me.

Except, of course, it hadn't happened that way. Blaze's mother, Joanna, had arrived while I was waiting—*panicking*. They must've found her information on him when they removed his personal items to take him for scans. I'd been sitting in the hospital room alone for what felt like forever when she burst through the door, sobbing that *her Blaze had finally found love.*

Someone had already told her that I, Blaze's girlfriend, was in the room, and again, my stunned silence only confirmed the falsehood.

Her arms came around me and jarred me from the shock, but

by then, she was crying, telling me all about her youngest son and how he's been so lost, and to hear that he's been staying in Maine because he found someone, was such a relief to her. Even if I wanted to correct her, Joanna Stevens talked a mile a minute, and by the time I could get a word in, the doctor came to give us both an update.

As wrong as it should've felt to sit silent and listen to a stranger's medical prognosis with his family, who believed me to be someone I wasn't, the way Joanna squeezed my hand made me glad I was there.

I remembered how Mom was when Kit was in the hospital, injured and unconscious. I remembered how many times she pulled me or Frankie or Jamie to her and swore she didn't know what she would do without us there. That was Joanna, devastated and afraid, and she had no one to lean on except me.

I'd squeezed her hand back, and with that small action, I was no longer an uncommitted participant in the ploy but a willing player. I'd stepped out of the shallows of the lie and into the deep end of deception.

I'd excused myself to get a cup of coffee and buy myself a couple minutes to think. *What would Frankie do?* No. Following through on this kind of fabrication is how Frankie ended up camping out at the inn with the man who'd then sold it to me. How she'd ended up pregnant and falling in love with him. Sure, it had worked out for her, but that was because it always somehow worked out for Frankie, no matter how much trouble she got herself into.

We were twins. There was no way *both* of us were born with that kind of luck.

No, I had to go back and tell her the truth. I was just the innkeeper who cared that Mr. Stevens was okay. I'd explain the runaway assumption and how I truly never meant for it to go this far. She would understand. She was already so kind to me. And I'd be happy to sit and stay with her until the doctors knew more. Just because I wasn't his girlfriend didn't mean I didn't care.

Just because I wasn't his girlfriend didn't mean I didn't care. I'd been repeating the mantra and my apology when I'd run into Mr. Tall, Dark, and Doused with Coffee.

For those minutes, there was no Blaze, there was no inn, there was only the racing of my heart and the flutter in my stomach, things I'd never felt before. But when he'd abruptly ended the conversation, I was convinced it was nothing more than my shot nerves wreaking havoc.

In retrospect, havoc was preferable to this.

"Wade, this is Lou Kinkade. Blaze's girlfriend," Joanna continued her introduction, having somehow completely missed his low accusation when he saw me.

I tugged my hand back from where it rested on top of Blaze's, almost as limp and cold as his, and stood, wiping the clamminess of my palms on the fabric of my pants.

Dark brown eyes glowed as they met mine, embers of disbelief popping and flickering in their depths. Under the heavy thump of my pulse, I noted the warm fluttering in my stomach again, inexplicably, the same as before.

"Hi—Hello again," I said, my voice cracking. I forced myself to swallow and quickly turned my head to Joanna, blurting out, "I met Mr. Stevens briefly when I went to go get some coffee."

I could only handle one lie, and I was hardly doing that. Plus, it felt like anything more than a few seconds under the heat of his stare, and he'd literally melt the truth from my bones.

"Miss Kinkade." There was an icy edge to his tone as he extended his hand to shake mine.

My tongue tumbled around in my mouth, searching for what to say as I placed my hand in his. His big palm completely engulfed my smaller one, a sizzling sensation shooting up the length of my arm and feeling like it collected as the base of my stomach.

"I'm so sorry about your brother," I managed, my eyes lifting to his. It was the truth—probably why it was easier for me to speak.

The hard angle of his jaw pulsed like a rock with a heartbeat. "So, you're Blaze's girlfriend?"

This was my chance to tell the truth. To cut this lie off at its small root before it had a chance to grow.

"For how long?" he asked not even a second later.

Could no one wait for an answer to one question before they asked another?

"Oh, Wade. Haven't we all been through enough tonight? Stop interrogating the poor girl," Joanna chided.

*Interrogate...*My jaw dropped, panic exploding as though he'd just pinned my head to the execution block. I'd forgotten...*He was the lawyer.*

Scrambled bits of online articles flipped through my brain. Wade wasn't just Blaze's brother. He was the lawyer in the family. He was the one who'd sue me for Blaze's fall...and now for everything that came after it.

Telling the truth was always the right thing to do, but I couldn't bring myself to do it. Not right now. Not at two in the morning. Not the way he was looking at me—questioning me like he didn't trust me even as his brother's girlfriend. I couldn't imagine the trial he'd put me through if I told him the truth...and I didn't want to imagine it. Not tonight.

"I'm not interrogating her. I just asked a question..." Wade trailed off, clearly a question he still expected me to answer.

"Not very long," I said softly. Going on about five and half hours now.

His eyes narrowed, scrutinizing my answer like he was a human lie detector.

Blaze had been staying at the inn for almost three months. Would he have told his brother if he had a girlfriend? Was that why Wade looked so skeptical? *No.*

My eyes fluttered, and the memory of Blaze flashed when I'd confronted him about leaving his door open and the bitterness of his words: *"Don't look at me like that—like my brother."*

"You don't say," he muttered under his breath.

Pulling my hand back, I pressed it to my chest and swayed. "I'm sorry."

"Enough, Wade." Joanna drew me back to my chair, and it was a good thing because my legs felt like they'd run empty of strength. "I'm just so glad you're here, Elouise. That Blaze found you here."

Words knotted in my throat like a ball of yarn, so tangled that all I could manage was a small smile and nod as she took my hand.

In my periphery, Wade moved to the corner of the small room, far enough away that it felt safe to take another look at him. The brother. The lawyer.

He was taller than Blaze. I'd never had to tip my head so high those few times I'd talked to Blaze at the inn. The shape of their eyes was the same, though not the color. And while Blaze was muscular—unless every photo on the internet had photoshopped his abs—there was an unsuspecting strength to Wade. I'd felt it when he grabbed me—steadied me. Underneath his fitted suit was an equally fit body.

But the most unexpected thing about Wade Stevens was how my body both wanted to be closer to him yet knew it was safer to stay away. Like a living flame, his presence made me tingly and warm, but too close—close enough to know the truth—and that heat would leave me as nothing but ash.

"He's going to be okay," I said, patting the top of Joanna's hand like I could convince us both and distract myself from the man who seemed to be assessing me far more than his brother.

"I just wish the doctor could do something for him. My poor boy..." she sniffled.

"Why was he drinking?"

I tensed at the rumble of his voice.

"Don't, Wade," Joanna begged, shaking her head. "I can't handle this tonight."

"Can't handle what? The truth?" he countered calmly with only the slightest glint in his eyes that gave away how her words affected him. "I want to know what happened to him, don't you?"

"No, you just want to be upset with him like you always are, and that's not helpful right now—"

"Dammit, Mom—"

"I'm sorry." I bolted upright from my chair. "I should go." *For a thousand and one reasons.*

"Go?" Wade's head cocked like he'd just caught me in the lie.

Boyfriend or not, I had a business to run.

"I don't...want to, of course," I stammered, pushing my glasses higher on my nose. "But the doctor said there's nothing more we can do tonight—for right now—except wait. And unfortunately, I have an inn full of guests, and I don't have anyone else I can leave in charge for a whole night and breakfast..." I trailed off and crouched by Joanna. "I'll come back tomorrow," I told her, her watery smile and nod steadying the uneven keel of my heart.

"Thank you for everything, Lou." She reached up and cupped my cheek. "I'm just so glad..."

"You own the inn where Blaze was staying?" His stare felt like a hand around my throat, tightening as he asked.

I straightened. "Yes, the Lamplight Inn."

Wade folded his arms over his chest, and suddenly, his suit didn't seem like it fit the muscles underneath. "And that's how you two met?"

"Yes," I said and quickly added before my answers were forced to become less truthful. "I need to get going."

He left me so rattled that I almost headed for the door without saying goodbye to the most important person to me. *Supposedly.* Thankfully, I caught myself and, giving my back to his brother, I went to the head of the bed.

For a second, I stared at the man I was supposed to be dating. Blaze looked even more handsome, if that were possible, though I still didn't feel even a twinge of visceral attraction to him. Maybe it wasn't handsome. Maybe it was simply more peaceful. In spite of his injuries. In spite of the cuts and bumps and bruising. There was no crease in his brow. No worry in his eyes.

I didn't know what demons he was fighting—except for maybe the one that growled behind me—but I felt for Blaze. I really did. The way he'd holed up in that room, never using his fame as leverage...never even letting the knowledge of his fame get out. I swore no one but Harper and I knew he was staying in Friendship, as though he was hiding from some kind of expectation he thought he'd never escape.

I sighed and bent over him. A girlfriend would've kissed him on the mouth, but I couldn't bring myself to do it. So, I pressed my lips to the side of his head, promising, "See you tomorrow."

"I'll see you tomorrow, sweetie," Joanna sniffled again. "Thank you for everything—"

"Please, don't." I smiled and then moved away from her side before she could say anything that would make me feel more horrible than I already did.

Frankie would've simply ignored the skeptical man observing me from the corner and left, but I couldn't. Wade had a right to be skeptical and a right to be worried, so I cordially murmured, "Goodnight," and then bolted from the room.

I thought it would be easier to breathe—to think—once I was out of that room. It wasn't. My breaths were just as shallow as I headed for the exit, the weight of the charade as crushing as an anvil strapped to my chest.

I should just go back and tell them the truth. Tell them I was scared what would happen to him and to me and to my inn and things got out of control. But then, a vision of that crisp, coal-burning gaze flooded my mind, and my pace picked up.

Tomorrow. After I slept. After I handled...my business...I'd figure out a plan to explain. Maybe I could catch Joanna alone. She seemed like she'd be more sympathetic to the domino of events that led to my deception. Much more so than Blaze's brother.

Wade Stevens hardly seemed sympathetic to his comatose

brother, why should he have any more understanding for me? He hadn't even wanted to hear my apology for spilling coffee all over his shirt.

No, Wade struck me as the kind of man who'd exact as much punishment as he possibly could for my crime before branding me with an L—not for Lou, but a scarlet letter for Liar.

"Miss Kinkade."

I shivered and turned slowly on the sidewalk, praying the sound was a figment of my runaway thoughts, but I wasn't so lucky.

Wade had followed me outside, somehow seeming even taller when he was this close. His stare should've cooled me far more than the crisp middle-of-the-night air. Instead, I only felt that dangerous warmth as it swept over me.

Did he know I was lying?

Was he going to confront me here away from Joanna?

"Mr. Stevens," I croaked, sending up a silent prayer that the death of my dreams wouldn't take place on the hospital's sidewalk.

"I'm taking you home."

Air whooshed from my lungs, and it took a second for his words to register.

"What?" I started. "No, that's not necessary. You should stay here with Joanna—"

"How do you plan on getting home then, Miss Kinkade? Because I'm hazarding a wild guess that there are no taxis around here, let alone ones roaming the streets at 3 a.m."

I stiffened. "I..."

My frazzled brain hadn't put the pieces together until that moment. I'd come in the ambulance, so I had no car to drive back.

Shoot.

I could call Max, but he was already holding down reception at the inn. Maybe if Jamie was there...No. I pressed my hand to my stomach. If my oldest brother came here—any of my family, but Jamie especially—and learned somehow, or was told by the very skeptical suit standing in front of me, that I had a boyfriend... *No.*

The only person I would trust to go along with the ruse until I could figure out a solution was Frankie. And my twin sister had a newborn baby, so there was no chance I was calling her right now. I'd sooner walk.

"You're right. I don't have a car here," I admitted, my shoulders slumping in defeat. "I'm sorry. If it's not too much trouble, I would appreciate a ride."

"No trouble at all." His hand twitched at his side, and when I heard a car engine turn over behind me, I realized he'd remote-started his car.

"Thank you."

It was going to be okay. It was only a car ride. Friendship was fifteen minutes away. I could pretend to sleep and avoid any more of his nosy questions until I decided what I was going to do. It would be fine. Nothing worse could happen tonight.

Just as the anxious beat of my heart started to settle, Wade opened the passenger door for me and said casually, "I'm going to stay in my brother's hotel room while he's here in the hospital."

No amount of cushion or suppleness in the luxury leather seats could soften the sudden blow of his words.

Stay... in his brother's... I couldn't breathe, my chest tight to the point of bursting as he closed the door, the sound like a gavel ringing in my ears declaring his verdict. *Wade planned to stay at the inn. With me.*

They said lies were like dominos, one toppling forward into the next. They were wrong. My lie was like quicksand, pulling me deeper into its mire, and the more I tried to get out, the harder it pulled me under. The closer it drew me to him. And the more dangerous it became.

Chapter Four

Wade

Elouise was either too tired or simply incapable of hiding her deer-in-headlights expression when I said I was going to stay at the Lamplight Inn, and it only further confounded my opinion of her, which was troubling for a man like me.

I dealt in opinions for a living. The opinions of my clients. The opinions of a jury. Of a judge. Opinions—right or wrong—were currency in my world, and I was the metaphorical banker. I traded on the opinions of the jury, sold them my opinion of my client, and bought the opinion of the judge. Not literally, but with evidence and case presentation. And I was damn good at it.

But while I'd normally be able to form that very first opinion of someone within moments of meeting them, my opinion of Elouise Kinkade wouldn't stop changing. Trying to understand her was like trying to hit a moving target.

On the one hand, when she'd crashed into me, my instant opinion was one of genuine, shy sincerity. Every word, every action as she tried to dry my shirt and tie, when she insisted on pouring me a cup of coffee, and even just now, when she realized she had no way home... was like looking through a stained-glass window. Not only could I see through to every thought, every motive, but her emotions colored everything from her cheeks to her tone.

And that kind of inherent honesty, hidden in plain sight, was so unbelievably—unexpectedly—attractive to me. All I wanted was to know more. All I wanted was to know what her hair would feel like between my fingers and just how many shades of pink I could turn her porcelain skin.

But when I did learn more, my opinion of Elouise veered drastically off-course. *Blaze's girlfriend.* The very thought made as much sense as driving the wrong way down a one-way street.

It wasn't true—couldn't be true. And it had nothing to do with her.

"Is that alright with you?" I asked and pulled up directions to the inn, watching Elouise from the corner of my eye as she buckled her seatbelt, her expression somber like she'd just clicked the final nail into her coffin. "Miss Kinkade?"

"I'm sorry?" Her lashes fluttered, dusting a fresh coat of pink onto her cheeks.

Tension rippled through me, and my cock swelled. I guess there were some parts of me whose opinion of Elouise didn't change. She was beautiful, and I was attracted to her regardless of who she was... or wasn't.

"Is it a problem if I stay in Blaze's room, Miss Kinkade?" I repeated, unable to temper the edge in my voice.

"No, of course not," she murmured.

The navigation dinged, and my hand tightened on the wheel, making the next turn toward Friendship. My focus dissolved into the shadowed road ahead, the full moon lending the palest gleam through the canopy of trees.

My gaze darted to her, catching the way she worried her bottom lip between her teeth and stared blankly out the window. Dammit. My jaw tightened, caging the swell of frustration that wanted to escape from my chest.

Blaze didn't have girlfriends—didn't *do* girlfriends. The media knew that. His friends and coworkers knew that. Even Mom knew that. And I had a folder of NDAs from his casual hook-ups to prove it. One—maybe two—nights was business as usual for Blaze.

Not this. Not her.

So, either my brother had completely changed who he was... how he'd lived... in a matter of months, or all of Lou's stained-glass emotion was nothing but a smoke screen, and my opinion of her was wrong from the start.

Whatever the truth, I was going to get to the bottom of it.

I glanced over, seeing her head was now tipped back and her eyes closed. Even if she could fall asleep in the span of a few seconds, the anxious clasp of her hands in her lap told me she wasn't sleeping.

"Can you tell me what happened earlier? When he fell?" I asked, my voice betraying my exhaustion.

The long column of her throat bobbed, and slowly, her eyes opened. I wished I could say for certain that her unsteady inhale or her downcast stare were signs she was hiding something, but in the impossible chance she was actually dating Blaze, reliving what happened tonight—what happened to him—would make anyone equally as unsettled.

Her tongue swiped across her bottom lip, and she began slowly, "I was downstairs at the reception desk, finishing up my nightly checklist. I went to grab water from the kitchen and heard a door slam upstairs. His. There are only a few rooms, and it's an old inn, so I know the creak of each step in the staircase and the sound each door makes when it opens and closes."

Again, I didn't just hear the truth in what she said but the emotion that tinted it. Lou noticed that minutiae because she cared deeply about every piece of the building. It was in her voice. It was in her description. This inn was like family to her. *And not the estranged kind.*

What if she saw things in Blaze that no one had seen before? What if that changed him? *No,* I assured myself. It wasn't possible. The fact that he drunkenly fell down a flight of stairs was proof he hadn't changed. This was typical Blaze, and Lou was the piece that didn't fit.

"I heard him coming down the steps, and something didn't feel right, so I hurried back, but I didn't see—couldn't stop—" She broke off as her breath caught so harshly she started to cough. "I'm sorry." She held her hand to her throat.

"Don't apologize." I couldn't stop my interruption.

She apologized too much. At least a half-dozen times since I'd met her only a few hours ago, most for things that weren't her fault. My brother being too inebriated to stay upright was definitely not her fault.

"The next thing I knew, there was a loud crash. Several of them as he fell... and then it was quiet." And so was she, her voice whittling into almost a whisper. "And he was just lying there on the floor. Not moving. Blood on his head. On the floor..."

I glanced to her at the exact moment the moonlight caught on a solitary tear as it tumbled off her cheek and landed on her thumb. The instinct to reach over and wipe it away was as surprising as it was strong, and I quickly buried it.

I had no room for my emotion, only facts if I was going to protect Blaze from people who would try to exploit him. Lou seemed genuinely distraught over what happened, so I decided not to push her for more, at least not from that part of the story. The only thing I didn't trust right now was 3 a.m. Wade with any more of her tears.

"How long were you seeing Blaze?" I changed course as we entered into Friendship, the sleepy streetlights welcoming us to a veritable ghost town.

"Not very long," Lou repeated her answer from earlier. Was she distracted or purposely vague?

"What does that mean?" I pressed.

There was a reason the devil lived in the details, and that was why I asked for them. Lying was difficult, and the more someone had to work to keep up the ruse and fill in the fabrication, the harder it became.

"He checked in only a few months ago... in April."

"And that's how you met? At the inn?"

She nodded and curled into the passenger seat like she wished she could disappear into the black leather and avoid me altogether.

So, Blaze hadn't come here because of her. He'd come here... and found her.

"And the Lamplight Inn... it belongs to you?"

"Yes." Her head bobbed with a surprising burst of enthusiasm. "I purchased it last year and finished the restorations."

"When did you open?" I heard myself ask, not because there was any insight to be gleaned from the answer, but because I wanted to see that eagerness light up her face.

"Officially? The middle of January, right after my sister had her wedding here, and we had some friends and family stay."

"Very impressive." I made the mistake of looking at her when I said it. Her lips parted at the praise, and a bright pink stained her cheeks. *Fuck.* How would she look if I really praised her? If I kept praising her? What sounds would those full lips... "And you run it by yourself?" I croaked, my dick deserving the kind of pain it was in.

What the hell was I thinking?

"Yes. For now." Her tongue swiped along her bottom lip. "Sometimes my family helps out here and there, but it's mine. I live in one of the suites, so it makes it convenient to be there..."

And to be around my brother all the time. My jaw started to tighten as we pulled up in front of the two-story brick building.

If someone had painted a postcard of an idyllic New England inn on the coast and then magically brought it to life... well, this was it. The wrought-iron fence was more quaint than foreboding, and the single candle in every window lit like beacons of hospitality, beckoning weary travelers inside.

I parked out front, and the car wasn't even off before Lou was out of it and rushing to the front door. I followed a few steps behind her.

As soon as we entered, the younger man hunched over the reception desk looked up and relief doused his features when he saw Lou.

"Lou. Thank God. Is everything okay?" He rushed over and wrapped her in a big hug. He had to be one of the family she was just talking about, the way she melted into his embrace.

Was my brother this gentle with her? Did he praise her, too? A raw, burning sensation gripped my chest, and I jerked my eyes away.

I shouldn't be thinking those things. In either scenario, whether she really was Blaze's girlfriend or was pretending, it was wrong.

"Yes. I mean, no, but yes. He's stable for now," she answered, and I ignored how it got easier to breathe when the man let her go. I was the next focus of his attention, and Lou turned and introduced us. "Max, this is Mr. Stevens. Blaze's brother. Mr. Stevens, this is my cousin, Max."

"I'm sorry about your brother," the cousin said as he extended his hand, his smile pure sympathy.

I shook it. "Thanks."

"Thanks for holding down the fort for me, Max," Lou said and linked her arm through his. "I can handle everything from here, if you want to head home, and we can talk tomorrow." She guided him to the door like she couldn't get him out of the building fast enough.

I gritted my teeth. Did she not want me to talk to him? And why not?

"Are you sure—"

"Yes." She nodded. "It's been a long night. Please..."

Or was she bone-tired and wanted to go to bed? After the night she'd had, it was equally as plausible.

"Alright. I'll call you tomorrow," Max conceded.

As soon as she closed the door behind him, Lou faced me, her glasses dipping a little on her nose, but she was too tired to notice.

"I can take you upstairs to your brother's room."

Without waiting for my reply, she made for the staircase that wrapped up the right-hand side of the hall to the second floor. Her pace slowed on the first couple of steps, pain creasing her brow as though she were reliving those last moments of Blaze's fall.

When we reached the top, my brows rose silently when she used a giant metal key to unlock the first door on the left, open it, and turn on the light.

"This is—Oh no..."

I stared over her shoulder into Blaze's room. It was a disaster. Worse than a disaster. Clothes and sheets and blankets... everything was everywhere. The chair tipped over, a lamp on the ground. *Jesus.*

"I'm sorry," she choked out, her voice catching on the sob she clearly tried to hide. "I didn't realize—Just give me one minute, and I can clean this."

In another time and place, it would've been comical the way she hopped through the room, trying to avoid stepping on Blaze's clothes. My brother clearly couldn't care less about them since he'd thrown them on the floor.

Instead, I only saw another victim of my brother's emotions. One who was desperate to clean up after him and try to put him to rights.

I knew because I'd been one, too.

There was something about being an older brother. A kind of protectiveness that just seemed innate. I remembered when Blaze was little, before we'd been forced apart. I remembered sharing my toys and teaching him how to ride a bike. I remembered pretending never to be able to find him when we played hide-and-seek because I loved the way he smiled and laughed when he thought he outsmarted me.

I'd never forget the time he'd been hiding behind the couch in

Dad's study. He'd been so excited I'd missed his hiding spot that when he jumped out to try and scare me, he'd knocked over a side table and shattered the vase sitting on top. I told him it would be okay, that it was an accident, but it wasn't okay. Dad was furious.

The next time something like that happened, Blaze and I were racing our bikes down the driveway. He lost control at the end and crashed into the side of Dad's car. That time, I told Dad it was me. That the scratches on the car were my fault. I braced for the same anger... but it never came. There was annoyance. Frustration. But in the end, he thanked me for telling him and told me to be more careful in the future.

Even though we were only kids, it didn't take long to learn we wouldn't be treated the same.

At first, it was a last resort if something bad happened. I'd take the fall because the fallout would be less. But as time went on and as Dad started to hound Blaze for other things—grades, school, his interest in acting—that was when he began pushing the limits. Purposely acting out. Causing trouble.

One night, Blaze stole the keys to Dad's Mercedes and drove to the movies. He was fifteen, and it came back with a dent in the bumper. I remembered pacing the kitchen until he got back and then demanding what he'd been thinking. Blaze tossed the keys at me and said, *'What does it matter? It's not like he'll ever punish you for it.'*

And that was the moment I realized my brother hated me. All those years I'd protected him, he'd only grown to resent me because, to Dad, I could do no wrong.

After that, things got bad. And once Blaze moved to Hollywood and became a celebrity, things got worse. And still, every time he or Mom called, I came. To protect him. To hide the mess. And somchow, that only made him resent me more.

"Goddammit," I muttered and strode into the room. I wasn't going to make her clean up his mess alone.

While Lou started by righting and up righting all the furniture and decor, I bent and picked up piece after piece of Blaze's clothes. He was always like this—a tornado when he felt like the world was closing in on him, and Mom always cleaned up in his wake. *Was that what Lou was having to do? Take care of the man she was dating like he was a child?*

Another surge of anger went through me, frying the already frayed ends of my nerves.

Was Blaze taking advantage of her caring nature? Or was she looking past his flaws for the payout his fame promised?

Silence chewed through the minutes like a flame down a fuse, and when the room began to look hospitable again, and Lou started to strip the bed, my fuse ran out.

"What happened here? Why did he do this?"

She stilled, her eyes dropping. "I don't know." Bending forward, she tried to wrangle the fitted sheet off the farthest corner as though I wasn't standing right there and able to help.

Was she innocent, or was this all part of her ruse? I hated that I couldn't tell.

"I don't believe that," I said bluntly and unsnagged the elastic corner to help her. "I don't believe that the woman he's dating—the woman he's basically living with"—*what else would you call the two of them inhabiting the same building*—"doesn't know why he was drunk and left this disaster moments before falling down the stairs."

Now, her cheeks bloomed bright red, and it was the only spot of color on her.

"I don't... I mean... I don't know what happened." Lou balled up the dirty sheets and dropped them on the floor, bringing her gaze to mine. "I was downstairs working in the kitchen. When I saw him earlier, at dinner, he was upset." She shuddered and went to the chest of drawers, pulling out a fresh set of linens from the bottom one.

"You went to dinner? I thought you were the only one who works—"

She shook the fresh sheet open with a loud snap. "No, we

didn't go to dinner. He ordered food to the inn, and I brought it up to his room."

That didn't sound like Blaze, either. My brother loved going out. Loved being seen. *Loved being loved.*

"And you didn't ask him why he was upset?"

A quiet fury flashed in her eyes. "I tried. I started asking questions, and we... argued."

"About what?" I grabbed the other side of the sheet to help her again, seeing how she was determined to put it on single-handedly.

She tucked the sides of the sheet, her movements frantic. "It's personal."

"My brother's in a coma, Miss Kinkade," I ground out. "Personal isn't really going to cut it for me right now."

She flinched, the tension in the room rising with each breath, but for as accommodating as she'd been, for as quick to please as she'd appeared, I'd suddenly come face to face with a fortitude I hadn't expected.

I didn't know what infuriated me more, the thought that this woman was out to take advantage of Blaze or the idea that he'd found someone who seemed quiet and pliable on the outside but, when tested, had a backbone of steel.

She finished arranging the pillows back on the mattress, and I realized she wasn't going to answer me, no matter how hard I glowered at her.

My sudden admiration of her snapped my restraint. It didn't matter what my opinion was of Lou Kinkade or if she liked me—or now hated me—my first responsibility was protecting my brother. And if the last decade was any proof, when it came to Blaze Stevens, everyone was guilty until proven innocent.

"So, what was it? Were you trying to pressure him into a relationship?" I demanded coldly.

"What?" She started to round the bed, her brow furrowing.

"Were you trying to blackmail him?" Gone was the last of my finesse.

She tripped and saved herself by catching the back of the chair she'd righted earlier. When she looked at me, her eyes were giant amber orbs behind her glasses, her cheeks void of every fleck of color.

"Are you... are you serious?"

A distant part of me—the one in the center of my chest that obscured rational thinking—winced at the damaged tremor in her voice. But I ignored it. I had to.

"Serious?" I laughed bitterly. "Yes, I'm serious. I'm the serious one. Not Blaze. The only thing serious about the 'relationships' Blaze engages in are the signed NDAs he gives me. And still, those women try to find some way to swindle money from my brother's fame, fortune, or his family."

Her eyes widened with every word, but I couldn't stop. My tirade was born from years of ballooned frustration pricked by a single traumatic event. My brother—my little brother—was in a coma, and I hadn't been able to protect him. I'd witnessed all kinds of theatrics over the years when it came to Blaze's women, and if this woman, no matter how different she seemed, was trying to take advantage of him now...

Guilty until proven innocent.

"So, which one is it this time? Did you think he was promising a relationship when it was only sex? Is it a sex tape you threatened to leak because he doesn't want a relationship?" My shoulders heaved with the weight of my growl. "Actually, it doesn't even matter. Just tell me how much money you want to drop the act, or go ahead with whatever your little plan is and face every legal resource at my disposal."

Her visible, instinctual flinch brought my self-loathing front and center. I hated myself for having to think this way. For having to talk to her this way. But in all these years, I'd never been able to protect my brother by being a hero. The only way to keep him safe was by becoming the bad guy.

"Now, I understand..." Lou said softly, almost in a daze.

She came toward me like a lamb approaching a lion, holding

my stare until she was in front of me. Again, I felt her fortitude rush like a gale wind against my chest, invisible yet powerful.

"Understand what?" I rumbled, my eyes burrowing into hers.

I wanted to understand what happened, what my brother was thinking. But most of all, I wanted to understand the hot, electric undercurrent running through my veins right now. I wanted to understand the instinct to reach for her, to undo her hair and run my fingers through its lengths, and then to bring those innocent-seeming lips to mine and taste the whole of her truth... and bring color back to her cheeks.

I needed to understand why the hell I wanted my brother's girlfriend so damn bad.

"Earlier tonight, when we argued... he told me not to look at him like that. Like you do," she answered slowly, her stare glinting. "Like the way you're looking at me now."

"And what way is that?" Even as I bit out each word, I knew I'd regret the question.

And I did.

Her answer chewed right up what was left of my justified cruelty. "Like I'm a disappointment."

Goddammit, Blaze.

"Look, Miss Kinkade—"

"I don't care what you think," she declared, lifting her chin even though it made the quiver of her bottom lip painfully obvious. "I told you the truth. He was upset. I don't know what happened. I was working all day, and when I went to bring up dinner, I tried to ask if everything was okay, and he wouldn't tell me. So, I came back downstairs, and that was the last I talked to him. Maybe he was coming down to explain. To apologize—" She broke off with a small cry, her hand covering her mouth.

It was nothing. The smallest, weakest of sounds, and yet it pierced right through my chest as though it were a blade with a tip that targeted the heart.

Dammit.

"I'm going to bed. I have to get up in three hours to get breakfast ready…" She broke off and wiped the back of her hands on her cheeks. "I'm happy to answer any other questions you have tomorrow, Mr. Stevens."

She walked around me and out of the room without a backward glance, the soft sound of her muffled cries hitting my chest like lashes of a whip.

"Fuck," I groaned and rubbed my hands over my face. I'd fucked up, but to go after her now would only dig the proverbial hole deeper—deeper enough to bury myself in.

Closing the door, I set my alarm for three hours from now. I'd meet her that early so I could make amends. I wasn't sorry for not believing her. There was something off about all of this—her and him and what happened tonight—but I'd been an asshole about it, and I shouldn't have been.

I didn't even bother to undress, lying on top of the covers in my coffee-stained clothes and closing my eyes. *Dammit.* I reached down and adjusted my cock. I shouldn't be hard right now. Hell, I shouldn't have wanted her in the first place. Not when I saw her. Not when I learned who she was. And definitely not now after I'd pretty much guaranteed her hatred of me. I shouldn't be wanting what I couldn't have.

Hopefully, three hours of sleep would fix my momentary lapse in judgment, too.

Chapter Five

Lou

"Just tell me how much money you want to drop the act, or go ahead with whatever your little plan is and face every legal resource at my disposal."

I tensed, channeling all my indignation into the stubborn lid of the jam jar that refused to open.

I didn't know who I was angrier with: Wade for saying the things he had... or myself because the undercurrent of the accusation was true: I was a fraud. Lying for my own benefit. Not for money but for mercy. For my dream. And no matter what Frankie would argue, the ends didn't justify the means.

And the things Wade said... if I were really Blaze's girlfriend, I probably should've slapped him. I'd thought about it. I pictured myself walking up to him. I heard the crack of my hand on his cheek, saw the look of surprise on his face, and felt the triumphant surge of retribution in my tingling palm. Then I blinked and realized the person I'd been imagining wasn't me. Not when I was being dishonest with him.

Was I?

I didn't know why Blaze was upset last night. *Truth.* I did try to ask him when I brought up dinner, and he wouldn't tell me. *Truth.* I wasn't after any of his money. *Truth.*

All I'd done was tell him the truth and look at how he reacted.

I let out a deep sigh, giving my arm a moment's break before I attempted to open the lid one final time.

I should've been braver. That was what kept me awake in bed —tossing and turning over the lie I'd told—when exhaustion dictated an instantaneous sleep. I should've braved the storm and admitted to the entire misunderstanding rather than layering tiny truths on top of the lie. My grandmother, Gigi, had a saying for that: *like putting lipstick on a pig.*

I buckled down on the jar once more.

I could still fix it—still make it right. I squeezed the lid tighter, my teeth locking with the effort. I'd go to the hospital, talk to Joanna, and tell her everything. Apologize for everything. And hope Blaze woke up.

The lid started to give.

And then I'd pray that Wade Stevens didn't decide to sue me anyway.

The lid flew off the jar like one of those popper toys, spinning dramatically in the air, sending a spray of blueberry jam onto the floor and tablecloth, and then proceeding to land with the perfect position and speed to send it rolling along the uneven dining room floor, careening toward the entry to the hallway like it was trying to make a break for it.

"Crap," I muttered, setting the open jar down and grabbing a napkin.

This was the kind of thing that happened after a hard night and only three hours of sleep. *The kind of thing that happened when your fake boyfriend's brother was sleeping upstairs.*

Sinking to my knees, I began to wipe up the dark globs of Mom's famous blueberry spread.

"What a mess..." And I wasn't just talking about the jam.

"Is it?"

I stilled at the rumble of his voice, the texture of it still too fresh in my mind for my skin not to lift in an armor of goose bumps. *Maybe it was just my imagination.* I turned, air fleeing my lungs in a quick stream at the sight of him.

There was no imagining the man who filled the doorway into the dining room. Not the way his shoulders spanned the space and stretched the t-shirt he had on to the limit of its seams, the fabric pulling over the breadth of his chest.

Was Wade wearing his brother's clothes? My gaze narrowed, scanning over him to confirm. I saw the small hole in the shirt right near the waist, almost impossible to notice except that the dry cleaner had tagged it in front of me when he stopped to pick up Blaze's weekly laundry. Now, it confirmed my thought. And the same with the jeans. Muscled thighs filled out the worn denim that, along with the shirt, I'd returned to Mr. Stevens's—Blaze's room two days ago after they'd been cleaned.

Of course, he was wearing Blaze's clothes. What else did he have to wear? His coffee-stained suit?

I jerked, suddenly realizing just how far off course my thoughts had derailed... and how long I'd been staring.

What a mess.

"Just a little," I said, wiping up the last drop and preparing for another standoff as I rose.

How had I not heard him come down the steps? Was I that oblivious? No, this was just what happened when you lived a lie. I was too busy worrying about what to do next than to focus on what was happening now.

"Here you go," he said and extended his hand, the rogue cap perched between his fingers.

"Thank you." I took the lid, sacrificing my fingers to blueberry stains since that was what it took to keep my hand away from his. "Have you heard..."

"No." Wade shook his head.

I fought the rush of disappointment. If I could just know Blaze was okay, I wouldn't be so worried about telling them the truth.

"Okay. Well, I won't have breakfast set up for another fifteen minutes, if you could come back then."

Setting the lid on the table, I stuck my sticky fingers, one by one, in my mouth to clean them, all the while hoping Wade would move from the doorway so I could flee to the kitchen.

He didn't move. He didn't even respond. Hazarding a glance in his direction, I found him staring at me. Specifically, the tip of my finger poised between my lips as I sucked the last of the berry sweetness off.

Not staring—glaring. He glared at my hand as though it had pushed his brother down the staircase last night.

My finger popped from between my lips, the noise punctuating the tension. I quickly dropped my hand, drying it with a fresh napkin, and stammered, "I just have a few more things to put out for breakfast. Can I get you a coffee or a latte while you wait?"

"I'm not here for breakfast, Miss Kinkade," he said, his tone taking a marked rasp.

"Oh." My cheeks burned. I wasn't ready for this conversation. I hadn't even had my coffee yet. "Well, you should be. The pastry of the day is a rosquilla, which is a Spanish donut. They're similar to American donuts but a little smaller. A little more delicate—"

"Miss Kinkade—"

The more intent he was on interrupting me, the more desperate I became to talk my way out of the room.

"They remind me more of a churro with taste and the slight crisp—"

"Please."

I went still except for where I continued to wipe my fingers with the napkin. They were clean, but I couldn't stop the repetitive movement.

"I came to apologize for the things I said last night."

I sucked in a breath, the napkin falling from my fingers onto the floor. What he said was so unexpected that I felt my head spin for a moment. My eyes fluttered, and the world settled with him in front of me, picking up the small piece of garbage like a peace offering.

"I'm sorry for what I said about you and my brother... for what I implied," Wade continued, the t-shirt charting with its stretched fibers just how deep his breaths were. "It was inappropriate and uncalled for and disrespectful, and I hope you can forgive me."

I was frozen. My feet. My hands. My tongue. *This was the moment,* a small voice inside my head whispered. This was my chance to set the record straight. To apologize as well. To assure him I didn't want any money from him, and that I'd acted in panic. *Was that the right thing to do? Would he forgive me?*

Did I need him to forgive me? Or did I need him to just not sue me?

"However, I understand if you can't," he added while I still fumbled for the right response, the napkin crushed in his grip like a casualty of his contrition.

My heart tumbled in my chest. *The moment was slipping.* There was nothing for me to forgive, not until he knew the truth.

"Mr. Stevens..." I faced the table and tried to take a steadying breath. Maybe I could get the words past the fear gripping my throat if I wasn't looking at him—if I wasn't staring straight at my could-be executioner. And maybe if I had a distraction to temper my racing heart...

I grabbed the first thing I saw: an unopened jar of strawberry jam.

"Here, let me," he offered, taking the preserves and popping the lid off with ease.

Whatever I'd been about to say—to confess—died the way kindling does in the presence of a flame as his fingers brushed mine.

"No mess," he murmured and handed it back to me.

And just like that, I lost my nerve and found myself sequestered back in the realm of worst-case scenarios.

I was happy... and what if the truth would destroy that?

My throat bobbed, fighting the swell of emotions. "Thank you."

I set the jar on the small tray next to the toaster oven with the rest of the spreads. Without prompting, Wade began opening the remaining jars, carefully resting the lids on top until they were ready to be used. My mouth went dry, watching the flex of his forearms, the muscles defined by the veins that ran along them. Man, that suit really hadn't been doing very much for him—*Elouise.*

Moving to the end of the table, I picked up the three big boxes of pastries and brought them over to the large platter I had centered on the table.

"Are these the donuts?"

"Rosquillas."

"Rosquillas," he repeated, taking the top box and noting the Stonebar Bakery emblem on top.

"They're made at a local bakery by this lovely Ukrainian woman, Ella, and delivered fresh every morning." And they were a luxury treat I was happy to pay for.

He set the box on the table and opened the lid, his head tilting to the side. "Interesting."

"Have one," I encouraged. "They're delicious."

His gaze hooked on mine for a second before he carefully pulled out one of the rings, examined it again, and then took a bite, chewing slowly.

After seconds that stretched forever, I had to ask, "So, what's the verdict?" I winced at my choice of words and added, "Good, right?"

His eyes snapped to mine, and I looked away, focusing my attention on unloading the pastries from the box and arranging them on the platter.

He made a low, rumbly sound of enjoyment. "Very good." More than *very good* judging by the way he devoured it and then stared at the platter lined with a dozen more.

"You can have another one." I opened the second box and

held it out to him, watching him consider the temptation—and then consider me.

Heat dripped like a leaking faucet low in my stomach, something molten and aching and arguably catastrophic building inside me. I told myself it was the late night, the stress, the panic that made my stomach flutter and my heart stampede around him… I was wrong.

He took another pastry. "You get these every day?"

"Not these specifically. Ella makes all kinds of international pastries, and they're all delicious. I'll get some repeats every month, just because some are my favorites, but gosh, she probably has enough recipes to go several months without repeating a single one."

"So, you enjoyed these before opening the inn?"

"Yeah," I blushed and went to unpacking the remaining boxes. At least if we were talking about this, we weren't talking about his brother. "I used to work at the local coffee shop in town for years—a decade. The owners would get some of her pastries there but only on the weekends."

"And you wanted them every day?"

I glanced at him. Had I imagined it or was there something different in his voice when he asked about what I wanted?

He looked away first, convincing me that I'd imagined it.

"Pastries are my guilty pleasure." I stiffened. *Guilty. Pleasure.* My streak of regrettable word choice continued. I picked up a rosquilla and quickly added, "But I think the chouquettes are my favorite."

"Chouquettes?" He picked up the empty boxes and began folding them up smaller and smaller to be discarded.

"They're French puff pastries sprinkled with sugar pearls. Your brother called them a bedazzled donut hole." The memory came unbidden, along with my small smile. Too fast for me to do anything to stop it.

"Miss Kinkade…"

I didn't know what Wade was going to say, and I didn't want

to find out. So, I blurted out the question lingering in my mind in the few hours we'd been apart.

"What you said, is that really... what happens?"

His brows rose. "That Blaze gets threatened? Extorted?"

I nodded, taking a bite of the pastry.

"Yes," Wade said gruffly. "Well, they try, but that's what he has me for, I guess."

I swallowed, the tightness in my chest excruciating. "I'm sorry."

I wasn't extorting him, I reminded myself. I wasn't trying to harm him at all. I was just so afraid of losing everything I'd worked so hard for. And even with Wade's apology, it still felt safer to tell Joanna first. Maybe if I had her sympathy...

"Don't apologize." There was an edge to his order, and it made me shiver as I took another bite of the pastry. "It's the price of fame... and of being Blaze."

"Well, he's lucky to have you looking out for him."

"Did he sound like he felt lucky to have me as a brother?"

Guilt stabbed my chest. Regardless of what he'd accused me of, I never should've brought up Blaze's comment. It wasn't my business—their relationship wasn't my business. But that didn't stop me from noticing that the pain on Wade's face when he heard what his brother had said was the same look of pain Blaze had when he said it.

"I'm sorry."

"Please stop apologizing for things that aren't your fault," he begged with a low rasp. "You weren't the one who said it. You were just the messenger."

It still didn't make me feel any better about it.

"To be fair, when he said it, he sounded like all of my siblings have at one point or another in our lives when we've wanted to strangle each other." I popped the last bite of my rosquilla in my mouth and then grabbed a bagel. I needed a little more substance for breakfast, especially after last night.

"How many siblings do you have?"

"Two older brothers and a sister." I sliced my bagel and pushed it into the toaster, realizing then that I'd left out I was a twin. The notion struck me like I'd betrayed Frankie. We were always a package deal. We'd come into the world as a package deal. Why hadn't I wanted him to know the other half of me?

Because Frankie was the part of the package that always stole the show.

"But my siblings would all do far less legal things if someone tried to extort me."

He made a low sound so close to a laugh that I took it as evidence that laughter from him was, in fact, possible. "I guess I would, too, if I wasn't a lawyer."

I watched the timer tick down on the toaster when footsteps above us drew my attention. My head tipped up. "Oh. If you'll excuse me. I have to grab a few more things before everyone—"

"What can I do to help?"

"Oh, you don't have to do anything, please," I said on instinct and opened the toaster. My bagel wasn't done, but that didn't mean the metal wasn't scorching when my fingers bumped it in a rush to take out my food.

I cried out and would've dropped it on the floor if Wade hadn't been quicker. He caught the bagel and quickly set it on the table as I doused my burned fingertips one by one into my mouth.

Good job, Lou. Good job. How I wished I had Frankie's hot wax-calloused fingers right now.

Wade stalked to the beverage dispensers on the far table. One for ice water, another for hot water, and then two containers for coffee and decaf. In a blink, he'd returned with a cup of cold water and a deep growl as he pulled my fingers from my mouth and doused them in the water.

The relief I felt was nominal compared to the fresh burn of his grip around my wrist, gentle but firm. His hand looked so big where it held me. Those veins I'd marked on his arms were closer now. Distractingly close. *He* was distractingly close.

My head tipped up slowly. The broadness of him that

stretched his brother's clothes seemed to stretch the seams between molecules of oxygen in the air, making them weaker. Making them less. *Making it harder to breathe.*

And when I did drag in a deep inhale, it was of a leathered, amber musk with a hint of pine. There was no growing up with my candle-making twin without being tested on all the scents she used.

"Are you alright?" Wade demanded, his voice lower... rougher than before.

"Yes," I murmured, unable to curb the breathlessness from my voice. As the pain cooled, it only made it more obvious how other parts of me had started to burn. "Thank you."

"Let me help you."

My eyelids fluttered. The air crackled with unstable attraction. Imbalanced. Forbidden. A kind of sensual, static electricity that made me want to ground my mouth to his.

Was this... My gaze lingered on his firm lips. Frankie had been the first of us to have a first kiss—*of course.* She'd talked it up—the heat, the sparks—a gross embellishment as it turned out when I'd finally kissed Dave Jenkins junior year. Nothing like Frankie said it would be. But now...

Now, Wade and I weren't even kissing, and I felt the sparks. The charge traveling along the skin of my lips. The jagged exchange of warm breaths. The hunger like my own little black hole, pulling all other thoughts... worries... fears... into it and obliterating them, leaving nothing but the want to kiss him.

"Please..."

Danger, my mind warned.

"I'm really fine." I swallowed again and tried to pull my hand back. "You're a guest. You don't have to help me."

Wade tightened his hold and let out a low growl. "I'm not a guest, Miss Kinkade. I'm your boyfriend's brother."

My jaw went slack, my eyes glued on his mouth. I wanted to push the words right back through his lips and lock them away with my own. I wanted to kiss him in spite of everything—in spite of every reason I shouldn't, and for some even greater inexplicable reason, his lips slid apart like he wanted to kiss me, too.

What was happening to me? How could he make me feel this way without hardly touching me? Who was this man, and what was he doing to me?

My boyfriend's brother.

My fake boyfriend's brother.

My fake, comatose boyfriend's brother who was already suspicious of me.

I sucked in a sharp breath, my body jerking like a bucket of ice water had been dumped from my brain.

"Yes," I said huskily, my throat working to swallow. "You are."

I lifted my fingers from the water when something caught Wade's attention—*someone* I realized.

"Lou?"

I'd know that voice anywhere because it was my own. *My sister was here.*

Chapter Six

Lou

Panic sank like a stone into my stomach, shattering the churning heat.

"Frankie." My unmetered heartbeat took another tumble, and I almost knocked the cup of water out of Wade's hand as I went to greet my twin.

She stood in the doorway in a pair of burnt orange pants and her favorite navy sweatshirt that read *Mama Bear* on the front. Her hair was loose around her face. It was always loose whenever she didn't have the baby with her. And even though she smiled at me—and at Wade—curiosity at who he was and why we'd been standing so close lined her gaze, and that put me on edge.

A curious Frankie was unpredictable.

My breaths turned shallow as I approached her. The story I'd spun pulsed like a live grenade in my palms. One wrong more inadvertently—or advertently—on her part could pull the pin and send my entire life up in smoke.

"Hey, what are you doing here?" I asked, quickly hugging her and trying to steer her from the room and as far from Wade as possible.

"And what do you mean, what am I doing here? I came to see if everything was okay." Her brow creased, but more importantly, her feet remained rooted where they stood. "Max told me about the accident last night when he stopped to pick up candles this morning for his summer bundle."

Max.

I nodded slowly, adrenaline firing off warning flares in my brain. "Frankie—"

"Hello." Wade's smooth voice by my side made me shiver.

I smiled quickly, hoping he wouldn't notice how fragile it was, how it cracked and quivered, ready to break under the slightest pressure. Frankie noticed though. She looked at my smile like I'd just put a Band-Aid on a bullet hole.

"Hi, I'm Frankie Collins," she greeted. It was still strange to hear her use her married name. Less strange at how effortlessly she absorbed it as though it was always meant to be a part of her. "I'm Lou's sister. Obviously," she tacked on with her usual brash.

"Nice to meet you. I'm Wade—"

"Frankie, can I talk to you a minute about Logan?" I interrupted him, grabbing my sister's hand.

Frankie's brows lifted at the mention of her newborn son, Logan, but didn't protest.

"If you could excuse us. I'll be right back." I shot Wade a brief, apologetic smile, and pulled my sister toward the kitchen and away from a conversation that could ruin everything.

Two steps into the hallway, and I heard footsteps upstairs. *Crap.* People were awake and heading down for breakfast.

I looked over my shoulder to Wade, "If you could let any other guests who come down know about the buffet, and that the yogurt will be right out..."

"I'll take care of it," he said, the promise calming me way more than it should. *So much for not needing his help.*

"Lou, what's going on? Who was that? Are you okay?" Frankie demanded as soon as I closed us in the kitchen.

"No." I sagged my back to the door and buried my face in my hands. "I'm not okay."

"I see that."

"Is it that obvious?"

"To me? Yes." She folded her arms. "And you're a horrible liar, so I know you didn't bring me in here to talk about Logan."

Apparently not that horrible...

I pushed away from the door and went to the fridge. I needed something cold. I needed to *be* cold. My face was on fire. My body was still coming down from the thousand-degree moment when I'd wanted to kiss Wade, one kind of panic turning into another when Frankie showed up.

"Is this about what happened last night with Blaze?" Her voice lowered. "Max told me it was him who fell down the staircase."

I groaned and opened the fridge door, basking in the chill for a very long second, and then reached for the boxes of individually wrapped yogurts.

"Something bad happened," I began, setting the yogurt on the counter and wishing I could crawl back into the fridge and take its place.

Frankie's shoulders slumped. "Oh, Lou. I'm sorry Blaze got hurt, but I'm sure he's going to pull through just fine—"

"That's not it." Just the thought of telling her what I'd done paralyzed me. I'd never shied away from telling my sister anything before, but this...

"Are you worried about what will happen? Oh, Lou..." She came over and pulled me into a tight hug. "You can't think like that. It's not good for you."

"No, he's not—he won't be," I protested. "He'll hate me when he learns what I've done."

I felt the truth building in my throat, swelling the same way nausea would.

"What you've done?" She laughed softly and then tipped back from the embrace to look at me. "Unless you pushed him down those stairs, what could you have possibly done to make him hate you—"

It swelled and rose and burned, and then it was bursting out of me, my body desperate to expel the truth that was causing so much turmoil.

"I pretended to be Blaze's girlfriend, so I could go in the ambulance and be at the hospital to make sure he wasn't going to die and his family wasn't going to sue me—"

"Wait, what—"

"But now, he's going to live, and when I tell them that I've lied to them, they're still going to sue me, and I'll lose the inn and everything I've worked for—"

"Elouise Margaret Kinkade." Frankie shook me. My runaway ramble halted as she stared at me with wide, disbelieving eyes. "What. *Exactly.* Did. You. Do?"

I heaved in a broken breath and formed the words more slowly, each one like another nail in the coffin of my dreams.

"When the paramedics came last night, they said I couldn't go in the ambulance because I wasn't family. But he wasn't waking up, Frankie. His head was bleeding, he reeked of alcohol..." I trailed off and drew a tremulous breath as my sister's hands moved to cup my cheeks, holding my head steady when it felt like my mind was going to spiral out of control. "I told them I was his girlfriend, and they let me go."

"You..."

I swallowed hard and nodded.

"You...lied?"

I winced and grabbed hold of her wrists. "Well, technically but not intentionally..."

"Of course, not intentionally." She rolled her eyes.

"He asked two questions one right after another. I was trying to answer the first one, but he didn't give me a chance. My *yes* came out as he asked if I was Blaze's girlfriend, and before I could correct him, he was letting me in the ambulance, so I didn't correct him..."

"Stop." She jostled me. "Stop and breathe."

Breathe. Right.

"I didn't mean for it to go this far," I said after a big inhale and turned away from her, opening the freezer and pulling out the bag of ice I used to fill the serving tray to keep the yogurt cold. "I thought we'd get there, and the doctor would tell me he passed out from the alcohol, and that with some fluids and meds, he'd wake right back up. I hoped."

I shuddered, not even feeling the icy cold cubes on my fingers as I spread them around the tray, recalling the doctor's voice. *'It could be a couple of days to months before he wakes up. If he wakes up.'*

"I told myself it was only the one EMT that misconstrued, and that as soon as I knew he was okay, I'd just leave, and it would just be a little misunderstanding."

"But that's not what happened." Frankie grabbed one of the boxes, opening it and arranging the small yogurts in the ice.

"Worse," I croaked.

"Lou..."

I pushed the ice around the tray in silence until it started to even out around the yogurts.

"The paramedics told the hospital staff. It was like... wildfire." I wiped my hand on the side of my linen pants and then went to the pantry cabinet to get the granola. "Honestly, I couldn't even think about correcting them. I was too worried if he was okay. Plus, he was alone... no one should be alone like that. Even unconscious. But before I even got an answer, his mom arrived.

"I didn't realize she lived in Boston—that his family was from Boston. I thought they all lived in California. I thought I had time

—" I broke off and took another steadying breath. "The nurse told her I was Blaze's girlfriend before she even walked in the room, and when she did..."

"What happened?" Frankie came closer and took the big bag of granola out of my hand.

I peeled my eyes open, my bottom lip trembling as I answered, "It was like Mom when she saw Kit in the hospital after the bombing."

That was all I needed to say to convey the depth and breadth of Joanna's pain, sadness, and love... and why I couldn't bring myself to rip the rug right out from under her when she clung to me for support.

"Oh, Lou."

"Yeah," I said, my voice a little hoarse. "It's bad, isn't it?"

"I mean..." Frankie tipped her head. "He is a celebrity who got injured on your property *and* his family are lawyers. And you are... you. You panicked the one time a guest got a splinter on the railing. I'm sure seeing him unconscious and bloody... worrying about him... the inn... you had to do something, and if pretending was the way to get answers..."

"Oh god. It's something you would've done," I groaned. "I didn't think it was *that* bad."

Frankie pursed her lips. "Rude."

That made me smile just a little before it crumbled under the weight of guilt. "What do I do?" I asked in a whisper. "I can't keep lying. I have to tell the truth and apologize."

"Yes. You do."

Wait. What? I balked and stared at her in confusion. "You're agreeing with me?" I choked. "Who are you, and what have you done with my twin sister?"

She rolled her eyes. "I'm agreeing in theory."

I exhaled. *There she was.* "Frankie—"

"You should tell the truth and apologize when Blaze wakes up."

"What?" I stammered. "Then he'll know—"

"He already knows." She came closer to me, cupping her hands over mine on the counter. "Lou... that man has been holed up at your inn for weeks. You've brought food to his room—picked up meals from restaurants for him when they wouldn't deliver. Gone to the grocery store for him. Gave him the mini fridge from your room. Folded his dry-cleaning. Made him fresh coffee at ten o'clock at night. And kept his secrets."

I wouldn't have called respecting his privacy as keeping his secrets but the rest she wasn't wrong about.

"Blaze knows who you are—what you've done for him. When he wakes up, he will forgive your white lie and be your biggest ally."

I hadn't lied to hurt anyone, especially Blaze. I didn't care who he was or how much money he had. I cared about my inn. My dream. I cared that if I lost it, I'd fade into the background for good. If I kept up the story until Blaze woke up...

"Just tell me how much money you want to drop the act, or go ahead with whatever your little plan is and face every legal resource at my disposal."

I sucked in a sharp breath, Wade's accusations from last night like a knife against my throat. If I told the truth now, when he hardly knew me—when there was only a fragment of trust between us, Wade would lump me right in with all the other women who'd betrayed his brother, and he'd make me pay. Even after his apology, I hardly knew him—couldn't trust him. Why should I expect him to trust me? Trust my intentions?

But if Blaze were awake... if Blaze could tell him... I chewed on my bottom lip. Either I was losing my mind, or Frankie's idea was sounding more and more reasonable. Except...

"What if he doesn't wake up?" Worst-case-scenario-Lou asked softly, pulling my hands back and moving to the cupboard where I kept the granola, removing the bag, and pouring some into the serving bowl I'd gotten out earlier.

"Lou, you lied about your relationship with Blaze but not about who you are." Frankie's gaze softened. "You're not a liar.

You're a good, caring person who was really afraid and worried for Blaze, and now, you have the chance to show that—to let his mom get to know that Lou. So, if it does come to that, and you have to explain it to her without Blaze's support, she will understand *why* you did what you did."

I blinked, slowly processing what she'd said… and what I hadn't. *I hadn't mentioned Wade.* I'd told her about Joanna. I'd told her my fears, but I hadn't told her the root of them.

"Frankie… she's not the one I'm worried about."

My sister furrowed her brow. "What are you talking about?"

I picked up the bowl of granola and handed it to her to carry, somehow finding it had been easier to explain my lie than it was to explain Wade.

"Joanna seems nice… understanding. But Blaze's brother is the lawyer… and he's here, too."

Her eyes bulged. "He is?"

"You just met him." I swallowed hard. "Wade is Blaze Stevens's older brother."

"Wade… the man out there? Thinks you're his brother's girlfriend?" she asked with unmistakable incredulity.

"Yes." A tingle ran down my spine, recalling the look in his eyes—the feel of his gaze on my mouth just moments earlier. I shuddered and picked up the tray of yogurts.

"Lou…" The corners of her mouth tipped, and she gave this kind of chuckle that made me feel like I'd missed something.

"What?"

She tipped her head. "The way he was looking at you when I came in…"

"Like he didn't believe I was Blaze's girlfriend?" I held back a groan and moved toward the door. We couldn't stay in here any longer. "This is why, even if I went with your plan, it wouldn't work. He's a lawyer. He finds the truth for a living. He'll realize—"

"No, he won't." Frankie shook her head, her smile tipping mischievously.

"How can you say that? You're the one who said I'm a terrible liar."

"Because of the way he looked at you, Lou… he didn't *want* to believe you're his brother's girlfriend."

Great. "So, I'm already failing…"

"No, you're not," Frankie said and reached for the door with her free hand, holding it open as she leaned closer and murmured, "There's a difference between thinking something is a lie and not wanting it to be the truth. And the man out there, he doesn't want your relationship with Blaze to be true because then, he'd be guilty of wanting his brother's girlfriend."

My steps faltered. She had to be wrong… *right?* I pushed the thought aside for a different concern that struck me.

"You can't tell Mom or Jamie or Kit—anyone about this, Frankie." The last thing I needed was my family trying to fix this for me, or worse, to be forced to lie to them, too. That was where I drew the line.

I held her stare until she nodded, and then led the way back to the dining room.

I didn't know what I was expecting, but it wasn't to see Wade selling Mrs. Tisdale on some rosquillas.

"They're a Spanish-style donut. I'm not a sweets person, but I tried them for the first time this morning, and I've already had two. Come find me in ten minutes, and I'll probably have finished my third."

"Well, that certainly is high praise…" She sighed. "Alright I'll give them a try."

"You won't regret it." He grabbed two from the platter with the tongs.

"Two of them, Mr. Stevens?" The older woman protested.

"They're small, and calories don't count on vacation." The briefest smile crossed his face as he placed them on her plate—a smile that disappeared as soon as he saw me.

"That's the look right there," Frankie murmured from behind me.

My eyes immediately snapped to the floor, and I hurried to the other side of the table and set the tray of yogurt down, quickly arranging the bowls and spoons.

"Call me if you need anything," Frankie said and hugged me again.

"Thanks." I stiffened when Wade came over to us, catching her just before she could leave.

"Heading out so soon?" he rumbled, and I felt that electrical imbalance begin to crackle again in the space between us.

"I have to get home to my son. He's only eight weeks."

"Congratulations."

Frankie beamed. "Thank you. It was nice to meet you, Wade, and I'm so sorry to hear about your brother."

Air plummeted like a hot knife into my lungs. *She'd called him Wade.*

It shouldn't matter, except Frankie was always first for everything, and for my entire life, I'd been fine with that. I'd been fine in the background. Safe in the shadows. Until now. Until the first time we'd said his name... and it had come from Frankie.

It didn't matter. I pushed out a long breath. He was my fake boyfriend's brother.

"Thanks," I heard him say before the newlyweds came up to me, all smiles, and captured my full attention.

"Thank you so much for your recommendations yesterday, Miss Kinkade. Our dinner last night..." The wife sighed.

"Good, right?" I beamed, all of my own troubles suddenly locked behind a closed door of cordiality and cheerfulness.

"Amazing," the husband chimed in. "Hey, by the way, what happened last night? By the time we got back, we only heard there was an ambulance..."

I balked, my heart starting to thud. I'd been so focused on what to say to the Stevens family that I hadn't even thought about how I was going to explain this to the guests.

"There's nothing to worry about," I said quickly, figuring I should say at least that much. "There was a minor injury for one of the guests—"

"And an ambulance was called out of an abundance of caution," Wade said, joining the conversation like some kind of cavalry. "As Miss Kinkade said, there is nothing to worry about and everyone is fine, and while she appreciates your concern, she also respects the privacy of all her guests."

I couldn't tell if it was his tone, his stoic expression, or simply the power of his presence that made the couple clam up and their eyes go wide. Or maybe it was because he had spoken for me.

"Please, help yourself to breakfast. The pastry of the day is a Spanish rosquilla, and they are delicious," I gushed nervously and stepped to the side, hoping to distract them from how Wade had firmly put them in their place.

As soon as they went to the table, I grabbed Wade's arm and pulled him to the side.

"I can handle my guests," I said, my voice hushed.

He stared and then slowly turned to where my hand was still holding him. I yanked it back like his skin was the equivalent of a hot stove and crossed my arms.

"And I'm responsible for handling my brother's privacy," he said in an equally low tone.

I winced. "I never would've told them—"

"I didn't say you would, Miss Kinkade. But it would be nice to feel like I can do something for my brother right now."

My jaw went slack, my stomach knotting tight at the expression on his face. I'd seen it far too many times in my own family, especially after everything that happened to Kit, to not recognize it now: the frustration of feeling powerless to help someone you loved.

My heart broke a little for the cool, collected man in front of me. Wade wanted to protect his brother—had protected his brother for so long—but hadn't been able to save him from this.

"You're right. Thank you. I'm sorry," I said and dragged my tongue over my lips.

"Stop apologizing." He sounded like it was more than the apology that had irritated him.

"Okay," I murmured, shifting my weight. "Do you want to take some breakfast—some of the rosquillas with you to the hospital for your mom?"

His eyes narrowed. "Are you trying to kick me out?"

"What? No," I stammered. "I just hate to keep you. I'm sure you want to get back to the hospital to see your brother."

"Don't you?" His eyes narrowed.

"Of course," I answered on a rushed exhale. "Of course, I do." *Be honest about who you are.* "I just… I have responsibilities here. For right now, at least until my cousin gets here to cover the front desk for a few hours."

"I'll wait," he declared.

"For me?" I squeaked. Why would he do that? Why wouldn't he just go—

"It doesn't make sense for two of us to drive over there. I'll wait, and we can ride together."

My jaw opened and shut, my brain fishing for some other excuse. "I don't know. I think you should—"

"Miss Kinkade," he interrupted, lowering his head to be sure no one else heard him. "Clearly, my brother told you enough to give you an idea that our relationship wasn't exactly… close. And after meeting our mother last night and seeing our… interactions, I think you might agree when I say it's probably better if you are there… as a buffer."

My eyes went wide, and my hand bumped his arm as I reached to adjust my glasses. "Oh."

A buffer.

Wade's jaw ticked. "You would be… helping me."

My chest tightened. I was a helper. For my whole life, I'd

helped my family and friends in pursuit of their own dreams. Mom's business. Frankie's candles. The Maine Squeeze. And Kit's art gallery. When I couldn't figure out my own future, I'd focused on helping the people I cared about succeed in theirs. Maybe this was the first thing I could do to show them—*show him*—that helping people was part of who I was: a good person who'd made a small mistake.

"I see. I mean, of course, if you want to wait, I can ride with you."

"Wonderful." Wade clipped his chin. "I have to make a few phone calls. Just let me know when you're ready."

Chapter Seven

Wade

"Everything okay?" I asked as Lou slid into the passenger seat, slightly flushed from hurrying to where I was parked out front of the inn waiting for her.

"Yes, sorry." She settled the pastry box in her lap and clipped her seat belt. "There's just two check-ins this afternoon, so I wanted to make sure everything was prepared for them."

While Lou finished her morning tasks, I'd spent the couple of hours making calls from Blaze's room. First, to the hospital's in-house legal counsel, formally requesting that everyone involved in my brother's care team sign an additional NDA to ensure his privacy while he recovered. Once I had their lawyer's agreement squared away and the NDA emailed over, I called the two people I had on speed dial for when... anything involving Blaze happened: his agent, Mark, and my private investigator, Mikey.

Mark's frustration quickly dissolved into dismay. As tired as he was of trying to rein in my brother's antics so Blaze didn't tank his career, he also genuinely cared about my brother, and I got the sense he felt a similar pit of guilt in his stomach. *How had we not been able to stop this?*

My private investigator, on the other hand, made a good living by being unemotional in the face of potential catastrophe. He made an even better living by being on retainer with me and forming contacts in all the major tabloids and celebrity entertainment blogs. Media was nothing more than modern-day espionage. A game of who knew what and when. Who was going to say too much. Who could be paid to keep silent. And who could be paid to turn traitor.

If anyone—any guests at the inn or anyone at the hospital—had leaked anything to the media about what happened to Blaze, Mikey would be able to find out, and I'd be able to do something about it.

I'd be able to do something to help him.

Only after I made sure every angle of my brother's situation was covered did I switch my focus back to my own business. I called Tim Heller, the other senior partner at my firm, and told him what happened.

Tim didn't sympathize with Blaze—*'a man has to take responsibility for his own actions'*—but he did empathize with me. *'You have to do what you feel is right, Wade.'* Countless times over the years, Tim had taken my side when Dad railed at me for coming to Blaze's legal aid, whether it was paying people off or threatening to sue.

Tim's condolences were heartfelt, and he already knew what I needed from him: to take over the mock trial and continue the preparation for our client's case without me. It went unspoken that I jeopardized not only our client but the firm's reputation by putting Blaze first. Dad would've been furious. Tim didn't question it.

"Do you need more time? I'm in no rush."

And I was under no reservations for what waited for me at the hospital. My distraught mother. My unchanged, unconscious brother. The destructive tension of trauma and broken family relationships.

"Oh, no. I'm ready. I was just caught in conversation on my

way out," she said, her hands knotting nervously in her lap as I pulled away from the curb.

"What did they want?" The couple who'd asked questions this morning at breakfast had been taking photos of the inn and selfies outside. They'd stopped Lou on her way to my car, catching her almost at the perfect time to speak to her alone.

I'd watched her face glow as soon as they had her attention. It was the same way she treated every guest who approached her at the buffet, like a flower that bloomed only under their attention. For those moments, she came to life, beautiful and vulnerable, and when finished, folded herself back into the shadows.

I saw it with everyone she spoke to. From her sister to the guests at the inn. Lou opened for everyone else. Gave them everything she had. And then closed back up.

I wondered if she opened that way for Blaze, too. I wondered if he'd even noticed. I certainly did this morning when I'd cared for her burned fingers. For those few seconds, I had been her entire world. More than that—I'd wanted to be. Until reality reminded me she belonged to him. *My brother.*

Fuck.

What the hell was I doing... wanting her like that. Guilt slipped like a knife through the throat of my thoughts, and an exhale hissed through my lips.

"They were asking for recommendations for things to do. Lunch spots—nothing about Blaze. I didn't say anything about your brother," Lou stammered quickly, her cheeks turning red while her knuckles clutched white around the box of rosquillas she'd brought for Mom.

My jaw flexed.

If I hadn't been such an asshole, her nervousness—how she'd wanted to avoid me earlier—would've made me suspicious. But I had been an asshole. I'd been tired and upset and... afraid for my little brother, and I'd lashed out at someone who hadn't deserved it. Someone I'd hardly spoken to before nailing her character to the stake and burning it.

No wonder she was still uneasy around me. An apology didn't mean much coming from a man like that.

"I know," I said and decided to change the subject. I didn't want her to be anxious and I didn't want to be... frustrated, and the only way to do that was to not talk about my brother. "You didn't tell me you were a twin."

She stiffened.

Shit. I didn't mean for it to sound like I was interrogating her. *Way to go, Wade.*

"I..." she drew silent for a moment and then let out a nervous laugh. "I'm sorry. I'm so used to people knowing about Frankie and me... or knowing about Frankie..."

"She likes the spotlight, doesn't she?" Two seconds was all it took to realize the sisters were the very definition of yin and yang, with Frankie Collins being the extrovert who naturally drew attention.

"You could say that." Lou's smile loosened, and her eyes lowered, her body sinking deeper into the seat... like she was trying to fold in on herself again so her sister could shine.

"I know what it's like to have a sibling who enjoys the attention." *A little too much in Blaze's case.*

Lou only responded with a quiet noise, and I realized we were back on the subject of my brother. Where I didn't want to be.

I cleared my throat. "Who is covering at the desk for you?"

I didn't know why, but when Lou said cousin, I'd been expecting the man from last night, Max, to show up again and resume his post. Instead, it was a younger blond with a bright smile and blue eyes.

"Oh, Harper." Lou adjusted her glasses, her button nose wrinkling adorably for a second. *Fuck.* My hand tightened on the steering wheel. *Adorable* was the kind of thought that was off-limits. "She's my cousin. Max's younger sister."

"I see," I rumbled, watching her attention shift to the window and the scenery passing outside, and I noticed her hands start to relax a little. Talking about the inn and her family calmed her. "Harper... like the honey?"

Her head snapped toward me, and her brows creased. "How did you know..."

"I saw the jar on the table this morning." *Harper's Honey,* the sticker read, a cute, illustrated bee completing the logo.

Her pink lips rounded into the perfect 'o,' and desire zipped through me, unexpected and powerful like a bolt of lightning.

My cock hardened inside my jeans. *Fuck.*

My cock hardened inside my brother's jeans... for my brother's girlfriend.

There might be no law against coveting your brother's woman, but that sure as hell didn't mean it wasn't wrong.

"She started just about a year ago—beekeeping. It was a hobby, and then it grew. Now, she has a small plot on my mom's farm where she has her hives."

"And she sells her products where? In town? Online?" I didn't really care where I could get a jar of honey. However, I did care that the more I asked about this, the less Lou's fingers dented into the pastry box.

"Right now, just to a few local businesses, but the demand has been growing. She's dealing with a few things while perfecting her product. The flavors. The logo. Her brother, Nox, is working on custom jars... But then she'll launch online."

"How many cousins do you have?" It seemed like at every turn, there was another one popping up.

"Just those three. Max, who was at the inn last night. He's thirty-four. Nox, who is twenty-nine like Frankie and me. And then Harper is the youngest at twenty-one."

"Sounds like a big family."

Mine was the opposite. Mom had no siblings. No distant relatives she cared to know. We had cousins on Dad's side of the family, but I'd met them only once at his funeral. They lived on the other side of the country, and our families had never been close. I never asked. I didn't have to, not with how our own nuclear family was barely held together with frayed threads.

Meanwhile, Lou had relatives showing up at the drop of a hat to help her.

"They're the best. We would do anything... for each other." She looked at me and smiled. Not the small, shy smile I'd seen countless times in the last twenty-four hours, but a smile that was wide and bright and full of personality. *Full of genuine happiness.*

My stomach tensed. This woman loved her family. There was no doubt about it. And I had no idea what that feeling was like.

A low sound rumbled from my chest. No matter how many times I tried to stop it, the notion that Lou wasn't my brother's type just wouldn't let up. It wasn't even her physical appearance, though more often than not, Blaze preferred bleach blondes. It was the whole package.

My brother always found himself entangled with younger women—usually college-aged party girls. The ones posting provocatively on social media, inviting attention—inviting him. He went after the ones looking for a good time because that was all he was looking for. Of course, some wanted more. More money. More fame. A jump-start to their acting career.

But Lou Kinkade was none of those things, and it was simultaneously both what attracted *me* to her and what should've sent Blaze running for the hills.

"Oh, good. You're here." Mom stood and rushed from Blaze's bedside, enveloping Lou first in a hug.

It didn't come as a surprise whom she was more relieved to see.

"How is he?" I asked when she finally reached for me, her embrace a fraction of what she'd just given a veritable stranger.

"No change." Her expression fell as she turned toward the bed, but when Lou placed her hand on Mom's arm, her expression lightened a little bit. "They took another scan earlier this morning, and the doctor said the swelling has started to go down slightly, not as much as he had hoped to see, but he said some is better than none."

I stared at Blaze's serene face, the beep of the monitors a distant echo in my ear. "Does he have any idea why it's going slow?"

Mom didn't answer right away, and immediately, I knew it was because she didn't want to. "He thinks it's because of the alcohol that was in his system, but now that they've flushed that out, he thinks the improvement will go quicker."

I bit the side of my cheek, willing myself not to say anything. I could be hard on him when he woke up—would be, even though, if the past was any indication, it wouldn't change anything. My brother had no incentive to reform because every time he failed, he failed up. *Maybe because I kept saving him.*

"How are you? Did you get any sleep? Eat anything?" Lou changed topics like she sensed the changing tension.

"No, not really. But I'm alright—"

"I thought you might say that," Lou broke in softly, extending the pastry box to her. "So, I brought some fresh Spanish rosquillas which are like donuts, and some yogurt for you."

Mom's eyes went round... and then watery. "You're so sweet," she gushed, taking the food and hugging Lou again. "So thoughtful... I'm just so glad Blaze found you. It's been my only consolation all night."

Jesus Christ.

It was a small miracle my phone started to buzz at that moment, giving me a legitimate reason to excuse myself. This was what I meant by failing up. Blaze ended up in a coma while he just happened to be dating the only woman who truly cared and wouldn't take advantage of him.

"Let me know as soon as you hear anything," I told Mikey and ended the call, looking up to see Mom coming out of Blaze's room.

For a woman who was always put together, her straight face trained to withstand the greatest of trials, it hit me now how ragged and exhausted she looked. It was like she couldn't let herself believe the doctors when they said Blaze should make a full recovery. It was just going to take time.

"What's wrong?" I rasped and met her a few steps from the door to Blaze's room.

"Nothing," she said as she reached up and absentmindedly rubbed her neck. I didn't doubt that she'd spent the remainder of the night in that chair by Blaze's bedside. "I was going to go get a cup of coffee. I wanted to give Lou some time alone with Blaze. The poor girl..."

For loving my brother, the thought came unbidden. *Unwarranted.* What kind of asshole mentally judged his degenerate younger brother while said brother was in a coma?

What kind of asshole desired his younger brother's girlfriend while said brother was in a coma?

This asshole right here.

"Who called you?" Mom asked.

"Mikey." My hand tightened on my cell. "Just trying to keep ahead of any media attention."

Immediately, Mom cupped her hand over her mouth, her gaze awash with fresh worry. "Do they know?" she whispered loudly.

I couldn't lie to her even if I wanted to. When it came to the press, we all had to be ahead of the game if there was any chance of keeping this under wraps.

"Not sure. Mikey said he heard rumblings, but if someone does have any information, they're keeping it quiet right now."

"Oh, Blaze." Mom shook her head, not bothering to hide how she wiped a tear from her cheek. "They wouldn't publish something about this. He's in a coma, they can't—"

"They won't," I interrupted her and took hold of her shoulders, trying to stop her from spiraling. "I spoke with the hospital council this morning. They're all signing NDAs."

The fact didn't seem to comfort her. "What if it's too late? What if they already know..."

I stiffened. "About the alcohol?"

She let out a cry and stepped out of my hold. "Don't start with me, Wade," she snapped defensively. "I don't want to hear how your brother brings this on himself. You don't know that. You don't know what happened. You don't know anything about your brother."

I gritted my teeth, forcing myself not to flinch as each accusation hit me like a whip flayed against my back. I wasn't going to say any of that, but there was no point in trying to deny it. I *had* said it plenty of times in the past for her assumption to be warranted and my denial to be doubtful. But this outburst—her anger—was mostly a product of emotion and exhaustion.

"Why don't you head over to your hotel for a few hours? I know Miss Kinkade brought you some breakfast, but you could shower and take a nap?" I suggested, urging when I saw she was about to refuse. "I'll be here... Miss Kinkade will be with Blaze until you get back."

That seemed to comfort her—Lou being here, not me. Some of the rigidity of her posture started to deflate, and she looked over her shoulder, debating.

"I'll call you if anything changes."

"I know you will," she said quietly, looking back at me. "I know how much you care about him, Wade. I just wish..."

"I know." I reached out and pulled her in for a hug. It was awkward and stiff. Not like the ones I'd seen her share with Blaze over the course of my life, but it was still a hug because I wished, too.

I wished Dad hadn't been like he was. That things had been different. That I knew more about the unconscious man in the hospital bed than just all of the legal problems I had to clean up.

"Go. Rest. He wouldn't want you wearing yourself thin." I pushed my hands into the pockets of Blaze's jeans.

Mom nodded, running the back of her finger under her eyes once more. "Thank you."

I let out a deep exhale, my feet rooted in the hall until she disappeared toward the exit.

Slowly, I shifted my gaze to Blaze's door, knowing what was behind it: Lou, bathing my brother in adoration and concern. Her wide eyes and soft words. Her face opening for him. Not nervous. Not anxious. But beautifully flushed all the same.

Fuck. Maybe I should go get some coffee. Give them their privacy like Mom wanted. It was the right thing to do. And I always did the right thing.

Always had done...

I found myself walking up to the door. *Just to look—to make sure—*I peered through the narrow blinds and saw Lou sitting on Blaze's bed, one of his hands clasped between both of hers in her lap.

Tension thrummed through me. *She was talking to him.* I moved my hands from my pockets to rest on the frame on either side of the door, not caring how it looked to anyone walking by that I was so obviously spying.

It wasn't like I could hear her.

It wasn't like it mattered.

Lou wore her every emotion out in the open. The nervous fidget of her fingers. The sad quiver of her full bottom lip. But it was the guilt... goddamn, it was the guilt in her eyes that gutted me.

I knew guilt. Learned it. Studied it. My entire life was predicated on discerning guilt from innocence, and while there might be a whole hell of a lot that screamed *innocent* about my brother's enigmatic girlfriend, there was also something undeniable in the way it whispered *guilty* in my ear.

But what the hell was she guilty about?

Annoyed, I tried to will myself to look away, to step back, but my annoyance only grew when I could do neither. I shouldn't be spying. I shouldn't care about what was going on, what she was saying to him, or how she was touching him. Yet, the sight of her small hands clutching his like she was the one holding on for dear life felt like a hot poker straight to my gut.

I tipped closer to the glass until it began to fog with my breath.

My jaw locked tighter and tighter, but I couldn't look away, watching the stroke of her hand along the back of his. Soft. Tender. I stared until everything else faded, and I imagined her hands on me. Touching. Stroking. And my hands on her, wrapping the soft length of her braid around my hand. Directing. Encouraging. I'd tip her head back until her soft lips fell open in that perfect 'o' again. Hold her steady as I fed my cock into the heat of her mouth... *That's it. Fit my whole cock like a good girl, Lou.*

Fuck. I jerked, banging my head on the glass because I was a fucking idiot.

Lou immediately looked over, and since there was no hiding my presence, the only thing I could do was pretend I'd knocked to alert her that I was coming in.

"Sorry to interrupt," I grunted as I opened the door.

Even with my interruption, she hadn't moved or changed her hold. I wanted to walk right over and pull his hand from hers so she'd stop stroking it—and so my imagination would stop running wild.

"It's okay," she said and gave her head a small shake. "I was just talking. Joanna said hearing my voice would help." Her shoulders sagged. "Do you think he heard me?"

I clenched my teeth. "I don't know." *But I wish I could've.*

"Where's Joanna?"

I grabbed the back of one of the chairs against the wall and carried it with one hand to the other side of the bed. *Better to keep Blaze between us. Remind me exactly where I stood in their relationship—outside of it.*

"I told her to go back to the hotel and get some rest," I said and took a seat, finally able to adjust my cock now that my waist was hidden.

"Oh, good. It won't help anyone if she runs herself ragged."

"Why does it sound like you're speaking from experience, Miss Kinkade?" I asked, my gaze still locked on her.

Those lips parted dangerously, and even though she kept herself facing my brother, it only gave me a straight-on view of the rapid thrum of her pulse along the smooth column of her neck.

She swallowed, her eyes lowering for a second. "My brother, Kit, was injured in the Boston Marathon bombing. He wasn't running... he just happened to be in the city that day..." she trailed off, but I didn't say anything—didn't move—because I needed her to finish the story.

The emotion she carried in her expression, in her words, in her voice, it was like a drug. Maybe if I was more like Blaze, I'd know better how drugs felt in my system, but I wasn't. So, I was blindsided by the swell of need I felt to know more about this woman.

"His injuries were severe, and he needed so many surgeries. Mom—our mom was inconsolable, afraid of the worst. My other brother, Jamie, fought so hard to get her to rest. I remember—" Her voice caught. "He tried to tell her that killing herself with worry wouldn't make anything better, but she just kept repeating, 'What am I going to do, Jamie? What am I going to do?' And I just remember going up to her and telling her that she had to be here for him when he pulled through. It was all she could do—all any of us could do. Hold ourselves together so we were there for him when he woke up."

Air pushed in a slow stream through my tight lips. I'd lost count of the number of times I'd consoled Mom because of something Blaze did or something that happened to him. I only wondered one time if she'd worry the same if it were me in trouble rather than her youngest—her baby. I didn't like the answer I imagined, so I never wondered again.

"I'm sorry," I said in a low voice, amazed by the picture of emotion on her face. It was so pure—like she'd stepped right back into that memory to recall the pain.

"Don't apologize for something that's not your fault."

I jerked, surprised to hear my own words turned against me. "Touché, Miss Kinkade."

"Just Lou," she demanded with sudden insistence, the strength of it retreating as she added, "Now that you know there are two of us."

There is only one of you, I wanted to growl. I wanted to cup her face, hold her eyes to mine, and tell her there was only one of the woman who made my blood burn and my body ache. If there were two, it would be easier. If there were two, it wouldn't be a problem. But there was only one of her, and she belonged to my brother.

Lou.

I ran my tongue along the insides of my teeth, the damn thing like a tiger assessing the bars of its cage. I shouldn't want to sink my teeth into the intimacy and taste the sound of her name. It was wrong. More than wrong. She was my brother's girlfriend, and I should keep the boundaries clear.

But instead, I found myself breaking them and wondering if maybe my younger brother and I had a little something in common after all.

"Lou." My voice rumbled over the single syllable. Small and soft and subtle. *Just like her.* But I'd be a fool not to think the nickname wasn't dangerous. Like a taste of belladonna on my tongue—the perfect poison to my morals.

Instantly, the color in her cheeks deepened, and that flutter of her pulse I'd been watching now raced. The way she sat—turned so she was in profile to me—I could follow the measured inhale and release of her breath, her chest rising, her breasts straining against the tight beige top that had been mostly hidden by the oversized blazer she'd had on in the car.

I gritted my teeth and inched my legs wider to relieve some of the pressure on my cock. *Fuck.* I forced myself to look at Blaze, thinking it would help.

It didn't.

I'd never once been jealous of my little brother. Not for his fame or his fortune or the way he managed so effortlessly to get everyone to love him, but that was what I felt right now: jealous that he was the one who got to find all the ways to make her blush.

"Is that what he calls you?" I heard myself ask.

"Excuse me?"

"My brother." My jaw pulsed. "Does he call you Lou?"

Her brows furrowed together, and she pulled her bottom lip between her teeth for a single, tantalizing second before answering, "What else would he call me?"

I waited until my gaze captured hers before letting the feral words escape from my lips, "Something sweeter. More intimate."

I should've stopped, but the rose color in her cheeks deepened with every word, and suddenly, I needed to see how many different shades I could turn her skin.

"He should call you something no one else would call you," I said, my voice gravelly.

Her throat bobbed. "Like what?"

My good girl.

I sat forward so suddenly the chair jerked, and I banged my knee against the side of the bed.

"Shit," I ground out, gripping my knee like the pulsing pain was any competition for the throb of my cock.

"Are you okay?"

No. Far from it.

Blaze might be the one who had an NDA for all of his liaisons, but as far as I knew, I was the one with the praise kink.

And when I looked at the woman in front of me, the way she worried over my brother, all I could think was that he never would've treated her like I would. Never would've worshipped her like I would. And the thought made me want to punch a hole in the wall.

"Fine," I said, finding my voice but unable to let go of the scowl on my face.

"Did he have... nicknames for his other girlfriends?"

I wanted to think she was asking out of jealousy, wanting to know more about my brother's checkered past, but I couldn't find any trace of the emotion in her voice.

"They weren't his girlfriends."

Lou ducked her head, but not before I saw her grimace. "Right."

Dammit. I wasn't trying to hurt her with who my brother was, but there was a reason the saying existed how a leopard couldn't change his spots.

I let out a slow breath and stared at my brother's sleeping face. For the first time, I let the thought in that this could've been so much worse. Many of the problems he'd had over the years could've been so much worse, but this... this could've been death. *And I wouldn't have been able to protect him from it.*

"Why don't you like him?"

My shoulders stiffened. "Who said I didn't like him?" Even my tone made the question sound ridiculous.

"I don't think it needed to be said."

I turned back to my brother, wishing I felt, even for a second, an ounce of dislike. Maybe that would make things easier... if I just hated him.

"What I don't like is that I wasn't surprised to get the call that Blaze was in the hospital—that he was drunk and ended up in a coma," I said through tight teeth. "What I don't like is that my little brother seems to have everything, still tries to fuck it all up, has everyone jumping to save him, only to come out unscathed enough to do it again. What I don't like is that there doesn't seem to be anything I can do to stop it... or to help him." My voice cracked at the end.

"I'm sorry."

"Stop—" I bit back a curse. The last person I wanted to take responsibility for Blaze was her. It felt like the sun apologizing for not being able to stop the night. "Keep saying sorry, and I'm going to assume you actually feel guilty for something."

Her eyes blew wide behind her glasses, her sharp inhale making her whole torso quake. And then the color in her cheeks appeared again, almost like my very own lie detector test. I inched forward in my chair, and I caught the subtle way she tipped back.

"Do you feel guilty for something, Lou?" Her name shouldn't have purred from my chest like it did. It shouldn't sound intimate when it was supposed to be an interrogation.

Her lips parted, the flutter of her pulse skyrocketing against her neck. There was something she wasn't telling me, and in that moment, I was sure of it.

"What is it? What aren't you telling me?" I coaxed, my voice dipping to a tenor reserved for times when I was with a woman and near a bed.

And then the machine by the bed began beeping loudly, making Lou jump and stealing both of our attention.

"It's not reading. What happened—"

I stood and then saw the problem. "The sensor on his finger —" I reached over the bed for the finger clip just as she did, our hands colliding right next to my brother's.

Heat seared my skin, my eyes snapping to hers. One slip of my finger against the sensor, and she'd know my heart was racing, too. She'd know there was something I wasn't telling her. Something I felt guilty for, too... *Wanting her.*

"It fell off," I muttered, releasing the clip to her hold and returning to my seat.

She fumbled to attach the monitor back on Blaze's finger. As soon as it picked up a signal, the beeping stopped, and her shoulders visibly sagged with relief. Without lifting her eyes from his hand, she said softly, "I feel guilty because this happened to him, because it happened while... he was with me."

I ground my teeth. "Don't do that," I warned. "Don't make yourself responsible for his actions."

For years, I'd taken responsibility for Blaze's actions, hoping it would protect him. Shelter him. Hoping it would give him the kind of love and support our father wasn't capable of. It hadn't done either of us any good.

"I know. But we argued, and he wasn't okay, and I couldn't—"

"That's not your fault, Lou. He had a problem with alcohol —has for a long time."

"W-what?"

I stared at her, unsure why she was looking at me like I had two heads. Blaze was an alcoholic. Hell, even with all my interventions, I hadn't been able to keep that out of the tabloids.

"He's an alcoholic," I repeated, slower this time. "He was in rehab. Mom paid for him to go to a very good"—*and very expensive*—"program, and he couldn't even stick it out for the first week before running away up here."

Not only had Mom paid for it—because she didn't even want to try to convince him to register himself on his own—but the soonest availability had been six months out, so she'd called me, and I'd offered my legal services to the facility at no charge for an entire year if they agreed to take him in the next round of admissions. All of that, and he'd checked himself out after a few days.

Decades, and I still hadn't learned that I couldn't help a man who wouldn't help himself.

"I don't—He didn't—" She shook her head, gathered her thoughts, and spoke again. "He didn't drink."

"What?" She couldn't mean what I thought she meant. It didn't make sense—wouldn't be possible. "No," I told her. "He was good at hiding it, but he was an alcoholic."

"You're wrong," Lou insisted, her voice small but all backbone as she stared me down.

"Just because you didn't see it, didn't mean he wasn't doing it," I said, my jaw clenching as I tipped forward, fighting my ingrained urge to argue and prove my point when I knew someone was guilty. "I'm sorry, but he had a problem—"

"And I'm telling you, he didn't drink while he was here," she said, her back ramrod straight. "I was in his room every day. There was no alcohol in there. No empty bottles. No hidden stash. He never had alcohol when he ate. Never had alcohol on his breath."

In his room. On his breath. Everything she said made the knot in my stomach turn tighter. It was one thing to know the concept of her being Blaze's girlfriend, but it was another to hear... to have to think about her being close to him every day. In his room—in his bed. Talking to him. Kissing him.

The angry urge to argue was suddenly cannibalized by the roar of jealousy surging through my veins. Hot and ravenous and violent. My mind flitted with visions of the two of them. Smiling. Laughing. Enjoying a meal together. And then an image of her—naked. Those long braids unraveled into chestnut waves, draping her pale skin. Her limbs tangled in white sheets. Her pink lips parted with pleasure as my brother—

Fuck.

Fucking fuck.

"Then what happened last night?" I demanded, frustration stretching my tone taut. "You saw him. You know what the doctors said was in his system. Why his brain—the swelling is recovering slowly. You saw the same room that I did..."

Like the flip of a switch, I watched all her emotions clam up, and the nagging suspicion that she was hiding something scratched the inside of my mind like nails on a chalkboard.

"I don't know what happened," she replied after a second, her voice lacking most of its former strength. "But it wasn't the Blaze I knew."

The Blaze she knew wasn't real—couldn't be real.

"Well, maybe you didn't really know him."

Her sudden inhale pierced the stillness of the room, and I

cursed myself when she stood from the bed and quickly excused herself from the room.

"Dammit, Blaze, what have you done?" I muttered, wondering if he'd hear me, too, as I added in an almost soundless whisper, "What am I doing?"

I didn't want to be an asshole, but I couldn't sit here and pretend like the man in the coma deserved the woman sitting by his side. As much as I loved my brother, I couldn't feed the fallacy of who Lou believed my brother to be. And if that made me an asshole, then so be it.

Who was I kidding? I was an asshole from the moment I'd wanted to kiss her... from the moment I'd imagined if she were mine.

Chapter Eight

Lou

"Oh, Lou, what a lovely space you've created," Joanna gushed as we descended the last steps back to the entryway, finishing up the tour of my inn. "I'm so glad he found this place... and you."

"Thank you," I said softly, guiding her away from the reception desk and Harper's curious gaze.

I owed my cousin big time for covering for me every afternoon for the whole week so I could go to the hospital. More than that, I probably owed her some kind of explanation, but I didn't know what was worse to admit to, the truth or the lie. So, I opted for the weak excuse that because of the NDA, I wasn't allowed to say anything. Whether it was her love for me or her true adoration of all things Blaze Stevens, I was glad she didn't press for more details.

Miraculously, I'd managed to keep any of the rest of my family from meeting Wade. It wasn't too hard. They were busy with their own lives, most of them with their young children, and I was good at pretending I had everything under control even when I didn't. I never considered that a lie, just simply survival.

"Here, why don't we sit," I said as we walked into the living room and motioned to the two armchairs tucked in the corner.

The seats were hidden from Harper and far enough away from the couches by the fireplace that we wouldn't disturb the newlywed couple who was perched on one of them, talking and looking at photos on their phones. Young people these days sure took a lot of photos.

"Thank you for bringing me here—showing me," Joanna said and sighed. "I didn't realize how much I needed a break."

There'd been steady improvements in Blaze's condition, but not drastic. Not enough for my ally to awaken.

All week, I'd sat by his side and Joanna's, listening to her stories about Blaze when he was little, hearing the love in her voice when she spoke about his career. It was easy to get Joanna off on tangents about Blaze. She was a proud mother. And it wasn't just for selfish reasons that I tried to keep the discussion on him. It seemed to bolster her spirits when she could gush about all the things he'd accomplished. But today, I couldn't keep the conversation on him.

Joanna began asking about me and my relationship with Blaze again. What the inn was like. What Blaze thought when he got here. What he'd been like over the last few months. How he liked being up here. What his plans were.

My vague answers backfired when Wade chimed in from his silent, solitary post in the corner and suggested Joanna come back with us and see the Lamplight Inn for herself. Maybe he'd wanted a break, too, clearly having a more conflicted perception of Blaze's past and present. *And me.*

After our conversation at the hospital, Wade and I skated through our interactions as though gliding across thin ice, afraid to say or do something that would crack through the surface and send us both sinking into depths that felt dangerous on so many levels.

Waiting for Blaze to get better so he could vouch for me seemed a reasonable solution in theory, but in reality, it was reckless. Especially when there was no denying my attraction to Wade. In the span of a day, I'd gone from no lies to two, and the irony was it was easier to lie about a relationship I didn't have than to hide feelings I definitely felt.

"This truly feels like a special place. No wonder Blaze loved it," Joanna went on, reminding me which one of her sons I should be thinking about. "Even the scent in here smells like—"

"Home." I took a deep breath and pointed to the candle that was lit on the coffee table closer to the couches. "My twin sister has a candle business. She made the scent especially for me—for the inn. It's vanilla and tobacco. A strange combination, but the sweet and smoky—"

"It's comforting." It was her turn to finish for me. "It sounds like the two of you are very close."

It was the kind of thing most people assumed because we were twins, and they weren't wrong. But sometimes, they also assumed that *close* meant *the same.*

"We are. Always have been. We're very close with our two older brothers, too. Well, half brothers, technically."

My and Frankie's dad had never been in the picture. From the time we were born, it had always been Mom, Jamie, and Kit, so it was hard to remember the distinction.

"That's so... wonderful." Her eyes saddened, and she began to fuss with the end of the black silk scarf she wore around her neck. "I wish my sons were closer."

My throat tightened. After a week of intruding on their family dynamic—or diffusing, depending on who you asked—the regret layered into Joanna's every expression was as obvious as the tension between Blaze and Wade had been from the start. Another feat, considering one of them was unconscious.

I reached over and took her hands in mine. "I'm sorry." As soon as the words were out, I winced. *Stop apologizing for something that's not your fault.*

Her smile was weary. "Don't apologize, Lou. If it's anyone's fault, it's mine."

I should drop it. Even if I was Blaze's girlfriend, even if I was sort of part of this family, it still wasn't my place. But I wanted to know. I should want to know about Blaze, but just like every conversation that had come before this one, the curiosity bubbling up from the center of my chest was only about Wade.

Every story she'd told, I'd hung on the smallest kernels of information about the older, stoic brother who seemed content in the shadows. I wanted to know more about the man who made my stomach flutter and warm shivers cascade over my skin.

And then I felt the unmistakable drop of a tear on my hand.

"What happened?" I heard myself ask, her pain pushing my curiosity over the edge.

"Nothing... and everything," she said with a sigh, brushing the back of her hand to her cheek. "My husband was... a flawed man. He had this idea of who and what he wanted his sons to be, how he wanted them to follow in his footsteps. But that was never Blaze. Blaze was always carefree. Imaginative. Playful. Always acting out stories from TV or movies and dragging his brother along with him."

The idea of Wade acting... anything... made me smile.

"My husband couldn't understand him—was hard on him. Too hard. And for every extra bit of hardness that he was, I became softer. Every time he praised or favored Wade, I tried to give something extra to Blaze." She took a deep inhale, her shoulders sagging as it released. "I didn't realize until too late that I'd been so worried about making up that love to Blaze that in the process, I wasn't there for Wade like I should've been."

I squeezed her fingers, words unraveling from my throat before I could stop them.

"Sometimes, we act in the moment to protect someone or something we love, and it's only looking back that you realize it wasn't the best thing to do. But just because it wasn't the best thing to do doesn't mean it was a bad thing either."

With the words out, all that remained was the knot in my throat. This was the moment. I saw it—felt it. This was the opportunity to tell Joanna the truth about me—about Blaze and me.

"You're so easy to talk to, Lou. It's no wonder Blaze fell for you," she said, her voice picking up a measure of strength as she smiled. "I know I keep saying it, but I truly don't know how I would be... handling this if you weren't here."

With every word, I watched my chance slip away. I felt the truth sink deeper and deeper into my stomach, buried under the weight of how much Joanna was relying on me.

"Blaze wasn't in a good place before, and just knowing he had you—knowing you were what kept him here, safe—brings me so much comfort, and I want to say thank you even though it doesn't seem like enough."

I tried to swallow—tried to free some kind of response—but I was speechless. I couldn't speak the truth but neither could I continue the lie. Thankfully, Joanna didn't wait for a reply before she stood and pulled me up with her and into a hug. Instinctively, I hugged her back even as my eyes darted to the other side of the room, afraid of who was seeing... listening... to all of this, but the young couple was distracted, taking a selfie in front of the fireplace.

"Thank you, Lou," she murmured again, and all I could do was nod into her shoulder and squeeze my eyes shut.

What am I doing? As she pulled back, I scrambled for something to say but was spared when the grandfather clock positioned in the opposite corner of the room chimed.

"Oh, dear. It's getting late. I really should get back to the hospital. I want to sit with Blaze a little before I go back to my hotel," she said, starting to get flustered as she gathered her things.

"Please, sit," I begged, my voice cracking. "I'll go get Wade and tell him you're ready."

After we'd returned to the inn, Wade went to make some calls for work while Joanna and I talked. His accusation that day at the hospital still festered between us like an open wound. *Maybe you don't really know him.* I didn't know him. I just couldn't admit to it.

I barely registered Harper's stare as I made for the staircase, all of my focus trained on placing one foot calmly in front of the other. *Don't run. Don't run. Don't run*, my heart hammered in my chest.

Was I holding back the truth because I didn't want to hurt her? Did I really think the woman who'd just said all that wouldn't forgive me? Or was I simply using someone else's pain to justify my lie?

I stopped in front of Wade's door and knocked loudly, my mind spiraling. I should've told her. I had the perfect chance. It would've hurt, would've disappointed her, but it would've been better in the long run.

The door whipped open, my knuckles swiping air.

"What?" Wade growled, and I realized I hadn't just knocked once. I'd kept knocking, lost in thought. No wonder he was...

Naked. *He was naked.*

My jaw dropped, eyes gulping in the sight of the bare-chested, towel-clad, glowering guest in the doorframe. When Harper first explained who Blaze Stevens was, the explanation had come with several visual aids—movie posters, YouTube clips—all to showcase his Hollywood physique, and none of which provoked even a fraction of the appreciation I felt right now. *For his older brother.*

I leap-frogged right over embarrassment for knocking and landed straight on mortification, unable to stop staring at the gorgeous man in front of me.

And if I thought it couldn't get any worse, instead of greeting him with *Wade,* the only word that slipped from my tongue was, "Wow."

Broad shoulders. Muscled chest. A ladder of abdominal muscles that led to his waist. All of it streaked in rivulets of water from the shower. His tapered hips were wrapped in the white terry towel he held cinched in one hand at his side. Wade held it so tightly, there was no chance of it slipping... but he held it so tight, it was impossible not to notice the large bulge in the front grow distinctly larger.

My breath caught, my nipples tightening to the point of ache. And the heat... it swelled in my stomach, between my legs. It cracked and popped like kindling catching flame.

"Lou." The low rumble of Wade's voice grated on my skin, an edge of anger to it.

My eyes snapped up, and I realized the crack and pop wasn't from the heat—it was from the thin layer of ice we'd been navigating, shattering under the weight of desire.

"What's. Wrong?" Wade punctuated each word like it was a sword pulling from his chest.

His wet hair curled, and water dripped off the ends, one droplet landing on the edge of his upper lip. My tongue instantly darted out and swiped over my own as though to lick it away.

"Sorry," I murmured, and this time, it wasn't lost on me that he didn't correct me. *This, most definitely, was my fault.* He'd been showering and I'd banged on his door like it was an emergency... and now, we were here.

A deep sound came from him. The stacks of muscles on his abdomen rippled, pushing the low, rough noise up to his chest and then higher through the pulsing of his throat and past the clenching of his jaw and the tight line of his lips. It wasn't like I hadn't heard him growl in displeasure before, but this time... the displeasure seemed to be lacking the *dis* and lingering on the *pleasure.*

"I'm sorry. Your mom wants to go back to the hospital," I blurted out and folded my arms.

His focus darted to my chest for a split second, and his jaw flexed. "I'll be right down."

I jumped when he slammed the door and then looked down, a fresh burn of embarrassment running through me when I saw the outline of my hard nipples pressed to my thin blouse. *No wonder he was furious.*

I spun and fled to the bathroom in my room, flipping the faucet on to cold and splashing the icy water on my face.

If he didn't hate me before, I was certainly giving him even more reason to now. Eyeing him up like I'd never seen a naked man before—like I'd never felt desire before. It didn't matter that I hadn't. It mattered that I shouldn't. Not like this. Not with him.

I shouldn't be attracted to my fake boyfriend's older brother, and I *definitely* shouldn't be so foolish as to let him realize it.

I was a ball of ungrounded electricity until they left. A ball of tangled, unstable electrons ready to combust with one more look or a single touch. Thankfully, when I went back downstairs, it was only Joanna waiting for me at the desk to hug me goodbye and tell me she'd see me tomorrow. Wade had gone to pull the car up front.

I sagged with relief as I closed the door behind her. I had the rest of the night to put some distance between me and Wade. Between me and my emotions. Hopefully, that would be enough.

"Is it true?"

I stilled at Harper's voice and then turned.

This time, I felt the heat leave my face as surely as I'd feel water running down my cheeks. "Harper—"

"Lou," she interrupted, her nostrils flaring. "Are you *dating* Blaze?"

My mouth opened. And then shut. And then opened again.

There was a wounded look to her expression, like I'd betrayed her, but I wasn't sure how. *Because I hadn't told her the lie I had to pretend was true? Or was it something else?*

"I..." I closed my mouth and swallowed.

"That's a yes." Harper wasn't as bold as Frankie, but she

didn't beat around the bush either. "Why didn't you tell me? And don't tell me it was because of the NDA. I already knew he was here. I already knew..."

My heart pounded in a tympanic thud inside my chest, beating to the tune of a tale I didn't want to keep telling. But like some kind of Pied Piper, I followed along the beat, afraid the truth would risk more than my dream.

"It just... happened, Harper," I said like it was even remotely close to an explanation. "I'm sorry. I've never done this before, and I didn't want to make anything more of it..." I trailed off when it was clear my excuses weren't helping. Harper's eyes glistened with tears, and her cheeks were pink.

Why was she so upset?

Of course, she had a crush on Blaze. Between her and Wade, they'd made it seem like every breathing female who came into contact with Blaze Stevens had a crush on him. But would they really cry to hear he had a girlfriend?

"Harp... what's wrong?" As soon as I stepped toward her, she flinched and cracked through the stone of her stance.

"Nothing," she stammered and spun, jerkily collecting her notebook and purse from behind the desk. "Nothing's wrong."

"Harp—" I couldn't catch her before she sped past me and out the front door.

I didn't have the strength to chase after her... or the ability to with no one to watch the inn.

Slowly, I turned in the hallway, seeing not the emptiness of the space but all the memories bursting from its seams. From Blaze, unconscious at the base of the steps. Joanne, tearful and grateful sitting in the living room. Frankie, eyes twinkling at the mess I'd gotten myself into. Harper and her tears. And him... Wade... The hot flicker in his gaze, the tension in his body, the stretch of that towel...

Oh no.

No, no, no.

I went to the kitchen, hopped up on the counter, and pulled

down a bottle of wine from the top shelf. It was one of the bottles left over from Frankie's wedding. I'd stashed it in here thinking I'd pop it open to celebrate the official opening of the Lamplight Inn, but then I'd just gotten too busy. And now... this was no celebration but commiseration.

I fished in the drawer for the corkscrew and, a few seconds later, had the bottle open. The liquid glugged into a mug because I didn't feel like searching out a wine glass.

It was only a matter of days... hours... until Harper told the rest of my family, and then I'd be back at that same fork in the road again: lie or truth. The lies had spiraled, and now, telling the truth seemed even riskier than before.

"Crap," I muttered and turned the bottle upright, having poured just about half of it into the mug while lost in thought.

I hung my head for a beat. No sense in trying to pour it back. I'd just dump whatever I didn't drink, I decided, bringing the mug to my lips and taking several healthy gulps. It was a sweeter red, but truthfully, I wasn't going to be picky.

Taking my very full mug of wine, I grabbed my laptop from the desk and went into the living room. With all the back and forth to the hospital while trying to keep everything moving steadily at the inn, I hadn't had much time to work on the wedding packages that I'd told Max I'd give to him for his friends. Now seemed like as good a time as any to work on them. There was no chance I was going to be able to sleep right now anyway.

I needed a distraction from the box I was in—a box that had been so clearly defined at the start: Let Blaze's family believe we were together until he woke up. Now, that lie was starting to chip into my reality, the box bending and blurring at the corners.

As I started to dig into my spreadsheets and drink deeper from my cup, it became clear that lie wasn't the one worrying me.

Lying about being Blaze's girlfriend was a problem, but the worst lie—the dangerous lie—was the one I kept telling myself: that I wasn't attracted to Wade Stevens, my fake boyfriend's brother.

CHAPTER NINE

WADE

"WHAT HAPPENS if he doesn't wake up?"

That was what Mom said to me when I left her at Blaze's hospital room door. I didn't know what to say, wouldn't have known what to say if it wasn't for Lou, if she hadn't shared with me about her own family's trauma.

"You can't think like that, Mom. You just have to be here for when he does," I'd told her, and then she'd hugged me, but not in her normal embrace for me, the one that was quick and efficient, but the kind of embrace she usually reserved for Blaze. The one that held on. That gave as much support as it took.

In that embrace—in that moment—I realized how easily Lou could've changed Blaze's life because it was with that same kind of ease that she'd changed mine.

I drove back to the Lamplight Inn consumed with thoughts of her. The way she so easily gave of herself to others. The way she sat and talked to an unconscious man like conversation could keep him alive. It couldn't, but it definitely did keep my mother from going off the edge of sanity.

The way she never asked anyone for anything—not even a ride home when she had no car—as though her greatest fear in life was to impose on someone. Even the way she dressed and did her hair, always folding herself into this nice, neat little package that remained tucked into the background.

As the streetlights became sparse in the stretch between Stonebar and Friendship, so did the lightness of my thoughts. Mom kept calling Lou an angel, which only served to remind me just how sinful the rest of my thoughts about her were.

I dreamed about unraveling her thick braids and combing my fingers through her honey-brown hair. I fantasized about her full lower lip and the sounds she'd make if it were caught between my teeth. And I imagined the color her cheeks would be when I praised her for taking my cock.

And then, invariably, I'd remember that all those fantasies were my brother's reality, and the cold slap of envy would jar me back to the moment.

I pulled my car into the spot out front and parked. It was late —almost ten thirty. Lou locked the front door at nine, so I used the keypad to let myself inside. The light above the reception desk was on and would stay that way until Lou turned it off in the morning when she came down. I breathed in deep, grateful that the only distraction I'd have to face tonight was the woman in my dreams.

I headed to the staircase, my foot on the first tread, when a flicker of light caught my eye. *A candle.*

I frowned. It was too late for any of them to be lit. It was dangerous. I strode toward the living room and stopped short when I saw her. *Lou.*

The candles all along the mantle of the fireplace were lit, streaming an unsteady bath of light over the far end of the room and the woman who'd dozed off on the couch. I took a few steps into the room and paused, seeing if she would wake, but she stayed just as soundly sleeping as Blaze was in the hospital.

What was she...

I looked closer, then noted all of the papers that covered the coffee table in front of the couch, arranged in various stacks. There was also a pile of magazines and a small arrangement of business cards, and Lou's laptop rested precariously on the edge of her lap.

My nostrils flared. She shouldn't be working this late. One of the many things I'd learned about Lou over the last week was that the woman stuck to her schedule. Not that she had much choice. The inn was her business—her baby. She was the only one responsible for making sure things stayed on track. And that meant a nine thirty bedtime and a five a.m. wake-up.

So why was she down here working at ten thirty?

Moving quietly through the room, I stopped just in front of the coffee table and let my eyes roam over her. Her fitted, short-sleeve tee shaped to the slope of her shoulder and the full swells of her breasts. The loose blazer that would normally hide every curve from her neck to her hips was draped over the pillow on the other side of the couch. Her chest moved in a soft rhythm of sleep.

It would be so easy to just pick her up and carry her to her room, to lay her on her bed and kiss her like my very own Sleeping Beauty.

But she's not yours, the surly, sexually frustrated voice inside my head reminded me.

"Lou," I said with a low rumble before I did something I'd regret.

She exhaled with a soft noise and then turned her head away from me. *Dammit.* One more go, and if she didn't wake up, I'd carry her.

"Lou, it's time for bed." I bent and gently placed my hand on her arm.

Instantly, her eyes sprung open and it took her a second to focus on me—to realize this wasn't a dream, and when she did, she gasped and jolted upright.

"Oh, no." She pressed the backs of her knuckles to her cheeks, feeling the color in them. "What time is it? Was I sleeping?" she asked like she couldn't believe it, her gold eyes sparkling back to life.

"You were." I turned my attention to the array of papers and images on the table. "What are you doing down here?" My eyes narrowed. Floral arrangements. Furniture and tent rentals. Musicians. Catering. "Are you planning a wedding?"

Cold spread through my chest like a shard of ice had been stabbed in the center. *Was she planning her wedding with...*

"Yes." She sat taller and then instantly went stiff, her head snapping up with a look of horror on her face. "No. I mean, no. Not for me. I'm—" She broke off at the turn of my frown, already hearing the echo of the apology forming in her throat. "Max's former business partner wants to have his wedding at the inn. I've always thought about offering event services here, but it just hasn't been at the front of my plate until now. I told him I'd put together options and vendors and—"

Lou set her laptop on the table and bumped a stack of papers off the edge.

"On no!" She tried to catch the pages as they tumbled into disarray, her dismay quickly turning into a whimper of pain as one of them sliced her finger. "Crap," she muttered and stuck the wound between her lips.

Desire sucker-punched my gut as her full mouth closed around the tip of her finger. Her wide, innocent eyes looked at me behind her square glasses. Her hair was still braided back, but some of the strands had started to loosen from their hold. My hand curled at my side. I wanted to loosen the whole of her. Her hair in my fingers. Her innocence in my praise. And her mouth with mine.

Fuck.

It wasn't like I hadn't seen this before. That first morning at breakfast, I'd watched, tortured, as she sucked jam off her fingers.

This shouldn't have felt any worse than that. Except it did. It felt so much fucking worse.

The way I wanted her had buried like a seed deep within my gut, growing and spreading in the shadows where I thought I could ignore it until I couldn't. But I had to. It was like I was drowning. Needing to breathe, though it was impossible.

Wanting her, but knowing I could never have her because she belonged to Blaze.

"I'll get it," I offered roughly and dropped to my knees, carefully retrieving the papers from every corner of the carpet.

"Thank you," she said after a moment. "I've just been behind… and I really want to get something together for Max's friend and his fiancée. They want to have their wedding here in September…"

I shuffled the papers together and then tapped them on the coffee table to straighten them out. My gaze found hers over the edges. "So, you're going to add wedding planner to your job title as well as innkeeper?"

"No," Lou said with a small smile as I handed her the stack. "I just want to have all of the options ready for… whoever wants to get married." As she took the papers, one last sheet caught my eye where it hid underneath the couch.

"One more," I grunted and reached for it, not realizing just how far it had slid until my face was precariously close to her legs in order for my arm to reach. "What do we have here?"

I fished out the sheet, realizing it wasn't like the rest.

The others had been printer paper, but this was a torn-out page from a magazine with a full-page image of a bride and groom kissing at the head of a dining table that was covered in white roses and candles while their family lifted champagne glasses in celebration. Across the top, the title read *Intimate Vintage.*

"Nothing." She plucked it from my fingers and quickly balled it up as garbage as though it was something I shouldn't have seen.

As though it was a secret. *Her secret.*

I rested one hand on the coffee table and the other on the edge of the couch, almost intentionally boxing her into her seat.

"Is that what you want?" I demanded low.

"What?" Lou looked at me with wide, doe-eyes, the flickering candles highlighting the gold flecks tucked along the perimeter of her irises. "No," she said, though the pink dusting her cheeks confessed otherwise. "Just ideas. Inspiration. For guests."

She was a terrible liar. So terrible it was fucking adorable. And attractive. And... my chest went tight. If it wasn't inspiration for guests, then I was right, and if I was right, then...

I picked up the crumbled magazine page and peeled it back open, only this time when I looked at the image, it was Lou in the simple white wedding dress.

"Do you ever let yourself want something, Lou?"

She stilled at my question and then jerked her gaze to the papers on her lap. "What? Of course," she stammered and pretended to arrange them again.

Liar. I watched her pulse tick and tumble along the slender column of her throat. I wanted the truth. I needed this truth.

A gravelly sound emerged from my chest, followed by my husked demand, "When was the last time you did something you wanted?"

Lou shivered and slowly lifted her head. Her cheeks were a sultry shade of red—a guilty shade of red. *A hungry shade of red.* The same hunger had colored her skin when she'd looked at me earlier tonight. I'd tried to convince myself I'd imagined it. Fantasized it. But I hadn't.

Lou wanted me, too.

My cock grew harder. Ached harder. Pained harder. I tried like hell not to be attracted to my brother's girlfriend, but goddamn, she was the most beautiful woman I'd ever seen.

Some women were beautiful in an explosive kind of way, like a firework in the night sky or a rainbow after a storm, forcing you to stop in your tracks and take notice. But Lou... Lou was gorgeous in the way the trees change in autumn or the sun sets on the horizon. An exquisite kind of beauty that existed only for those who would take the time to stop and savor it.

"Why does that matter?" she murmured, her eyes fluttering.

"It matters to me." *Because I wanted to savor it.*

Because I wanted to savor her.

I grunted and shifted my weight. It would've been a good time to stand and get some distance, except there was no way to do that without putting her eye-level with my throbbing hard cock. Then I would be the one under scrutiny.

"I… bought my inn," Lou said firmly, the pink tip of her tongue sliding along the curve of her lips. And I wanted to chase it with mine. To taste her mouth. Her skin. To feel the warm velvet of her tongue knotted with mine.

"And before that?"

Now, she pulled her bottom lip between her teeth, worrying the flesh for a second. "I ran my brother's art gallery."

"And you wanted to do that for you or for him?"

"I wanted to do it," she answered.

"For you or for him?"

A tremor of irritation went through her. "He was going to throw away all his paintings…"

She'd done it for him, and we both knew it.

"And before that?"

Her chin notched higher, but all that did was give me a better view of the unsteady clamor of her pulse. "I worked at The Maine Squeeze as a barista."

"For you?"

Again, her lip rolled through her teeth. "I wanted to save money."

"For you, Lou?"

"They were short-staffed and needed someone," she said with a small huff and tried to grab the magazine image again. I tugged it back in time, but not before she lost her balance and started to topple forward.

Her hands landed on my shoulders, and my free hand

bracketed her waist, stopping her from crashing into me with hardly an inch separating her mouth from mine.

My jaw locked. Our eyes collided, and our breaths crashed together, one hot wave into another. A storm brewing, sweeping away all boundaries and safeties of the shore.

I should push her away, sit her straight, but instead my fingers only held the soft dip of her waist tighter, hungry for the feel of her bare skin under my fingertips. My gaze roamed up her torso. I could see the tight tips of her breasts pressing through the fabric of her top. I wondered if her nipples were red like her cheeks or if they would be once my mouth got ahold of them.

"Why does it matter?"

"Because what you want matters, Lou," I said, my voice hoarse.

Her eyes dropped to my mouth, and mine sank in tandem. I felt her swift inhale, the need for oxygen just a cover for the way she wanted me closer.

"What you want should be everything, Lou..." I was so close the tip of my nose brushed hers.

Her lashes dusted the tops of her cheeks, and when I went to reach for the side of her face, I forgot I held the magazine, and the edge of the paper caught the table and made a tearing sound.

Lou started, her eyes fluttering and then going wide, realizing what had almost happened. She quickly recoiled to the safety of the couch, her hands running along her braided hair as she stammered, "I'll... take it under consideration."

I looked back at the torn image, seeing Lou still as the bride, only this time, my brother's face replaced the groom's. Him and Lou... I dropped the ripped magazine page like it was fire between my fingertips.

Thinking of the two of them when I'd just been a breath away from kissing her—knowing he was the only one who had that right—it opened up a pit inside my chest. A green, gnawing pit.

"Is this what you imagined with Blaze?" I couldn't help the envious drop in my voice.

"No!" She exclaimed instantly and shook her head. "No, of course not."

I knew how the saying went—that a lady doth protest too much—but in this instance, it was wrong. There was no hesitation. No uncertainty. My head cocked. She'd been lying when she said the photograph wasn't inspiration for her own wedding, but she wasn't lying now.

"Why not?" I probed, feeling instinct and exhaustion take over. "Because you were with a movie star, so you imagined something bigger? Grander?" I growled before I could think better of it.

Everything about Lou Kinkade screamed subtle intoxication, not the kind of outlandish extravaganza Blaze created everywhere he went. They were opposites. Their personalities. Their lives. Their families. Sure, opposites attracted, but not like this. I knew that fact like it was written in my blood and carved in my bones. I knew it because Blaze and I had always been opposites, had always liked opposing things. I knew it because Blaze was never attracted to the kind of woman who attracted me... and Lou Kinkade had wholly, unsettlingly attracted me.

And now I was desperate to find something wrong with this beautiful, kind, and smart woman, so I would stop wanting her the way that I did.

It was driving me insane... and turning me into an asshole.

She looked at me, her wide brown eyes pierced with pain. *Shit.* And then her jaw locked tight, and she forced herself to swallow.

"No. Definitely not," she clipped and returned her focus to the piles of papers, reorganizing them into their original stacks.

Before I could think better of it, my hand slid forward on the table until it rested over hers. She stilled, and the candles flickered at the swift catch of her breath.

"Then what did you picture with him, Lou?" I demanded, my voice cracking. Maybe if I could picture it, too—the two of them married—I'd stop picturing her with me. Pressed against me. *Moaning underneath me.*

Her throat bobbed, and for a second, I swore she was going to yank her hand away and run. But then her chin dipped in a kind of deep resignation I didn't fully understand.

"I didn't picture anything with your brother," she admitted softly. "I never imagined myself marrying him."

It was a damn shitty thing to feel pure joy that my brother's girlfriend never considered marrying him. Unadulterated relief that this shy, independent woman knew she was better off not hitching her bright future to Blaze's falling star. But that relief was short-lived.

Lou thought of everything—had everything planned, everything on a schedule. I didn't care who the man was. There was no way she'd date someone and not think about where it was leading...

"Why not?"

Now, she pulled her hand back, reaching up and tucking a stray strand of hair behind her ear.

"Why, Lou?" I pressed, feeling myself inch closer because I had to know.

All week, I watched this woman cater to everyone else's needs—her guests, her family, my brother, my mother, and even my own—and never did I see anyone ask about her. Even when I tried, she buried her own needs like they didn't exist. Like she was created only to fill the needs of others. And I hated the thought that Blaze had had that—and that he'd taken advantage of it.

Lou pulled her bottom lip between her teeth, worrying the full flesh before she slowly turned to me and lifted her eyes to mine.

"Because he is who he is, and I'm me," she said and let out a soft, strangled laugh. "You know this. You saw it from the start. We're from different worlds. We don't belong together. Not like that."

"Is that what you really think?"

Her head dipped, and I growled, the sound bringing her eyes back to mine.

"Please, Wade, it doesn't matter," she begged, her breath escaping in a soft rush. "What I want... doesn't matter—"

Her words felt like a hot knife twisting between my ribs. I hated the resignation in her voice. I hated more that Blaze was the reason it was there.

"Bullshit. Of course, it matters," I bit out, my voice deepening as something uncontrollable awakened inside me. "Is that what he told you? That what you want doesn't matter? Because he's a selfish idiot if that's—"

"No!" Her protest erupted like something exploded inside her chest, sending her rocketing off the couch with its force. "It doesn't matter what I wanted because we weren't together."

Her hand slapped over her mouth, her pupils blowing wide.

I stood slowly, swearing that I couldn't have heard her right. "What did you just say?"

Lou drew a tremulous breath, her fingers sliding to hold her throat as she repeated unsteadily, "We weren't together."

Air fled from my chest like a prisoner freed from the war inside me. *They aren't together.* The knowledge snapped my restraint—shackles I hadn't known were so strong until they were gone.

She wasn't his.

In three words, the gravity of her relationship with Blaze—the rules, the boundaries—was eliminated from the atmosphere, no longer pulling her toward him... and out of my reach.

"Because of this? Because you wanted a future, and he didn't?" I demanded with a low voice, knowing that was *exactly* like something my brother would do.

Blaze was selfish and self-centered, not in a cruel way but a careless one. Then again, he was usually at least smart enough to make clear from the beginning that any kind of future with him was off the table.

"Is that why you argued that night? Why you broke up?"

She made a strangled sound. "No—"

I stepped closer, my face lowering as I growled, "What did he want, Lou?"

"I don't know," she murmured huskily, her breath catching as her gaze lowered to my mouth. "I don't know what he wanted... but it wasn't me."

A kind of fury I couldn't explain came over me. To see this beautiful, kind woman who spent her whole life catering to the needs of those around her feel unwanted was... *criminal.*

It was fucking criminal.

"Then he's an even bigger fool than I thought," I rasped and reached up to cup her face, forbidding her eyes from looking away.

"W-What?" The sincerity in her voice killed me. She truly didn't fucking understand how lucky Blaze should've felt to have her—*to have had her.*

"He didn't deserve you, Lou. Not even fucking close."

For Lou Kinkade, not wanting anything more for herself was a habit. A habit my brother had fostered. *A habit I wanted to break.*

I groaned and dipped my head lower. "If you were mine, you would never question what I wanted."

Her eyes grew hooded. "And what is that?"

A deep rumble hummed from the center of my chest. "To give you everything you want."

Her breath hitched. "Wade..."

My cock swelled at the sound of my name on her lips. It was a plea she didn't know how to make. And I could've simply answered it—could've lowered my mouth to hers and kissed her. But I wanted to hear it—*no, I wanted her to hear herself say it.*

"What do you want, Lou?" I asked, my thumb stroking along the edge of her bottom lip.

When I kissed her, I wanted it to be because she'd asked—because she'd wanted it. And I wanted her to know it was me, not Blaze, who gave her what she needed.

"Tell me what you want, angel." My gravelly encouragement purring from deep in my chest.

I felt the warm release of her breath, a forbidden filament about to be set on fire.

"I want you to kiss me." The words—her want—felt like the most precious gift, and I was damn sure going to make sure she knew it.

"Good girl," I praised and then crushed my mouth to hers.

Chapter Ten

Lou

I wanted to tell him the truth.

It was all I wanted—and I tried. I tried to tell him Blaze and I weren't together, but he didn't understand. He misinterpreted. And then the things he said… the things he promised… the way he looked at me. Somewhere in the midst of all that, the truth had changed. *My truth had changed.*

In this moment, the only truth that existed, real and breathing inside me, was that I desperately wanted to kiss him.

I wanted the heat of his mouth crushed to mine. The firm of his lips branding my skin. I wanted to know what every moment I'd spent around him had promised. The look in his eyes. The barely tethered restraint of his body. The raw promise of his words. I wanted to know what it was like to be wanted by a man I desired. Even if it was only for one kiss—only for a few seconds. I wanted to steal those seconds for myself.

Just once.

Mine.

I whimpered at the press of his mouth. Firm and hot, it

charred my lips, scorching the sensitive flesh, and all I wanted was more. *All I wanted was him.*

Maybe I wanted him so badly, this was still part of my dream. Maybe I was still asleep on the couch and had only imagined the man kneeling at my feet. The one who'd looked at the magazine picture and knew immediately it was for me. Known why I'd picked it.

I wondered if he knew I'd looked at the photo and saw his face staring back at me.

It was a crazy thought. Almost as crazy as kissing my fake boyfriend's older brother. But whether I was delusional or dreaming, I didn't want this to end.

Wade cupped my face, the expanse of his hands stretching onto the sides of my neck, marking the gallop of my pulse.

"Open your mouth for me, angel," he ordered and tipped my head back, his tongue teasing the seam of my lips until they parted. He growled. "Good girl."

My gasp was extinguished by the way his mouth devoured mine. He was everywhere—tasting, exploring, claiming. Everywhere all at once, and I was dissolving the way Frankie always explained a candle loses to its flame. Not melting, but vaporizing. Every hot stroke of his tongue drew desire up my body, evaporating it into pure want.

Pure ache.

I felt something for Wade that I'd never felt before for anyone. A yearning I tried to ignore—tried to box up and put aside like I'd done with so many other wants over the course of my life, but it wouldn't let me. *He* wouldn't let me.

He deepened the kiss, and I heard a bottomless groan break from his chest. "So fucking sweet, angel. You have no idea how I want you."

He wanted me.

Wade. Wanted. Me.

I felt swept away by the subtle power of him. Unmoored by the desire thudding through my veins. Like a ship without a compass, I knew what I wanted—where I wanted to go—but I needed him to guide me. *And he did.*

His tongue stroked along mine, coaxing it to spar with his. Our mouths tangled together until I felt the wet friction of each lick as though his mouth was anchored directly between my thighs.

It had been too long since I'd been kissed, but no length of time would make me forget that I'd never been kissed like this. Searing and starved and desperate. Shivers cascaded along my skin with each stroke of his tongue.

How was it another person could supply my body with warm electricity? How was it that another person could make me come alive?

How was it that this kiss didn't feel horribly wrong?

It should have. The hard press of his lips. The way he held me prisoner to his body. The invasion of his tongue into the depths of my mouth. It felt warm and wet and wanting... and it should've felt wrong.

He was Blaze's brother. Even though I'd said we weren't together—even though it was the truth—there was still a minefield of lies lying in wait between Wade and me, and yet, somehow, his lips managed to find a safe path to mine. Somehow, the kiss only felt right—*only felt true.*

"God, you taste so fucking good," Wade rumbled, taking my bottom lip between his teeth and biting it until I gasped. With a groan, he soothed the worried flesh with his tongue and then kissed me again.

Deeper, this time, until my mind was in a continuous spin, and all I could do to not lose my balance was for my hands to climb the lapel of his jacket and then wind around his neck, flushing my body to his.

Goose bumps invaded my skin. He was so hot, so hard. The feel of his broad chest was like a wall of hot stone against mine.

And lower… there was no mistaking—no guessing about the size of him as his erection wedged into my stomach.

"He didn't deserve this—he didn't deserve you," he ground out, but I didn't have the words nor the strength to correct him.

My heart thudded in my ears as my hands locked around his neck, trying to anchor myself in the storm of pleasure that whipped through my body. Waves of heat rolled through my veins. My nipples drew painfully tight, the thin bra I had on suddenly chafing the sensitive flesh. And between my thighs… I squeezed them tighter, the pulsing ache in my core so strong it made the whole of me feel on pins and needles.

"Wade…" I shuddered as his mouth moved to my cheek.

"What do you want, angel?" he asked again, decorating the edge of my jaw with bites and licks until he reached the sensitive corner of my neck.

My throat tightened. He was like some kind of gorgeous genie asking me what my wishes were. Begging to make them come true. My lips parted, but my tongue was still lost from the dizzying demands of his kiss.

I wanted more of his heat. More of his touch. More of his kiss. I wanted more of him before I remembered he could never be mine.

"More," I whispered hoarsely, feeling his lips close on my earlobe with a gentle tug.

The sound that came from his chest was ragged, like steel wool torn in two. Wade lifted his head just far enough and just long enough for his eyes to find mine. They flickered and sparked like charred embers about to catch fire—a blaze that would consume me with him.

Our tongues tangled until I felt like I was spinning. My stomach turning into sparkling knots. My core tightening into a hot ache. And then I was falling—or he was falling. No, sitting. *And I was on top of him.*

Wade took my seat on the couch and, with his hands on my waist, pulled me onto his lap, my knees finding their spot on either side of his legs. Instantly, the clench of my thighs was replaced by the pressure of his hard arousal straight under my core.

"Go ahead, angel," he cooed in response to my gasp. "Take what you want from me."

His hands tugged on my waist, encouraging me to rock against him, the pressure sending a shot of pleasure arcing through me. Without thought, I repeated the movement. I chased what my body wanted. *Needed.*

"Good girl," Wade growled his approval, and it broke loose something inside me. Something that would allow for more than a kiss. Something that needed more than a kiss.

He claimed my mouth again, and this time, I kissed him back with abandon, meeting the hot invasion of his tongue and letting the waves of pleasure sweep me away. My body moved with a mind and hunger of its own. Rocking and bowing. Ebbing and flowing. My hips ground my core against his thick ridge, desperate for more of the friction.

My head fell back, my eyes closed as his mouth burned a path along my neck and then lower. I wanted his mouth lower. I wanted his lips on me, his tongue. I wanted to know what it felt like... Needed to know. My fingers threaded into his hair, clutching his head as he moved down my neck.

"Tell me what you want, angel," Wade muttered, his lips resting on my collarbone.

I trembled and sucked in a breath, realizing at that moment that I hadn't been holding onto his head but guiding it down my neck and toward my breasts.

His hot breaths came in angry spurts against my skin. "Tell me," he ordered, rougher this time.

He knew what I wanted. His thumb stroked along the underside of my breast like a thoroughbred pawing at the gate. He knew what I wanted, but he wanted to hear me say it... and I wanted him to call me a good girl again.

"I want your mouth... on my breasts."

His ragged groan made my nipples pebble tighter. "Good girl."

I whimpered, another bolt of pleasure spearing through me. His praise was like bait on a hook, catching me every time and reeling me closer and more desperate for him.

Wade took the sleeve of my shirt and, with one swift yank, pulled it and my bra below my breast, baring me for him.

I had a single moment to feel the cold air on my skin—a single moment where Wade paused, his gaze worshipping the sight his mouth was about to desecrate. A single moment to process the feral sound that broke from his lips before they covered me.

"Wade..." I gasped... or moaned... or both as my head lolled back, pleasure churning through my insides at the feel of his lips and tongue.

He licked and bit and sucked in some combination that felt like nothing short of magic, the way it spelled pleasure through my body. His other hand rose to my shoulder and pulled down my other sleeve, the fabric of my top now rolled and wedged underneath my breasts.

"So perfect," he cooed, his fingers stretching over my newly exposed skin.

Between the swirl of his tongue and the roll of his fingers, I lost myself in the onslaught of sensations, like a tornado with no center. No safety. No reprieve from the pleasure. My hips began their frantic chase, grinding along the ridge of his cock, chasing the friction that promised to ease the ache.

"That's it, angel," he purred against my skin. "Take what you want. You deserve it. You deserve everything."

A strangled whimper broke from my throat. I couldn't stop even if I'd wanted to. I'd never felt the urge to orgasm like this before. Not with my fingers. Not with my vibrator. And certainly not with a man.

If someone came downstairs right now, I could only imagine the sight they'd be treated to: the innkeeper straddling one of her guests on the couch, half-naked in the candlelight with his mouth and hands on my breasts. It was so wrong—so forbidden and exposing. It almost tempted me to believe it wasn't real, but there was no way any dream could make me feel the way he did.

"Wade," I panted, my body coming apart at the seams.

He groaned. "Say it again," he ordered, his voice strained. "Say my name again."

"Wade."

Somehow, his name became the translation for everything I needed. It meant *more.* It meant *please.* It meant *yes.* And above all, it meant him.

I couldn't give him the whole truth, but I could give him this part—the knowing that he was the only man who made me feel this way. The only man on my mind.

"*Wade.*"

"Good girl," he chanted, and another tremor rocked me.

I'd never had a nickname. Frankie had a slew of them because of all the trouble she got herself into, but me... I was always sensible. Rational. I was always Lou. Except in Wade's arms. Then I became something hungry and wanton. I became his angel. *His good girl.*

"Come for me, angel," he ordered like it might kill him if I didn't. "Come for me all over his jeans, so there's no question who you belong to."

My hips ground harder. Faster. I chased the rub of the fabric against my clit and distantly wondered why there was any fabric at all between us. Pleasure spiraled and arced. And just when I felt it whip me over the edge, my release erupting through me, his lips sealed back over mine.

It wouldn't be until later I realized it was so he could swallow my scream.

My body stiffened and quaked and then fractured on my orgasm. And Wade held me through the storm. His mouth fed me oxygen when it felt like my chest had forgotten how to breathe. His arm locked around my back, holding me upright when I worried my spine would turn to Jell-O. And his hand on my waist guided me along his cock, leading me through the waves of pleasure that threatened to drown me.

"Lou..."

His voice reached me through the fugue. *What just happened?*

What had I done?

The sound of my heavy breaths was so loud inside my head. Was breathing always this loud? What about the pound of my heart? How long had I been like this? How long would it continue?

"Look at me, angel," he said, but his knuckles under my chin didn't give me a choice. He lifted my face like it was nothing. Like he couldn't feel the thousand-pound thoughts stacking in my mind.

I'd kissed him. I'd...ridden him. And then I'd orgasmed in his lap.

My eyes flung open, and I scrambled off the couch—off him, unable to miss the dark spot on the front of his jeans where my release soaked not only my own clothes but left a wet spot on his jeans. *Oh god—on Blaze's jeans.*

"Come for me all over his jeans, so there's no question who you belong to."

My core clenched traitorously at the memory of what had sent me over the edge.

"Wade..." I pressed the back of my hand over my mouth and then brought it to one cheek and then the other, feeling the heat buzzing under my skin.

"Don't say it," he ordered, and the apology disintegrated on my tongue. But it didn't change the sentiment storming in my chest. This was still wrong. A mistake. He still believed I was involved—though not currently—with his brother. He still believed my lie.

"We shouldn't have done that."

Anger tore through him like a bolt of lightning. It didn't help that while I'd found release, he hadn't. The wet denim stretched threateningly by the thickness of his cock.

"Because of my brother?" Wade ground out low.

"Wade—" I broke off when he stepped closer, invading my space and my scrambling sanity.

"Did Blaze ever make you feel that way?"

My chest tightened. I didn't want to answer because the answer wasn't the whole truth. "Wade—"

"Did he?"

I sucked in a breath, the hot, electric air loaded into my lungs. I shouldn't give him an answer. It was wrong. Dangerous, even. The worst-case scenario was...bad. But how many other times in life would I have this moment?

"No," I admitted. Blaze had never made me feel this way because he'd never had the opportunity. He'd only been a guest. A person I knew in passing, even in spite of his fame.

"I know you feel guilty because you argued—because of what happened to him, but you don't owe him this, angel. You don't owe him the feelings that you have for me."

My breath caught like a knife punctured through the center of my chest.

"I don't care what happened. I don't care that you were with him. I don't care that you were his once. I care that you've never been with a man who gave you what you wanted. Who praised you for your desire. Who worshipped every inch of you... for you."

I couldn't speak. Forget the truth, I couldn't even find a semblance of acknowledgment for the things he said.

"I care because I want to be that man," he finished a little softer, his thumb brushing my cheek like a match softly caressing the strike paper. A little more pressure, a little more determination, and he'd have my body on fire again.

"Wade..."

"But I won't... can't care if Blaze is who you want."

He wasn't. But the words stayed locked in the prison of my guilt.

The heat of his touch disappeared, and I stood there, watching as Wade turned and strode from the living room and disappeared upstairs. Only when the click of his door echoed down to me did it feel safe to breathe again.

Numbly, I collected the stacks of papers I'd organized on the coffee table, tidying them all into the folder folio I'd labeled *WEDDINGS* on the front.

You kissed him, Lou. You wanted to kiss him.

I shuddered and looked for the magazine page, the one that started this all, but it was nowhere to be found. Had he taken it?

You wanted to do more than kiss him.

The ache still lingered between my thighs—a hungry pain in spite of the pleasure he'd given me. I looked toward the stairs, wondering how he must be feeling because while I'd found relief, he hadn't...

I wanted Wade. Blaze's older brother. It was wrong and impossible and forbidden... and all because of my lie.

It took two tries before the tightness in my throat would let me swallow. I fished for my cell phone. I had to tell Wade the truth.

> I can't do this anymore. I'm telling Wade the truth tomorrow. I never should've let it go this far.

I sent the message off to my sister in a hurry and then gathered my things, returning them to the reception desk before heading up to my room. When I reached the second floor, I paused and stared at Wade's door. I could knock... I could tell him right now...

Or I could have this one night.

In the end, I took the Cinderella option. One night dressed up in the lie that let me live in the fantasy with the man who was everything I wanted. Tomorrow, I'd step, glass slipperless, into the reality that Wade Stevens was instead the man who could take everything from me when he realized I wasn't who I said I was.

Chapter Eleven

Wade

I WANTED her like I hadn't wanted anything in a long time.

The hum in my veins. The ache in my body. It was something entirely animalistic and not rational. Not the way I'd goaded her downstairs. Not the way I'd led her mouth to mine—her body on top of mine. Animalistic to want to prove myself as more—as right for her instead of my brother.

But she still held back.

Her hesitation was as obvious as the damn blush in her cheeks, and I hated the thought that it was because of Blaze. Even if they weren't together, she still wanted him, and that meant I had to stay away. Unfortunately, I'd already tasted her. The sweet warmth of her mouth, her tongue like sugar the way it dissolved against mine. The honey of her skin, her flush making it even sweeter...

I threw off the covers with a groan and pushed myself upright. I ran my hand through my hair and glanced at the clock. "Dammit." It was too fucking early. Or late, I guess, since I hadn't slept.

I reached for my water bottle, the plastic light in my hand

since it was almost empty. I popped the cap, and no sooner did I bring it to my mouth for a swig than my phone started to vibrate on the nightstand.

"Shit." I grabbed it and swiped to answer. "What is it, Mikey?"

There was no good reason to call someone at four thirty in the morning. No *good* reason for my private investigator to call at any time of the day or night. His calls only spelled bad news.

"The Chronicle is printing something today about Blaze's whereabouts," my inside man rumbled.

The Celebrity Chronicle was the worst tabloid offender. They were notorious for their celebrity news and getting stories that no one else seemed to be able to get—stories that bordered on lies, defamation, and harassment. But they were stories that sold, which meant they had the money to deal with the lawsuits that inevitably came their way.

They'd been a real pain in my ass since Blaze's first movie deal. Initially, I'd gotten them to back down with the threat of legal action, but once Blaze became famous enough...well, the reward for their trashy drama was worth the risk, and the higher his star shot, the harder they fought for the story of his fall.

"Fuck. Today?" I stood and threw on the light, my footfalls landing hard on the floor as I grabbed some clothes.

God, I wished Blaze had brought a single suit with him. Who was I kidding, he probably didn't own one. He liked the small-town, rugged celebrity persona. It seemed to cater to everyone.

"Yeah."

"Is that really all the warning you got?"

"You know I call as soon as I hear anything concrete," he replied, and as pissed as I was, I believed him. I paid him too well for the alternative to be the case. "They've really kept this one under wraps. I'm not sure how or why. My contact at the printer called me when he saw the first run come through."

"Who talked?" *Who was I going to have to sue?*

"Not sure—"

"What's the Chronicle's angle?" I pinned my phone to my shoulder and tugged on the jeans I'd discarded last night. I should've washed them—at least the spot where Lou had soaked them, but I couldn't bring myself to do it. I wanted to wear her desire for me with pride. On these jeans. On my mouth. On my cock.

I turned and banged my knee into the corner of the bed. "*Dammit,*" I hissed.

"He couldn't tell me. Everything was already packaged up for distribution by the time he saw it. It was a real hush-hush job." Mikey sounded just as pissed about the fact as I was.

"Shit." When the tabloids kept it extra quiet before print that usually meant they thought they had something good. Which meant they had something bad. *Like a story about how my brother drunkenly fell down the stairs and ended up in a coma.*

"Alright. Thanks for the heads-up."

"I'll let you know if I hear anything else," my PI said and ended the call.

I shoved my phone in my back pocket. Briefcase. Keys. Wallet. Room key. I was ready and out the door in a couple of minutes.

Unfortunately, even if the magazine didn't hit shelves until stores opened, the Chronicle would drop the story online at five a.m. I'd dealt with them enough times to know their publishing timelines. Once it was online, all bets were off on how long it would take for the hordes of reporters and fans to get to the hospital and start to harass the staff. The sooner I got there to prepare everyone, including Mom, the better.

As I headed for the stairs, I paused for just a second to look at Lou's door. Shrouded in shadow, I hoped at least she'd gotten some sleep. If she hadn't, was it because she was thinking of me or thinking of Blaze?

Fuck.

Why her? Why did I have to want my brother's girlfriend?

Ex-girlfriend.

I told myself the distinction mattered—that it had been a

boundary that felt like a law if I'd broken it. I told myself it was only hearing the law didn't exist that allowed me to kiss her. I told myself a lie. Deep in the recesses of my mind, I knew I would've broken every law, committed any crime, just to kiss her.

I considered knocking to tell her what happened and that I was leaving, but I decided against it and hurried downstairs. It was better she stayed here away from the publicity mess. Who the hell knew what kinds of things they'd assume or write about her—about her and Blaze—if they saw her at the hospital.

I gritted my teeth. I didn't want the world to have any other opinion of Lou Kinkade other than that she was mine.

"Someone had to have talked to them."

"I promise you, Mr. Stevens, no one on your brother's care team would've revealed anything. That's not how we do things in a small town," the nurse insisted.

"I want to speak to Dr. Cooper."

"He's not in yet—"

"Then get me his cell phone number," I demanded firmly and strode back into Blaze's room.

I checked my phone again like that would make the minutes tick by faster and then peered out the window as though I expected to see them start to line up around the block for a look, or a comment, or an inside scoop.

Air hissed through my tight lips. *God, I hated the press.*

"Wade."

I turned as my mother entered the room, her face stricken and her hands shaking as she closed the door. "Mom."

She looked at me and then at my brother, and when I realized she wasn't able to take another step, I went toward her and pulled her to my chest.

"Why can't they just leave him alone?" she whispered, heartbroken against my chest.

"Because there's too much money to be made in misery." And if that wasn't the principal tenet of the mainstream media, I didn't know what was.

"It's all my fault." Her tears started to leak through my shirt.

"No, it's not," I rumbled. It was decades ago that she'd first spoken to them, thinking it would help Blaze's career. "Whatever it is, I'll handle it," I promised and checked my phone again.

Two minutes.

"That's my fault, too," she said and pulled back from my hold, her eyes shimmering. "I'm sorry I never stood up to him."

Her words tightened a band around my chest. When Dad and Blaze had it out, I was always the one who stepped in to take the fall or defend Blaze. Mom never argued with Dad. Not that he was abusive or she felt threatened. She was just a people pleaser. She wanted to make Dad happy just as much as she wanted Blaze to feel loved. So, while I was sacrificed on the altar as the perfect prodigy, Mom would rush away to take care of Blaze and unknowingly widen the divide between us.

"It's in the past," I told her roughly, opening my cell and refreshing the Chronicle's home page.

"No." She stopped me with a hand on my arm. "He's in the past, Wade. We aren't."

My eyes flicked up to hers, holding them for a second before I looked back to my phone.

"Where's Lou? Is she okay?"

I gritted my teeth, my thumb slamming on the screen to refresh. "She's fine. Sleeping, I'm assuming. I didn't want to wake her for this. I thought it would be better if she... wasn't here."

The reporters... paparazzi... they were ruthless. They were the 'get the shot now and apologize later' type of people. Intrusive. Abrasive. Soulless. And they weren't the kind of people Lou would know how to handle.

She was too trusting. The kind of person who left her purse

tucked behind the reception desk at various points throughout the day, unguarded. I knew she left her room unlocked during the day, too, trusting that the other guests either didn't realize or that they wouldn't invade her privacy. I didn't judge her for it. It was a small-town mentality, and it worked in a small town.

But Blaze Stevens wasn't a small-town phenomenon.

"You're right." Mom nodded and took up her post at Blaze's bedside, my brother still breathing evenly and lying completely unaware of how the world was turning and transforming around him. "I don't want them to scare Lou off—to ruin what she and Blaze have. It must've been so precious to him that he didn't tell me—tell anyone about her."

My throat went tight, and I gritted my teeth, the truth barreling around like a wrecking ball in my mouth.

She wasn't his. He didn't care for her the way he should have —the way he should've cared about all the things that mattered. His friends. His career. His family. He was reckless with it all, and Lou had been no exception.

She wasn't his anymore. *She was mine.*

But I swallowed the words instead. With no change in Blaze's status over the last week, Mom needed this kind of hope. She needed something good to hold onto. And she definitely didn't need to hear that I'd been the one kissing Lou last night. That it was me she'd wanted. My lap she'd ground herself on until she came.

Mom didn't need to know that a future hadn't been in the cards for Lou and Blaze and never would be. Not if I had anything to say about it.

My phone refreshed, and it took a second for the breaking news headline to update.

And then my heart dropped into my stomach.

Blaze Stevens hiding away in Maine with new girlfriend!

I scrolled, my eyes scanning so fast that my head started to pound. Friendship. The Lamplight Inn. Elouise Kinkade. Pictures of Lou and Mom in front of the inn yesterday, Lou's face bright and smiling as Mom held her arm. I read it twice before a string of vicious curses broke through my lips.

"What is it, Wade? What did they write? They can't print about his medical condition. They can't cross that line. I don't care if I have to go to their CEO myself, I won't let them—"

"Mom," I growled and grabbed her shoulder to stop her where my words failed. "It wasn't... they didn't write that he's in the hospital." I turned my phone so she could see.

Her brow creased, then lifted, and then her hand covered her mouth in a gasp. "Oh, no. Not Lou..." She looked at me, tears threatening to fall. "You have to help her, Wade. They'll eat her alive."

Chapter Twelve

Lou

"Thank you for calling the Lamplight Inn. This is Lou speaking. How may I help you?"

"Hi, Lou. This is Mack. I'm a reporter from the *Shore Report*, and I was wondering if you had a couple minutes to talk to me?"

My heart fluttered. Had someone told them about the inn? Was I getting press already?

"Yes." My head bobbed as though he were in front of me, and I clutched my phone tighter. "Of course."

"I'm on my way up there now, but I'm so glad I got you on the phone before things get crazy. So, what can you tell me about Blaze Stevens?"

An arctic wind blew through the butterflies in my stomach, freezing their wings, and settling a graveyard of ice into my bones.

How did he know about Blaze? What was going on?

My eyes flicked to the steps, expecting Wade to walk down them any minute and rescue me from the phone call. Foolish, since he'd left early this morning before I was even up. *Without saying anything.*

"I'm sorry. I... I can't talk about that," I stammered, knowing I had to say something to stop the conversation.

It didn't matter. The reporter went on like he hadn't heard me.

"How long have the two of you been seeing each other? Is it serious? Rumors are he left rehab for Maine. Was that because of you? How did you meet?"

I frantically tapped to end the call, dropping my phone onto the desk like it was a hot pan I grabbed barehanded from the stove.

What was happening? How did he know—

"Lou!"

I spun, seeing Frankie come down the hall from the back entrance to the inn, holding Logan in his carrier. I expected to see determination on her face. Instead there was only worry.

Was it really that bad of an idea to tell the truth?

"Frankie—"

The phone rang again. I froze, afraid it was that reporter calling back. I wouldn't have answered if it was, but this call was a different number.

"Lou, we have to talk." Frankie rushed toward me, insistence brimming in her eyes.

I was prepared for this—I had to be after sending her that message last night. I knew she'd want to come convince me otherwise, but after that kiss, after everything that happened... I couldn't let this continue. And I couldn't argue with her about it right now. I had to take a phone call.

Holding up a finger so she'd know she had to wait, I answered the phone, "Hello, thank you for calling the Lamplight Inn. This is Lou speaking. How can I help you?"

"Hi, Lou, this is John Mascarin. My wife and I are checking in this afternoon, and we just got to town and are trying to find parking."

"Oh, of course. You can park right out front, and I can help you if you have bags—"

"That's why I'm calling. Is there an event going on? The street is completely packed."

"No. No event that I'm aware of," I said, my voice shaky even though I should be confident. I knew the event schedule in town like the back of my hand. I would know if something was going on. "Just double up, and I'll come out and take your bags, and then I can direct you to the private lot in the back."

I happened to glance at Frankie, her eyes wide and nodding like she knew why I was directing guests to the small lot that usually only I or my family used.

"Thank you so much. We're pulling up now."

"I'll be right out."

"Lou, what's going on—" Frankie started before I'd even hung up.

"I can't talk right now. I have to go help a guest. He said there's something going on in town..." I trailed off as I sped away from her.

"Not in town, Lou. Here," she said.

I stopped with my hand on the doorknob. "Here?" My brow furrowed, and that was when I heard it. The commotion outside. No. It couldn't be. I pulled open the door and stopped short.

"Miss Kinkade! Is Blaze Stevens staying at the inn with you?"

"Where has he been staying?"

There was a mob of people on the sidewalk along the fence. Cameras. Phones. *A crowd looking for a man who wasn't here.* My stomach sank like a stone and rooted my feet to the entrance. How did they know? Who had told them?

"Is he going to a rehab program here?"

"Are things serious between the two of you?"

"Lou, you can't go out there right now." Frankie put her hand on my arm, trying to draw me back inside.

I wanted to agree with her. I wanted to slam the door and call Wade and figure out what was happening—what had happened. But then a car honked, causing a commotion in the crowd. The dark sedan stopped just out front, its four-ways flashing through the moving bodies.

I couldn't go anywhere. I had guests that needed help.

"I'll be right back."

"Lou—"

I shrugged off her hand and went outside, closing the door firmly behind me. I knew she wouldn't follow, not with Logan.

My feet carried me toward the gate, toward the chant of cameras and the call of inquisitors. I wondered if this was how the women of Salem felt when they were walked to the stake. Ready to burn because of a lie.

"Lou!"

I froze at the boom of his voice, sure I was imagining it, until I saw Wade slaloming through the group of people, warning them as he went.

"That's private property on the other side of the fence. I'm going to have to ask you to step back." He didn't give them much of a choice, his arms firmly pushing a path through the crowd to the gate.

"Hey! Who are you?" One of the paparazzi shouted at Wade, fighting to follow him as he stepped through the gate and onto my property. "She didn't invite you either—"

Wade spun and slammed the gate just before the man could come through. "I'm Miss Kinkade's attorney. So, either you respect her privacy, or I'll sue you until the only photos you can sell are ones of your feet."

He left the man gaping in disbelief, and I was, too, until his hands landed on my shoulders.

"Are you alright?" His eyes burned as they raked over me, smoke swirling in his gaze. As soon as my chin gave the slightest dip, he declared with a low voice, "You shouldn't be out here. Let's go back inside where we can talk."

My head jerked. "I can't." I tried to shrug out of his hold. "I have guests checking in. I have to help them with their things and show them where they can park—"

"Let me handle it."

My stomach rolled. "No, I couldn't—"

"It wasn't a choice, Lou," he growled. "Where are they?"

I tried to swallow but nothing felt like it was working. I didn't understand what was happening. Why it was happening. *Why it was happening now?*

"Over there." I lifted my arm and pointed limply in the direction of the car with the hazard lights blinking.

"Go inside," he ordered curtly and then released me.

I took a step back, watching as he strode through the gate, the sea of cameras parting in front of him with every footfall. Folding my arms, I moved back another foot, unable to take my eyes off Wade as he greeted the couple and lifted their duffel bags from the trunk. As he did that, I saw him explain to Mr. Mascarin how to go around the block and then turn into the small drive marked *Private*, which would bring him to the gravel lot at the rear of the building.

"Miss Kinkade!" An obnoxious shout caught my attention. I wasn't sure what it was about that particular one, but my attention snapped to the call. A cacophony of shutters went off. "How does it feel to be dating Hollywood's most infamous heartthrob?"

Air whooshed from my chest like a punctured balloon. *The world knew my lie.* I squeezed my eyes shut like that could stop everything from spinning—like it could stop the darkness from creeping in.

"Lou."

My eyes popped open to a broad wall of chest and Wade's musky scent hitting my nostrils. With him in front of me, I couldn't see the crowd, the cameras, the flashes. I couldn't see anything but him.

"Go inside," he ordered, his deep voice perfectly treading the line between stern and soothing.

He followed me in with the guests' things, and I closed the door behind us. My hand stilled on the doorknob, frozen stiff as though I'd turned to stone.

The world believed my lie.

"Hi Wade, so good to see you again." I heard Frankie greet as I breathed in slowly.

"Frankie. Good to see you."

I exhaled even slower.

"What's going on out there? Did something happen?" she asked the questions that were all tangled up in my brain. She was always the half of us who found her way—or made her way—when we were lost.

Just breathe, I thought, drawing another breath of air into my lungs as I waited for his answer. Frankie would get to the bottom of it—figure out what was going on while I stood here.

I tipped closer to the door, wishing I could just melt into it. Melt away.

"Lou." His voice cracked quietly behind me.

I stiffened, and then his hand rested on my shoulder, and all the tension started to seep out of me.

"It's alright."

I turned, glad that he didn't release me. His hold seemed like the only thing reaching me through the darkness.

"It's not alright. There are... paparazzi outside. They think... they know..." I couldn't form a complete sentence, fear and anxiety working like landmines in my brain, blowing up all paths to coherency.

"I'm going to fix it," he swore, his hand sliding to the side of my face. My eyes fluttered shut, and I turned ever so slightly into his hold, letting the heat worm its way into my skin and settle my racing heart. "Lou—"

He stopped and half-turned, both of us looking down the hallway past Frankie to the back door that creaked open.

"My guests," I croaked. "I need to welcome them."

"Don't worry about them. I'll handle them," he swore.

I needed to help them—help everyone. I needed to tell the truth. Fix this. *Stop this.* I swayed, the thoughts pummeling me from every side.

"I need to sit down," I mumbled, my head feeling light.

Instantly, he was guiding me into the living room and over to the couch. Sitting down felt like I was sinking into the quicksand of memories from last night. Him on his knees in front of me, staring at the magazine page I'd ripped out, telling me I deserved more than his brother.

"Wade—"

"Stay here. I'm going to handle your guests, and then we'll talk," he said gruffly, and as soon as he stepped to the side, Frankie was there waiting, bouncing Logan on her chest and scrutinizing Wade's every movement until he disappeared from the room.

"How is this happening?" I whispered, my throat too tight to speak with any volume.

"Lou, you don't even know what is happening—"

"I know that they're here for Blaze—because they think I'm dating him." I framed my hands around my throat like I could forcibly hold my pulse back from racing.

"How—"

"I don't... It doesn't matter. I have to tell them the truth." It was the only solution, and I felt more determined than ever. "I can't... Strangers, Frankie. Strangers think I'm with... that Blaze and I..." Air whipped in and out of my lungs like it was on a yo-yo, one I couldn't seem to catch.

If strangers knew, it wouldn't be long before the rest of my family did.

"Lou, just breathe for a second, okay?" Her voice was sterner now with one hand on her hip and a baby in the other. "Just breathe."

I wasn't sure how long she repeated the instructions, her voice echoing like it was my own inside my head. Sometimes—most times—I looked at my twin like she was the devil on my shoulder, always getting into mischief, always encouraging it. But sometimes—those times when I was at my worst—she was the angel on the other, soothing me with the kind of composure only someone who thrives in chaos can have.

"Nothing good comes from rushing. Just breathe and calm down. Wade obviously knows what's happening. Let's see what he has to say."

My head snapped to the reception desk, reality finally grabbing hold of the reins. I couldn't freak out. I had a job to do—a dream to protect. And that meant my guests came first. No matter what else was going on around me—*or happening to me.*

When I looked, I only saw Wade coming down the staircase, his stride barely restrained as his heavy steps thudded on the wood floor.

Where was the couple checking in? What just happened?

"Wait." I stood and started to move toward him. "The Mascarins. I need to check them in—"

"Already done." He gripped my shoulders and guided me back onto the couch. I went willingly. My wits might've regained some strength, but my knees hadn't yet.

"How—"

"Lou, you leave enough details for everything that your nephew here could've checked those people in without a problem," he ground out, glancing at Frankie's baby. "I got them their key. Room 206. I gave them the tour. Told them about breakfast. Time. Place. Gave them the map of town."

My jaw slackened. *How did he...*

"I've been living here the last week, Lou. I've seen how you do your job—how well you do your job," he said, his chest rumbling.

A familiar kind of heat prickled in my cheeks. It wasn't that I didn't know he'd been watching me, but to hear him admit to it. To know he'd watched close enough to be able to replicate it all to some degree.

My gaze dropped to his lips. My brain was too frazzled to shy away from the boundaries we'd crossed last night. I wanted to kiss him again. I wanted to be consumed by something other than my thoughts and worries—by something other than what everyone else around me needed. But I couldn't kiss him again. I knew that the second I'd stopped kissing him last night.

I swallowed and pushed the thought aside. I couldn't think about that now. There were... paparazzi... in Friendship.

"What happened?" I asked, lifting my chin to meet Wade's dark gaze. "What's going on?"

Wade glanced toward the hall, and I saw the newlyweds had come downstairs and were standing at the reception desk, hovering over my activity book, scanning the pages, and not looking at us. Still, Wade came and sat beside me on the couch, his body tensing when his knee brushed mine.

My eyes flicked to Frankie, wondering if she saw the sparks that erupted on my skin.

"Someone leaked information about Blaze... about you... to the Chronicle," he said, keeping his voice low. "I got a call from my... from the guy who keeps an eye on the press for me. For Blaze." He was being delicate about it, but it was only because I'd seen them together—seen him with his Mom—that I picked up on the truth. Wade kept an army at his fingertips to fight his brother's battles. "It was early this morning, and he didn't know what story was running, just that it was about Blaze."

"That's why you left."

He nodded. "I thought it had someone there. That it was about his injury, and I wanted to prepare the hospital team, and Mom, for..."

"That. Out there." My head tilted toward the windows, knowing they were still out there, waiting.

"Yeah." He cleared his throat, his jaw muscle flexing tightly. "As soon as the digital article published and I realized... I came right back to warn you."

"Can I see?"

He hesitated, debating for a moment before giving in and pulling out his phone. I held it with both hands so it wouldn't shake as I read the article—read about me. Saw the photos someone had taken of me and Joanna when I'd been giving her a tour of the inn.

"Oh god..." I pressed my fingers to my mouth. This was a

disaster. All I'd wanted was to make sure he was okay... and now the world thought I was Blaze's girlfriend.

"Frankie, can you get her some water?" Wade asked, but his focus never left me.

In my periphery, I felt my sister look at me. I could've nodded, but I didn't need to. Instinct. Twin-stinct. Whatever it was, it kicked in after a moment, and she headed for the kitchen, leaving Wade and me alone.

My eyelashes fluttered onto my cheeks, the burn of tears stinging behind them. "I'm sorry—"

His deep growl frightened the words away, and before I even realized a tear slipped free, I felt his hand on my cheek, his thumb catching the droplet.

"I'm the one who's sorry," he rasped low. "I should've been here. I had no idea... have no idea how they found out." Tension rippled through him like a crack through stone. "I'm going to fix this, Lou. I promise."

"I'll just tell them. We aren't together. I'll just tell them, and then they'll go away, right?" My voice lifted at the end with an unreasonable amount of hope that it was that simple.

That if I just told them all the truth, everything would be fine again. *Normal.*

Wade's jaw locked, and my pulse slowed to a drugged thud.

"What is it? What's wrong with the truth?"

"Nothing," he muttered, but the firm line of his lips grew even thinner. "You're right. If you tell them the truth, they may leave you alone."

My brow pulled together for a second before his words clicked like puzzle pieces into place, and I saw the whole picture.

"But they won't stop looking for Blaze," I said, my voice hardly making any sound.

"No, they won't. Not until they get their story."

Right now, the paparazzi were here, outside the inn, waiting for a glimpse of the movie star. If I told them the truth, then they'd go looking elsewhere... and the story they'd find was exactly the kind Wade tried to save his brother from.

"You want me to let them believe it." I wasn't sure if I was asking or telling, but whatever it was, my assumption was right.

Pain pulled his features tight. After last night, it was the last thing he wanted, but it was what he needed in order to protect his brother.

"No, you don't have to, Lou—"

"No, it's okay. I'll do it," I interrupted. It was the least I could do—go along with the lie that I told, the problem I'd created.

His gaze locked with mine. For a second, we didn't say anything. We didn't have to. This wasn't what either of us wanted—to have Blaze back in the middle of everything. But if we didn't, it was only a matter of time before they hunted him down to the hospital and printed who only knew what about why he was there.

"I'll do it," I repeated.

"It would only be for a few days. I'll talk to Blaze's doctor tomorrow about arranging a transport for my brother. If we can move him to another hospital—another bigger, more secure facility, then you can tell them the truth and put an end to this..." he trailed off when Frankie returned with a glass of water.

"I'm sorry about all of this," Wade apologized again and rose stiffly.

"Can I offer a suggestion?"

"No," I exclaimed, water sloshing to the edge of the glass as I stood.

"Lou—"

"Frankie—"

"I think we can fool them into going away," she insisted, a devious tip to her smile.

Wade stilled, her idea hooking into his brain. But I knew better. I knew that look in her eyes.

"How?" Wade asked.

"I think with a few well-placed comments and a good

disguise, we can make them think Blaze and Lou are getting out of town now that they've been found out."

I chugged another gulp of water and wished it were something stronger.

"Go on," Wade said and folded his arms.

"I can have our family slip information to some of the reporters or in front of some of them that Blaze and Lou are going to leave Friendship and head back to Boston for a little—"

"No, Frankie, I'm not getting our family involved in this."

"Lou, the press is literally on your doorstep, and your new... relationship... is plastered all over the internet. They're already involved whether you want them to be or not."

My throat tightened. Her words hit me like a wave into my chest just as I was coming up for air. This was no longer a lie that only Frankie and I knew. No longer a lie that strangers knew. It was... everywhere. It was now a lie that Jamie, Kit, their wives, Mom, Gigi, my cousins... all the people I cared most about in the world just found out I was dating a famous Hollywood actor through a tabloid.

I sank back onto the couch, catching how Wade reached for me, but then stopped himself when he saw Frankie watching.

"All I'm suggesting is we plant this information. Make it seem like you're trying to make a break for it before even more attention shows up here. I'll get Chandler, and we'll go out there and politely ask them to please respect our guests. Allude to the idea that we are taking charge of the inn because you're leaving."

"But then what?" I let out a weak whimper. "It's not like we can actually leave. Blaze isn't here. I can't put someone else in charge of the inn for... days at a time. And they're not going to take town gossip as fact."

"You don't need to actually leave, Lou. They just need to think you have, and to do that, you just need to pretend."

"Pretend?" I croaked and shook my head. "I can pretend, but I can't fake Blaze. This isn't *Weekend at Bernie's.*"

She stared at me, her expression deadpanning, *Really?* And then her eyes dragged slowly to Wade.

"You want me to pretend to be Blaze." Wade didn't miss a beat.

Frankie shifted Logan to her other hip and replied, "You're already wearing his clothes. Throw on a ball cap and some shades. Blaze's car is parked out back. The windows are tinted enough that if you drive by slow enough that they can see Lou, they'll assume you are Blaze."

"And then what?" I asked hollowly. "They're going to try and follow us. Do we fake it all the way to Boston? Do we pull some stunt driving feat and lose them off our trail?"

"Nope." She popped the end of the word like a triumphant flag capping her conclusion. "You head out of town and divert to Mom's house. It's far back off the road, and with everything in bloom, you'll be out of sight within seconds. They'll continue to race toward Boston, and in the meantime, you can spend the day at the house with everyone. By the time night rolls around, you can take the back way to the inn, and if they're not all gone, you can borrow some of my clothes for a few days, and they'll think you're me."

My head was shaking no, but by the time she finished, I couldn't find the actual word to disagree with her. It was a crazy plan, and there was still Wade's suggestion to consider.

The longer they were here, the more likely they were to find out the truth about where Blaze was... and why he was there. And I couldn't let that happen. I didn't know Blaze—not like Wade thought I did. But I knew the look of a man haunted by his past and trying to change his future, and if it were my brother—if it were Kit in that hospital bed, I would do whatever I could to give him the best chance at defeating his demons. I couldn't fight his battles, but I could do my part to protect his peace.

"Lou..."

"I think we should do it," I said quickly and set my glass on the table. "Frankie's plan, that is. I think... it's the best chance we have to get them to go away."

And once their threat was gone, I'd tell Wade the truth. The whole truth.

Wade's jaw ticked. "Okay."

"Alright." Frankie nodded like a general commanding her troops. "I'm going to head to Mom's and assemble the troops. By the end of the day, everyone will think you and Blaze are in panic mode and trying to get out of town. And tomorrow, we'll pull a Kinkade family shuffle."

"A what?"

"Kinkade family shuffle. It's like a Kansas City shuffle, but with Kinkades." She grinned. "Tomorrow, they'll be looking for who left, and you'll be going right back to where you started." She paused. "After a day at Mom's."

And that was when I realized Frankie's ulterior motive. She wanted me at Mom's. No... My brow creased, watching her say goodbye to Wade and then give me a wink.

She wanted me and Wade to come to Mom's.

Chapter Thirteen

Lou

"Miss Kinkade." Mrs. Tisdale strode up to the desk, patting her silk scarf down against her chest. "I was hoping to go out shopping today, but I see there is still a kerfuffle outside—"

"Yes, Mrs. Tisdale, I'm so sorry about that. If you would prefer to use the back exit and follow the gravel alley to your left, it will take you to the next intersection where you return to Maine Street," I instructed, dragging my finger along the path on the map resting on the counter like I had several times earlier today. "No one should bother you, but if they do, my legal team has advised to simply reply that you have no comment."

My legal team consisted of Wade who'd outlined a clear framework for my guests on how to handle the media attention outside. He didn't give them any information about Blaze, though I was sure by now most of the guests knew which celebrity caused this commotion.

"I see." Her eyes narrowed as she looked me up and down, and then declared, "Well, I hope you get a ring from this young man after all this trouble."

At this point, I was too numb to be shocked, but I couldn't

correct her even if I wanted to, and after yesterday, I didn't want to.

I'd held the truth in my hands, a fragile, heartfelt apology, ready to give to Wade as soon as I saw him. And then one look at his torn expression, and I'd let the truth slip right through my fingers so I could help him by holding onto the lie. A lie that was so twisted and convoluted that I felt like I was walking a tightrope with my eyes closed. A lie Wade thought could protect his brother.

"Have a nice day," I called belatedly after Mrs. Tisdale, watching her retreat toward the back door of the inn.

I stepped away from the desk and moved almost blindly to the first window in the living room. Resting my shoulder on the frame, I carefully lifted the curtain back with one finger.

The last twenty-four hours had been... not a whirlwind but a cyclone, with the inn sequestered in the eye of the storm.

Inside, Wade and I orbited each other in our own atmospheres of distraction, avoiding any conversation about what happened between us two nights ago. It wasn't the right time to talk about it, which made it all the more obvious that the kiss—and everything after it—was all we thought about when we were around each other.

So, we did our best not to be.

I'd hyper-focused my attention to my guests. To making their stay feel as normal as possible even when stepping outside meant they were assaulted with questions. And Wade focused on his brother. He wouldn't risk going back to the hospital, but he had been on the phone with Joanna, and then on calls with... I don't even know who or how many people to try and figure out who'd leaked his brother's whereabouts.

Outside, the Friendship police did what they could to break up the collected camera-wielding crowd out front that had spilled from the sidewalk and onto the street. Unfortunately, that didn't do a whole lot to deter them.

Frankie said they'd infested the town like a band of

cockroaches. Roaming. Listening. Waiting. Some had left when the police had shown up, but most were biding their time, waiting it out for their perfect shot. There were a handful of them still out there, roaming on the sidewalk, taking photos of Friendship and the inn from a distance like they were tourists.

Wade said they would do that, too. Pretend to be something else in order to get close and get what they wanted. *Not unlike what I'd done.*

I swallowed hard, feeling the tightness in my chest and then the way it erupted like a warm flutter of confetti as heavy footsteps approached. I never knew someone could come with a warning sign—physical, chemical alerts that went off whenever Wade came close.

I'd expected to have to look out for the big memories from that night. The power of his kiss, the force of my orgasm, those were like waves coming in the distance that I could try to avoid. But it was the little ones, the look of his hair making me remember its texture to grip, the scent of his musk drowning my lungs, the rumble of his voice—not the sound itself, but the way it felt against my skin. Even the sound of his footsteps brought me back to the moment he walked away—the moment he promised to give me everything if it was him I wanted. Those were the dangerous memories, catching me off guard and sweeping me away like a riptide.

I remained peering out the window when he stopped just behind me. My right hand toyed with the end of my braid like it was the strings I was trying to keep together.

"What if they don't believe it?" I asked quietly.

"They will," Wade said, his voice ebbing like a warm wave.

I couldn't take my eyes off the people milling along the sidewalk. The lenses on some of their cameras looked like weapons. "How do you know?"

"Because people will believe anything when it's something they want to believe," he said. "I've dealt with this enough to know."

"I didn't realize—"

"How popular Blaze is?" Wade finished.

"I guess." I shifted my weight.

"You wouldn't believe how people will just show at the whisper that he might be somewhere..." Wade trailed off and cleared his throat. "Are you ready?"

Ready. The word sounded foreign to my ears.

I hadn't slept. Between the distractions that didn't feel numerous enough, all I'd thought about was Frankie's plan. Not the sitting in a car and letting myself be seen part. That wasn't much of an act, even though there was a lot weighing on it. But going to Mom's after. Bringing Wade. Letting my family think...

I shuddered.

They'd wanted me to find someone... to find love... and now, not only had they learned about my first 'relationship' in a decade through the gossip mill, but that relationship was a lie. I was lying to the people I loved.

But I owed it to Blaze. To Wade. If this was the consequence of my lie, that it should hurt me, too, then I would take it.

"I'm ready," I said and let the curtain slip from my fingers, blocking the window once more as I turned to Wade.

My breath stumbled when I looked at him. They weren't twins, but goodness, did he look like his brother.

Even though he'd worn Blaze's clothes before, there was something different about wearing them to intentionally impersonate his brother and wearing them out of necessity. The faded jeans seemed to hug a little tighter. The tee fit with a little more attention. And the leather jacket... it was the same one Blaze was wearing the night he fell. To top it all off, Wade sported a Red Sox baseball cap—something Blaze had been photographed wearing countless times.

The only marked difference from a distance would be the length of his hair. Blaze's light brown locks were longer and unruly, while Wade's were trimmed short. It made me nervous even with the hat on... even though we'd be inside a car.

"Is Frankie here?"

My sister and Chandler were going to cover the rest of the day for me. After that, Jamie's wife, Violet, was going to help me at the desk and with the phones for the next few days to keep up the appearance that I was gone.

"Yeah, she and Chandler walked in as I was coming down. I think he went to unload some things into the fridge, and she was going to change a diaper."

I nodded and turned robotically toward the back door. It was time. *One step after another. That's all*—I gasped and looked down at my hand now armored inside a bigger, tanner one.

His fingers squeezed mine, bringing a familiar ache back to life —an ache I couldn't think about now.

"I'm sorry about all of this, Lou."

I shuddered, knowing I was the one who should be apologizing. "Don't apologize for something that's not your fault," I reminded him.

We went to the back of the building. I hugged and thanked my sister and brother-in-law again, trying to hide the fear in my voice. Still, Frankie looked at me like she had this all figured out—like she knew how this was all going to work out.

Wade held the door open for me, the little back lot eerily calm compared to the front of the inn.

I stepped out into the warm breeze, the sun hanging like a yolk in the late afternoon sky. For the first time in my life, I wished the weather was horrible. I wished it was raining and stormy, the sky filled with dark clouds… anything that would help our plan.

"If I'd been better—done better—Blaze wouldn't be the way that he is," Wade said low, leading the way to Blaze's car.

I don't know why, but I always pictured famous celebrities riding around in their massive Suburbans or G-wagons. Of course, that wasn't Blaze. He'd pulled up to the inn in a black Audi sports car, so small and low to the ground, I was surprised it fit him, let alone the single suitcase he'd brought.

"Sometimes I think that about Frankie," I admitted, the lights flashing as Wade unlocked and opened the passenger door.

"Really? She doesn't seem like the type to get into trouble."

I laughed. I couldn't help myself. The sound burst from my stomach like the swell of a geyser.

"She is all trouble," I said and then tempered it with, "Well, not as much since Chandler and Logan, but our whole lives... she's been the bold one. A prankster. This plan of hers? This is the kind of thing she's known for. From the time we were young, she was the one who always spoke first, spoke the loudest, and once she had an idea in her head, there was no stopping her."

I sank all the way down into the bucket seat, wishing it went deep enough to make me invisible through the window. Wade closed the door and rounded to the driver's side, muttering a curse as he hit his head getting in.

"And how could you have changed that?" he wondered, starting the car and putting it in reverse.

"By being more," I said softly, unsure why I was telling him this.

It didn't matter—shouldn't matter to him. *Wouldn't matter, if he knew the truth.* But with my heart hammering against the front of my chest, it beat down the wall I should've kept up—the wall that kept me from getting closer to him.

Wade's jaw pulsed, and then he put the car back in park.

"What—"

"What does that mean?" he asked with a low growl.

I inhaled quickly, shocked that he wanted to know—needed to know so much he put the entire plan on hold.

"Wade..."

He pulled off Blaze's sunglasses and looked at me, his dark eyes pinning mine hostage. "I want to know what you mean."

What did I mean?

I wasn't sure I'd ever verbalized it before, not even to myself.

"I mean... I was always quiet. Shy. Unsure. And when I think about it now, I think Frankie tried to compensate for me. She tried to be louder, bolder, harder to ignore. She tried to spare me the attention I was afraid of. So many people think she's too much." I swallowed of the lump in my throat and then forced the last words out. "But it's because of me. It's because I wasn't—"

"Don't," he stopped me, his knuckles white where he gripped the shifter. "Don't ever say that."

Heat stole across my skin, thieving worry, frustration, and fear, and leaving instead the want to be closer to him. To trace the hard line of his jaw. To kiss the sudden anger from his mouth.

"Isn't that how you feel about your brother?" I said instead, watching his nostrils flare.

"It's not the same," he muttered, sliding the sunglasses back on and putting the car in reverse.

The car moved the way I imagined a panther would, all instant response and smooth agility. As we pulled down the alley, I gripped the handle on the door, my breaths growing shallow, and my other hand fidgeted on my lap.

Wade stopped at the stop sign on Maine Street. Even though the coast was clear, he didn't pull out right away. Not until he'd slid his hand from the console and claimed mine.

I wished I could say it was for show. I wished I could say the way it made me feel was just for show.

I wished I wasn't falling for everything this lie was making me feel about my fake boyfriend's older brother.

Wade drove slowly, giving the photographers plenty of time to spot the car that stuck out like a swanky sore thumb in a sleepy small town. I knew the moment the first one realized we were coming because Wade's fingers tightened on mine. He tugged on the lip of the visor, keeping it low against the rim of his sunglasses, and drove forward.

"The police will keep them away from the car." Wade's low voice rippled through the small cab as we got closer.

I saw the moment the spark turned into wildfire. When the squinting and pointing of a few people suddenly turned into a swarm of focus.

In the daylight, there were no camera flashes, and I realized that was worse. The flash of light was as much of an alert as it was an assault. It gave away who was watching—who wanted to see. Without them, my head snapped side to side, unsure where to look. Unsure where the danger was coming from.

Sure enough, no one got too close. With some of those lenses, they didn't need to. Then people started trickling into the street. Between parked cars. Along the roadway. Everyone inching to get a little closer than the person next to them. Pushing. Bumping. Intruding. The few police officers were now on alert, shouting at people to stay out of the road.

It would've been easy for Wade to hit the gas and blow past the crowd, but that wasn't the point. We didn't want to leave any question—any doubt. We wanted to give them this show.

Like a movie playing through the windshield, the scene suddenly went into slow motion. A man on my side of the car started causing a commotion—pushing in front of people, shouting, pointing—and the police officer instantly went to intervene. But it was a smoke show. A decoy.

As soon as the officer was diverted, a second man a few feet farther down the sidewalk stepped into the street.

"Wade." I sucked in a breath, watching the man stride right into our lane without a single worry that he'd just walked into oncoming traffic. *Anything for the head-on shot.*

Wade hit the brakes. He didn't have a choice. There was traffic in the other direction, and even if there wasn't, this paparazzi wasn't going to let us by without a good shot—one that would clearly show it wasn't Blaze Stevens in the driver's seat.

"Shit," Wade muttered, keeping his head ducked down as his hand slammed into the horn.

The reporter didn't care. He came closer. His camera firing like an automatic weapon.

I looked in the rearview. The officer realized something was wrong, but he was older and heavyset and wouldn't make it to us before this reporter got the shot he wanted—the shot that would ruin this entire plan.

We were so close. We'd made it so far.

My jaw went slack, my pulse thumping in my ears. I turned to Wade, but aside from the horn, there wasn't anything he could do.

"Look at me, Lou," Wade ordered.

My heart tripped, the photographer swarming closer in my periphery. In another second, he'd be close enough, and this would all be for nothing.

The commotion around me started to blur. The sounds fogged together until nothing but his voice was strong enough to cut through them.

"Look at me, angel." The tenor of his command... the promise buried in the rumble...

I turned my head. I couldn't see Wade's eyes through the sunglasses, but I felt the heat of them just as I had the other night, stoking an ache I didn't know bones and blood could make.

His lips parted like a crack of lightning through the darkness before the low power of his words made the silence quake.

"Good girl."

The praise erupted like a firework in my mind, not with thought but with instinct. In the single second that we had, I unclipped my seatbelt and launched myself across the console, crushing my mouth to Wade's.

It was bold. Brash. Without thought. *It was more.*

He stiffened, his surprise coming as swift as it disappeared. A low groan rolled from his chest, and an instant later, he cupped the back of my head and held me to him, his tongue pressing through the seam of my lips.

It was supposed to be a diversion. A last-ditch attempt to hide Wade from the camera and preserve our plan. But the instant my lips touched his, the idea that it was a diversion became nothing but an excuse to kiss him again. To taste the way he wanted me and feel the way he made me ache. An excuse to go back to that moment where he made me feel everything and then promised that there was more.

Wade's hand hooked into the notches of my braid like it was made to hold his fingers—made for him to hold me close as he deepened the kiss. My mouth opened, and my head tilted on instinct—a habit formed from a single night. A habit of wanting him.

Heat coiled through my body. I hardly felt the console digging into my side, only the hardness of him pressed to my front. I wanted to climb onto his lap even though there definitely wasn't room for that. It didn't matter. I ached for this. For him. For this thing I'd never felt before... never thought I'd wanted.

This thing I'd risk anything to try and hold onto.

And that was what frightened me the most. That I couldn't stop myself from wanting Wade Stevens just as surely as I couldn't reverse the lie that brought him into my life.

There was a loud bang on the hood. Three of them in sequence. And I jerked back, startled.

"Lou," Wade growled, holding me steady. "Don't move."

I wanted to tell him I couldn't—that I needed a moment to rewire my brain to the rest of my limbs after that kiss—but my mouth also seemed to forget it existed for any purpose other than to kiss him. All I could manage was a slight nod as he tipped ever so slightly to look out the windshield.

"It's the police," he rumbled low, his heavy breaths mirroring my own. "They've cleared the road. We're safe."

My sigh of relief was audible as I carefully pushed myself back into my seat. The police had the crowds contained to either side of the street—everyone where they were supposed to be.

The car moved forward, steadily gaining speed as we reached the edge of town. Neither of us said a word, our eyes flicking to the rearview, expecting at any moment for cars to follow. As soon as we passed the last of the buildings, Wade sped up, my back pressing harder into the seat as the car picked up speed like a race-horse finally let through the gate.

"Do you think they realized?" I asked, my voice hoarse as we got closer to Mom's house. "Do you think we're safe?"

I swore I saw Wade flinch at my second question, and his hand definitely tightened on the wheel. He looked tense. Uncomfortable. Maybe it hadn't been enough. The kiss. Maybe that photographer got too close—

"From the paparazzi... yes," he said with a strained voice. His answer was meant to relieve me, but there was too much meaning behind it for that to matter.

I'd saved the plan with that kiss, but what I'd risked with it...I bit my lip, looking in the side mirror one last time as we turned onto Mom's driveway. Another few seconds and we'd gone past the first rim of trees that obscured the rest of the driveway—and us—from sight, and another minute later, Mom's beaming modern farmhouse appeared ahead of us. My family's cars parked like sentries out front.

We'd made it, but we weren't safe.

At least I wasn't. It was one thing to keep up a lie to strangers from the confines of a car. It was another to hold up the farce in front of my family. My mom. My grandmother. My brothers. I wasn't safe from their scrutiny.

Nor from the man sitting next to me.

How did I continue to pretend like his brother was a barrier when Wade was the only man I'd ever wanted?

Chapter Fourteen

Wade

I SLOWED the car to a crawl as we approached the Kinkade homestead. The last thing I needed was to greet Lou's entire family with my dick standing at attention.

Buried between pockets of forest and farmland, the two-story white farmhouse rested at the end of the winding drive, hugged by a wraparound porch, the sunlight glinting off the large stretches of windows.

I had the same feeling driving up to it as I did the night I'd pulled up in front of the Lamplight Inn. *Welcome.*

"Just park next to the truck." She pointed to the massive Ford.

"Looks like quite a crowd," I murmured, scanning down the line of a half-dozen cars out front. From what Lou had told me about her family, I got the sense this kind of crowd was a common occurrence here.

"My family likes to get together," she said, folding her hands together as her eyes hopped down the line of cars. "That's my brother Jamie's work truck. He does carpentry and makes custom furniture out of a renovated barn deeper onto Mom's property. You'll meet him and his wife, Violet. Next to that is my brother

Kit and his wife Aurora's minivan. They're expecting their first baby in October."

"The artist?"

She nodded. "The truck with the MaineStems decal is my cousin, Max's. Next to his, the navy sedan belongs to my mom. The VW bug on the other side of that used to belong to my sister, but she gave the car to Harper just before Logan was born."

"The one who makes the honey?" I confirmed and pulled next to the massive black truck, putting Blaze's sports car in park.

"Yeah." Lou gave a small smile. "She calls it her VW bee... instead of beetle."

"Got it," I grunted and turned off the engine, the silence settling like a frost between us.

"The last car on the end belongs to Harp and Max's brother, Nox, but he's not here," Lou went on, and I turned to her, realizing she looked almost as nervous as she had when we left the inn. "He left for Italy last month. He went to study glassmaking in Murano for the summer."

"Lou—"

"I think he felt a little lost in the family, which I can understand. Everyone kind of has their own thing, and he would just work odd jobs for everyone. It makes you feel like you don't have a place—" She broke off when I placed my hands over hers, her head snapping to me.

"What is it? What's wrong?" I asked low, my eyes flicking to the rearview. "No one followed us, Lou. The plan worked... so far."

"I know," she said and pulled her hands free to reach for the visor, finding the mirror and starting to fuss with her braids. *Always making sure every piece of her was tucked into place and out of the spotlight.*

"Then why are you nervous?"

Her tongue slid along her bottom lip, my body instantly tightening, the taste of her still lingering on my tongue.

"Because..." She drew a trembling breath, her train of thought fractured as a woman appeared on the porch.

Judging by the wisps of white wisdom streaking her hair, the rosy warmth of her cheeks, and the familiar set of eyes on her face, I bet I was looking at Lou's mother.

"Elouise?" the woman squinted.

"Crap." I heard Lou mutter under her breath. She smiled big and waved and then quickly looked back at me, her throat working to swallow before she said quickly, "My family didn't know about Blaze and me."

My brows pulled together, and I felt my head tip as the thought settled unevenly into my mind. "But..."

"Frankie knew. And Harper... recently found out. But the rest of them didn't know until... this." She shivered at the last and then unclipped her seatbelt, opened the door, and beelined for her mother.

"Hey, Mom," I heard her greet the older woman as she headed for the steps.

They didn't know about her and Blaze... and they never would have if it weren't for me. The band around my chest cinched tighter. I yanked off my cap and tossed it onto the dash, the lip hitting the window with a thud. *Fuck.* I got out of the car and followed to join her, hating myself with every step.

"Mom, this is Wade Stevens. Wade, this is my mom, Ailene Kinkade," Lou made the introduction as I joined them on the porch.

"Mrs. Kinkade—" I extended my hand, but she cut me off as she took it.

"Ailene, please." She smiled. "It's a pleasure to meet you, Wade, though I'm so sorry it has to be under these circumstances."

My eyes flicked to Lou, catching the practically imperceptible flare of her nostrils. "Me, too."

"Please, come inside. Everyone is excited to meet you," she said as though it were the most natural thing in the world to welcome your daughter's (ex-)boyfriend's brother, who you'd only found out about twenty-four hours ago, into your home.

Lou's family was nothing like mine. Not in size or character or smiles.

I met her brothers first, the two men standing just inside the doorway and filling either side of the hall so that we were forced to walk single file through them like some kind of security check.

Lou went first, swallowed up in each of their bear hugs. They talked softly, but not soft enough for me to miss how they asked about her. If she was okay. Jamie, the auburn-haired eldest, cupped her face and tilted it side to side as he asked, his expression unreadable. But her other brother, Kit, hugged her and then held her in front of him by her shoulders. He was the one whose worry smoked from his gaze.

"I'm fine," I heard her tell him, but he looked unconvinced. I would be, too. *Fine was never fine.*

For as much as I watched the way they passed Lou between them like she was an egg they were trying not to drop, I also watched the two of them. The looks they shared. The unspoken dialogue weaving an undercurrent through the silence. All things I never had with Blaze. What would it have been like if I did? Would we be like the two of them? *Would Blaze be in this situation at all?*

Ailene followed Lou through the greeting line, her sons reaching for her shoulders and nodding as she passed through. Their deference to their mother was as palpable as my own, though I wasn't sure Joanna ever looked at me like Ailene looked at them.

"Jamie. Kit. This is Wade Stevens."

"Pleasure."

"Nice to meet you."

Their tones were pleasant, but when they gripped my hand, it was firm. Assessing. "Thanks for having me over," I said, letting my chin dip.

"Come now, boys. Let the dear man inside for the rest of us," a trembling but lively voice ordered, accompanied a second later but a tiny, elderly woman with bright purple hair and a devil-may-care smile. "Hi, I'm Gigi." She waited for no one before introducing herself, ambling in front of me and craning her hunched form to look up at me through her thick lenses.

"Pleasure to meet you. I'm Wade." I took her wiry hand to shake it gently and couldn't hide my surprise when her grip tightened impressively around my hand.

"So, you're my granddaughter's boyfriend's brother..." She didn't ask it or even look like she wanted my confirmation. She said it like she wanted to hear the words out loud as she looked me up and down to decide whether they were true or not. "Are you sure you're not a movie star?" She squinted up at me. "You sure look handsome enough—"

"Gigi!" Lou hissed and reached for her grandmother's shoulder, trying to pry her away. "Wade is a lawyer."

Her purple permed head wobbled on her thin neck as she regarded me, pinched her mouth tight, and then smiled wide. "So, you're one of those."

I chuckled even as my brow creased. "Not many people say that with a smile."

"What do you mean 'one of those?'" Lou demanded and folded her arms.

Lou's sudden defensiveness on my part intrigued her grandmother, her aged, alert eyes darting between us. The moment Lou realized, her cheeks turned bright red.

"Never mind—" Lou insisted, flustered, and then reached for my arm. "Here, let's go in the kitchen so you can meet the rest of my family—"

"What I mean, Elouise, is that he's one of those people who lives by the rules."

"Oh—"

"And knows exactly how to break them," Gigi finished smartly and winked at Lou before sliding her hand into my elbow and pulling me with her. "Now, come, meet the rest of the family."

She led us into the kitchen, the large island rounded with warm faces of people I subsequently met. Jamie's wife, Violet. Kit's pregnant wife, Aurora. Harper and Max, I already quasi-knew. The room quickly filled as we joined them, but it didn't feel crowded. Not like Blaze's hospital room when it was just Mom and me and my unconscious brother. There I felt my lungs struggle to breathe and my body itch to escape. But not here.

Here, I didn't feel like a stranger. Ironic, since this family wasn't mine.

"We decided on a charcuterie and dip dinner," Violet said. "We've got the hummus bar here to start, and then we'll put out the charcuterie boards on the table." She pointed over her shoulder to the dining room which stretched over to the left of the kitchen, whereas the front opened up into the living room.

As the group started to talk, I began to piece together the smaller things—things I'd noticed but not recognized. The scent of the house. It was different than the inn but warm and inviting all the same. There were candles on every end table, a sign of Frankie. The dining table was not only expertly made but made with care. Her brother, Jamie, must've hand-carved it. Everything was connected. Open.

I could see straight into the living room. On one wall hung a giant painting of a lighthouse beaming over calm seas. One of Kit's, I had to assume. And on the other wall, a dozen framed photographs of everyone in this room and some who weren't in varying configurations. In this home, family was the focus. And the difference with mine was like day and night.

We'd never had photographs in our house. Dad preferred to frame diplomas or expensive art, and Mom only kept an old photograph of Blaze and me on her nightstand. We were maybe nine and ten... it was probably the last time we'd hugged each other.

"So, Lou... you and Blaze Stevens? I can't believe it," Aurora gushed, her tone nothing short of pure excitement. "I absolutely loved him in *Works of Love.* And the one where he played the tornado wrangler, oh, what was—"

"Swept Away," Harper finished for her and sipped from her can of seltzer, her hip propped against the counter. She was part of the circle around the island but slightly distanced from it. I wondered why.

"Yes." Aurora giggled. "That's it."

"Careful, Aurora, I think you're making Kit jealous," Violet teased, drawing everyone's attention to the way Kit stared fiercely at his wife.

Only when she looked up at him did she flush and lean into his hold. "Oh, he knows he doesn't have anything to worry about." Her tone turned serious, husky even for a second, before she quickly added, "I don't think Blaze is broody enough to be my type." She winked at Kit and then looked at me. "Your brother is a phenomenal actor. And I'm just so happy for you, Lou." Her attention finally rested on her sister-in-law. "It's like a fairytale."

I didn't even realize how tightly my fist was clenched on the counter until Gigi placed her hand on top of mine, side-eyeing me in a way that felt dangerous.

"I wouldn't say that—"

"More like a miracle since you didn't even know who he was when he first came to the inn," Harper chimed in.

"He booked the room under Blaze Turner—"

"But he didn't show up in disguise."

"I don't know," Lou stammered, tucking a wisp of hair back behind her ear. "I didn't recognize him—"

Harper snorted. "I had to show you three different trailers before you remembered who he was."

Lou opened and shut her mouth, her lips pursing for a second before she replied, "I don't watch a lot of movies."

"Wade, can I get you something to drink?" Ailene asked. "The boys are having whiskey sours."

"Sounds great." I nodded, watching as Jamie took up the task so his mom wouldn't have to.

"So, tell us everything. He came to stay at the inn, and then what happened?" Aurora propped her elbows on the counter and cradled her chin on her folded hands.

All eyes around the island went to Lou—including mine.

"What do you mean?" Lou grabbed a carrot, dunked it in the bowl of hummus and quickly shoved it in her mouth, an obvious effort to delay answering.

This was my fault. They had no idea about her and Blaze and never would have if I hadn't asked her to do this. If I hadn't begged for her help. Now, she was having to rip off the scab and relive a relationship that hadn't worked out... all to protect my brother.

"What do you think she means?" Violet chimed in, resting her elbows on the counter and propping her chin on her hands. "Who made the first move?"

"Blaze, obviously," Harper said and snuck a hand through the crowd for a piece of pita.

"You think?" Aurora asked, grabbing a piece of celery. "I don't know. I think Lou knows how to go after something when she wants it."

Her eyes swung to mine, meeting at the memory of the other night when what she'd wanted—who she'd wanted—was me. And now, I had to stand here and listen as they asked her to relive her relationship with my brother, the man who hadn't deserved her.

"So, tell us how it happened, dear." It was Gigi who spoke, her smile beaming as she reached for her granddaughter's hand. "We're so excited to hear."

For some reason, the old woman looked at me then. Almost

like she saw the tension crawling like a swarm of ants under my skin. I didn't want to hear about it—didn't want to think about it. No matter what I knew or heard or had seen, it didn't feel right to think of Lou as anything other than mine.

"I..." Lou tried to swallow. "I don't know." She paused, her eyes meeting everyone else's except mine. "I saw him a lot because he didn't really go out. He'd try to come down before the breakfast crowd, and we... would talk."

"So, you were friends first? How romantic. Keep going," Aurora begged.

One by one, hands reached across the counter and dug into the spread of food, but all I could see was how they reached for information. Prying it from her when she clearly didn't want to talk about it. But she would... because that was Lou, giving everyone else what they wanted.

Giving me what I'd asked for.

Lou hesitantly continued her story, and with each detail, it grew harder to breathe. Like being trapped in a burning building, I didn't even need to be near or see the flame. The smoke alone—the remnants of their relationship—was enough to suffocate me.

"Wade." I stiffened at the sound of my name, only then realizing the glass held in front of me.

Dammit, how long had Jamie been waiting for me to take it?

"Thanks." I grabbed the tumbler like it was a lifeline, hauling it to my mouth just as Aurora lifted her drink to toast and forced me to stop.

"To Lou and Blaze."

All the color drained from Lou's face, but she didn't say anything. Couldn't. My fingers tightened around the glass so hard I swore I heard it crack.

I extended my glass toward the collection in the center, feeling like I had to break the bones in my arm in the process. Even when I finally brought the alcohol to my lips, the burn down my throat wasn't enough to clear the smoke of her story from where it embedded into my chest.

"How come you didn't tell us?" Jamie probed, trying his hardest not to let the edge of accusation come through his tone. It came from a good place, but that didn't make it any better.

Lou stiffened. "I wasn't sure... anything would come of it."

"Still, Lou, we would've been happy for you," Kit's voice was almost identical to his brother's, the way it was laced with betrayal.

Lou's eyes glistened, and I wanted to reach across the counter and throttle them. A pretty poor choice for someone who was a guest in their family's home.

"I'm sure it was my brother's decision," I broke in, the words clipped. "Sharing things... publicly... too soon has never really worked out for him."

I met Jamie's gaze, the two of us staring in silence for a second that felt longer than necessary before Lou jumped back in nervously, "He's right. Plus, Blaze is a movie star, and I run an inn. It didn't seem... likely."

He was also a self-centered ass, and she was an angel.

"Fairy tales rarely are," Violet declared again, beaming first at Lou and then up at her husband. "Just think... when he wakes up and hears everything you did to protect him."

A clacking sound drew everyone's attention to Harper, who'd collected one too many jars of jam in her arms to carry into the dining room.

"I'll help her," Lou jumped at the chance to escape and quickly fled the room.

"Is Harper okay?" I asked Max, who stood beside me. It was hard to miss his sister's irritation.

Max sighed. "She's just dealing with some guy—another local honey company who's causing some backlash online. Trolling her posts. Making accusations."

I tensed, instantly on alert. "Does she need a lawyer?"

"No. Not yet, I don't think." He glanced over at his sister, Harper, and Lou in a conversation among themselves. "I think it's just at that painfully annoying stage, where every time he does or says something, it's like her soul is stepping on a Lego."

"Ouch." I winced at the thought.

"It always happens when you're starting out. When you're joining a market that other people think they have all the rights to. I told Harp that I went through it with my business, and it all worked out. You just have to muddle through for a little."

"Well, if something changes..." It was the least I could do for the way Lou was helping my family right now.

"I appreciate that." Max smiled and clapped me on the back.

"Boys, why don't you grab the meats from the fridge and put them out?" Ailene asked, and Max and her sons moved to comply. I would've gone to help—anything to get some of the tension to move from my body—but I didn't get a chance. Gigi came over to me as soon as the space opened.

"How's your brother doing? Frankie told us a little about what happened. What a shame. That poor boy."

"He's okay. All things considered." I cleared my throat. "We're thinking about moving him to a facility in Boston as soon as I'm sure the media has cleared out of town."

"So, Lou will have to go all the way to Boston to see him?" Aurora asked, dismayed.

Shit. I wasn't thinking when I said that.

"If it's for the best care..." Violet suggested.

Lou returned then. "Food is ready."

Within minutes, everyone circled the dining table, filling our plates with the charcuterie that overflowed it. There wasn't enough room for everyone to sit in one place, so pockets of conversations started to form, coursing through a variety of topics.

I ended up with Gigi and Ailene, answering their questions about my work—my office, my family. Listening as they shared pieces of Lou's childhood with me like the information would magically be transmuted to my brother. The entire time, only part of my focus could be dedicated to them. The majority of it stayed locked on Lou, where she sat with her sisters-in-law.

Some people—most people—change when they are around family versus when they are talking to strangers. Especially introverts. But even people like my brother, who was charismatic and carefree in public, became someone drawn and tense in private. At least, he had the last time I was alone with him, but that was a while ago... and maybe it was the company and not his character.

Lou, on the other hand, effused the exact same generous spirit and easy smile with her family as she did with the guests at the inn.

She didn't see it. I wasn't sure if the rest of them did either. But the way Lou drew everyone into conversation was as effortless as the way the sun shined. She talked and tugged at their lives and interests until I overheard all about the new hotel contract Violet had just secured for Jamie's furniture business, how long it took Kit to figure out the instructions to build the crib for their nursery, and that Max worried his best friend was having second thoughts about his wedding.

I listened as Aurora shared about her latest research, a ripple of laughter running through the room every time she pronounced the Latin classification of the mollusk she was studying. And even her mother, Ailene, was pulled into the fray, excitedly outlining her ideas for the blueberry festival she hosted at Stonebar Farms at the end of the summer.

Lou hinted that she wasn't enough. That everyone else in her family was a bigger piece of the puzzle, especially her twin. She didn't see that she was the glue between all of them. The one that brought all their different edges together. That flowed through the rough patches and sharp corners.

She thought she wasn't seen, but that wasn't the same as being invisible. Air couldn't be seen, but that didn't mean it wasn't formidable—didn't mean it wasn't elemental. It didn't mean she didn't have the power to shape and sway everything around her.

Even I didn't come away untouched when the conversation returned to me. Violet shared that she, too, had come from a generational family business with a father that was particularly callous.

"I had no idea until I came here that family was what you make of it—*who* you make of it." She smiled, glancing around the room before her eyes fell on her husband, who pulled her hand to his mouth and kissed it.

"Well, I think Harper would be happy to have Blaze as a part of ours," Max chimed in, nudging his sister with his elbow.

"Max," Harper hissed, furious.

"What? You have all of his movie posters hung in your room—"

"Not anymore," she huffed and punched him in the arm. "He's dating Lou."

I looked at Lou, our eyes locking for a long second before she pulled her gaze away and turned to her sister-in-law.

"Here, let me take your plates," she declared, building herself an exit from the conversation.

As Lou took mine, our fingers brushed. Like paper over an open flame, my skin started to curl and my nerves started to char, the way I wanted her burning holes through me and my resolve.

Somehow, I ended up talking to Max and Harper in the doorway between the dining room and the kitchen, where Lou and her sisters-in-law were cleaning up. As much as I tried to pay attention to what Max was saying about his friend's upcoming wedding—and the advice Harper was trying to give him—all I could hear was the hushed tones of the women a few feet behind me.

"So... tell us the details," Aurora begged. "What's Blaze really like? Is he as charismatic as he is on screen?"

My body stiffened. I wasn't prepared for this. I wasn't prepared for her family to not have known she was seeing my brother... wasn't prepared for all the questions I'd have to listen to her answer.

I had no right—no reason to be jealous. But I was. Every moment. Every breath. It filled me with envy for my brother. I was jealous of the man who'd lost this gorgeous woman because he was lucky enough to once have had her.

"Yes... but also more reserved in private."

My fist balled, and my vision started to blur.

"That makes sense. It had to be hard to be in the spotlight like that all the time. People always wanting to see you—photograph you."

"Is he a good kisser?"

My head jerked, but I caught myself just in time before I gave away which conversation I was really interested in.

"Aurora," Violet chided. "It had to have been magical."

"W-why?"

It took everything in me not to turn and look at her.

"Because you don't hide a kiss or a boyfriend from your family if it's not," Violet reasoned. "You hide something that you want to protect—to preserve. You only hide something that is too good to be true but somehow too forbidden to be yours."

"No."

Blood thumped in my ears. I didn't want to hear this. I didn't want to hear that anything Lou had with Blaze was magic. I didn't want to hear about anything she had with Blaze.

"Where did it happen?" Aurora asked.

"In the living room at the inn."

I stiffened. *That was where we'd first kissed, too.* The thought turned my stomach. *The both us of...*

"So, what happened?"

I didn't have to look at her to know she was blushing—to know she was hesitating, searching for any reason to get out of answering the question, but there was none. Words bubbled in my chest—an excuse to go in there and save her from the conversation, but they died on the tip of my tongue when I heard her.

"Well, it was late one night, and I was working on wedding stuff for the inn—for Max. I'd fallen asleep on the couch, and when he walked in, he startled me, and I knocked all my papers onto the floor."

I couldn't breathe. At first, I thought it was a twisted coincidence when she'd first kissed us both in the same place, but now...

"He helped me gather them and we were... close. Surrounded by my inspiration for weddings and after a week of..."

"Electricity?" Aurora offered.

Lou must've nodded because she continued, "It was something unstoppable."

"Did he kiss you?"

Until this moment, there was a kernel of my brain that still thought she could've experienced almost exactly the same situation with two different men.

"No. I kissed him," she answered, and that kernel evaporated.

They'd asked about her first kiss with Blaze... and she'd told them about the kiss she'd shared with me instead.

"Incredible," Aurora gushed.

"I love that for you," Violet added.

"Wade?"

I blinked and saw Max and his sister staring at me strangely.

"Excuse me," I murmured and walked around them. I needed space. Fresh air. A second to think.

Earlier, Max had taken a phone call on the back deck of this house. His friend, I assumed, since that sparked his frustrated conversation with me when he came back inside. Now, I headed for that deck like it was an oasis in the middle of a desert. A drink of cool rationality in the midst of the hot turmoil churning inside me.

I didn't know how long I was out there for or how deep I was in thought until a low voice rumbled behind me.

"Did you know?"

I tensed at the low voice. Jamie had joined me on the back deck with two glasses in his hands, one of them containing another cocktail for me.

"Thanks." I took the glass, tapped the edge to his, and immediately took a healthy sip, swirling the taste in my mouth before swallowing.

Jamie didn't drink though. He stared off the back of the deck and raked a hand through his auburn hair, dislodging what looked like a wood shaving from between the strands.

"Did you know about them?" He repeated his question and then felt the need to clarify, "Lou and your brother."

My teeth clenched, and I shook my head. "No." Another sip. "My brother and I aren't close."

He glanced at me, grunted, and finally took a swig from his glass. "Family can be tough."

I couldn't stop the bitter sound that pushed through my lips. "Yours seems anything but," I told him, taking another drink.

"Only because we've been through a lot," he admitted with reserve. "There was a time when Kit and I hardly spoke. After everything that happened to him, I couldn't break him out of his shell no matter what I did or said, and the frustration... it drove a wedge between us for a while."

"The worst thing is wanting to help someone you love and having them hate you for it." I swirled the liquid. "Damned if you try to help, damned if you don't."

"Yeah." He nodded solemnly. "Took me awhile to learn I couldn't be everyone's training wheels making sure they didn't fall. All I could be was the safety net, there for them if something happened."

The door opened behind us and Kit joined us on the deck. "Are we talking about Lou?"

No. I went stiff.

Jamie cleared his throat. "Siblings."

Kit came and stood between Jamie and me, his arms folded over his chest, his expression unsettled. "Does Lou seem like your brother's type?"

I choked.

"Kit—"

"I'm serious," Kit interrupted Jamie. "I'm sorry. If you want to tread lightly, that's up to you, but someone has to come out and say that none of this makes sense. Tell me I'm wrong."

Jamie didn't respond, the muscle in his jaw pulsing.

"Exactly," Kit rumbled and looked to me. "I just can't believe Lou would date your brother. Nothing against him, but Lou is... soft. Shy. She doesn't like to be the center of attention, and she hasn't been interested in dating in..." He huffed. "I know they say not to believe the tabloids, but none of this—nothing about the two of them makes sense. Am I wrong?"

I swallowed, taking a second before I replied, "No."

"You of all people should know that opposites attract," Jamie countered.

"And for her not to tell us?" Kit returned, rubbing a hand along his jaw. "Why wouldn't she tell us? When has she ever kept anything from us?"

Anger fumed under my skin. Even though I understood where they were coming from—why they said the things they did —I couldn't stop the fury from bubbling in my veins.

I tossed back the rest of my cocktail, the alcohol clearing a path down my throat, and then my hand slammed the glass down on the railing, harder than intended.

"I think she didn't tell you because all your sister ever does is cater to everyone else's wants and what they want from her. And for once, maybe she wanted something unexpected... something she was afraid she shouldn't... and she didn't want to hear how it was wrong from the people she loves the most."

They slowly looked at each other, Jamie's head dipping in a sign of tentative surrender. Kit on the other hand...

"Whatever the reason, if he hurts her—"

I stepped right into his space.

"I would never let anyone hurt her," I swore, my promise rough and hewn as though drawn from the very marrow of my bones, and then turned and stormed inside to find Lou heading toward me.

"Frankie just texted me." She held her phone in her hand as

though I might ask to see it. "She said she's pretty sure the coast is clear."

My jaw clenched and released.

"Should we go—"

"Yes," I didn't even wait for her to finish.

"Great." She sounded as relieved as I felt, but for a completely different reason.

She didn't want to answer any more questions about a relationship that no longer existed... and I needed to know why she'd described her first kiss with Blaze as ours.

Chapter Fifteen

Lou

"How was it?" Frankie wrapped her arms around me as soon as we got back to the inn. "Are you okay?"

"It was fine—I'm fine." I sighed and hugged her, my eyes closing for a second in the safety of my sister's embrace. "How was everything here? Any problems? Did the check-out go okay?"

After asking to extend their visit for two more days—a request I was happy to accommodate—the newlywed couple was scheduled for a late check-out this afternoon, right in the middle of the fray.

"No hiccups at all. Well, except for Logan's." She smiled and turned to Chandler who held their son cradled to his chest while talking to Wade. Looking back at me, she asked, "What are you going to do?"

I lowered my head, watching Wade from underneath my lashes. He'd had his eyes on me all night at Mom's *as I made up lies about my and Blaze's relationship,* and then wanted to leave so suddenly but hadn't said a word on the drive back. I knew why. It was the same reason Jamie was always quiet when he'd pick us up from one of Frankie's failed pranks when we were younger: He wanted unobstructed time to talk, and car rides didn't last long enough for the conversation he wanted to have.

"I don't know." The real question was: *What was Wade going to do with me?*

I worried my bottom lip between my teeth. Had I said something he realized couldn't be true? Had my brothers said something to him out on the deck? Had Max?

The way Wade stormed outside in the first place had put me on edge, so I'd checked in with Frankie, not the other way around. I wanted to know if the coast was clear because being at Mom's... having to lie to all of them... I was just waiting for the other shoe to drop.

"They're going to be so upset with me," I said softly to my sister so Wade wouldn't hear.

"Who? Mom? Jamie and Kit?" She made a *pfft* noise and reached for my hand. I hadn't even realized I'd been pulling on a thread at the end of my sleeve. "They can't be upset with you for living your own life, Lou."

"I think they already are." Our brothers had been skeptical and broody all evening.

"They're upset because you broke out of your mold. Because you did something they didn't know about, and that's never happened before. It doesn't mean you did something wrong. It just means they're having to realize they were never entitled to every detail about your life."

I squeezed her hand and gave her a small smile. Frankie did know how to put things in perspective.

Our conversation lulled for a moment as Wade and Chandler went into the living room to look outside. The street had been clear when we drove by. I didn't expect it to be any different now.

"You know the reason Chandler and I stayed at the inn that whole week?" Frankie asked, her eyes still focused on her husband.

My brow creased. *Was this a trick question?*

"Because you lied about the inn being haunted, and Chandler

called you on it, so you both had to stay," I recalled the beginning of their relationship.

"Yes... but no," Frankie said, one corner of her mouth tipping. "We ended up in a predicament because of a lie, but we stayed at the inn because of the truth." She looked at me then—my bewildered expression—and her smile widened. "We stayed because we felt something for one another. A little bit of loathing at the time, yes, but also attraction. Connection. We stayed in the lie because the truth was we didn't want to be apart from one another."

I blinked slowly. They'd stayed in the lie in order to stay together. *Was that why I was so eager to live in mine? Because the moment I told Wade the truth, I risked losing the only man I'd ever felt something for?*

"I see," I murmured.

"All I'm saying, Lou, is don't get so lost in the little bits of lies that you miss the raging current of truth running underneath them all."

"Raging?"

Frankie shrugged. "It felt like the right word to describe the tension between you and Wade."

My jaw dropped and then snapped shut when the guys returned to the reception, Wade's eyes immediately hunting for mine.

"We should get going, Frankie," Chandler rumbled, and my sister nodded, approaching her husband and taking the baby from his arms.

"Say goodnight to Auntie Lou," she cooed, giving me one last half-hug as I kissed Logan's forehead.

I stood frozen in place—Wade, too—as my sister and Chandler left, feeling that very raging tension spinning tighter and tighter until the door closed behind them.

"Lou..."

Slowly, I regarded him, my lips leaking every last drop of oxygen from my lungs.

How could I miss the truth? How could I miss the way a single look from him made my nerves fizzle like a water droplet on a hot skillet? How could I miss the way his kiss made me feel or how it was all I wanted?

Trying to keep hold of the little lies was like trying to catch a fish with my bare hands. They slipped and twisted, desperate to escape, but the truth was I needed to hold onto them a little longer so I could have a little longer with him.

Wade stepped closer, his eyes darkening as they roamed my face. "We need to talk."

Warmth prickled the swells of my cheeks. "Okay."

He stiffened, and then I heard it: the vibration. His jaw muscle fired as he reached for his phone. The slight sag in his shoulders told me who was calling before he did. "Joanna."

I nodded and watched him head into the living room, taking the call in a low voice.

Should I wait? My pulse thumped as I looked to the reception desk, instinctively reaching for my daily checklist that Frankie had dutifully marked off everything she'd done. *What did he want to talk about?*

Air pinched into my lungs, the stream narrowing with each breath. I wasn't missing the truth... I was afraid of the consequences. I was afraid of what would happen to the tender and untried parts of me if Wade couldn't get past my lie. I was afraid of what I risked damaging—*or losing entirely*—if I gave into wanting the man who made me feel things... want things... I'd never wanted before.

Within moments, the hallway felt bereft of oxygen, so I headed upstairs, my heart thudding like footsteps in my chest. I just couldn't determine if they were running from how I felt about Wade or running toward him.

As soon as I reached the top step, my head swung in the direction of his room. A habit it had formed over the last two weeks.

And there I stopped, my heart sinking like an anchor into my stomach, holding me in place.

The door was distinctly cracked open.

"Lou."

I jumped when he came up behind me and blurted out, "Did you leave the door open earlier?"

It was a dumb question because I was the last of us upstairs. Maybe I missed it. It was possible. But the way my head always turned toward that room lately, no matter which direction I was going, made it incredibly unlikely.

"No." His voice was a low growl as he moved around me, holding an arm in my direction to signal that I was to stay back. Still, I followed ever so cautiously as he pushed open the door to the room and flicked on the light.

The room wasn't that big. It only took a second to scan and see it was empty, at which point we both went inside. Unlike the first time we'd both gone inside Blaze's room, uncertain of what we'd find, everything was neat and tidy.

"Is anything missing?" I asked quietly, still feeling the violent thud of my pulse.

As far as I could tell, nothing looked out of place.

Wade didn't answer right away, taking a couple of minutes to do several passes through the room, checking different spots every time. The closet. The desk. The dresser. The desk chair. The bed. Underneath the bed.

He stopped, his hand on the narrow desk drawer. "Did you have anything in here?"

The drawer was slightly ajar. Not enough to stand out, but enough that it hadn't been closed all the way. And there could be a hundred reasons for that, I told myself. It was a vintage piece—one that Jamie had restored for me—and the drawers in those moved with the sturdy but unsteady effects of age.

"No." I shook my head. The answer should've been a relief. Even if someone had gone searching through the drawer, there'd been nothing in it to take. So why did it feel like my heart was beating out of my throat?

He shimmied the drawer open and put his hand inside, retrieving only a pen from the space, and it instantly made him frown.

I moved closer, trying to get a closer look. "What is it?"

"This pen is one of the monogrammed ones my firm gives to clients. Or family members."

"So, Blaze put it there?" And if he had, was there something else with it? Something that was missing?

"He probably dropped it in there or it rolled in there. Who knows."

Wade was probably right, but after everything that happened today and then seeing the door cracked open, my nerves were having a hard time leaving *fight or flight* territory.

Until he looked at me, and then I had no choice.

"Lou..."

"I don't... I don't want to talk about Blaze anymore."

Wade stepped in front of me, the size of him, the leather musk of his scent, the heat of his body as it wrapped around me, I was caught in his presence as surely as a moth to a flame.

"Neither do I," he said, his voice rough. "I want to talk about why you lied to your family."

My pulse erupted, all the little lies exploding like a giant firework in my chest. Panic seized my throat. "Wade—"

I must've swayed because his hands were on my shoulders a moment later, either to save me from falling or to stop me from running.

"I want to know why, when they asked about your kiss with my brother, and you told them about our kiss instead?"

My jaw dropped. *Our kiss.* That was what he was talking about, not the other lie. Yet, I felt no relief.

"You..." I croaked, my throat lined with sand. "You heard that?"

He'd been listening when I'd described my first kiss with Blaze to my sisters-in-law, only it hadn't been a kiss with Blaze because there'd never been a kiss with Blaze. There'd never been anything —anyone but Wade.

"You told them about *our* kiss, Lou. Why?" he growled, one hand sliding to frame my chin in his fingers.

I shivered. My mind circled between all three moments—this one, the one from earlier when I told them, and the kiss itself. Like a bird searching for a safe place to land, but there was no escaping this. No escaping him.

"I..." Words tangled in my throat, and my tongue quickly swiped along my lips like it would help free them.

All it did was bring his face closer to mine, the warmth of his ragged breaths rushing against my skin. My eyes fluttered, my gaze sinking to the firm curve of his mouth. *A place to land.*

"Tell me, angel." His palm cupped the side of my face, and I couldn't hold back the truth any longer.

"Because yours was the only one I could remember." *His was the only one that had been magic.* "Yours was the only one I want to remember."

With Wade, there only was the truth: I wanted him. And his brother had never been a thought in my mind.

"Lou..." he groaned and crushed his mouth to mine.

Like magnets held apart since those minutes earlier in the car, our tongues collided with electric hunger. The kiss turned devastating in the span of a second. An assault of tongues and teeth. Of desire and ache and exactly what Violet had said earlier: *forbidden.*

All over I felt it now—my skin sizzling off the heat that thumped through my veins. I wanted him. That was my whole truth and nothing but.

I panted when he drew back, my hands reaching for him, clutching the fabric of his shirt—holding on for dear life.

Wade angled my face, his thumb brushing over my bottom lip like it marked his prey. "Did his kiss not make you feel the way mine did?"

Ache pulsed in my core. The possessiveness in his voice, the greediness of his gaze as it raked over my face, it made it hard to breathe hearing him jealous of something that never existed.

"No," I answered breathlessly. There was no comparison. *It was impossible.*

"Good," he growled.

My reward was his mouth again. Another kiss that went deeper than the last, each stroke of his tongue seeming to reach into the very depths of my stomach and stoke the heat licked down between my thighs.

My head spun—we were spinning, and I didn't even realize it until his foot shoved the door behind me, and it closed with a thud. I jumped, unsteadily finding his gaze.

"Wade..."

"And what about his touch?" He demanded low, his hand cupping the side of my neck and tilting my head so his mouth could find my ear. "Did it make you tremble like mine does, angel?"

Heat drenched my pussy. There was something about the sound of his voice that brought me pleasure. That made goose-bumps rise to my skin and heat rush between my thighs. Especially when he called me *angel.*

I shook my head against his palm, letting him feel the guilty confession against his skin.

"Say it." Wade's teeth nipped at my ear lobe, and I gasped, the sensation so fleeting, I couldn't tell if it was pleasure or pain that left the small brand on my skin.

My throat worked to swallow but ultimately conceded to the tightness. "N-no. It didn't."

"Good girl."

My knees went weak, and my exhale tripped when his hands slid to my hair, gently tracing the ridges of the braid along the left side of my scalp. And then oxygen ceased to matter altogether when he took a half step back.

"Take your hair down," he said, eyes glittering and jaw tight. "I want to see you."

It was wrong to let this continue. Wrong to race toward intimacy on a path built by deception. But I wanted him to see me. The real me. Hair down. Desires exposed. Pleasures unfettered.

I wanted to hold onto this truth.

I lifted my hands, pulling the ties from my braids one after another. As I combed the sections free, I watched Wade's gaze darken as though I were stripping naked in front of him and not just letting my hair down.

A deep sound of appreciation erupted from his chest when I finished, making my nipples tighten against my shirt.

"Good girl." His hungry praise made my core throb like it had the other night, and all I wanted was for him to ease it. And to ease his, too. And he knew it.

"Tell me what you want, Lou," he rumbled the same way he had in the living room.

The way that made me feel powerful. And bold. And wanted.

"I want you to kiss me."

Groaning, he cupped my face and angled it to his. The feel of his fingers on my skin was like bait on a lure, my head tipping and turning, trying to catch more of it. But instead of kissing me, his hands slid back to my scalp. The feel of his fingers through my unbound hair was like dynamite to my senses, pleasure exploding as his mouth took mine.

Each kiss seemed to go deeper. Like each lick and stroke of his tongue could rewrite the history of any kisses that had come before. Like he could single-handedly erase any other man but him from the memory of my mouth.

I wished I could tell him I could hardly remember who I was when he kissed me, let alone my fake relationship with his brother.

"What else?" Wade muttered when it was clear I'd be completely incoherent if he kept kissing me like this. "Tell me what else you want."

He ordered like he didn't already know—like his hands

hadn't already slid to my neck, one teasing the neckline of my shirt where it dipped onto my chest.

"I want you to touch me," I confessed, feeling how it lifted some of the guilt off my chest. Maybe it was never the lies that oppressed me, but the way I tried to fight the truth of how much I wanted him.

His lips moved to my neck, an animal sound clawing from them and over my pulse. The fabric of my shirt bunched, my arms lifting like a needy marionette as he pulled it over my head and let it drop to the floor.

My breath caught when his hands landed on my back—at the clasp of my bra—and then that, too, was gone, my nipples pebbled and aching where they rubbed against his shirt.

I found his heady gaze for only a second before he kissed me again, dragging me into that sweet oblivion. The next time I came up for air, he was sitting on the edge of the bed, and I straddled his lap, exactly like I had the other night.

"Wade..." I sighed, my head tipping as his teeth scraped down my throat onto my collarbone and then lower on my chest.

"So beautiful, angel." His palms slid from my waist to cup my breasts, weighing them and tipping them to his gaze. "Every night I've dreamed of you like this... every goddamn night..."

I was gasping even before his lips closed over one tight peak, flooding my veins with desire. My hands dug into his shoulders as his expert mouth licked and sucked and teased. A hot, wet torture was what it was. Lips and tongue on one breast, his hand on the other, until I couldn't breathe without begging for more.

"Tell me, Lou. Tell me what you want."

Through the murky churn of ache, a deeper-seated want emerged.

"I want to touch you."

Wade growled, swirling my nipple with his tongue like he needed one last taste before he drew back and lifted his arms.

My eyes went wide at the gesture, heat burrowing a fresh path between my thighs. I grabbed the fringes of his shirt and pulled it up his broad torso and over his head, his muscles rippling as his arms came back down.

I reached out, gingerly at first, my finger starting at the corner of his neck and tracing along the ridge of his shoulder. They curved then onto the swell of his pecs, the tan of his skin gleaming bronze under the sheen of sweat.

"Tell me what you're thinking."

My finger paused for only an instant before the tug of need drew me into uncharted yet unavoidable territory.

"I wanted to do this." My confession oozed out in a husky whisper. "When I saw you in the towel that day." My fingertip moved over the flat of his nipple, marveling at how the muscle in his chest pulsed like I'd shocked it to life.

His skin rippled under my touch. A low rumble sounded from his chest, urging me on. And I didn't hesitate.

"I wanted to trace all these lines. Ridges," I murmured and spread my fingers onto his abdomen, letting them sink into the grooves between the muscles like mortar between bricks. I didn't stop when a strand of my hair spilled over my shoulder or immediately try to tuck it back. And I didn't shy from his obvious, appreciative gaze as it heated my bare chest, my nipples tight and tingling, aching for the return of his mouth.

"I wanted you to." Wade's tone was dark. Urgent.

His hands gripped my hips and pulled me hard against him, and I gasped. The thick length of his arousal was unmistakable where it wedged between my thighs.

"Wade..." I breathed, my body recalling the rhythm it found the other night. The slow friction of my core grinding against his cock.

"If you would've come in instead of knocking, you would've known," he said hoarsely as I began to rock faster. "You would've found me in the shower with my hand on my cock, groaning your name."

My lips broke apart, a cry tumbling out.

"I wanted you then," Wade swore, capturing my gaze. "I

wanted you from the moment you spilled coffee all over me—" He broke off with a groan and reached for my face, his thumb stroking over my cheek. "From the moment I saw this pretty blush on your cheeks, I wanted to see the color on every inch of you. On your mouth." He stroked my lips. "On your breasts." He cupped and thumbed my nipple. "And here..."

I shuddered as his whole hand wedged between us and cupped over my sex.

"I wanted to see this pussy pink and weeping for me."

At that, I wasn't sure there was a solid piece left to me. My body, my bones, everything seemed to have dissolved into liquid, molten lust.

"Is that what you want, angel?"

I let out a small cry and tipped into him, sure that my lips couldn't form an answer unless they were attached to his. But before I could kiss him, he moved back and tightened his hand on my waist.

"I want to hear you say it." Wade's gaze was sparkling and tumultuous, the reflection of stars on unsteady seas. "I want to hear the words, Lou. I want you to tell me what you want because you never tell anyone, and I want that part of you to be mine, too."

Air crackled in and out through my lips, each breath like an ember landing on dry kindling, my body just waiting to go up in flames.

"I want this. I want you," I said huskily, my throat working to carve out the words. "I want to be yours."

He growled low.

"Only yours," I promised, and it set him off.

Maneuvering us with a dexterity I didn't possess, he laid my back on the bed and rose over me, his hands working the waist of my jeans. Another blink, and I felt the cool caress of air on my hips and legs, the rest of my clothing gone in an instant.

There was a soft thud, and I was sure it was my clothing

landing on the floor, but it felt like it was his gaze landing on me. Pinning me. *Marking me.*

Tension rippled through his patchwork of muscles as his gaze roamed over me. It milked heat from my skin and sent it pooling between my thighs until I had to bite my lip and squeeze them together, the pressure unbearable.

Wade's eyes snapped to mine. *Fierce.*

"I'm not like him, Lou," he said, air hissing through his teeth as he pressed his palm to the front of his jeans where they stretched over the bulk of his cock. "I'm not unsure or indecisive. I don't play around when I want something. And I definitely don't fucking share."

I shivered, his possessive tone like fire catching on the brush of goosebumps on my skin. I didn't realize my eyes had fluttered shut until his hand gripped my chin, lifting my face to make sure I was looking straight at him before he spoke again.

"I want you to be mine, Lou," he murmured, his voice strained. "But that means you're only mine... and everyone is going to know it."

The implication was like an eclipse, bright and rare, but also dangerous. For everyone to know it, they'd have to know I wasn't with Blaze.

"Is that what you want?"

"Yes," I said, knowing I'd never responded so quickly in my whole entire life. And it was with a voice that didn't sound like mine yet sounded more like me than ever before.

"Good girl," he growled, making my desire surge at his praise.

He flicked open the front of his jeans, and my jaw went slack. I'd imagined this part so many times, too, after the towel hinted at what was underneath. After I'd ground out my orgasm on his length. I wanted the rest of what that night promised—of what he promised. *All of him.*

Wade stripped and straightened, all air bleeding from my lungs as I looked at him. He was... beautiful. *Big* and beautiful.

And wanted me like a beast, the way his hand instantly gripped his cock like he had to physically hold it back from me.

I shivered, feeling another rush of heat from my pussy.

"Spread your legs for me, angel," he commanded like he knew what was happening to me, how I was melting at the sight of him.

My chest heaved, and I pried my tight legs apart. My teeth caught on my lower lip to hold back sound when I saw how wet the insides of my thighs were. I was so desperate for him, even more so when I saw how he stared at me. Hungry and fervent and wild.

"Good girl," he rasped and dropped to his knees, his hand gripping my knee and then sliding up my thigh. "The blush of your cunt is so much prettier than I imagined..." His praise dissolved on a groan as his fingers slid along my pussy.

I bit my lip harder, but it wasn't enough to stop my hips from bucking to his touch.

"God, you're so wet. So fucking perfect," he said reverently, gliding through my slick seam until his fingers found my clit.

"Wade..." Either my eyes closed, or I lost my sense of sight as his played over the aching bundle of nerves. Swirling, stroking, pinching.

"Look at me, angel."

I quaked, forcing my eyes open and into the clutches of his.

"*Good girl,*" he cooed deeply and pushed a thick finger inside me.

My hands curled into the covers, my body tensing and then squeezing along the delicious intrusion. In and then out. My gaze blurred from the pleasure and then focused on the sight of him stroking me. *And himself,* I realized in a stupor of desire.

Every few breaths, his hand that gripped his cock below the edge of the bed jerked hard. *He wanted me that badly.*

"Wade," I cried out, my back bowing toward him.

"I know, angel," he swore. "You're so wet for me, but you have to relax. I don't want to hurt you."

You could never hurt me, I wanted to say, but the words died in my throat as the stretch between my thighs intensified with another finger.

In and out, the rhythm began again. Faster. Rougher. And then he curled his touch against a certain spot that made my heart stop with pleasure, a choked sob bursting from my lips. I was so close...

"Tell me what you want, Lou," Wade said roughly. "I want to hear it from your mouth, too, not just these greedy pink lips."

"You," I begged with abandon. "I want you inside me."

And then he was gone, muttering something between a curse and a groan as he fished through his brother's things until he found what he was looking for. A condom.

I pushed onto my hands, mesmerized by the sight of him rolling the rubber down his thick length. I tried to stop myself from tensing, but I couldn't help it. He only seemed to swell larger under the grip of the condom.

No wonder he'd wanted to prepare me.

"Look at me." Wade's voice coaxed my heavy gaze to his as he stepped in front of me. His fingers swept over my clit, bringing me right back to the edge.

"When I'm done with you, angel, you won't remember fucking him either," he swore with a violence that made me gasp.

He was talking about his brother. And then the slippery little lie slid out of my grasp, the truth surging in its wake.

"We weren't together," I choked out desperately.

Wade froze, his fingertips stilled at my entrance—every part of him hard and stiff except the fire that churned in his eyes.

"You weren't together?" he repeated, his voice dangerously low.

Something didn't feel right about his question, but I could pinpoint what it was.

"N-no. We were never together."

A ragged groan ripped through his lips, and then his fingers pushed through my entrance once more, the sensation sparking a single, lucid thought in my mind.

He thought I was talking about sex.

He thought I meant Blaze and I had never been together sexually.

"So, you're telling me this tight little pussy is all mine?" His heavy breaths pummeled heat onto my skin.

My mouth opened, but I couldn't form words. His fingers were moving too fast—too perfectly positioned—that my body was too caught up in a race for release to rescue the truth that was trampled over in the process.

"Yes. Yes, Wade. Yes..." I whimpered as his fingers worked over my clit right to the peak before he pulled away, leaving me gasping and sputtering, my heart threatening to give out.

And then he was between my thighs. The narrow of his waist pinned them wide as he lowered over me. He peppered kisses along my jaw to my ear while he positioned himself at my entrance, the head of his cock so much larger than what was there before.

"You know why you were never his?" he rasped along the shell of my ear, and I felt the flex of his hips, the blunt head of his cock notching into my pussy.

Because I never wanted him, I thought, but I was long past being able to form words, let alone the truth.

"Because you were always mine." And then he pushed forward, his length stretching me—pushing my tight muscles apart to make room for him. To form my body to his.

My head tipped back, silent gasps of air filling my lungs.

"Relax for me, angel," Wade cooed against my ear, and I felt the sheen of sweat on his shoulders as he tried to hold himself back. "Relax so you can fit all of me."

I didn't know how to relax. I didn't know how to work any part of me right now when it felt like he was tearing me in two. The pressure peaked on unbearable, and then his fingers began to comb my hair back from my face and neck, from my chest, his mouth marking every inch of skin that was exposed.

The tenderness did something to me—loosened something inside me.

"That's it. Relax so I can give you what you want," Wade said with a low groan, filling me with what seemed endlessly through a small tug of pain until his hips connected with mine, the whole of his cock lodged deep inside my core. "*Good girl.*"

I shuddered, the praise hitting my senses just as he started to move, rocking in and out in short thrusts that slowly grew longer. Harder. Faster. Desire scrambled the simplest of functions. Breathing. Thinking. Seeing.

Our hips started to slap together. The electric sound of skin as it chased a powerful release. I felt him rub along that same spot his fingers had found each time he drove deep, the coarse hairs at the root of his cock caressing my clit as he pulled back.

"Please, Wade," I choked. "*Please.*"

He shunted harder and growled, "Look at you, angel, taking my cock like such a good girl. Your tiny little pussy stuffed so full."

Lust choked me.

"You're mine. My good girl." His words filled me. *Consumed me.*

Within minutes, my fingers dug into the skin of his back, and I clung to him as the promise of release whipped all rationality into sweet lunacy. I lifted my hips to meet his thrusts, knowing I would be bruised and sore from the chase tomorrow. But I didn't care. Couldn't care. All I cared about was him.

"That's it. Take what you want. Come all over me." Wade's voice broke through it all, a kind of leash leading my body exactly where I wanted to go.

"Wade…" I panted, spiraling toward the edge and then fearlessly falling over it with a cry.

I arched into him, my climax pulling every one of my muscles tight before snapping them free. My core clenched and rippled along his length, my orgasm breaking and reforming my body around his.

"*Good girl,*" Wade ground out, the words dissolving into a

bone-deep groan as he thrust deep inside me once last time and then held himself against my womb as he came.

I felt the jerk and pulse of his cock inside me, distantly wondering what it would be like without the condom between us. *Another want.*

I wasn't sure how long it took for my eyes to peel open, finding him gazing down at me, his fingers sliding through my hair. The way it felt, the way it made me feel, I never wanted to tie it back again.

"You're mine, Lou."

My breath caught, watching his lips lower to press a gentle kiss to mine.

"All mine."

Chapter Sixteen

Wade

I WAS out cold all night. Dead to the world. And what a hell of a way to die, I thought, my chest rumbling as I came back to life.

And to an empty bed.

Shit.

I sat up, my hand sliding to the empty spot next to me. It was cool. Lou had been gone for a while.

Did she regret it? It was the first and only thought that came to my mind as I reached for my phone.

It was early. Too early for even the sun to be up and dripping light through the blinds on the windows. Too early for even Lou to be preparing for breakfast.

"Shit," I muttered and threw the blankets off, realizing all the things I hadn't done last night.

My body had been too wrung out, too completely spent to do anything but fall asleep with Lou in my arms and my cock softening inside her. Once she was finally asleep beside me, I'd barely had the wherewithal to pull the condom off, wrap it in a tissue, and drop it on the floor to be cleaned in the morning.

It had been a while since I'd been with a woman. Not for any particular reason but a mix of work, stress, and disinterest. And I was now paying the price. I should've gotten up and cleaned her —cleaned the both of us. Should've talked to her. The things I'd said...

Groaning, I spun to the side and stood, picking up the discarded tissue and not bothering to turn on a light until I reached the bathroom.

I looked myself in the mirror. *'When I'm done with you, you won't remember fucking him either.'*

Except she hadn't fucked my brother.

I hung my head, and my eyes caught on the tissue I was about to toss. My brow drew tight, unmistakable streaks of blood stained the tissue.

She hadn't fucked anyone.

The realization was like a sledgehammer to my chest. *Lou had been a virgin.* And I fucked her... not gently. Not like I should have.

I swallowed hard and fought to steady my breathing. I'd been so concerned—so fucking consumed with making her mine. With the primal need to claim her, to fuck my brother out of her system, I didn't even realize I was her first.

I felt honored... and like the biggest fucking asshole. No wonder she disappeared this morning.

I balled the tissue and tossed it in the trash, leaving only my guilt to stain my hands. I'd told her she deserved more—deserved better than my brother, and then I'd gone and done this.

Dressed in a pair of Blaze's sweats and another one of his tees, I went quietly downstairs, following the muffled sounds of movement coming from the kitchen. Of course, she was preparing for the day, even though it was way too early.

"Lou."

The spoon in her hand clattered onto the island as she gasped, "Wade."

"Sorry," I mumbled, closing the door behind me and moving deeper into the room. "Are you alright?"

"Yeah." She flushed. "Are you?"

"Why didn't you tell me?" I asked, unable to answer her because I wasn't alright. I was coming apart at the seams, harboring this insatiable need for her yet afraid I'd never have her again.

Her eyes balled like a deer in headlights. "Tell you?"

"The truth," I said when I reached the island and gripped the edge of the butcherblock top. "You said you were never with Blaze—"

"I can explain—"

"Why didn't you tell me you were a virgin?" I rasped, watching her chest cave in with her exhale. "If I would've known, Lou... what I did... what I said..." I broke off, my eyes closing.

Soft hands rested on my chest, and I sucked in a sharp breath as I opened my eyes again and stared down at her upturned face.

"If I'd wanted you to know—if I wanted you to do something different—I would've told you," Lou murmured.

I shuddered, her words like a balm to my worry. I cupped her face, tipping it to mine.

"So then why did you leave?"

Her lips peeled apart, lashes fluttering to her cheeks.

"Because I've never done this," she admitted softly. "Because I don't know what happens next, and I was afraid..."

"Look at me," I rasped when her gaze dropped to the center of my chest. Without hesitation, her golden-flecked irises found mine again. "What were you afraid of, angel?"

"I was afraid you might regret it," she said, her throat working to swallow. "Because of your brother... because of me... because I wasn't..."

"Don't," I warned, my jaw clenching violently. "Don't overthink this, Lou, because I promise you, the reality is simple."

She let out a weak laugh. "Is it?"

I couldn't argue that there were times—parts of this situation—that were anything but simple, but not this part. Not her and me. Not us.

"Ask me what I want," I said, knowing how many times I'd asked her the same question last night.

"What do you want, Wade?"

I moved closer, my hand sliding from the side of her neck to the end of her braid, tugging the tie off of one and then the other.

"You," I murmured, combing her hair free. "I want you. Whether I should or shouldn't, I want you more than I can explain, Lou. I want you so much it hurts—" I broke off and took hold of her wrist, dragging her hand down my chest all the way to the front of my sweats so she could feel my cock. "I want you so damn much it physically hurts to not be inside you."

Her expression softened, the worry in her eyes drowned swiftly and suddenly by desire.

"I want you, too."

With a groan, I sealed my mouth over hers, her lips opening instantly for me. For more. So, I gave it to her. I slanted her face, angling her perfectly so my tongue could delve deep into her heat and devour every sweet corner of her innocence that had been mine.

"I should've been gentler with you," I rasped, trailing my mouth along her jaw as my hands worked into the loose strands of her hair.

"I didn't want you to be," she said breathlessly, turning her head so her lips met mine.

I tugged her head back and kissed her hard, the eager slide of her tongue promising me that she liked it.

"And what do you want?"

"I want you to be not gentle with me now."

A ragged groan ripped from my chest, my forehead resting on hers. "Lou..."

Whatever I wanted to say died a sudden death on my tongue as she palmed the length of my erection.

Growling savagely, I slammed my mouth back on hers, kissing her until we were both breathless and I had her back against the island. My hands had moved to her waist, finding her skin underneath the edge of her shirt.

"Wade..." she moaned as I kissed and bit along her jaw, scraping and soothing her soft skin.

I wanted to savor her—at least a little of the way I should have last night. But Lou had other plans. The moment I found the pulse of her neck, she reached between us again and squeezed my cock, dragging her small hand up and down its long length.

"Fuck." I spun her so suddenly that she let out a small cry. "Keep that up, and I won't even make it inside you, angel," I rasped into her ear, feeling her shudder against me. "Put your palms on the island."

My hands toyed with the skin at her waist, waiting until her small fingers splayed over the wood.

"Good girl," I praised and hooked my fingers under the waistband of her leggings, drawing them down her legs... and finding nothing underneath them. "Fuck, angel. No underwear?" I palmed her bare ass, sinking onto one knee as I stared at her slick, pink pussy that was completely bared to me.

"I didn't plan on being down here long..." She ended on a moan as I pushed two fingers inside her.

She winced a little as I stroked inside her. She was still tender from last night, but that didn't stop her from drenching my fingers with want.

"Don't stop," she begged, like she heard where my thoughts were going.

Groaning, I bent forward and bit into the fleshy part of her ass, curling my fingers into her G-spot at the same time and marveling at the way her knees went weak.

"I can't stop, angel," I murmured, standing straight but keeping my fingers working on her pleasure. "I can't stop wanting you." I reached for the band of my sweats and stopped with a curse. "Fuck." My teeth ground together. I was zero for two on being prepared for her—for this. "Condoms are upstairs."

"I'm on birth control, and I..." Her breath hitched. "Well, it's only been you."

I stilled, my breath morphing into a beast that clawed in and out of my lungs. "Lou... are you sure?"

She pushed back on my fingers. "Please... I want you."

I groaned like my very bones were breaking and tugged my sweats down over my hips.

Sliding my fingers from her heat, I gripped the meat of my cock and wiped her desire along its length.

"Fuck, Lou..." Placing my other hand on the small of her back, I held her forward and lined myself up at her entrance, dragging my tip through her arousal.

"Do you feel what you do to me?"

She moaned and tried to press back against my cock, but my hand on her spine stopped her.

"Answer me."

"Yes," she panted.

I rewarded her by pushing just the tip into her heat, savoring —and slowly dying—at how her body clutched and tightened on me for more. It was so much hotter this way. To feel her desire right on my bare skin...

Letting out a hiss, I yanked my hips back.

"*Wade!*"

"Promise me you're not going to disappear from my bed in the morning ever again."

"I promise," Lou whimpered. "I promise. Please..."

"Good girl," I said and gave in because I couldn't hold out any longer.

I worked the head of my cock inside her, gripped her hips hard, and buried myself inside her with one fast thrust.

We both cried out, but I didn't give a shit who heard. I was in heaven. Playing by the rules meant I'd never fucked a woman without protection before, and this was more than I could imagine.

And I proceeded to be the *not gentle* she swore she wanted.

I pulled out and thrust even deeper. Harder. Faster. I stared down at where my body disappeared into hers, everything the darkness had hidden last night now on full display. Her swollen pink pussy spread around my shaft. Her desire that slickened and dripped from my cock.

"You're so good, angel," I croaked. "The way you feel around my bare cock, so wet and hot, wanting me to slide so fucking deep..." I ended on a groan, feeling my hips bottom out against hers.

"Please, Wade." She used the island as leverage, pushing off her hands and back onto my cock, meeting each thrust with a lust of her own.

"You were made for my cock," I said, moving faster. The knot of pressure started to tingle at the base of my spine, and I knew my release was coming.

I pressed on her back, bending her more forward, so the change in angle made me hit that sweet spot buried inside her pussy.

"*Yes,*" she whimpered, each thrust now making her breath catch.

Holding her hips hard with one hand, I snaked the other around her front and searched for her clit, feeling her body spasm along mine when I found it.

"Be a good girl and come for me. All over me," I rasped, circling my fingers and making her gasp for air.

My thrusts grew faster. Shorter. More frantic as my release started to drown me. I couldn't hold out. She felt too fucking good.

"That's it," I cooed, feeling her pussy tighten. "Come all over me... make me come with you."

Lou cried out as she came apart, and the next thing I knew, white spots erupted in my vision as my orgasm washed through me, carrying me with her. I pinned her against the island, my cock pulsing hard inside her and pouring every drop of my release against her womb.

This time, exhaustion wasn't going to steal my aftercare.

I carefully pulled out of her and reached for some tissues first. Once those were used, I wet a cloth with warm water and gently cleaned us both. Next, I righted her leggings, silently enjoying the idea that she'd be leaking my cum all morning.

"Lou..." I turned her to face me, lightly brushing her hair back from her face. "Are you okay?"

Her smile was everything. "Perfect," she answered huskily, making me groan, and then her eyes went suddenly wide, a small cry escaping her chest. "You don't think anyone heard?"

I chuckled. "I think we're safe," I murmured. "But if you disappear from my bed again, I can't make any promises."

She blushed. "I won't."

"Good." I kissed her again, slow and deep. "Now, what can I do to help you with breakfast?"

Her lips parted, and then she smiled the kind of smile that made me feel like I'd just taken the world off her shoulders.

"You can help me arrange the Vatrushkas."

I felt my eyebrows raise, and she laughed.

"They're a Russian pastry similar to a Danish," she explained and scooted by me to grab one of the boxes off the end of the counter, opening the lid for me to look at the circular pastries stuffed with blueberries in the center. "They've got a blueberry and ricotta-like filling in the center."

"Interesting..." I murmured.

"You can have one... after you arrange the rest on the platter." She closed the lid and set it next to the tray while I went to the sink to wash my hands.

We worked a few minutes in silence, me unloading the Vatrushkas and Lou slicing the fresh fruit.

"Can I ask you something?"

I paused at her voice and looked over my shoulder. "Anything."

"What did my brothers say to you yesterday? You came inside looking... upset."

My teeth ground together, recalling the conversation I'd had with Kit and Jamie.

"I was just... on edge. They were only being protective of you." I placed the second to last pastry on the plate and then picked up the final one in the box for myself.

Lou hummed. "Overprotective?"

"Isn't that what brothers are for?" I grunted and took a bite.

"Is that what you are? For your brother?" she countered softly.

Her response unsettled me. I'd been upset by the overbearing way Lou's brothers had spoken about her, yet I couldn't help but think I treated Blaze the same way.

I swallowed and answered, "I had to be. Our father was... tough."

It was hard to talk about anyone in my family, honestly. I hadn't been close with them in so long. It was hard to find the right words to say. It was like looking at a picture on a postcard, easy to see but hard to describe if you'd never been there. And if I'd never been close to my family, it was hard to talk about anything more than the image.

"How so?"

"He had expectations, and he didn't know how to handle people who didn't meet them."

"Blaze," she said softly, knowing.

I nodded and took another bite. "He was hard on Blaze. Cruel. I didn't want to be like him, but it was the only way to keep his anger off my brother."

"That's tough in a different way," she said thoughtfully. "It's hard to be outside of the mold, but when you're in the mold, it's hard to see everyone else not realize the mold is more like a cage."

I stared at her, the sentiment striking right through the beat of my heart to my very core.

"Is that how you feel?" I asked, moving closer to her again.

Her hands stilled in the middle of arranging the pineapple

slices on the plate. She lifted her gaze to mine and murmured, "Not with you."

"Good," I rumbled, tracing my finger along the curve of her cheek. "But you shouldn't feel that way with anyone, Lou."

She looked away and then murmured, "I'm working on it."

Lou fixed the last of the fruit on the plate before moving it to the end of the counter. She looked around, satisfied with what we'd accomplished so far, and then glanced at the clock. It was still about forty-five minutes until the buffet needed to be ready.

"I think I should shower quick and then put everything out."

"Whatever you want," I said, covering the pastry platter and the fruit with plastic wrap.

We walked to the kitchen door, and when I opened it for her, she stopped and looked at me. "What happens now? With us, I mean."

I watched the color in her cheeks deepen.

"What do you want to happen now?" I said low.

The way this question caught her off-guard was jarring. She was so surprised, so unaccustomed to anyone asking her what she wanted, that it caught her unprepared every time.

I was going to change that.

"I want... to be with you," Lou answered hesitantly. "I want to be here with you."

I stayed quiet, soaking in the sight. She was so damn beautiful like this, courageously vulnerable. Lou put herself out there even though she wasn't sure about the response.

"Then that's what happens now." And then I picked her up and carried her upstairs to my shower.

Chapter Seventeen

Wade

"I like the second closing better, but you can try them both with the mock jury if you want and see which does better," I said, only part of me focused on the conversation with Tim.

Tim had been doing this long enough—had worked at Dad's firm long enough—that he really didn't need my input, but he was the kind of guy who wanted to keep me in the loop since this was originally my client, and I appreciated that.

But not as much as I appreciated the woman I was falling for as she welcomed a new set of guests with a beaming smile, both of her cheeks dimpling.

For a week, Lou and I lived in a bubble. One that existed almost magically inside this damn inn where nothing could touch us—or what we'd found together. Not the press. Not our families. Not the lie the world believed.

The thing was, Lou was mine. I'd known it in an instant. *She. Was. Mine.*

And I'd made a point to make her mine every chance I got. Every night in my bed. Every morning before the sun came up. Every moment when I could steal a kiss.

We'd fallen deeper into a routine over the last week. Every morning, I'd wake up, and we'd have sex before breakfast. Sometimes in bed. Sometimes in the shower. Sometimes in the kitchen. On the island. On the floor. Yesterday, against the fridge. Then I'd help her get the buffet ready.

She usually had to tell me twice where the pastry of the day was from. The first time, I was always too caught up in the sparkle in her eyes to pay much attention to anything else.

Then she'd spend the rest of the morning at the reception desk while I worked on my laptop in the living room, responding to emails, checking in with Tim, and sometimes, taking calls upstairs in my room.

I'd make us lunch. Sandwiches were my specialty for how many times they'd served as dinner when I worked late at the office.

Dinner, we'd order in and eat with a classic movie playing on the TV in the living room. Lou was pleasantly surprised how many guests sat and joined us for the show.

And then I'd count down the minutes until she was done working and I could take her upstairs, the anticipation for the moment it would be the two of us alone again suffused into every second. Every breath. Every heartbeat.

By the time she turned off the light at the reception desk and locked the front door, I was vibrating with need.

Lou was in my blood. In my bones. I'd gone so long alone... not caring... not needing the hassle of even no-strings sex, and now, I couldn't get enough. I couldn't get enough of the slow and lazy sex. The hard and fast fucks. I couldn't get enough of the way she responded to my praise each and every time like it was the only thing she needed.

Fate—possibly disguised as my degenerate brother—had brought us together and now it killed me to keep it a secret. To know that outside these walls, everyone had to believe she belonged to Blaze. But not for much longer.

I planned to talk to Mom this afternoon about moving him to

a facility in Boston... and tell her that Lou wasn't his girlfriend. Hadn't been from the night of the fall. From the moment I'd set eyes on her.

But until that happened, we'd stay here where I didn't have to hide that she was the only thing I wanted. It would be a long time before I would miss going out or being in public... hard to when every night, Lou was in my bed, and my cock was inside her.

Like she heard my thought, her eyes flicked to mine, and she blushed. Instantly, I had to adjust my seat, my jeans pinching my cock as it hardened.

"I trust your judgment," Tim replied, forcing my attention back to the call.

"You should trust yours. You handled this case better than I would," I admitted.

"You left a pretty detailed game plan."

I had, but that didn't change that Tim had put in the effort, made the plays, and was going to come out on top. "A game plan is only as good as the players who execute it."

"Thanks, Wade."

"No, thank you. I can't tell you how much I appreciate you taking on this case for me so I can be up here." The words stilled me, and I wondered if I'd ever said them to Tim before.

I wasn't cold or perpetually unimpressed like my father, but had I ever been grateful? I'd never had time to be. I'd been working... or putting out the fires Blaze left in his wake.

It hit me then that maybe I wasn't grateful because I didn't have anything to be grateful for. Until her.

"Of course. I've got everything here under control. You just worry about taking care of your family."

"Thanks," I repeated as he ended the call.

I was taking care of Lou, but Blaze... Mom... I didn't know how to take care of them. They'd always taken care of each other. And now... God, I just wished Blaze would wake up.

Every day, Mom called with the same news. Consistent improvement but without consciousness. I heard the wear in her voice. I felt the strain it buried in my chest. But there was nothing I could do. For her. For my brother. And I wasn't sure there was a more painful feeling than helplessness.

Reaching for my plate from breakfast, I ate the last bite of my Nazook, an Armenian flaky pastry with a crumbled walnut topping. It was easily my favorite pastry out of the two dozen or so I'd had since coming here. Lou said it was just because I liked saying the name. *Na-zook.* I told her it was because of the way she smiled at my pronunciation.

The things I would do to earn that smile... and a blush.

Taking my plate and empty coffee mug, I headed for the kitchen. Once I'd loaded them in the dishwasher and started the cycle, I returned to the hall, slowing when I saw Lou wasn't at the desk anymore. I took the stairs two at a time to find her.

"Lou?" I called when I reached the top of the steps.

"In here—" *Thud.* "Ow."

I rushed into her room, the bed perfectly made... and untouched for days. It took a second to locate her on the far side of the room, rifling through a large closet.

"What are you doing?" I got to her just as she untangled herself from the coats and cleaning supplies.

"Julie—the guest I just checked in—asked if I had a steamer. She's here for a friend's wedding this weekend and wants to steam her dress."

"And you have that... in your coat closet?"

She smiled and lifted her arm, in her hand a steam wand. "Yeah."

I chuckled, holding her arm as she stepped over the shoe boxes on the floor. Clearly, they were what she'd stumbled over and caused her to bump her head.

"You okay?" I cupped her cheek and playfully turned her head side to side, pretending—but not really—to examine for injuries.

"I'm fine."

My fingers stilled on her braid. "Why don't you wear your hair down?"

Another blush. "Habit." She tried to look away, but I caught her chin and lifted her face back to mine.

"Maybe we try to form a new habit?" I suggested, my voice husky. "Kind of like the one we've started in the mornings where you're already wet for me—"

"Wade!" She quickly stepped around me, but her eyes danced when they caught mine over her shoulder.

I chuckled and bent to clean up the boxes on the floor.

"I'll get them—"

Too late. I already had them in my hands and cleared a spot on the floor in the closet. And that was when something caught my eye.

"Lou…" I carefully grabbed the edge of the framed canvas and pulled it out. "What's this?"

Her throat bobbed. "A painting of the Lamplight Inn."

My lips pulled tight, shooting her a look for being purposely obtuse. "More than the inn, Lou."

The painting was of Lou standing at the gate of the inn, her arm on the bronzed post holding the sign and a huge smile on her face.

"Kit painted it for me right after I opened," she murmured.

"And it, too, belongs in the coat closet?" It was a rhetorical question because it didn't. The artistry alone demanded for it to be hung and admired, but the fact that it was of the Lamplight Inn and its beautiful innkeeper…

"No." She sighed. "I just… haven't found the right place to hang it yet."

"What about above the reception desk?"

Her brow furrowed, and I watched the color in her cheeks saturate to a deep red, a shade of warning that meant I was getting close to something too sensitive.

"No, I have Frankie's photo there," she said so factually you'd think the photograph was carved into the wall and the entire building would fall down if it were removed.

"Lou… this is your inn. Your dream. Why do you want her

front and center?" I murmured and stood, closing the closet door and resting the painting against it. After everything she did, everything she had done to get her business up and running, she deserved every credit.

"Because Frankie—" Lou broke off and pulled her bottom lip between her teeth.

I went to stand in front of her, hooking my fingers under her chin. "Because she what?"

"Because she's always been there... in front."

"Is that what you want?"

"It's how it's always been with us."

"Not what I asked, angel."

Her throat bobbed. "I just mean—I never been—I don't know how to be the center of it all."

My chest rumbled, and I lowered my head close to her ear. "I think you do." I looked over my shoulder and pointed at the painting. "I think that woman knows exactly how to be front and center for her dream. And she's certainly been front and center in all of mine."

I felt the warm catch of her breath, her head turning so our lips were floating just apart.

"Wade..."

My gaze roamed over her face. The wide frame of her glasses hiding her brilliant eyes. The tight tuck of her braids obscuring the soft waves of her hair. "What are you afraid of, Lou? Why don't you want to be seen?" I traced my fingers down the ridges through her hair, curling them at the tie on the end.

Lou reached up and grabbed my hand, stopping me from pulling the tie off.

I knew it.

Turning my hand, I took hers and brought it to my mouth, pressing my lips to her knuckles. Her eyes dipped and then returned to mine.

"Letting them see all of you doesn't take away anything from Frankie. You're twins, not two sides of a scale that have to balance out," I promised her. "Choosing to step into the spotlight of your own life doesn't mean hers dulls."

"I know that," she said, but sounded unconvinced.

"Okay," I said, not wanting to push it. "Well, I don't think that painting should stay in the closet. So, maybe we'll just leave it out here until you find a spot for it."

"It's fine—"

"Or I could take it into my room and hang it in front of the bed..." I drawled slowly.

"No, it can stay right there," she chirped, the cord to the steamer falling from her hand. Remembering what she'd been rushing to do, she backpedaled toward the door. "I have to bring this to Julie. I'll see you downstairs."

I watched her scurry from the room, taking a moment for myself to appreciate the painting once more.

Kit hadn't just painted the Lou who worked at the reception desk. He'd painted his sister, who'd worked tirelessly for her dream and who, for the single moment she posed in front of the inn, was proud to be in the spotlight.

That was the Lou I saw every night when it was just the two of us. The one who took her hair down and dragged my mouth to hers. The one who told me what she wanted—begged for it, demanded it, took it—and the one who greedily and shamelessly clamored for my praise.

That was the Lou I wanted everyone else to see. Well, not at those moments. Those moments were mine. But I wanted everyone to see the Lou that Kit saw in this painting. The one who deserved the attention she fought so hard to hide from.

I'd just closed the door to her room when my phone started to vibrate with the very last number I wanted to see. My body stiffened like it was bracing for impact.

"Please tell me you're calling for something else—anything else," I answered Mikey's call.

"I'm sorry, Wade," my PI replied.

I should've known this bubble we were in had gone on for too long to do anything but burst.

"Shit." Air hissed through my lips. "One second." Instead of heading downstairs, I went into my room, shut the door, and strode over to the windows as though I could see whatever catastrophe was about to happen. "Alright. How bad is it?"

Did they realize we'd been lying? Did someone at the hospital finally break? Did they know where Blaze was? What happened to him?

"Wade—"

Fuck.

"How bad, Mikey?" I ground out my fist, flexing at my side.

"It's a baby, Wade."

"What?" My voice didn't even sound like my own.

I stumbled back, the word like a swift kick to the chest. I was prepared for a lot of things—life and being a lawyer had taught me preparation was the key to any success. But even with that, even with everything Blaze had put me through, I hadn't been prepared for this.

A baby.

"They have a paternity test. They're running a story that Blaze is going to be a father."

I felt like I was falling off the edge of a cliff or out the side door of a plane. I careened backward, unsteady on my feet, until my legs hit the edge of the bed, and I sank onto the soft landing. The mattress could've been made of metal for all I could feel right now.

"Wade?"

"Yeah, I'm here," I muttered, shaking my head. "You're sure? Any chance it's fake?"

After everything our father had put him through, Blaze made it clear early on that he had no intentions of ever becoming a father himself.

"Always a chance in this industry, but I'd think there would be plenty of other stories to run—other things to focus on rather than risk the repercussions of faking a paternity test without any kind of basis in fact. Plus—"

"What?" *What more could there be?*

"Well, there's something else," he added, clearly regretting whatever it was. "The report was dated only a few days before your brother... before he went into the hospital."

My brow creased, trying to slog through the jungle of facts and emotions inside me. "So, he just found out?"

"With postage, I'm thinking he found out the morning of his fall."

The picture of what happened that day started to take shape in my mind like a castle forming out of a thousand grains of sand.

Lou insisted that Blaze wasn't drinking—wasn't his usual careless, carousing self while he'd stayed here. But that day was different. She couldn't argue with the blood alcohol level in the tests the hospital had run. He was drunk when he fell. He was agitated that day, she'd said. And now, I knew why.

He'd gotten proof that he was going to be a father.

"I see." I swallowed over the boulder in my throat. "Do you know who the mother is? I'm assuming she leaked it to them. But why—Jesus," I swore loudly and pinched the bridge of my nose. "Is she upset because Blaze moved on—because they wrote he had a new girlfriend?"

"Wade—"

"Or did she try to get ahold of him, and he didn't respond because he's been in the hospital, and now she's trying to force his hand—"

"It wasn't the mother," Mikey said loudly.

I stilled. "What? What do you mean? Of course—"

"My source said that the paternity test came from Blaze."

"No." The word flung like a spear from my chest, ready to fight that assumption at any cost. "Not a chance he would reveal that. Not without talking to me. It has to be the mother—"

"It's not."

My stomach turned with dread. "How do you know?"

Mikey cleared his throat. "Because the piece... the article is that the baby is why Blaze came to Maine. Why he's in hiding with his new girlfriend."

"Lou..." *No.*

"The story they want to break is that he got Lou pregnant, and now he's trapped in a small town." Mikey's words were like a knife straight through my ribcage and right into my heart.

Lou wasn't the mother, but they didn't care about that. They cared about the story—a story I'd asked her to feed into. A story she'd propped up to protect my brother, and now, they were going to drag her name through the mud.

"What do you want me to do?"

"Find the mother. I have a feeling she's going to be just as much a victim of this as Blaze."

I hung up after Mikey's muttered goodbye, my gaze swimming in and out of focus like the tide rushes and retreats along the shore. *A baby.* And there was nothing I could do about it until the story broke. Nothing except prepare Lou and my mother.

If Blaze would've just called me. The thought brought me to a place I didn't want to go.

My attention swam back into focus on the desk in front of the bed, thinking back to the drawer that was slightly ajar when we got back from Lou's mom's house that night, empty save for a pen. *Would Blaze have put the paternity test results in there?*

I lunged off the bed and opened the drawer. *Still empty.* Of course, it was still empty. It wasn't fucking magic—*Crunch.* The distinct sound of paper being crushed echoed in the room. *Shit.*

I pulled on the drawer again but didn't stop there. Reaching along the sides, I felt for the latch on the glides and freed the drawer from the rails. Sure enough, as soon as I removed it from the desk, a mangled piece of paper fell onto the ground.

Setting the drawer on top of the desk, I dropped to my knees, grabbed the letter, and opened it.

***Probability of Paternity**: 99.999999%*.

My brother was... or was going to be a father.

My gaze did laps over the page like it made it any easier to process. At some point, I noticed the date on the letter. It was just a few days before his fall. Mikey was right. He probably opened the results that morning and then shoved them in the drawer in a hurry where they got caught.

Was this the reason they'd fought? The thing that ended their relationship before it really began? Had Lou known about Blaze's child this whole time and not told me?

And if this was where the paternity test had been the whole time, who'd found it to leak to the press?

Chapter Eighteen

Lou

"If she wants more ideas for vendors, just let me know." I handed Max the folder I'd finished putting together yesterday for his friend's bride, Daisy. I texted and told him he could pick it up today, and he'd been waiting at the desk when I'd come downstairs.

His eyes widened at the size of the packet, flipping briefly through the contents. "Are there any vendors left in the state?"

I flushed. "I wanted to be thorough."

"No, I know," he said quickly. "I'm really grateful, Lou. Seriously."

"It's no problem. I'm excited to start offering weddings here." My attention flicked to the large photograph mounted behind the desk, mentally reassuring myself that this was why it needed to remain. For marketing. For business. Hanging a painting of myself wouldn't do anyone or the inn any good.

When I looked back, Max seemed lost in thought—and not a good one, the way his mouth turned in a frown.

"What is it? Did I miss something?"

He snapped out of it and patted the folder. "No. This is awesome. It's not that."

"Then what is it?" I probed gently.

His hesitation was noticeable. "I just... I don't know. Todd is... off, and I'm worried about him."

"Off? Like cold feet?"

His head wavered. "I don't know. He's been avoiding me the last couple of weeks, and when we do talk, he won't talk about the wedding."

"I'm sorry," I offered, wishing I could do more to help. "Planning a wedding can be stressful, especially when you're also having a baby. Maybe it's just taking a toll."

"Yeah." He shifted his weight. "It's just Daisy offered for them to go to the courthouse and skip the whole planning part. She was fine with something small—something just the two of them. She doesn't have any family, and Todd isn't on great terms with most of his."

The picture I'd torn from the magazine the night Wade had first kissed me came to mind. I would've given it to Max with the packet if I had it, but somehow, that picture had vanished into thin air. It wasn't in any of my papers. Not left in the room. At least not that I could find. I finally gave up and assumed it had been found crumpled on the floor by another guest who'd thrown it away. It wasn't important, I told myself, even though I'd thought of it countless times in the last few days.

Because of Wade.

"Todd didn't want to do that?"

"He didn't seem like he knew what he wanted. That was why I suggested the inn. Seemed like a good compromise. Plus, I hated to see them go to the courthouse. Daisy hasn't had it easy, and with the pregnancy, she deserves—" He broke off, whatever he was about to say next was like a stopper to his thoughts. "Anyway, he's just been distant, but I'm sure everything's fine. He gets in these moods sometimes."

"I think we all get a little afraid of what the future holds, especially when something so good is right in front of us. The fear of losing it..."

His brows knitted together, making me think I'd said something more than I'd intended. But then the expression vanished, and his charming smile returned. "I'm sure it will work out." Max held up the folder once more. "Thanks again, Lou."

The door had just closed behind him when I heard footsteps on the stairs. *Wade hadn't been looking at the painting this entire time, had he?*

I turned and instantly saw something was wrong—something had happened.

"Wade?" I didn't even know what to ask as he descended the last of the steps, his expression darkening.

"Did you know about the baby?"

Baby? I grabbed for the ballast to steady myself.

"What baby?" The only baby that came to mine was Frankie's baby, but he couldn't be talking about Logan.

"Blaze's baby."

"Your... your brother's baby?" I gaped. "Your brother has a baby?" I repeated and realized I hadn't answered his question. "No. I had no idea he has a baby." Some of the tension seemed to seep from his shoulders with my answer, but it didn't stop my mind from spiraling. "What's going on? Is Blaze awake?"

I pressed my hand to my throat, feeling my pulse start to spiral against my fingertips. *If he was awake...*Like the flip of a switch, my body went into hyperdrive, flying through all the scenarios where I'd have to tell Wade the truth and explain why I'd kept it from him for so long.

I'd tried to tell him—

"No, he's not awake." He exhaled hard. "I just got a call from my PI. The Chronicle is running a story that Blaze has a kid."

"What? They have to be making it up, right?"

Wade's head gave a tight shake. "No, they're not." He reached and pulled something from his back pocket—a folded paper—and handed it to me.

I took it hesitantly, holding his gaze as I opened it.

"Oh my god..." It was a paternity test. A positive paternity test. "Where did you—"

"I found it jammed behind the desk drawer in his room," he said. "Look at the date. The results were from only a few days before Blaze's accident. If they were sent here—"

"They were. Oh god..." I pressed my hand to my mouth, my eyes dropping under the weight of the realization. "Not many people get mail here. Sent here. Sometimes packages if they're in town for an event. But a letter..." My voice trailed off, becoming threadbare as I finished, "That's why I remember it. A letter came that morning, and I slid it under his door. I had no idea..."

"It makes sense then... why you said he hadn't been drinking, but that day his blood alcohol level blew well over the limit."

I nodded, the movement feeling as clumsy as my thoughts putting all of this together. After everything I'd learned about Blaze Stevens from the moment he stepped into my inn, I could only imagine how the news would've affected him.

"Lou..."

I blinked and refocused on his face. "How did the Chronicle get this information? From the mother? Why now?"

"My informant said it wasn't from the mother. He's confident the source of their information was here."

"No..." I couldn't believe it. "Who? How..."

The chilling thought hit me like the first sweep of a winter wind, circling me with the memory of the cracked door. The open desk drawer, only a pen inside.

"I have security cameras outside. I can check the footage to see if anyone who wasn't a guest came in while we were gone, but Frankie and Chandler were here. I could ask her if she saw anyone strange..." It just seemed so implausible. Or maybe I just wanted it to be. "He's sure the mother didn't leak the information to the Chronicle?"

"Yeah," he said, his voice crumbling into a rumble. "If she did, they wouldn't be going with the assumption that the mother is you."

I felt the blood drain from my face.

"They found out you were together, and then we fed into their story. They think this is the reason Blaze came to Maine. Because you told him you were pregnant."

"Oh my god..." I didn't feel myself sinking—or Wade clutching me to him, holding me upright by strength and will.

"I'm going to fix this, Lou. I promise," he murmured into my hair, gently drawing my head back. "I'm going to prep a letter and send it as soon as they hit publish. Unfortunately, I can't... stop them ahead of time."

"I know," I said numbly, the shock starting to wear off, leaving in its place only the weight of the lie I'd armored myself with. "Wade_"

"I have to talk to my mom. I can't... she can't find out from the papers."

A fresh wave of panic crashed over me. "I'll have to tell my family, too..." They believed the story, and I couldn't let them read this and think that I... that Blaze and I...

But I had to tell Wade the truth first.

Wade's face was grim as his head dipped closer to mine, his palms on my face the only source of warmth. "I'm sorry, Lou. I'm so sorry for all of this."

I shook my head, the surge of tears as sudden and threatening as a tsunami. "It's not your fault," I choked out, the droplets spilling hotly down my cheeks. "It's mine."

"No," he swore and kissed me. Hard. The pressure of his mouth soothing the unsettling in my chest. "None of this is your fault—"

"Wade, we have to talk—"

"We will, I promise." His lips touched lightly to the corner of my mouth. "But I have to go talk to my mom. I don't even know how to tell her this, but I can't risk her hearing it from anyone else."

Once more, I balled up the truth and forced it away. "I'm coming with you."

"Lou—"

"Violet said she'd cover for me whenever I needed," I insisted. "You don't have to do this alone."

And knowing how close I could be to losing him, I didn't want to waste a single moment apart.

The car was silent on the drive to the hospital, but my thoughts were anything but. Blaze was a father—or was going to be a father—and the press thought the baby was mine. Soon, everyone would.

And it seemed like a rumor impossible to stop. Well, for the next nine months or so until no baby appeared, and they realized how wrong they'd been. But by then... all those months... *Oh god.*

I held my arm over my stomach, wishing Wade had let me carry the box of pastries inside. Instead, he clutched it in his hands like it was Pandora's box, a threat rather than a treat.

We headed straight for Blaze's room. Wade hadn't told Joanna we were coming. After we'd decided to stay away from the hospital to help insulate Blaze's condition from discovery, to call her and say we were on our way would've been an immediate red flag.

Wade slowed as we approached the door to his brother's room and then stopped, staring blankly at the handle.

"This is my fault," he said so low I almost missed it.

"No, Wade." I inched toward him, wanting to pull him to me, but I couldn't. Everyone in this building thought I was Blaze's girlfriend.

"If I wasn't... if Blaze and I weren't the way that we were... he would've told me," he insisted, his pulse thumping in his neck.

"He would've told me weeks ago when he found out. When he left rehab. I would've helped him. God... why didn't he just tell me..."

I reached for his arm, the familiar prickle of contact lighting up my skin. "Let me talk to her."

He looked startled by the suggestion. "What? No. You don't need to—"

"I know I don't need to, but I want to... and I want to tell her the truth." I swallowed hard. "She needs to know Blaze and I weren't together, and I need to be the one to tell her."

Joanna had already been through so much with one son. To see the look of pure anguish on Wade's face right now...well, if I could spare her that, I would. Plus, I wanted to apologize in person for what I'd done—for lying to her. Once I told Wade the truth, I wasn't sure if I'd have this chance again.

"Please, Wade."

"Alright," he agreed after a beat. "I'll wait out here." Even the anger brimming in his eyes wasn't enough to drown out the guilt that effused from the rest of him.

I reached and took the box from him, holding it with one arm and giving a gentle knock on the door with the other, and then let myself inside.

Joanna lifted her head from her arms. She'd been resting on Blaze's bed, and her eyes went wide when she saw me.

"Lou," she exclaimed and stood.

The mother who approached me now looked almost nothing like the woman I'd met that very first night. Her make-up was gone. Her clothes carelessly picked out and put together. Her hair pulled back in a severe bun that only accentuated the strain on her face.

The idea that she was losing her son was killing her, too.

"What are you doing here?" Even her hug seemed fragile.

"I brought something sweet."

She drew back, her watery smile widening when she looked at me. "Yes, you did."

My chest tightened. Guilt for the way she regarded me—the way she thought I was someone I wasn't—squeezed the inflexible cage of my ribs.

Clearing the lump from my throat, I lifted the box's top. "These are Nazooks," I said, revealing the glazed, rolled pastries. "They're an Armenian pastry with a walnut filling."

"They sound delicious." She reached in for one. "Thank you, Lou."

"Why don't we sit?" I suggested, unsure if either of us could remain steady for the conversation I was about to have.

She couldn't answer since her mouth was filled with the first bite of the Nazook, but she moved willingly as I guided her back to her seat. Setting the box on the end of the bed, I took a second chair from the wall and dragged it beside hers, taking a pastry for myself as I joined her.

"How is he?" I asked after a few bites and a few minutes spent staring at the comatose actor in the hospital bed.

It had only been a week since I'd seen him, but his hair had grown longer, the pelt of his beard coming in darker on his face. It was strange to think how, in some ways, time had stopped for him, but in others, it was moving on without him.

Before, when I'd visit, I would always go to the head of the bed and kiss his cheek. It didn't feel right to do that anymore. Not for anyone involved.

Her lip quivered. "No... change."

"I'm sorry, Joanna." I took her hand and squeezed.

"No, I'm sorry, dear. This must be so hard for you, too, and now to not be able to be here..." She let out a choked cry.

"Joanna—"

"I'm sure he misses you," she went on like she hadn't heard me—couldn't hear me. "I talk to him about you, though, since you can't be here. I tell him everything you've done—"

"Please," I cried out and grabbed her hand, peeling it from the blanket and pulling it between mine. "Please stop."

The dark pools of her eyes focused slowly on me as though

she were reeling herself back in from the depths that her despair had taken her to.

"What is it, Lou? What's wrong?"

Everything.

I bit my tongue to hold the word back, feeling my eyes burn with tears. I wanted to tell her then the truth about Blaze and me, but I couldn't. If I did, I risked her being unwilling to hear the rest of what I had to say.

"Joanna... I came here—Wade and I came here because something has happened. We learned something about Blaze, and Wade believes it's going to be published in the Chronicle soon."

She reached for her son's limp hand, squeezing his lifeless fingers tight. "They know he's here? They found out what happened—"

"No," I said quickly to reassure her. "No, they don't know that. But according to Wade's sources, they have reliable information that Blaze... has a child with someone. Not me." It was as close as I could come to the rest of my confession at the moment.

If the news wasn't so earth-shaking, her response would've almost been comical. The way her head tipped in slow motion from one side to another was like one of those blimps floating in slow suspension over reality.

"A... child?"

I nodded. "They have a paternity test that confirms it. It was... mailed to the inn the morning before he fell."

"A child..." She turned and looked at Blaze—stared at his sedate face for so long, I started to worry she'd gone into shock.

"Joanna..." I probed gently.

"I'm sorry." Her eyes glistened and she pressed her hand to her mouth. "Blaze was going to be a father. I just can't believe it..." Like the word triggered more pieces to connect, she turned to me, eyes wide in horror. "Oh, Lou. I'm so sorry."

"No—"

"Sometimes I don't understand why Blaze is the way he is. He purposely sabotages himself—sabotages the good things in his life. To have to learn about this... like this... To know he lied to you. I'm so sorry—"

"Please." I gave her hands a small shake. "Don't apologize, Joanna. Please. He wasn't the one who lied. I did." I swallowed, feeling the wrecking ball inside me let loose from its moorings. "Blaze and I... we weren't together."

I'd said the words so many times now and yet the truth still seemed elusive. I wondered if she'd misinterpret it, too, like Wade had each and every time.

"Lou..." Her brows furrowed tightly.

Like a match set to strike paper, the idea made the rest of the truth catch flame and crackle from my lips.

"The night of the accident, I was afraid for him—afraid of what had happened. Afraid he would sue me. I just wanted to make sure he was okay, but when they wouldn't let me in the ambulance, the EMT asked if I was his girlfriend, and I didn't deny it. And then it just spiraled. You were so upset, and I just wanted to comfort you. I never meant for this—for all of this. I never meant to hurt you..." My rant died into silence as tears ran down her cheeks.

It was what I deserved. I'd lied to her, and even if I hadn't meant to hurt her, I had.

"I see," she finally replied quietly, sitting so still I was afraid one movement would make her crumble.

I didn't know how long we sat like that, but it was long enough to convince myself I didn't belong by her side any longer.

"I'm sorry. I'll leave you alone." I went to pull my hands away, but she wouldn't let me.

"I don't think I ever believed it was true," Joanna spoke quietly.

"W-what?"

"I wanted it to be true," she informed me with a sideways glance. "I think I wanted it to be true bad enough that I was willing to ignore that it was too good to be true."

I sat there stunned. I couldn't have heard her right.

"The way I hoped for you was the way I hoped for so many things for my son. But deep down, I know he's not in a place to accept those things in his life no matter how hard I try or Wade tries... no matter how much it hurts him." Her jaw trembled. "I thought I might lose him, and it was easier to face that knowing he'd found someone to love, and who loved him."

The lump in my throat grew bigger. "I'm sorry I lied to you."

Her jaw trembled as she nodded and then managed a small smile. "You were trying to protect the thing you loved. I can understand that." The smile pulled tight before she continued, her voice thick with emotion, "You were there when I needed someone... in ways you didn't have to be... and that's more than most people offer anymore."

We sat in silence for several minutes. It didn't feel right to thank her for what she said... for her understanding... it didn't feel like enough. So, I didn't say it.

"Where's Wade?" She wiped a finger under her eyes.

"Outside." I glanced to the door. "He's... he feels responsible."

Joanna sighed. "He always does. He always was." She looked back at her youngest son. "Sometimes, I wonder if Blaze gets into the predicaments he does because he wants to test Wade's limits."

"Why?"

"Their father... well, he made it clear who his favorite son was early on, and as they grew older, the quicker he was to turn on Blaze. And the quicker Wade was to jump in and save him," she said, her tone somber. "I think Blaze is just trying to figure out the point at which Wade will abandon him."

"But he wouldn't," I said without even thinking—without hesitation. I'd seen the lengths Wade had gone to for his brother, the things he was willing to do—willing to sacrifice. He was willing to lie to the world about me—about us—to protect his brother.

"I know. But the way my husband made Blaze feel all his life... and the way he groomed Wade to fill his shoes. Not every fear is justified. Most aren't rational. And when it comes to someone you love, someone you're afraid of losing, well, those fears become a living, breathing thing, threatening to eat you alive."

Her words connected straight into the pit of my stomach, shining a light on exactly why I was afraid to tell Wade the truth. I'd never wanted someone the way I wanted him. Never thought I'd experience the things I did, the things I feel with him. And I was so very afraid of losing that.

"Lou..." She looked at me curiously. "Does Wade know? About you?"

My lips parted, air retreating from my lungs like it didn't want to be caught on the guilty edge of my answer. "No." I swallowed. "Not all of it. I tried to tell him we weren't together, but he assumed I meant... something different. I don't think he'll understand."

Her face softened.

"After all this, you don't think Wade is understanding?" A pale brow arched.

"I'm afraid to hope."

An eerie realization dawned on her face. "Oh, sweetie." She reached over and patted my hand. "Wade has always played by the rules. To appease his father. To protect his brother. If he feels the same about you... believing you were once Blaze's..." She trailed off and shook her head. "I don't think you have anything to be afraid of."

As much as her words comforted me, it was easy for her to say. Easy when she wasn't the one who'd never really had a boyfriend. When she wasn't the one who'd spent the last decade finding herself and settling into the idea that love wasn't in the cards. When she wasn't the one who closeted her deepest, most ached for wishes because that was easier than acknowledging the picture of the intimate inn wedding would never come true.

Joanna let out a heavy sigh and looked at her son and then back to me. "Maybe one day, Blaze will figure himself out, and if he's lucky, he'll find someone like you, too."

"Joanna—"

"A sister? A cousin, maybe?" She was teasing.

I grabbed another pastry and smiled, not bothering to tell her that my sister was married and—

"Harper?" I started, seeing my cousin's wide eyes in the window. I stood abruptly, hearing Joanna's sharp gasp. "I'm so sorry. My... cousin is here. I'll be right back."

Chapter Nineteen

Wade

"Wade Stevens."

I sat up straight, doing a double-take at the familiar wrinkled smile and purple perm of the hunched woman in front of me.

"Gigi?" I stood to greet her, and she immediately gestured that she was expecting a hug. "What are you doing here?" I asked, awkwardly embracing her.

"Oh, Thelma just had her hip replaced yesterday. I called to check on her, and she said they were going to keep her an extra day or two, so I figured I'd better bring her some sustenance. The food they serve here, not to mention the entertainment options..." She shook her head, not a single strand of hair moving.

I looked behind Gigi and saw Harper standing a few paces back.

"Hi, Harper."

The younger woman seemed to be in a daze, taking a second to realize I was talking to her before she came forward and greeted me with a loose hug.

"Hi, Wade." Her mind was definitely elsewhere, and for once,

I was sure it wasn't on my brother. She didn't even glance toward the two rooms closest to us.

"Excuse her," Gigi muttered, her mouth drawing tight. "She's dealing with a scoundrel, and I was hoping a visit with Thelma would help distract her."

"A scoundrel?" The word made me want to chuckle, but the old woman's expression told me it was no laughing matter.

"Adam Eastwood. Owns a bunch of bee farms in the area, Honey Trap Farms. Thinks he has a monopoly on the whole local honey business in Maine." She tapped her cane on the ground as though she wanted to rap the man over the head with it. "He's threatening some legal trouble. Saying her branding is too similar to his and some other blarney. Causing some ruckus online. Heaven forbid two honey farms both use a bee in the logo. Scoundrel," she grumbled under her breath.

"Gigi..." Harper shot her grandmother a warning look.

"I know, I know." She raised her hands in surrender and then looked up at me and added, "She can handle it, but that doesn't mean I still can't call him a scoundrel."

I nodded, recalling what Max had told me last week at Ailene's house. This must be the guy he was referring to.

It always surprised me the level of entitlement some people had for commonalities. Like using a bee to promote honey, a tooth to advertise a dental office, or a scale on a law office logo. There were concepts that belonged to an industry, not an individual, and I always wondered about the sanity of those who argued otherwise.

"If there's anything I can do, Harper, please let me know," I offered again.

After everything Lou had done for my brother, I'd be happy to take a look at whatever legal smokescreen was thrown in her path. Based on what Gigi said, it was probably something strong enough to deter a small business from fighting back, especially when fighting back would entail legal fees.

Her smile was fleeting before she changed the topic. "Where's Lou?"

I nodded to the room in front of me. "In with my mom and Blaze."

She finally turned and slowly moved to the window, peering through it as though it were a snow globe, wanting to be inside but knowing it wasn't possible.

"I'm glad I've run into you, Wade," Gigi started again, Harper sufficiently distracted.

"Oh?"

"I have something..." She dug in her purse, her cane swinging freely off her arm. "You know, I took this pocketbook because it was big enough to hold the jar, but do you think I could find it?" With another huff, she unhooked the cane from her shoulder and held it to me as though that was the thing holding her up.

I took the rod and waited another minute before she exclaimed, "Aha!" And held up a jar of blueberry preserves. I'd opened the very same jar enough times for the breakfast buffet to recognize it on sight.

"For you."

"Me?" My head cocked, and I lifted my hand. "Gigi, I don't need—"

"You do." She shoved the jar into my hand just as the door to Blaze's room burst open.

"Harper?" Lou stood in the doorway, her eyes landing on her cousin and then snapping to her grandmother. "Gigi? What are you doing here?"

"My word," Gigi huffed and planted her hands on her hips. "I'm ninety-five years old, young lady. If anyone here has the right to be at the hospital, it's me."

"That's not—"

"I was visiting Thelma down the hall. She had her hip replaced yesterday and is bored out of her mind. And starving." Gigi patted her cloud-like perm as if there were any force in nature that could cause her hair to move.

"Oh." Lou stepped out of the room. The door almost shut behind her when it swung right open again.

"Lou—oh."

Everyone turned to Mom who looked a little startled by the crowd she'd just walked into.

"Joanna, this is—"

"Hello, I'm Gigi, Lou's grandmother," the old woman interrupted Lou and approached my mother with a smile. "And this is Lou's cousin, Harper."

"We met briefly at the inn before..." Harper murmured softly, the information lost as Gigi claimed Mom's attention.

"Hello, I'm Joanna. Wade and... Blaze's... mom." Her voice caught on my brother's name.

"It's lovely to meet you." Gigi didn't even feign an attempt to shake Mom's hand before hugging her. "I'm so sorry about Blaze, but I'm so happy Lou has found your son." It was drastic, the way Mom's stiffness melted then into Gigi's embrace.

On the surface, Gigi could've been referencing Blaze—should've been referencing him since Lou's family thought they were together—but it didn't feel like she was talking about my younger brother at all. Not the way she said it. Nor the way her eyes flicked to me behind her thick-framed glasses.

She wasn't talking about me—she couldn't be. Lou hadn't told them... No, she'd lied to them about Blaze. About me. Still...

"Me, too," Mom murmured as they pulled apart.

"You know, Joanna, Harper and I were about to head down the hall to entertain my friend with a friendly game of Go Fish. Would you like to join us?"

"Oh." Mom looked over her shoulder, her expression crestfallen once more. "I would love to, but I can't leave Blaze. I don't want him to wake up alone."

"I can sit with him," Harper offered in a meek voice, banding her arms over her chest. "I brought a book with me. I could read to him. It's *Treasure Island*."

"A book? Harper Lee, I thought you were going to play Go Fish with us." Gigi sounded affronted.

"I was, but sometimes, you and Thelma start sharing stories, and all of a sudden, we're fishing for four hours."

Gigi harrumphed while Harper looked to Lou whose only confirmation of her cousin's statement was the color in her cheeks.

Meanwhile, Mom bit her lip and faced me like I could make the decision for her. I couldn't, but I did think it would be good for her to get out of Blaze's room for just a little bit.

"He did always love a good adventure," I said low. *No matter the consequences.*

Lou gently reached for Mom's elbow, the touch the soft encouragement she needed.

"Alright," Mom said, smiling a little. "If you wouldn't mind."

"Oh, the more the merrier. At least Thelma's stories about her trained cat, Constance, will be new for someone."

Everyone—even me—let out a small chuckle.

"Alright, I'll join you in a minute. I just want to talk to my son."

Gigi repeated the room number she was heading to and then took off at a far too brisk pace for a woman who held a cane but wasn't using it.

"I'll take Harper to Blaze," Lou murmured and then took her cousin's hand and let her into my brother's room, leaving Mom and me alone.

"Wade..."

"I'll find out who the mother is—where the baby is," I began before she could. I didn't know what else to say—what else I could do to make everything okay. "I've already got Mikey on alert if anyone mentions even a hint of this—"

"Wade." She pushed just hard enough to get me to stop and do the thing I was trying to avoid—looking into her tear-drenched eyes.

"I'm sorry," I rasped in spite of what Lou had told me. "I should've known—should've done something—"

"There's nothing to apologize for," she interrupted, curling her hand into my shirt and pulling me to her.

I stood stock-still the moment her arms encircled me. This wasn't like the halfhearted hug she always gave me. This was the kind of embrace usually reserved for Blaze—for the son who struggled with failure.

"He was never going to be your father—never going to be you," she said softly.

My jaw pulsed. "I never wanted him to be."

"I know." She pulled back. "But maybe you constantly protecting him—taking responsibility—makes him feel like you do."

"I don't want him to get hurt," I told her, my voice painfully taut. "I don't want... this... to happen."

"I know. Neither do I." Her smile was wistful. "But maybe all he's ever wanted from you was a big brother. Not a protector. Not a savior. And the same goes for me."

"Mom..."

"We had good intentions. We really did," she said, placing her hand on my chest. "But maybe all we've done is show your brother we don't trust him to take care of himself."

"I only want him to be happy." *And safe and not self-destructive.*

"So do I. But if this has taught me anything, it's that you don't know—can't know—how strong you can be until you're forced to break a little. And if we're always here, making sure nothing is ever broken..."

I followed her gaze back to Blaze's room. Through the window, I caught Lou and Harper sharing a pastry as they stood talking at the end of the bed.

Seeing her youngest son like this had definitely broken something in Mom and in me. Even though I hoped—believed—Blaze would wake up, it didn't dim the reality that he might not. That the fall could've been a lot worse.

The idea broke something in me. It broke my drive. My ambition and urgency to work like I had something to prove to a man who was dead. It broke the mold I'd lived in for so long, a mold made of Dad's dreams. It broke the rules I thought I had to live by and left me with a single thought: If I had fallen... if that were me in there... what would've happened? What would I have left behind?

What did I want to leave behind?

The answer to that question was nothing that I'd had when I'd arrived here... and everything that I'd found in Friendship.

"We were broken, too, Wade," Mom added, her lip quivering as she regarded me.

Family was complicated. Decades of memories piled into a wall between us, one that wasn't dismantled in a single night or week or month, but could be. With effort. Brick by brick, day by day, the wall could be repurposed—reformed into a bridge over all of the things that had kept us apart.

My jaw tightened, and I replied, emotion thickening my voice, "I think we can be strong again."

She smiled and then hugged me. The good kind of hug. The kind of hug that started us down a different path.

"You know, deep down I didn't believe it... knew it was too good to be true."

"What was?" I asked as we pulled apart.

"Lou."

I winced. "Mom—"

"I wanted to believe it though," she went on, insistent. "I wanted to believe Lou would be a part of our family." As she looked at me, my chest tightened. "And now, I think she still will be." Her watery smile widened.

Lou exited Blaze's room then, bringing our conversation to a swift halt. "I'm sorry." She blushed, sensing her interruption. "I can go to the waiting room—"

"Oh no, sweetie. It's okay. I should go meet your grandmother. I don't want them waiting on me." Mom went and hugged her close, and then hugged me again whispering, "Don't let her go, Wade."

Mom pulled away before I could tell her I'd never let Lou go. I couldn't. To let Lou Kinkade go would be like letting all the blood from my veins.

"Do you mind if we stop at the Pastry Queen on our way back?" Lou buckled her seatbelt as we pulled out of the hospital parking lot. "This way Ella doesn't have to drop them off in the morning."

"Sure. It's in Stonebar?"

"Yeah." She nodded. "Right on the main road, so just follow the signs for town."

I'd driven this stretch of road enough to know exactly where the left-hand turn was with the sign directing visitors to the seaside harbor.

The drive was insulated by trees and suddenly opened up to a sprawling town harbor.

Stonebar was larger than Friendship, drawing a bigger crowd with its lighthouse and harbor filled with lobster-scavenging boats. But today, the throng of tourists swelled for the donut festival going on.

"There's Max's storefront." The MaineStems boutique passed by on our right as we crawled closer to the store. "The Pastry Queen is up here on the right, so we can park—oh, right there!" Lou pointed to a car pulling out of a spot just ahead.

In another minute, I'd snugged my car up to the curb, and we were walking the rest of the block to the brightly lit and warmly decorated store.

"So, what's on the menu for tomorrow?" I asked, holding the door open for Lou.

She looked at me, smiled, and answered, "Schnecken."

Ella, the joyful Ukrainian baker, was a sight in and of herself. We'd caught her in the middle of filming a clip for her social media accounts and stood rapt as she tossed flour into the air and then threw nuts at the tray of pastries with exaggerated comedy.

It took her only a few minutes to finish filming, after which she washed and warmly embraced Lou and then me as though she knew me well by extension of knowing Lou.

After a fifteen-minute conversation about Schnecken and far too many samples, we walked out of the store holding two big boxes of pastries in our arms. Schnecken, as I'd learned, translated into 'snails' from German, and was more or less the equivalent of a cinnamon roll topped with a honey-pecan crumble.

"She uses Harper's honey for these?" I thought I'd heard her mention it, but she talked so fast and moved so wildly, there was a lot to take in.

"Yeah."

"Gigi said some guy is giving Harper problems..."

Lou frowned. "Adam Eastwood. He used to supply honey to a lot of the local businesses, and we—Mom would sell it at the Stonebar Farms store in town. She still does, but I think he sees the writing on the wall with the way Harper's honey is gaining traction. Ella just switched to using Harper's brand last month."

I hummed low, the picture coming in clearer. "So, he's trying to bully her?"

Never one to say a bad thing about anyone—even when it was the truth—Lou countered, "He's framing things that aren't a problem as if they were and letting the internet do his dirty work."

"Well, if there's anything I can do—"

"Thank you, but it'll be okay," she was quick to interject.

"Really, Lou, I'm happy to help."

"I know." Her head bobbed quickly, and she repeated with a softer voice, "I know."

We reached the car, and I opened the door for her, but instead of getting in, she set the pastry box down on the seat and straightened.

"Do you want to walk down to the harbor and check out the donut festival?"

My woman loved her pastries. I tensed. *My woman. Lou was my woman.*

"Sure." I closed the door and locked the car. "When do you have to be back?"

Lou checked her watch. "Oh, we have plenty of time. Violet was so excited to cover for me at the inn. She loves working with my brother, don't get me wrong, but she gets a little nostalgic for the hospitality business."

"She used to work for a hotel, right?" I tried to recall the bits and pieces I'd learned from the afternoon at her mom's house.

Lou nodded. "Her family owns Royale Hotels."

I tipped my head. I'd heard of the giant luxury hotel corporation before. They'd been really big a few years ago—a lot of good prospects on the horizon, but lately... "Why do I feel like they aren't doing so well?"

"Because they aren't," Lou said. "Violet was doing everything to revive the brand and really make it something unique, but her dad had in his mind that Violet's brother was going to take over the company, so he promoted him instead of her. That was when she came up here... and never looked back."

I hummed low. "Fathers."

In the span of a second, the word had taken on new meaning. Prior to this morning, *father* had been reserved for a man of admirable success in spite of his poor character. A title that left a bad taste in all our mouths. But now, *father* also belonged to Blaze. It was still hard to wrap my head around.

My head swiveled as we reached the start of the festival, tents lining the pedestrian street all the way to the harbor. I dragged in a deep breath, the air thick with the scent of sugar settling into my lungs like syrup.

"What if this is all my fault?"

Even in the middle of the milling crowd, I heard her breath catch. "Wade..." She stopped, forcing me to stop, too. "It's not."

A line for one of the tents swelled behind her, a group of kids bumping into her back. She was forced to step forward, and I reached for her instinctively.

"How do you know?"

"Because a relationship isn't built by one person. Two people share the responsibility for building it or breaking it."

"And what if me trying to build it is what broke it? Is what broke him?" Because that was certainly what it felt like, and after what Mom said... Every time I stepped in, Blaze stepped farther away. Every time I fixed a problem, the next one was only bigger.

And now, he'd found out he was going to be a father, and we were too broken for him to tell me.

"You didn't break him, Wade. You loved him and wanted to help him." Her hand rested on my chest. "But maybe he just didn't know how he needed to be loved... or how to tell you."

I'd never thought of it like that. I'd loved my brother the only way I knew how: by protecting him and then cleaning up all his problems. But maybe loving someone wasn't taking all their responsibility away. Maybe for Blaze, loving him meant trusting him to fix his own mistakes.

"Telling someone that isn't as easy as it sounds," I murmured and slid my fingers under her chin.

"No, it's not," Lou said, her breaths labored as I rubbed my thumb along her lip.

"It means being vulnerable... and trusting." Like she'd been with me—vulnerable every time I asked what she wanted. When she'd risked getting involved with her ex-boyfriend's brother.

Trusting me every time to give her what she needed.

"Yes." The word was a whisper, her hooded eyes pinned to mine.

"It takes a brave heart to tell someone how you need to be loved."

Lou's eyes flashed, and her tongue slid along her lips. "I guess it does."

Suddenly, the people, the conversation, the music, the festival... it all disappeared for her. My head dipped and I pressed my lips to hers, finding them the sweetest possible thing this festival had to offer.

I didn't mean for the kiss to deepen. For it to slide from something slow and tender into something impatient and ravenous. But it did, and I realized it was because I needed the honesty of her emotions. I craved it like oxygen. I craved her brave heart, the exquisitely empathetic part of her that went out on a limb for every goddamn person she loved. The part of her that went out on a limb for me. The part that was vulnerable and trusting for me.

It was the part I loved most about her.

I pulled back with a sharp breath. The tide of the crowd drew us apart, giving space to the huge realization that was impossible to ignore. *I was falling in love with her.*

But after what Blaze put her through, how was I going to tell her how I felt without scaring her off?

I shoved my free hand into my jacket pocket, colliding with the glass jar I'd forgotten I'd put in there earlier.

"Wade, I need—"

"Lou, why did Gigi give me this?" We spoke at the same time, but the jam jar I pulled out won over the topic of conversation.

Lou's eyes rounded as soon as she saw it. "Oh no." She whimpered and reached for it, but I quickly held it high.

"Oh no, what?" I probed and glanced up at the jar. "Is it poisoned?"

Lou shook her head. "Worse." Her groan turned into a strained laugh. "It's a premonition."

"A premonition? Like a fortune?" I looked at the jar again, my eyes narrowing on the label.

When Gigi handed it to me, my memory filled in the details of the label from what I'd seen on the ones Lou opened for breakfast, but now that I looked closer, I realized it didn't say anything about blueberry jam.

"Gigi gets... premonitions... for certain people. It's a word or a couple of words, and she puts them on a label on a jar of jam and gives them to the person. It's probably nothing—"

"It says Brave Heart."

Our eyes collided. *It takes a brave heart to tell someone how you need to be loved.*

"Maybe you're supposed to watch the movie," Lou said and yanked her gaze away, clearly avoiding mention of what I'd said earlier.

"It's two words."

"She's ninety-five. She probably made a mistake."

"Lou—"

"We should probably head back." She made a point to look at her watch. "I don't want to keep Violet there too long."

I swallowed down the rest of what I wanted to say—everything I wanted to say. She was afraid of what was happening between us. The way it happened. How fast it happened. I understood... but it didn't change how I felt.

Whatever it took, however she needed... I was going to love her until she felt safe enough to love me back.

Chapter Twenty

Lou

Brave heart.

Dammit, Gigi, how could you?

Even now, the drive back to Friendship passing in sedate silence, my heart still rushed like torrential rain against my chest.

How could Gigi know it was him? Had she known the whole time? *Had she told anyone else?*

I wanted to bury my face in my hands and sob. I didn't know how Frankie managed feats like this for her entire life, treading tightropes between truth and fib like the deftest acrobat.

Between protecting the inn, helping Wade protect his brother, and then protecting my heart... I was twisting myself in knots to keep it all balanced. The thing about knots, though, is when there are this many of them, there is no unraveling. You either hurt yourself to break free, or you suffer in their prison.

And I wanted to break free.

I wanted Wade to know the deepest truth: *that I wanted to be loved by him.*

Joanna had given me fortitude. Hope. The way she'd easily—graciously—understood when I'd told her the truth had given me so much hope for what Wade's response would be. But no amount of hope could unearth the seed of fear rooted deep in my stomach.

And that was why I didn't want to come back to the inn after leaving the hospital. I didn't want to tell Wade the truth in the place that was my home. My haven. The place that was now filled with so many memories with him, to have Wade hate me for everything would be the equivalent of sending the entire building up in flames.

So, I'd suggested Stonebar, knowing the festival was going on and having the pastry pick-up as an excuse.

We were away from everything—everyone. It felt safe to tell him, especially as we talked about his brother. It felt safe right up until I realized just how much danger I was in.

The things he'd said. The way he looked at me—kissed me. I felt the words *I love you* like every touch was steeped with them, soaked into pockets of breath, infused into each syllable. Wade Stevens was about to tell me he loved me… and the worst part was that I loved him, too, *but how could he believe me when I'd been lying all this time*?

"Lou."

I rushed to the back door of the inn and away from Wade, words caught in a net inside my throat.

Did I tell him I loved him first and hoped he'd forgive me for the lie? Or did I tell him about the lie first and protect myself—protect my heart—in case Joanna was wrong? And if she was wrong, how would I… how could I live knowing that confessing the lie was only half of the truth?

Like night leading into day, I'd lied about dating his brother, but it led me to him… to falling in love him.

Wade caught my hand before I could grab the knob.

"Lou." He pulled me to him. "What is it?"

My tongue felt like a sandbag weighing on the floor of my mouth. And then I saw it—Kit's minivan parked in the back next to Jamie's. I'd been too lost in thought when we'd pulled in to notice it in the spot where Violet had parked Jamie's truck earlier.

"Why is my brother here?" I blurted out. The blip in Wade's focus was enough to get me through the door.

The hallway was quiet—a heavy kind of quiet that hung suspended between the broad shoulders of my older brothers. As soon as we entered, they both looked up from where they stood on either side of the reception desk, their elbows propped on the counter.

"Hey. What are you guys doing here? Where's Violet?" I rushed closer, adjusting my glasses on my nose as my eyes flicked between them.

I'd texted Violet when we left Stonebar to let her know we were on our way back. Her response hadn't given me any indication she wasn't here... or that my brothers were.

"We need to talk, Lou," Jamie spoke first, his voice a low baritone, one that rarely boded well.

"Is everything okay? Is everyone okay?" Panic made my voice waver, a myriad of worst-case scenarios vying for front-row seats in my mind.

I didn't even notice my purse started to slide off my shoulder until Wade came beside me, catching my bag before it dropped to the ground.

I should've fixed it—*shouldn't* have stood there and let Wade take care of it and me in front of my brothers. But I couldn't stop him... and I was tired of pretending I wanted to.

"No, everything's not okay." Kit looked like a rubber band about to snap. His jaw. His fist. His gaze. Everything was pulled taut... and ready to unleash on Wade.

No.

Jamie stepped forward, putting a hand on Kit's chest and moving himself between Kit and Wade. He leveled Wade with a stare that would've stopped a freight train.

"What the hell do you think you're doing with our sister?" my oldest brother demanded.

My stomach sank into a pit of panic.

"Excuse me?" Wade growled, now equally on edge, and stepped in front of me.

"Wait. Stop." I scrambled to stop everything from imploding, thrusting myself in front of Jamie. "What are you talking about?"

"This," Jamie bit out, his teeth interlocked like a pressurized puzzle.

He held his phone up so I could see—so Wade could see, too—the image on the screen.

Oh, no. Air sank like an arrow into my lungs. *No, no, no.* The photo was taken not even an hour ago of Wade and I kissing at the festival on the pier.

"Where did you get that?" I asked, my voice like wisps of sound woven into fragile fabric.

"Max sent it to me."

My exhale whooshed out. *Max.*

I hadn't even thought about who might be in Stonebar. There were so many people, and I was so caught up in the moment with Wade that I hadn't even considered my cousin might be close by, finishing up at his shop for the night. The lights had been off as we drove by, but it was a foolish assumption to believe he wasn't still in town.

Kit shoved his way forward next to Jamie, threatening, "I don't care who you think you are or how angry you are at your brother, I'm not going to let you use our sister as a pawn."

My pulse galloped in my chest, watching as the three of them seemed to close in on each other like walls closing in around me. I struggled to breathe—struggled to see a way out of this without wrecking everything.

Wade tensed behind me but didn't move, his deep voice a presence all on its own. "I would never use Lou."

The way Wade said my name... it was powerful because it was precise. Not like how Kit referred to me. *Our sister.* I was an abstract term to them, and that was my own fault.

I'd done such a good job fitting myself into their lives, being who they needed me to be that the idea I had my own life outside of that box... that there was a *Lou* who existed independent of being their sister, was something I'd never asked them to see. Never wanted them to see. *Was it right to punish them for not being able to see through the walls I'd built around myself?*

"Then how the hell do you explain that photo?" Jamie demanded. "Because it sure as hell looks like you're not only disrespecting our sister but your brother, too."

"I don't have to explain it because it's none of your business," Wade fired back.

"Bullshit. She's our sister. It damn well is our business—"

"Well, she can explain if that's what *she* wants."

Jamie's attention narrowed on me. "What's going on, Lou?" he asked without even a flicker of doubt in his eyes.

Oh, Jamie.

I wanted them to know the truth. It wasn't that. But I didn't want to tell them like this—I didn't want Wade to find out like this. But neither could I lie to the two of them. Not again. Not for this.

It was one thing to shade in the outline of the 'dating Blaze' story at Mom's house, but it was another to look the two of them in the eyes, emotions heated, and give them some carefully carved story that was enough truth to stop them from realizing the entire lie.

"Lou—"

"Enough," I said softly. All their eyes were on me, but it was my brothers I felt the most.

They were here to protect me—defend me—and it wasn't their fault they had to. It was mine. Because all I'd ever shown them was the woman who hid her true self, tucked away in a closet, and let her siblings take the attention for her.

"Enough," I repeated, but this time for myself.

Enough hiding. Enough lying. A stillness came over me like everything that had been sent fluttering and flying had now found a place to land.

With him.

I turned to Wade, my gaze tracing the hard line of his jaw, the firm set of his mouth. Here was a man trained to defend people—to speak on their behalf—and still, he held himself back. When he had every right to defend himself against their accusations, he let them think the worst of him... for me.

My head swiveled back to my brothers, and I felt a surge of guilt. Not because I'd lied to them. Not because I still wasn't going to tell them the truth. But because the Elouise Kinkade they knew, the one they had to stick up for and fight for, was changing. Was *becoming* who she was meant to be.

A woman who didn't need her brothers, or even her twin, to show up threatening fire and brimstone to protect her.

That woman also knew there was only one thing—one truth that would stop their inquisition in their tracks. And it was the truth that would leave my heart in jeopardy.

I moved in front of Jamie and set my hand on his chest. How many times did he rock me to sleep when I was a baby? How many nights did I fall asleep listening to the beat of my half brother's heart? He'd soothed me so many times, and I just hoped that what I was about to say would be able to soothe him.

"I love him," I declared softly. Fervently. "That's what's going on." Every word felt like a firework that came from my chest, ignited by the spark Wade created and then bursting with my own strength. "I'm in love with Wade, and that's all the two of you need to know."

I loved my brothers. I would tell them the whole truth at some point. But I didn't owe it to them now—I didn't owe it to them before the man who'd been directly affected by it. The man who'd captured my heart.

"Lou..." Jamie said faintly. Maybe Kit did, too. I couldn't be certain. It was hard to hear anything over the screaming of my heart.

"I love you, Jamie. I love you both for coming here. For wanting to protect me—for having protected and sheltered me for so long. But now, I need to love you for knowing there are boundaries in my life and for honoring them."

Jamie processed the information, slow and steady, as was his way. And then, a tight stream of hot air exhaled from his lips, and his chin lowered.

"If you're sure," was all he could manage.

"I am."

Jamie hugged me tightly, and it was a brief relief before he moved aside so I could talk to Kit.

"I don't understand," Kit said, his voice more hurt than angry.

I took his hands in mine and clasped them tight. "I think you do," I told him. "The part of you that drew all of Aurora's sea specimens in secret understands what it's like to fall for someone you shouldn't."

Kit fought it for another second, his gaze flicking to Wade and then back to me. And then his chin lowered, resigned to accepting the situation because he understood the feeling even without knowing all the facts.

My brothers left with wary stares, simultaneously respecting that they had no right to the particulars of my relationship with Wade but not liking it. They would come around.

Slowly, I faced Wade, surprised by how soft his gaze was when it captured mine. I started to speak, unsure of what was even coming out of my mouth, until he stopped me.

"Don't say it, angel. Don't apologize for that."

Chapter Twenty-One

Wade

An apology was the very last thing I wanted to hear from the lips that had just confessed to loving me.

"They shouldn't have come here like that," she said softly.

I closed the space between us and framed her face in my hands. "Then let them apologize." At least that got her to smile a little before she let out an unsteady breath. "You could've told them the truth, Lou," I murmured, knowing she would have to soon anyway.

I didn't know vulnerability existed so deep in my heart until her brothers demanded answers, and she looked like it pained her to keep them at bay.

"I did tell them the truth, and I'll tell them the rest of it, but on my terms." She pressed her hand to my chest, her wide gold-drenched eyes glistening. "I'm tired of putting everyone else's wants above my own."

My jaw locked, my admiration of her knowing no bounds. "Good girl."

She shivered. "Wade, I need to tell you the truth."

Hope and fear vied for the tighter grip around my throat. "That you love me?"

Her lashes fluttered, warm tears hitting my thumbs like pelts of hot hail. "I do. I do love you." She took an unsteady breath as my thumbs swiped away one tear after another. "But I have to tell you about Blaze—"

"Lou," I stopped her right there, my hands tightening so she couldn't look anywhere but me. "I don't care about Blaze," I started, then corrected, "I mean, I do. I care about my brother, but I don't care about your past with him. I don't." A short breath rushed through my lips.

"Wade—"

I held her tighter. "Does what you're going to say change who you are or how you feel about me?

"No, but—"

"Then whatever it is doesn't matter, Lou. If you love me, then it doesn't matter how you ever felt about him."

Her lip quivered, and she shut her eyes for a second like she didn't have the strength to keep them open. "Don't cry, my brave heart," I said, catching a hot tear on the pad of my thumb. "What are you afraid of?"

Her eyes flitted wide, a hundred emotions spinning through them before she confessed in the softest whisper, "I'm afraid you won't love me back."

A deep growl rumbled from the caverns of my chest as I pulled her mouth to mine. "Then let me show you that you have nothing to be afraid of."

I kissed her then, aiming for tender but spiraling into something rougher as soon as her mouth opened for the smooth slide of my tongue. She licked and stroked hers along mine, coaxing—begging me to devour her with the kind of desperation that only comes from fear—the fear of being on the brink of losing everything you wanted.

She whimpered and clutched me tighter.

"Don't worry, angel, I'm not going anywhere," I promised and then lifted her into my arms and kissed her again.

We barely made it through the door before I was tearing at her clothes. I wanted her naked underneath me. Her tight, warm heat around me. I wanted her mouth fused to mine as she came.

"Take your hair down. I want to see you," I rumbled and reached for the waist of her pants. "Let me see the real you."

She reached for her braids as I worked the waist of her pants, the loose fabric falling to the ground and revealing her black lace underwear.

Kneeling, I gripped her hips and pressed my face to her, inhaling deeply as I kissed her stomach and then lower, marking each inch of skin bared as I drew the lace over her hips

"Wade!" She clutched my head when her underwear fell to the floor and my mouth latched on her sweet pussy.

"Already so wet for me, angel," I muttered, flattening my tongue to her and dragging it through her slit.

Her legs weakened, and I guided her back, my tongue feasting on her center until her back hit the door, and she bowed off it toward me.

God, she tasted so damn good.

With a growl, I grabbed her knee and lifted one leg and then the other onto my shoulders, so she only had me and the door for support. And then I devoured her, flicking my tongue over her clit, sucking on the small bundle of nerves until she soaked my mouth.

I ate up every drop of her sweetness until she trembled against me, a string of whimpers and cries weaving a cocoon around us until she orgasmed and bathed my tongue in her release.

I lapped slowly, savoring each drop as she slowly began to relax and her breathing settled. Carefully, I slid her legs from my shoulders and then straightened in front of her.

I buried my hands in her hair, pushing her head back so she was forced to look at me.

"This is you," I growled, my eyes raking over her. "Hair loose.

Pink cheeks. Perfect lips." I dipped my head close to her ear. "And your pussy soaking wet for me."

Moaning, she reached for my jeans, fumbling at the waist. My cock throbbed for her touch. For her.

"Tell me what you want."

"I want you inside me," she murmured, her voice husky from her orgasm. "I want your bare cock stretching me."

"Fuck." I ripped at my zipper, shoving my jeans down far enough to free my weeping cock.

Lifting her again, I held her to the door, positioned myself at her entrance, and drove home.

"Wade," Lou whimpered as the door rattled on its hinges. "They'll hear..."

"Let them." I pulled back and thrust even deeper. "Let them hear what a good girl you are."

Her head tipped back, her cry oozing through the wood as I fucked her against the door.

I didn't care about the rest of the guests. I was happy for them to hear just how mine their innkeeper was. But after a few more thrusts, I carried her to the bed where the angle was better. Where each drive buried the head of my cock into her G-spot, and she started to come apart again.

"I love you, Lou," I growled, feeling my own release prickle at the base of my spine. "Your kindness." My balls tightened. "Your generosity." My cock swelled. "Your honesty." I thrust harder. Faster. I felt her muscles coil, her body primed to fall apart once more.

She came on a cry, her body bowing and then shattering around me, wringing my orgasm from me. I shunted deep, burying my groan in the side of her neck as my cock pulsed inside her.

I rolled to the side, taking her with me and holding her close. "I love you, and your beautiful, brave heart."

Chapter Twenty-Two

Lou

There was only one truth left to tell, and I risked everything to do it.

I waited as the two bridesmaids who'd stayed through the long weekend took the last of the apricot-filled kifli from the platter on the table and then approached the reception desk to check out.

"Aren't they delicious?" I smiled. "The kifli are one of my favorites."

If Wade were downstairs, he'd be giving me a sideways glance right now because I said every pastry was one of my favorites. It wasn't a lie. I loved them all.

"Incredible," one girl gushed.

"Thank you so much, Lou," the other chimed in. "This place is seriously so amazing. No wonder you're so happy."

Happy. I felt myself blush. *I was happy.*

I was happy now. Not before.

Before this, before him, I'd been hiding. I'd been accommodating everyone else in my life, twisting myself into knots to please them, and I'd equated their happiness to my own.

Except it wasn't mine at all.

People pleasing had buried the real me. My wants. My needs. For the longest time, even my dream. And I'd convinced myself it was okay because I was pleasing people whom I loved. People who needed me. Family who loved me.

But love—their love—wasn't something I ever needed to earn, and it wasn't something that was ever at risk.

Wade had shown me that. By asking what I wanted. By giving me what I wanted. By seeing all my buried pieces and loving them when it would've been easier not to.

Because of him, I realized real love wasn't risked by having boundaries. And I hoped real love wouldn't be lost because of one small lie that spiraled into something I hadn't planned on.

"Thank you," I murmured. A strand of hair slid over my shoulder, a new sensation as I tucked it behind my ear. "So, heading back home today?"

I hadn't braided my hair this morning, and I had no plans to do so tomorrow or the next day or the day after that.

The braids were part of my disguise. My armor. The part of me that wanted to please everyone by only being all the things she wasn't. But not anymore. I was Frankie's twin, not her foil. And I didn't want to hide from all the parts of us that were the same.

"I think we're going to check out the donut festival this morning and then head home after lunch."

"Oh, perfect. You're going to love it." Memories from yesterday flashed through my mind. The food. The smiles. *The way Wade had looked at me.*

They thanked me again, gathered their things, and then left their room key on the desk on their way out. The hallway settled into silence, and a different memory crept out.

The thud on the stairs. Blaze's body tumbling like a weighted slinky down onto the floor. The dark pool of blood by his head. *The way I hadn't corrected the EMT.*

I shuddered and turned my gaze from the steps to the photo on the wall.

For my entire life, Frankie had stood behind me—or more aptly, in front of me. My own personal guardian angel... or devil depending on the situation and the trouble she was causing. My chest constricted as it hit me.

Wade was right. *I was afraid.* Of being seen. Of being similar. I was afraid, without Frankie, there wasn't enough of me.

But I wasn't afraid anymore.

My feet were moving before I even realized where they were taking me. My steps quiet as I ascended to the second floor, assuming that Wade was still on his video call in his room.

Thankfully, I didn't have to rummage or risk another bump on my head to find what I was looking for. The painting Kit had done still rested against the closet door, waiting patiently for its time to shine. Just like I had been.

I carefully brought it back downstairs, removed Frankie's wedding photo from the wall, and hung the painting in its place.

This was my inn. My future. And the man I wanted to spend it—hoped to spend it with—was upstairs, still believing I'd been his brother's girlfriend.

He said it didn't matter—that whatever I'd felt for Blaze or had with Blaze didn't matter, but it mattered to me. I couldn't put the past behind us when his version of the past was a lie.

Resolve knotted in my chest, and I ran through my truths in my mind again, prepared to tell him when he finished his work call and came downstairs.

I lied to you, Wade.

I love you, Wade.

Forgive me. Please.

My head jerked as the front door swung open, bounding off the stopper as Harper barreled inside, her face distraught.

"I knew it." She held up her phone like it was weaponized, and as she got closer, I saw her eyes were red like she'd cried the whole way over here.

"Harper—"

"How could you, Lou?" she choked out.

"How could I what? I don't know what you're talking about—"

"You cheated on him!" She was practically yelling now. "*With his brother!*"

She dropped her phone on the counter in front of me with disgust, the screen bouncing twice until it settled, a single, giant word headlined the screen.

CHEATED.

Underneath, it read: *Blaze Stevens's new girlfriend spotted kissing mystery man.*

The rest of the article swam in my vision. Letters blurring into dots. It didn't matter what it said. None of it was true. But Harper didn't know that. All she knew was this.

Cheated.

I swayed, past colliding with the present. Almost a year ago, Gigi had given me a jam jar with my own premonition. *Cheated.* I'd been upset and heartbroken, unsure how the word could mean anything good for my future. Never in a million years could I have anticipated *this* would be the scenario that would play out.

"Harper..." My tongue fumbled for solid ground.

"He's in a coma, Lou—unconscious—and you're out here screwing his brother."

Holding the edge of the counter, I tried to approach her, but she backed away like she was Blaze's knight, chosen to fight for him when he couldn't fight for himself.

"Please, Harper, it's not what you think—"

"Unless you're about to tell me this isn't you"—she grabbed her phone off the counter—"then I'm pretty sure it's exactly what I think."

Harper's sense of loyalty brandished like the sharpest sword, a weapon she rarely had cause to use, though I'd seen it handfuls of times before. But not like this.

She swiped her cheeks with the back of her hand, her lip quivering.

"How could you? How could you do this to him?" she

demanded, every question ripping away the weak ties still holding my story together. And then, too upset to continue, she turned and headed for the door.

"Harper, wait!" I caught up to her just past the staircase and grabbed her arm.

She spun on me. "I can't believe you," she charged again. "I can't believe his own brother—"

"Harper, I wasn't with Blaze." The words were firm. Steady. Pressurized from the truth being held hostage in my chest for so long.

"What?" Her lip quivered, brow tightening. "What do you mean—"

"I mean exactly what I said." As I spoke, I found myself standing taller, the weight starting to lift. "I wasn't with Blaze. I was never with Blaze. When he fell, I let the paramedics think I was his girlfriend so they'd let me go to the hospital with him. I needed to know he was going to be okay. He'd fallen on my property, and I was afraid..."

Her jaw dropped, a different kind of turmoil rolling in her eyes. "You... lied?"

I winced but slowly nodded. "I was going to tell everyone the truth, but then the papers..." I tried to reach for her, but she flinched away. "They ran the story that I was his girlfriend—that he was up here for me, and I was going to correct them, but I couldn't."

"Why?"

"Because if they knew he wasn't here for me, they'd have to wonder why he was here, and if they started looking for that reason... for him..."

The implication was clear, and she understood because only then did her expression start to soften when she realized I'd lied to keep them from hunting down Blaze at the hospital. That I'd lied to protect him.

But softening wasn't forgiveness, and her anger gave way to shadowed betrayal.

"But you lied to us. To your family."

The ball in my throat inflated. *Not Frankie,* I thought, but that didn't make any difference.

I'd lied to them because of Wade. Because if I told my family the truth, I risked them getting involved. I risked them jumping in to rescue me because I'd always been happy to be saved. I'd always been happy to let them help because Frankie never would. If I'd told them the truth, my brothers would've reacted like they had last night—blowing up everything to protect their little sister. Including my chance with the only man I wanted.

So, I lied to them because that lie protected the truth: that I wanted more time with Wade.

"I'm sorry, Harper." My voice cracked with emotion. "I never meant to hurt you."

Like last night, I didn't feel the weight of owing her an explanation. I'd made a choice to preserve something I wanted—something I'd never felt before and was afraid I'd never find again. Maybe it was wrong, but at the bottom of it all, whose happiness was I most responsible for? *Theirs or my own?*

"And that's supposed to make it okay?" Harper's voice lashed at me, and then she spun and fled back through the door.

I pressed my hand to my chest, my heart thumping in its cage.

I'd been her once—aware of the lengths I'd go to protect my dream. That all changed when I let the paramedics believe I was Blaze's girlfriend, and then, somewhere along the way, being with Wade had become my dream, and I'd been willing to lie to my family to give me a chance at having him.

Maybe one day Harper would know what that felt like, too.

Turning, I walked toward the desk in a kind of daze, and that was when I heard him, the slow, heavy pace of his breaths. When I felt the warm electricity of his presence.

My head snapped to the steps, finding Wade standing on the small landing at the end of the first flight.

I didn't need to wonder how long he'd been standing there.

His eyes glittered, like a hunter who'd just caught a wolf in sheep's clothing.

He'd heard everything.

My arms fell to my sides, my heart freefalling through my chest. "Wade—"

"You were never in a relationship with my brother?" His voice cracked through my apology as he descended the rest of the stairs, his steps slow and heavy like the fall of a gavel.

"When the ambulance came that night, they wouldn't let anyone but family ride in it with him—"

"So, you lied."

"No—yes. I didn't mean to. They asked too many questions. I said yes to one and they thought I meant yes, I was his girlfriend—"

"But you didn't correct them because you wanted to get in the ambulance."

Every word tightened the invisible grip around my throat, my pulse fluttering like a bird

"He didn't have anyone... I wanted to know he was going to be okay," I confessed.

"Because you were afraid of getting sued?"

"Yes. That too." My throat bobbed. It was time for the whole truth.

"And at the hospital?" His eyes narrowed into slits. "You lied to my mother."

"I don't—Everything happened so fast. They'd already told her who I was—who they thought I was by the time she came in the room, and then she was so devastated. I was still processing what had happened... a famous actor had fallen down my steps and was now in a coma. I couldn't... I didn't..." I drew a trembling breath, forcing myself to steady under his steely interrogation. "She was so afraid. Just like Mom had been with Kit, and I couldn't... I thought I could comfort her until the doctors helped your brother, and then I could explain the misunderstanding."

"The lie," he corrected flatly.

My mouth opened and then closed again as I conceded with a wordless nod.

"And even when I got there, you didn't say anything—didn't correct anything."

"I didn't think, Wade. I got caught up in how the story—the lie unfolded, and I was too scared to fight it."

He stepped closer. "Even when I said you weren't Blaze's type?"

I shivered, recalling our first argument that night. "Especially then," I admitted. "You accused me of being like all the other women who wanted to use Blaze for his money and fame—who were lying to get something out of him. If I had told you the truth then, when you were so bent on hating me, you definitely would've sued me."

It gave him pause. There was no hiding that. Nor could he deny it. He'd been livid that night, angry with his brother for putting himself in this situation, but even angrier that he hadn't been able to stop it. And to think—to know someone tried to take advantage of his unconscious state—Wade would've taken out his own frustration on the white lie.

"And is that why you kissed me? Why you fucked me?" he said coldly but without malice, the questions like a weapon with two ends, cutting us both as they left his lips.

I flinched, his words like a slap to the face, but still I didn't look away. Lifting my chin, I answered, "No. Not at all."

Again, he came closer, the heat of him making my skin prickle. "And I'm supposed to believe you? You lied to me. Every day—"

"I tried to tell you the truth," I interrupted him, once more feeling that overwhelming urge to fight—to claw and scrape and cling to the thing that I wanted. "I tried to tell you before the kiss—"

"You said you broke up—"

"No. I said we weren't together." I inched forward, feeling a little bolder now as our chests almost touched. "You assumed it meant we'd broken up just before his accident."

His eyes flared. "You didn't correct me."

"You asked me what I wanted, and all I wanted was to kiss you. And when that happened… what you made me feel… I wanted one night of unspoiled fantasies—"

"Enough," he ground out, the glint in his eyes sharpening. "And you said the same thing when I fucked you. You let me think it was only sex."

"I wanted you, Wade. I wanted you the way I haven't wanted anything for myself before. Not even the inn—not even the dream made me feel this way. You didn't just see me. You made me want to be seen. No one has ever—" I broke off, the sweetest pain tearing from my chest up my throat like a flame through a paper funnel. "And I just thought since you knew Blaze and I weren't together currently… that we'd never…"

"Fucked," he said flatly.

My chin jerked. "I wanted to live in the fantasy just a little longer."

"You mean the lie."

I winced again and murmured, "The way I felt about you was never a lie."

"Lou—"

"I'm sorry, Wade," I pressed on, lifting my hand to his arm. "I love you, and I'm sorry I didn't tell you the whole truth about Blaze and me. I was afraid of losing you—afraid of losing the first thing I've been brave enough to want for myself."

"I have to go." He shrugged my touch away, the slight movement hurting even worse than the harshness of his words.

"Please, don't leave. Just let me explain," I begged. I knew I'd made a mistake, and I was ready to make amends for it however I needed to, but I wasn't going to stop fighting for him. For what we had. "I want to fix this. Please, let me fix this. I love you."

This time, it was his turn to jerk as though struck. "Don't," he warned.

"Please..."

"I have to go because Blaze is awake," he snarled.

The world fell out from underneath me.

"Awake?" My voice hardly made a sound.

"My mom just called. He's out of the coma and is asking for me," he said, the words stacked, cold and hard, like an igloo wall around him.

"Oh, thank God." My hand fluttered to my mouth, the news freeing tears down my cheeks. *Blaze was awake.* "Let me grab my purse and call Violet—"

"Why would you come?" he interrupted harshly.

I grabbed for the edge of the desk, the question knocking all the air from my lungs.

"Wade..." I stared at him, wishing I could stop the hot tears that sliced down my cheeks.

"You were never part of his life. There's no reason for you to be there."

And then he turned and walked out of the inn, and I was afraid, out of my life, too.

Chapter Twenty-Three

Wade

They'd never been together.

I could hardly process that my little brother had come out of his coma because the entire ride to the hospital, I was too busy picking up all my memories of the past month, the truth having knocked them all askew like a wrecking ball through a Jenga tower.

"Oh, Wade, he's awake." Mom broke from her conversation with a nurse to rush toward me, wrapping her arms tight around me. "He's awake."

I hugged her back but couldn't say anything. When she moved from the embrace, the pure elation on her face dimmed. I knew why.

"Where's Lou?"

My haggard voice replied, "I told her there was no reason to come."

"What?" She gasped, her hand to her chest. "Wade—"

"I'm going to see Blaze." I didn't give her a chance to stop me or ask any more questions, moving to Blaze's room and letting myself inside, closing Mom and all of her heavy questions out in the hall.

For a second, he looked no different than he had the past several weeks, peacefully resting in the hospital bed, the monitors softly signaling he was still alive in there. And then he opened his eyes, his groggy gaze focusing on me slowly as I approached the bed.

"Wade." His whispered voice cracked.

"Blaze." The emotion in my own voice surprised me as I went to the side of his bed, sitting on the edge even though there was a chair pulled close. In that moment, he wasn't a famous actor or a reckless degenerate. He was my little brother who I almost lost.

"I'm sorry—"

"Don't." My ears grated on the words. First from Lou and now from Blaze. Suddenly, I couldn't stand another apology. "Don't apologize, Blaze." I took his limp hand and squeezed. "I'm just glad you're alright. You had us worried."

"How... long?"

I reached for the cup on the bedside table. Carefully bringing it to my brother's lips, I held it even when he lifted his hand to support it himself.

"Mom didn't tell you?" I said after he'd drank what was left in the cup.

"Crying," he answered, his voice a little less rough.

I nodded. "Just over three weeks."

I stood and went to the table on the other side of the bed where there was a pitcher of filtered water, stopping when I saw there was also a familiar purple box. I couldn't stop myself from lifting the lid and seeing the fresh pastries inside. *Kifli*. Lou must've sent them to the hospital this morning for Mom.

How many other mornings had Lou done that—looked after Mom when we couldn't be here? The way my chest tightened told me I already knew the answer.

No, she'd been looking after herself. Protecting herself.

I poured more water for Blaze and wished there was something stronger for me.

"I guess I took a pretty good fall down a flight of steps," Blaze said when I returned and handed him the cup. Even now, he attempted a smile. Like being at death's door hadn't fazed him.

"You'd been drinking," I said and found myself holding back the reason why. It wasn't like me. Normally when Blaze fucked up, I'd confront him with everything I knew...which was usually everything to know about the situation, and then tell him how I was going to handle it. How I was going to fix it for him.

Suddenly, I saw myself and how I'd been treating him our entire lives: like he wasn't capable of fixing anything on his own. My intentions were good, but my execution was misguided.

Kind of like Lou? I shoved the thought aside.

Blaze let out a heavy breath. "I'm sorry, Wade—"

"No," I cut him off and shook my head. "I'm sorry. I've been messing things up between us for a long time."

He stared at me. "Are you... apologizing?" He lifted his hand to the back of his head. "How hard did I hit my head? Am I still in a coma?"

I firmed my mouth and rolled my eyes. "Be careful, or you'll miss this opportunity."

His grin cracked wider, and there was my brother, the kid who even a coma couldn't hold down. Well, almost all of him. I saw the sadness buried underneath the brightness of his eyes—the shadows that Lou said were haunting him. I turned away, hating how she'd infiltrated every part of this moment—hating that I didn't hate her at all.

"What is it?"

I looked back at Blaze and smiled. "Nothing. Just glad you're awake."

He relaxed back into the bed. "So, about this apology."

Nodding, I went on. "I want things to be different between us, Blaze. I don't want you to think... I need you to know I'm not like him. I'm not like Dad."

"Wade—"

"Let me finish. Please." I sank into the chair Mom had pulled beside the bed and clasped my hands in front of me. "When we were younger, I always stepped in with Dad because I wanted to protect you, and I hate that he turned that into a wedge between us.

"I realized there's not much difference between Dad assuming you were going to make mistakes and me assuming you didn't know how to fix them, and I'm sorry for not realizing that sooner."

Blaze sagged into the pillows, his head swaying. "You were only trying to help me."

"Didn't mean I was doing the right thing."

"Well, in your defense, I was doing a lot of wrong things, and I honestly can't say I would've known how to fix them..."

"Are you defending me now?" I teased hoarsely.

"Be careful, or you'll miss this opportunity," he muttered, and we both chuckled. "We could both do better. Actually, I have to do better."

"Blaze—"

We both turned when the door opened.

Mom.

"I'm sorry, I was just talking to Dr. Cooper. He said if your scans look good, they will release you in a few days." Mom stopped as she walked by the table where I'd refilled his water and reached for the box. "Oh, Blaze, do you want to try a pastry? Lou—"

"I think he might want to rest," I interrupted.

There were a hundred other things to talk about right now. When Blaze would be discharged. Where he was going to go. What he was going to do. If he was going to tell me about his kid... and who the mom was. But now wasn't the time.

"Well, if you want a snack, these kifli are excellent." She set the box next to his water with a decided thump, glaring right back at me. "They're Hungarian crescents with apricots in the center."

"Oh, I love those," he murmured and reached for the box.

Smiling victoriously, Mom opened it and let him take his pick.

"I just had these yester—" Blaze grimaced. "I guess it was a few weeks ago now. I had these for breakfast at the inn where I'm staying. The owner is a pastry aficionado."

My blood started to hum, and I felt like an asshole. My brother had just woken from a coma, and still, I didn't want him talking about Lou. Not until my brain settled the score with my heart.

"I'm just… I'm so glad you're awake." Mom sniffled and sat on the edge of his bed, and I realized the three of us were closer to each other right now than we'd been in the last decade.

"Me too." Blaze smiled at her, his eyes growing heavy.

"You rest, sweetie. We'll be right here." Mom took his hand, and we sat in silence as Blaze drifted off to sleep. "Dr. Cooper said he'll be pretty tired for the next day or so because of the meds they had him on."

I grunted.

"When he's discharged, I was thinking he'd come stay with me for a little—"

"Mom," I stopped her.

Her shoulders slumped, resigned. "I know. I just… I worry."

"So do I," I told her. "But it's his choice. His life."

"Did he mention…"

"No." I sat forward, resting my elbows on my knees. "Also, his choice."

I stared at my younger brother, feeling for the first time a kind of peace. There was still a lot to talk about, a lot to overcome, but now I had the right tools.

It takes a brave heart to tell someone how you need to be loved.

I breathed out heavily. This whole time… the only reason I'd met Lou was because of her lie. The way I'd fallen in love with her, it was like fruit of the poisoned tree.

"I'm worried," Mom said quietly, her chin lowering.

"He's going to be fine—"

"Not about Blaze." She looked at me.

"Me?" I stared.

"Lou told you, didn't she?" Mom's lip quivered. "She told you the truth. I see it all over your face."

My spine zipped straight. "You knew?" I said, my voice lowering a notch.

Mom nodded slowly. "After Lou told me about the... report, she confessed they'd never been together."

I reeled. Mom had known. Not only had she known and not told me—she'd known and still treated Lou like family.

How?

"And you were okay with that? You let her think that lying to you about who she was was okay?"

"Oh, Wade. She didn't lie about who she was. She lied about dating Blaze."

I recognized the look on her face: disappointment. The strange thing was, I was never on the receiving end of this look, only Blaze. She always looked at my brother like this—like she loved him so much, and she couldn't stand to see the way he continued to jeopardize all the good things he had in his life.

But that wasn't me. I hadn't jeopardized anything. Lou was the one who'd lied.

"She lied, Mom." I repeated it like I was treading water, trying to keep my head afloat above my heart that wanted to drag me under.

"That's like saying the sun lied about being bright just because one day she was hidden by a cloud." Mom set Blaze's hand on the bed and faced me fully, bundling her arms over her chest. "She fibbed because she was afraid. For the things she cared about. For Blaze and me. For you—"

"No." I waved my hand to stop her, shaking my head. "She lied to save herself."

"Tell me, Wade, what part of the lie has benefited her?"

I stilled. "The whole part where she was trying not to get sued."

"Oh please," Mom snapped, her patience starting to wear. "Your brother had enough alcohol in his system to topple the Leaning Tower of Pisa. You never would've sued her. You would've lost miserably. And I know your father taught you to never take a fight you couldn't win."

I stood. "I'm not going to argue with you—"

"Because of her lie, she's taken time away from her new business and her guests to be here. To visit with me and your brother," Mom continued, her voice sure. "Because of her lie, she was scrutinized and then targeted by the media, putting her guests in discomfort, at best, and at risk, at worse—"

"Mom—"

"And for your brother—for you—she lied to her own family."

The ball of nails dropped to my stomach, wrecking a fresh path of havoc in my gut as I recalled her argument with Harper where I'd learned all this in the first place. Lou had lied to her mom, Gigi, her brothers… people she'd spent her life putting first. And because of Blaze… because of me… she'd put them second. *For me.*

It was getting harder to breathe. I tried to focus on Blaze, the slow and easy rise and fall of his chest where he slept in the bed, and for the first time in my life, I wished I could be him.

"She said she tried to tell you the truth."

"She should've tried harder," I ground out, anger, pain, and ache rolling around in my chest like a ball of nails and spikes.

We weren't together. How many times had she said that to me? How many times had I assumed it meant something else instead of listening to her?

"Life isn't like the law, Wade. It's not either innocent or guilty and nothing in between."

I couldn't listen anymore. I surged toward the door, surprised to hear Mom's footsteps coming after me. She'd always run after Blaze, never me.

"She lied because she was afraid. It doesn't change who she is... or that she's in love with you."

My fists balled. Knowing she loved me—knowing I loved her —knowing this was all fucked up made me want to punch something.

"Loving someone isn't an excuse for lying."

"No? How many times did you lie to protect your brother?"

I stopped short, her words like chains over my back.

"Even though it pushed you apart, you still lied to protect him."

"It's not the same," was all I could manage.

"Isn't it?" she asked softly. "You can be upset, Wade, but if you think this changes how that girl feels about you, how she felt about you even when she knew how risky it was... then the only one lying here is you."

Three days later...

"I have all your stuff moved into my apartment in the city. You're welcome to stay as long as you want."

I'd been back and forth between Boston and Stonebar for days, giving myself task after task to complete for my brother so I didn't have to think about Lou.

It didn't work.

"We haven't lived in the same house for over a decade," Blaze drawled. "I'd be careful making blanket statements like that until you see how much of a mess I make cooking and hear how loud I snore."

I chuckled and handed him a stack of clothes, which he took

with a grateful smile, and headed for the bathroom in his hospital room, leaving the door cracked as he changed.

"All your scans good?"

Because of the head trauma, initial brain swelling, and subsequent coma, the doctors had kept him the last several days to do several cognitive tests as well as repeats of all the original scans they did when he was admitted. At every checkpoint, he passed with flying colors.

"Cleared for take-off."

My laugh died when I thought about how much of a mess they'd see if the doctors scanned my brain right now. *Or maybe they would just see her.*

I couldn't stop thinking about Lou. The soft brown of her eyes. The shades of pink in her cheeks. The way she'd had her hair down that morning and hung the painting of her behind the desk. A small detail I'd noticed but hadn't processed until I went from seeing her all day to not at all.

I was the one who told her not to be afraid to be seen. I was the one who told her that no one would love her less for being who she was. And then, I'd been the first to walk away when she'd brought that final piece into the light.

The way her glasses made the tears in her eyes look larger as I walked away. God, I was an asshole, and I was paying the price.

Loving her… that fruit of the poisoned tree… well, it poisoned me. Every breath. Every thought. Every moment. Every dream. I loved her, and it was killing me how I'd hurt her.

And now I was the one living the lie, pretending as though I could figure out a way to go on without her.

There was some shuffling from the bathroom. "So, I guess I missed a lot while I was out."

"What do you mean?" I rested my hips back against the table.

"Apparently, I got a girlfriend who I then skipped town with, but not before the paps got some nice juicy make-out shots in my car, and then who came back to town and cheated on me… with my own brother."

Dammit. "You know your name is clickbait. They'll write anything to make a buck."

The bathroom door swung open, and Blaze stood there in jeans and a tee.

"Is that my jacket?"

I looked down to where I clutched the leather in my hands. It was his jacket. I'd just been wearing it the last couple of weeks, and it was the only thing I had left that still smelled like Lou.

"Yeah," my voice came out like a frog as I handed it to him and he took it, looking at me suspiciously.

"You're right. They will write anything. Mom, on the other hand... Apparently, the real story is you got a girlfriend, pretended to be me, and then fell in love."

I ground my teeth together. "Mom talks too much." I led the way out of Blaze's room, not sorry to put the hospital behind me.

While I'd been between here and Boston, I knew Mom had gone back to the inn. Blaze mentioned she'd gone to let them know how I was doing. *Because I hadn't. Because I hadn't gone back.*

"Wade, hold up." Blaze reached for my arm, slowing my punishing stride toward his car. "We need to talk."

"There's nothing to talk about. This isn't your problem—"

"I'm not coming back to Boston with you."

"What?" I stopped and faced him. This wasn't where I thought he was going with the conversation. "I asked what I could do, and you said you needed a place to stay—you said it might be good to stay with me for a little—"

"I know I did. This is all on me. I'm sorry." He hung his head sheepishly for a second. "Hopefully, you can forgive me for it though. The reason I can't come with you is because I enrolled in a six-month rehab program instead."

"You... did?" I blanked. My mind became a full white canvas of no response I was so shocked by the revelation. I was glad. Christ, I was more than glad, and it took a second to let the magnitude of that sink in.

"Yeah," he said with a slow nod.

"Wow, Blaze. That's great." I found my voice and reached to pull him in for a hug. "I mean, of course, it's not a problem—"

"You should hold on to the hug. I'm not done." Blaze strolled forward to the cement block at the end of the empty parking spot and then turned and sat on the low beam.

I knew where this was going. I'd assumed he'd already told Mom about the baby, but he hadn't said anything to me. I wanted to ask. Of course, I did. But this was his life—his story to tell. And God knew, we'd been estranged for long enough that I wouldn't blame him if he didn't think I deserved to know.

"Six years ago, I was seeing this girl on and off." He pinched the bridge of his nose and blew out a breath. "You wouldn't know her. I didn't have her sign... anything."

I made a low sound to acknowledge him.

"It was before my career was... where it is now, and she was this cute waitress at a diner I used to visit right off set. She was wholesome. Thought I was an extra in the show. Anyway, it wasn't anything serious—I made it clear I didn't want anything serious, as I usually do. When I finished filming, we went our separate ways, and I... I can't say I ever thought of her again. Horrible, right?" He laughed bitterly.

"Blaze—"

"Don't," he stopped me. "I know the image I created for myself. No point in sugar coating it."

My lips pulled into a tight line, but I did as he asked and didn't protest any further.

"Fast forward to three months ago. I get a letter forwarded to me from a law office in California. I assumed it was from, well, something else. Anything else, at that point. But when I opened it... it was from Megan's parents. The waitress, her name was Megan," he spoke, the facts coming in fractured. "She'd suffered an aneurysm and died unexpectedly, leaving behind a young daughter."

Our eyes connected.

"I guess Megan's sister is fighting them for custody, and while they were going through Megan's things, they found references to my name." His voice grew more rasped. "They said they believed I was the father. The timeline and everything..."

"You have a daughter."

He smiled and made a sound that was part laugh and part pure disbelief. "She's five. Her name is Paisley."

"Blaze—"

"Before you say... whatever you're going to say. I've thought a lot about this. For two months, I thought about how it was possible for me to be a father. Was it even true? What would I do if it was? What could I do? Did I even want to?"

In a former life, those questions would've been for me. Questions for me to ask—for me to answer. For me to jump in quietly and fix this entire thing for him. Not anymore.

"Everyone wanted a paternity test. Me. Her family. So, I took one, and when I got the letter confirming the match... I lost my mind a little. Drank too much. Fell down a bunch of steps and landed in a coma..." He trailed off and looked at me. "Sound familiar?"

"Vaguely," I murmured.

"I didn't know what I was going to do. Didn't know what I should do. Five years. I'd been a father for five years, and I'd had no idea. I was starting out a failure..." He paused and drew a deep breath. "But when I woke from the coma, I don't know. It was like the fog of the last thirty years of my life had cleared. I've spent so long hating Dad, and now, I have a chance to do the thing he never could—to be the father he could never be."

"You'll be a great father," I said without hesitation.

His eyes flicked up. "How do you know that, big brother?"

"Because you're nothing like Dad."

He smiled tight, turning his head to the side and blowing emotion from his chest with a loud exhale. "Anyway, the family—Megan's sister is fighting my custody. She doesn't think I'm... fit."

"Fuck her."

That got a small laugh out of him. "Apparently, she hired some investigators to spy on me... out here. Tried to fuel bad press so she'd have a better argument in front of the judge."

My muscles pulled tight. Mikey still hadn't found an answer to how or who had leaked the information about Blaze and Lou to the press, but now, it looked like I had my answer. It didn't matter who specifically it was, what mattered was it was someone with ill will toward my brother.

"I don't want to fight her," he said, knowing I would do it if he said the word. "I just want a chance with my daughter. I want a chance to be her dad. So, I told Megan's parents I'd go through therapy first. I feel good—better—but I've felt better before. I don't want to fuck this up, Wade. I can't. I won't."

"I know," I choked out.

"Megan's parents agreed to take care of Paisley while I complete the program. During that time, I'll meet her and have visits with her and calls so she can get to know me before she comes to live with me. Somewhere. I haven't figured that out yet."

Again, he wasn't asking me to figure it out for him.

"Whatever you need, Blaze. I'm here."

He smiled up at me. "I actually do need something—"

"Name it."

Blaze rose and came to stand in front of me, his gaze determined as it met mine. "My whole life, all you've done is save me from my mistakes. Picked up the pieces. Tried to put them back together—"

"I'm sor—"

"No." He shook his head and grabbed my shoulder. "My point is now it's my turn to return the favor."

My brows knitted together. "What?"

"You messed up, big brother," he informed me with a sad smile. "You know it. I know it. Everyone who's interacted with you in the last couple of days knows it."

"Blaze—"

"I know you've never made a mistake in your entire life, but

I'm here to tell you, it's going to be okay." He now held both my shoulders. "You fell in love with her, Wade, and yeah, Lou lied a little, and it spiraled, but the lie was always about me. Not you."

"You don't—"

"I heard everything you and Mom said when you thought I was asleep."

I frowned. "Eavesdropping?"

"I was the one in the hospital bed. If you didn't want me to hear, you should've taken your conversation somewhere else," he quipped and then added more quietly, "Mom filled in all the details. Everything that happened with Lou."

I let out a deep sigh and shook my head. "So, you're giving me advice now?"

"Well, I am the expert on fucking up."

I shot him a glare.

"I'm serious, Wade." He shook my shoulder. "Why are you doing this? You obviously love her, just forgive her—"

"It's not about forgiving her," I said low, meeting his eyes. I'd forgiven Lou before the door to the inn had closed behind me. "I can't forgive myself, and she shouldn't forgive me either."

I'd walked away from her. I didn't feel like I deserved to have her back.

"You're a lawyer, Wade, not judge and jury. You don't get to make that call. Shouldn't Lou get to decide what she wants?"

I drew a pained breath. *What Lou wants.* That was all I ever wanted to give her—what she wanted—and now, I was the one living in fear that after how I'd acted, what she wanted wasn't me.

My throat tightened. "Do you think she'll forgive me?"

"Yes."

I exhaled. "How do you know?"

"First, you only have to meet Lou Kinkade to know that girl couldn't hold a grudge if her life depended on it," Blaze said, releasing me. "And second, she loves you. She wouldn't have done what she did if she didn't love you. And when you love someone, you forgive them. Just like you've forgiven me more times than either of us probably care to count."

He sighed and stepped back. We stood there for one long second, finally seeing a path forward for the both of us.

His hand lifted, his keys dangling from his fingers. "Now, are we going to go get your woman or not?"

I snatched the keys from him and unlocked the doors. "Not with you driving."

He laughed and followed me to his car. "Fine. You can thank me later."

I shook my head, grinning. "For what? Bringing me to my senses?"

Blaze winked. "For falling down a staircase so you could fall in love while I was asleep."

Chapter Twenty-Four

Lou

"Are you the one dating Blaze Stevens?" The young girl at the desk stared at me like I was some mythical character come to life. *Blaze Stevens's girlfriend. A veritable unicorn—a.k.a. something that didn't ever exist.*

"No, I'm not," I told her, adding for good measure. "You shouldn't believe everything you read online."

"Oh man." She was genuinely disappointed. More than genuinely. "That was the whole reason I told my parents we should come here for vacation. I thought he'd be here." She let out a dramatic groan.

I wasn't sure what to say to that... planning a vacation around a celebrity sighting... I couldn't wrap my head around the idea. But there were plenty of people who could.

"I'm sorry."

"Yeah..." Her hand slid off the counter dejectedly.

"Do you want a pastry?" I lifted the box I'd stashed on the shelf under the counter, two massive cronuts sitting inside. Hopefully, something sweet would cheer her up.

"Sure." She reached over and took one with a small smile.

If I hadn't pitied Blaze before, I did now. The way people circled around him like vultures even when he wasn't physically around was frightening. Even now, in the days after that final article, they still called and asked. Stopped in. Left when they realized there wasn't a story.

Mostly though, I tried not to think about the recovered actor or his handsome brother. It was hard since Joanna had visited every day since Wade walked out.

She wanted me to know how Blaze was... she also thought she was helping to tell me how tortured Wade was. I didn't have the heart to tell her it only hurt to hear all that and know he still kept his distance. It hurt even worse to hear the hope in her voice.

"Lou."

I turned at Frankie's voice. I hadn't seen my sister since Wade left. I'd called her and told her what happened, sobbing from the floor in my room. She'd talked me down in the way that only Frankie could and said she wanted to come, but Logan was sick and then got her and Chandler sick, so she couldn't leave. It was better that way. I hadn't wanted to see anyone. I was afraid what they would see.

A woman who'd taken a risk and gotten her heart broken.

In a blink, her arms were around me, and I was crying silently into her shoulder.

"It'll be okay. You'll be okay," she promised, gently rubbing my back.

"I'm sorry," I murmured. "I'm fine, I promise—"

"Lou... I love it," Frankie cut me off, drawing back and staring behind me. "I love the painting. I love that you hung it here. I'm sorry, but I'm so glad my photo is gone."

"What?" I stared at her, dumbfounded.

"What?" She cocked her head.

"You didn't want your photo here? Why didn't you say—"

"No, I didn't mean it like that. I don't care where my photo is, I just never thought it belonged here."

"You got married here..."

She waved me off. "So, hang it in the living room or on the stairs or in the hall, but not here. This is your post, the beating heart of the inn. It's where you belong, not me. Not my wedding."

I blinked slowly and then nodded. "Why didn't you ever say?"

Her eyes widened and then turned soft. "Because I love you, Lou, and I'm happy to be what you need. I'm happy to be the focus or a distraction, but that's not what I want. All I've ever wanted was you feel safe enough to be who you are. To stand up for what you want."

I felt the tears threaten to spill again, and I quickly wiped my eyes. I was so tired of crying.

"I love you."

"I love you, too." Frankie smiled, and then her head turned toward the opening front door. "I'll let you handle that. I'm going to go find some pastries in the kitchen now that I can keep food down again."

I nodded and turned to greet the guest—

"Blaze?" I gaped at the man who'd walked through the door as though he were a dead man come back to life. In a way, he kind of was.

"Hi, Lou." The tousled hair. His tipped smile. The shadows still covered his eyes but not like before.

"Hi," I choked out. "It's good—I'm so glad to see you—to see you're doing alright."

"I am, thank you," he said, but all I could focus on was his eyes. They were just like Wade's.

I flushed and lowered my head. "Is there something I can do—"

"I wanted to apologize."

I balked. "No—"

"I'm sorry for how I acted the day that I fell. I wasn't... in a good place. And I'm sorry for how I left the room—"

"Really, it's no problem. It's fine."

"I also wanted to thank you for everything you did for me. While I stayed here, and then afterward."

Heat exploded into my cheeks. Embarrassment but also pain. I didn't want to be thanked for lying and breaking my own heart.

"Who... told you?" I swallowed.

"My mom."

"Then you know you don't need to thank me," I said and lowered my voice. "I'm so sorry for what happened and then for lying about who I was... to you. I just panicked, and then things spiraled—"

"Please, Lou. If anyone is an expert in the ways life can spiral, it's me." His grin tipped higher on the right. "I know I've got a few days left on the reservation, but I'm leaving town today, so I'm just going to get my things."

"Oh." My heart sank like a stone. "Of course." I forced a smile, trying to revive the sluggish beat in my chest.

Of course, he would come back for his things. Why wouldn't he? His stay was almost up? Why would I assume it would be Wade who'd return for all of his brother's possessions?

"I figured a place like this... someone is definitely waiting in the wings for a room to open up, and since I don't need it..."

"Thank you." There wasn't anyone waiting, but I appreciated his thought. "Do you need any help?"

Please say no.

I hadn't been in the room since the morning Wade had walked out. Even to clean it—something I could justify waiting at least a few days to do.

"I'll be fine. Thanks."

I listened to the disappearing sounds of his footsteps, exhaling deeply at the distant click of his door opening and then closing.

This was it. My eyes closed. *The end.* With that room locked —untouched—it was like a piece of this puzzle left unfinished. A loose thread left untied. A small sliver of hope that Wade would be the one to walk through those doors and pull me into his arms.

Instead, it was only the Hollywood heartthrob. I let out a

weak laugh. Harper would be beside herself to know the disappointment I felt.

"Lou."

I tensed, a shiver running up and down my spine.

No. I squeezed my eyes tighter. I was imagining things again. Imagining him. His voice. His musk. His warmth.

"Lou. Look at me."

My eyes flitted open, sure that what I saw in front of me was nothing more than an apparition. A figment of my desperate imagination. The shorter, light brown hair. The square jaw and straight nose. Full lips, the bottom one still thicker than the top. The slight cleft of his chin and that stare. Earthy and raw like timber set on fire.

"Wade." I breathed out his name, and he didn't disappear.

He was real. He was here. *But why?*

My heart cried out, begging to be put out of its misery. I thought of a thousand things to say, but they'd all already been said. *I loved him. I was sorry. I never meant to hurt anyone.* To repeat them only risked a repeat of the trampling over my heart.

"Your brother is upstairs." It was the safest assumption for why he was here—the thing I had to believe out of self-preservation.

"I know," he rumbled, eyes flicking to the stairs and then to the painting behind me before capturing mine once more.

The heat of his stare felt like a hand around my throat, holding me hostage with its strength. "Is there something else I can help you with?"

"Yes." He cleared his throat, and it hit me then that it wasn't anger pinching his jaw tight or making him rock side to side. He was nervous. "I need to rent a room."

"A room?" I blurted out stupidly, and then quickly reached for my tablet. *Business.* He was here for business. Still, my racing heart wouldn't quit. "Of course. Let me check for you." Normally, my availability would be sitting at the ready at the top of my head, but it had evaporated under his stare.

"Thank you."

"How long do you need the room for?" I kept my eyes focused on the screen, the booking app blurring in and out of focus.

"Forever if you have it—if you'll have me."

The world stilled. My heart fluttered like a butterfly free from its tight cocoon. I looked up, blinking slowly as the iPad slid from my hands and clattered onto the counter.

Had I heard him right? Had I really heard him?

"I'm sorry, Lou," he said, the weight of his voice pinning down my wild thoughts to reality. He was here. He'd come back. *To stay.*

"Wade..." My voice cracked as tears readied in the corners of my eyes.

"I'm so sorry for the things I said—how I treated you the other day. I can't—" He broke off with a huff. "I was shocked and upset, but there's no excuse—"

"I should've told you the truth sooner," I insisted, unwilling to be blameless. "But I was afraid of losing you."

"And I should've listened when you tried to tell me... but I was afraid I'd never truly had you."

"You always had me." My heart cried out for him. "Only you."

"I love you, Lou. I want you and this inn and this town and your family for all of my days. But mostly, I want to give you what you want," he said and reached into his pocket.

My brows pulled together as he slid free a folded piece of paper and set it on the counter. It wasn't paper, I realized as he began to unfold it. My heart stumbled. I knew exactly what it was.

He flattened the image I'd torn out of the wedding magazine weeks ago. The intimate celebration I'd envisioned for myself here at the inn... the fantasy I'd pictured with him.

"You kept it."

"If there's one thing the last three days have taught me, it's that I've kept every piece of you with me. Your smile. Your generosity. Your blushes. Hell, even your love of pastries..."

He reached his hand over the counter, holding his palm open for mine. When I set my fingers in his, he led me from behind the desk so there was nothing between us.

"I want to give you this future, Lou. With me," he said, and then my eyes widened as he slowly lowered onto one knee. "If you'll have me. If you want me—only if you want me."

It was better than any ring. He asked me to marry him with a reflection of who I was and what I wanted, and I felt pure happiness burst through me.

"I do," I said, pulling him up to me, happiness bubbling from my lips. "I do want you."

Relief snapped through him, and Wade hauled me into his arms. "I love you, my brave heart."

"I love you, too," I managed just before his mouth claimed mine.

The kiss was deep and hungry, swallowing me up in its desire until my toes curled and my knees turned to mush, and every other thought was wiped from my mind except one.

I was happy.

Epilogue

Lou

One year later...

"Is it everything you imagined?"

I turned, finding Frankie standing beside my chair. I could've answered her immediately, but instead, I took another glance around the dining room at the inn. Ivory cloths. Flickering candlesticks. Bouquets of white roses and lilacs. My and Wade's wedding was everything and nothing like I'd imagined.

It was the intimate elegance like I'd seen on the magazine spread... only better. Better because it was Frankie's candles that lit the table and Max's blooms that colored every vase. It was Jamie's craftsmanship that built the table itself, and Kit had promised us a wedding portrait to memorialize the special day.

It was better because it was Mom's fruit spreads layered into our wedding cake and a little bit of Harper's honey drizzled on top. And because the champagne flutes Wade and I drank from were made by Nox. They were the very first set of glasses he felt were good enough to sell—or give as a wedding present.

It was better not only because of my family but because of Wade's, too.

Ever since the whole truth came out, including how it had been the honeymooners, who weren't really honeymooners at all, who had been leaking fake news stories to the press, Joanna had surprised us all by deciding to stay in town. With Wade only commuting to Boston every other week or so and handling most of his work for the firm remotely from Friendship, Blaze finally had the space to figure out his own life now that he was a father.

"It's better."

My sister smiled wide—extra wide because she was holding back tears. She was also holding her stomach because she and Chandler were pregnant again. Logan was getting a baby brother.

"Love always is," she said and sighed, finding her husband's gaze from across the table. And then Gigi called to her. "Oh no," she groaned. "They're going to try and recruit me to their club. Help me," Frankie begged through the smile she'd pinned to her face.

I covered my mouth and laughed. "Sounds like a you problem."

Joanna and Gigi had started a Canasta Club that met weekly at the inn, the two of them manning the reception desk for a few hours while they played so Wade and I could go out. They were actively recruiting new members. Or holding them hostage, depending on who you asked. Harper didn't seem to mind joining in a game every once in a while, but she was facing her own challenges at her bee farm.

Even after Wade stepped in with some legal help, the online backlash from the smear campaign had lingering effects. But Harper had nothing if not grit, and in a lot of ways, I'd seen how the struggle had matured her. She wasn't going to give up fighting for her dream even when things got tough.

"Seriously, Lou—"

"Frankie, come down here," Gigi ordered with another frantic wave.

"I'm sure you'll think of something," I murmured encouragingly, watching her drag her feet to the far end of the table.

"Everything okay?" Wade wrapped his arm around my shoulders and nuzzled the side of my neck.

"Perfect." I turned to him, his mouth instantly claiming mine in a deep kiss.

For quite some time, I'd waited for the day when his kisses would stop spinning my head. For when the heat wouldn't sweep me off my feet and make my limbs melt into Jell-O. That day still hadn't come, but I wasn't waiting for it anymore.

There was a high-pitched shriek, and we pulled apart. Everyone's attention turned to the living room where Blaze chased Paisley around the chairs. His daughter had beautiful, golden curls, the most adorable laugh, and her father's eyes. Blaze caught up to her and scooped her into his arms, spinning them around.

"He looks good. They both do," I murmured.

We didn't see too much of the famous actor. After returning to his real world, Blaze finished his rehab program and went through the lengthy legal process to get custody of his daughter, Paisley's aunt fighting him tooth and nail along the way. The entire time, he'd been filming his latest movie.

Sometimes, Wade wondered if the coma changed his brother. If it reset something in his brain chemistry while he was sleeping. But then I had to think that maybe Blaze's coma had changed the people around him. It changed how Joanna and Wade saw him. How they treated him. How they thought they had to be there for him. And I wondered if it was the change in them that allowed Blaze room to finally grow into the person he wanted to be.

Or maybe, it was the smiling little girl in his arms. He certainly looked at her like she'd changed his whole world.

"Yeah," Wade agreed and then went tense, seeing Blaze take a call on his cell.

I put my hand on his leg. "He can handle it."

Blaze carefully put Paisley back on her feet and ushered her over to Joanna so he could step outside to take the call. As the little girl ran to her grandmother, I caught the tail end of Harper's stare following Blaze as he disappeared. She still harbored a crush on him, but surprisingly kept her distance whenever he was around. Though sometimes, the way Blaze looked at her made me wonder...

"I know." Wade took my fingers and squeezed. "I'm proud of him for handling it."

Wade was still learning he couldn't jump in and save his brother from whatever media scrutiny was headed his way. After Blaze left Friendship, Wade gave him Mikey's phone number, effectively pulling him out of the loop unless something legal had to be done.

Unfortunately, Blaze's new life wasn't providing the usual fodder for tabloids. The things they did print had become harsher. And according to Blaze, they were starting to print things about Paisley, and that was where he was going to draw a hard line.

"I wish he'd come up here more. I think Paisley would like it."

"I suggested it..." Wade trailed off. What he wasn't saying was that Blaze hesitated because he knew what happened wherever he went—he knew who followed. In the city, it was easier to hide in the masses.

"Excuse me, everyone," Frankie stood, clinking her knife onto her glass of water. "I'd like to make a toast."

"Oh no," I murmured, and my twin only smiled wider.

"To Lou. Everyone always thinks that I led our way into the world with my personality and pranks, but the truth is, you've led me," Frankie began, my eyes tearing as her voice trembled. "With your patience. Your graciousness. Your kindness and selflessness. You've led us all, and this whole time, I've only ever been trying to catch up to your goodness. When you do something, you do it right. Whether it's making lattes at The Maine Squeeze, turning Kit's stack of untouched artwork into a booming gallery, or transforming a forgotten inn into a cherished landmark, you always do it right on the first try, which is why I'm happy to see that for once, you took some of my advice when it came to love." Her watery grin turned into something mischievous as she wiped the tears from her eyes. "You lied and cheated and stole your way into Wade's heart, and I couldn't be prouder of you for it."

The entire table burst into laughter. My brothers shook their heads because... only Frankie. Mom and Gigi hugged each other and then Joanna, and my cousins chuckled and nudged each other.

When everyone quieted, Frankie shifted her attention. "And to you, Wade, because you won the Kinkade with the best heart."

Everyone lifted their glasses, but it was Wade who claimed my focus, his mouth finding my ear as he murmured, "The bravest heart."

I turned, losing myself in the love in his eyes. "I love you."

"I love you, too."

"To Mr. And Mrs. Stevens!"

The Gentleman

Max Hamilton knows how to treat a woman right. Open the door for her. Lend her your coat in the cold. And flowers. Always flowers. It was the reason he started MaineStems, his flower delivery service—to help more men be gentlemen. And one of those men is his best friend on his wedding day—even if the bride is the woman of Max's dreams.

Max will deliver the wedding day bouquet with a smile on his face and only his best wishes for the couple. A simple feat... if only the message in the card was one of everlasting love instead of instant betrayal.

Daisy Turner has been knocked up, stood up, and she's ready to shoot the messenger. Max is responsible for this—for her runaway groom—and she knows it. But now, he's her only shot. Not for a happily ever after, but for the next best thing: health insurance coverage.

Max will do anything to help Daisy and her unborn baby... including marry her. And he'll tell himself it's the gentlemanly thing to do. Bring her pickles at 2AM her. Rub her back when it's sore. But the way he wants her... that's the opposite of gentlemanly. And to tell her how he's always wanted her... well, only a scoundrel would do that.

When the timer on their convenient marriage runs out, will it be the gentlemanly thing to do to keep his word and walk away? Or will Max confess that Daisy has always had his heart?

Read here.

Other Works by Dr. Rebecca Sharp

The Vigilantes

The Vendetta

The Verdict

The Villain

The Vigilant

The Vow

The Kinkades

The Woodsman

The Lightkeeper

The Candlemaker

The Innkeeper

The Gentleman

The Beekeeper

The Glassmaker

Reynolds Protective

Archer

Hunter

Gunner

Ranger

Covington Security

Betrayed

Bribed

Beguiled

Burned

Branded

Broken

Believed

Bargained

Braved

Carmel Cove

Beholden

Bespoken

Besotted

Befallen

Beloved

Betrothed

The Odyssey Duet

The Fall of Troy

The Judgment of Paris

Country Love Collection

Tequila

Ready to Run

Fastest Girl in Town

Last Name

I'll Be Your Santa Tonight

Michigan for the Winter

Remember Arizona

Ex To See

A Cowboy for Christmas

Meant to Be

Accidentally on Purpose

Hypothetically

The Winter Games

Up in the Air

On the Edge

Enjoy the Ride

In Too Deep

Over the Top

The Gentlemen's Guild

The Artist's Touch

The Sculptor's Seduction

The Painter's Passion

Passion & Perseverance Trilogy

(A Pride and Prejudice Retelling)

First Impressions

Second Chances

Third Time is the Charm

Standalones

Reputation

Redemption

Revolution

Want to #staysharp with everything that's coming?

Join my newsletter!

About the Author

Rebecca Sharp is a contemporary romance author of over thirty published novels and dentist living in PA with her amazing husband, affectionately referred to as Mr. GQ.

She writes a wide variety of contemporary romance. From new adult to extreme sports romance, forbidden romance to romantic comedies, her books will always give you strong heroines, hot alphas, unique love stories, and always a happily ever after. When she's not writing or seeing patients, she loves to travel with her husband, snowboard, and cook.

She loves to hear from readers. You can find her on Facebook, Instagram, and TikTok. And, of course, you can email her directly at author@drrebeccasharp.com.

If you want to be emailed with exclusive cover reveals, upcoming book news, etc. you can sign up for her mailing list on her website: www.drrebeccasharp.com

Happy reading!

xx

Rebecca

Made in the USA
Monee, IL
07 April 2025

15290128R00184